Deception

DAVID GLEDHILL

ISBN-13: 978-1508762096

ISBN-10: 1508762090

"All warfare is based on deception"
Sun Tsu
"The Art of War"

CONTENTS

This book is dedicated to friends
lost in flying accidents over the years.
There is no greater gift than
to give your life in the service of your country.

PROLOGUE

The Beirut Suburbs, Summer 1985.

The man stepped from the shadows and glanced furtively up and down the rubble-strewn streets. His destination was close by but he had a strong sense of self preservation and an equally strong desire to arrive intact. Snipers dotted every street corner and he had no wish to join the ever growing casualty list in this God forsaken city. He moved briskly towards the entrance of the office block where he had arranged to meet his contact. The alternative would have been to walk in through the front door of the British Embassy on Serail Hill in the Beirut Central District but that would have attracted far too much attention. His immediate task was one which needed the utmost discretion.

It had been three days since he had been burdened with the knowledge. The documents were, without doubt, political dynamite and people much further up the decision making chain than he needed to digest the implications. First he had to make arrangements to get them out of the city and back to London and the diplomatic bag was about the only safe means out of war-torn Beirut. How the Syrian dissident who had passed them on had come by them was still a mystery but his credentials had seemed above reproach. He had checked his history carefully and the story that emerged was, undoubtedly, real but reflected a sad tale of repression and exploitation. Maybe passing on the plans was the only way to make amends. Either way, the documents would be analysed in London before hasty actions were taken. The veracity would be checked and cross-checked before the content influenced operational planning.

As he had leafed through the Operational Plan, the security caveats emblazoned across its cover he had, at first, been sceptical but, eventually, persuaded. It detailed exactly how the Syrian Army would recapture the Golan Heights from Israel. In a daring stroke, ground units would move in and isolate the Israeli units on the Heights after first knocking out the communications. They would be followed up by air strikes on the Israeli units as they regrouped. At its heart, the plan was simple but used overwhelming force to achieve the aim. Speed and surprise were the key and quite uncharacteristic of this part of the world where brute force and ignorance often reigned. Any Israeli retreat down the southerly slopes would be neutralised by a pincer force. Isolated from the command chain and overwhelmed by numbers, capitulation seemed likely unless massive reinforcement followed. In parallel, any response by the Israeli Air Force would be countered by the new Syrian Mig-29 fighters deployed forward to join the Mig-21s at Khalkhalah airbase at As Suwayda in the south. Israeli defence tactics were legendary but the plan was bold, detailed and seemed to have every chance of success. Crucially, and perhaps most worrying, once the Heights were retaken, SS-1 Scud B short range ballistic missiles would be moved into the forward base and protected by SA-6 surface-to-air missiles bringing the Israeli capital Tel Aviv within range.

A Russian made, short range, tactical ballistic surface-to-surface missile system, the Scud is descended from the German V-2 rocket and in Syrian service carries a conventional payload. After launch it flies through the upper reaches of the atmosphere before returning to Earth in a vertical terminal dive. In its original A version it had a range of 130 Km but, after upgrades to the B version, the range was extended to 300 Km. Simple gyros guide the missile during the initial boost phase which lasts only 90 seconds after which the missile flies unguided to its target. As a precision weapon it is useless but used indiscriminately against a civilian population, it can wreak havoc and generate psychological paralysis. Life in the Israeli capital would never be the same again with the population under constant threat from the air. Only a massive investment in an anti-ballistic missile defence system which might bankrupt the Nation could offer any hope of survival.

Threatening the Israeli capital with the missiles was one thing. Delivering on the threat was something he couldn't second guess. His initial but subtle queries had suggested that, to the best of his knowledge, Mossad, the Israeli Secret Service had no idea of the existence of these plans. Whilst they had probably war-gamed this very scenario many times, they could have no inkling that the reality might be so close. Undoubtedly, if the Israeli MOD knew the how and the when the attack might take place, they could easily reinforce and negate the threat. Kept in the dark, success was entirely possible. In the meantime, the plans were safely hidden and only he knew of their whereabouts. He was confident his hideaway was safe and no one would find them without his help. His careful plans included safeguards against disclosure both physical and mental. He had trained his mind to shut down under such duress but he hoped such an eventuality would never be tested.

Approaching the main entrance cautiously checking for obvious signs of a watcher, he satisfied himself that he was alone and pushed inside working towards the ground floor office where his contact should be waiting. The small glass door to the concierge's office was to his left and he checked carefully for signs of activity. At this time of day, most of the locals would be taking a siesta before the evening sniping warmed up again. All seemed quiet. Pushing open the door he stepped inside looking for his man from the Embassy. The office was eerily silent. As he moved forward, the foot poking out from behind the desk in the far corner rang subconscious alarm bells and he became instantly alert. Edging towards the prone figure, he didn't make it as far as the desk before a door at the far side of the room opened and a man, his face wrapped in a brightly coloured keffiyeh, stepped into the room holding a machine pistol. A barked command which was unintelligible despite his perfect Arabic stopped him in his tracks and he felt the cold barrel of a gun press into his neck from behind. He raised his hands meekly, survival being uppermost in his mind. Staying alive was of more concern than false bravado at this moment.

"Stay very still Mr Reeves."

The fact they knew his name raised an instant chill.

"Now lie down, put your hands behind your back and don't even consider trying to leave."

He complied submissively as his hands were bound tightly and, as his face dragged across the floor, the grit scraped his cheek raw. Manhandled to his feet he was pushed roughly against the wall, straining to catch the conversation in the background hearing only muffled voices. His captors were clearly Arabic speakers but the cultured accent of the leader suggested that he might not have been educated in the back streets of Beirut. There might be more to worry about than appeared at first glance.

The leader of the group picked up the phone and jabbed a few keys waiting for a connection. His voice made him easily identifiable and it would be a sound which haunted Reeves in his nightmares over the coming days. There was no way he could know but the voice on the other end of the phone line was not from Beirut. Despite the Arabic the recipient of the call used naturally, his harsh clipped tones had been cultivated in Moscow.

"We have him but I'm afraid the whereabouts of the package is still not clear. He doesn't have it with him," said the man in the keffiyeh. He listened intently to the response, signs of frustration evident.

"No, I have no idea what was in the package, do you?"

His facial expression said it all but he was not convinced the man on the other end was telling him everything he should know. His body language reeked of caution.

"I understand. We'll move him to the safe house and work out what we do to locate the goods once we have him secure. Leave it with me. I'll get back to you as soon as we reach our destination."

Prompted by unseen commands, hands hauled Reeves roughly to his feet and began to push him towards the street entrance. Outside the sounds of a vehicle which had pulled up at the door were audible even though he could not see past the blindfold which had been drawn tight across his eyes. He stumbled as he was dragged bodily down the corridor but the momentum carried him along between his captors.

Reeve's nightmare was only just beginning.

CHAPTER 1

RAF Coningsby, Lincolnshire

The minute hand on the clock clicked to 4 AM just as the phone rang. A hand stretched out from under the bedcovers and grabbed the handset.

"Anderson."

"Sir, sorry to wake you so early, it's Will O'Brien the Duty Ops Officer."

"Morning Will, it's a bit early for pleasantries!"

He glanced at the clock and groaned. It had to be TACEVAL.

The neatly tended married quarter patch was only a few miles from the busy airbase in the wilds of the remote county. Arranged around a large attractive crescent with lawned areas and a children's play park in the centre, the residents were exclusively military. As the siren on the large pole immediately outside his bedroom window began blaring out its doleful tune, he reflected on the fact that it was perhaps a good thing that most of the local residents lived or worked on the base. Lights snapped on in bedrooms as the cascade callout began; it was a well rehearsed routine. The order in which the phones began to ring around the square gave an indication of the resident's importance in the Station pecking order. In each bedroom groans were replicated as the enveloping darkness, coupled with the early morning call, slowly sunk into tired brains.

"It is Sir," said the operations officer "but this one is a bit out of the ordinary. I can't say too much on an open line but the Squadron has just been given notice to move. You're about to get a tasking to deploy overseas. The details are just coming in on ASMA and I thought you'd want to know immediately. Looks like Cyprus again for you."

He talked on for a few minutes passing only the briefest of facts as the Squadron Commander listened, his brain rapidly clearing as he digested the information, his interest growing by the second. As the man said, this was definitely out of the ordinary.

"The Station Commander's considering it now but I expect him to sound the hooter for a Station callout."

"He beat you to it Will. It sounded about 2 minutes ago. I'm surprised it wasn't you hitting the button. Can't you hear it in the background? We'll be popular in the village again today! My wife gets grief from the butcher every time we play the morning symphony. I'll get straight over to the Squadron now. Have my Execs been called out yet?"

"No Sir, I thought I'd get hold of you first."

"OK, leave that to me. Those on the patch are already out of bed but I'll make the calls to the flight commanders and SENGO. They all live out in the local area. I'll speak to you when I get to the Squadron."

The bleary-eyed Wing Commander reassured his wife as he dragged himself out of bed. She groaned, rolled over and covered her head with a pillow, immune to these early morning dramas. Making his way quickly to the bathroom to catch a quick shower before setting out he experienced a minor pang of guilt. The callout rules said "Do not pass Go. Go straight to the Squadron, unshaven and hungry." Despite those rules he would bring himself round first. His first coffee of the day could wait but he wanted to arrive at the Squadron in one piece and some cold water and the scrape of a razor across the chin would be an impetus to wake up quickly. A shave was a luxury he would give himself even if it would cause mutterings amongst his junior officers. "Do as I say, not as I do" would spring to mind later in the day.

He pulled out his copy of the call out list from his bedside table where it lived, positioned precisely for this situation. He began to make the brief series of calls before he set off so that his Execs would be able to mull over the implications as they made their way in to the Squadron. Unlike his own 5 minute drive, his flight commanders and his Senior Engineering Officer would take 20 minutes longer and might as well be productive during their drive. He felt just a little guilty at breaking the news of yet another call out so soon after the last exercise but he knew that, like him, a Station hooter was part of Cold War life. Each callout was, normally, remarkably similar but on this occasion there was a stimulating twist. He briefed each of his key lieutenants similarly starting with his deputy; one of the flight commanders of the fighter squadron.

"John, The shit's about to hit the fan. I need you in at the squadron now. We're on 48 hours notice to move and we need to get planning."

He began to rattle off a few details that he had picked up from the ops. officer hoping that the communications monitors were not active at this early hour. Needs must he consoled himself. If this was an exercise he had almost certainly just joined the list of bad boys who would make the "faux pas" list in the debrief. The questions from his deputy which the revelations sparked were inevitable and he was quick to cut off the discussion.

"I'll brief you when we get to the Squadron, John and I get a better idea of how this thing will shape up. This is an insecure line and I don't have the full story yet but let's say it's another trip to Golf Dispersal if you get my drift".

To understand the significance, an eavesdropper would have to know that Golf Dispersal was the home for the fighter detachments at RAF Akrotiri in the Eastern Mediterranean. Two words said a lot.

"Start thinking about what we'll need as you make your way in. Let's just say the mission details are way too interesting to speculate about until we've got the full facts. We'll decide who's going straight away and everyone will have time to pack later but we need to get some basic planning done; and soonest."

As he put down the phone the wail of the callout siren continued to split the air across the officers' married patch. Familiar to anyone who served during the Cold War the sound was identical to the air raid sirens which had blared out in the classic wartime movies such as *The Battle of Britain*, its low moan starting a cascade of frantic activity. It would take a bottle of sleeping pills to sleep through the cacophony. Urgent calls were already being made, starting with the most senior officers and working down to the most junior airman. Within 10 minutes, cars would be speeding in towards the fighter base from all parts of remote Lincolnshire ready to react to what everyone would assume to be the latest hypothetical crisis. The difference this time was that the events that were unfolding were no exercise.

Within minutes, Paul Anderson picked up his keys, let himself out of the front door into the dark street and climbed into the green camouflaged Mini parked on his driveway. As the engine fired up protesting its innocence, he reversed out into the road amid a cloud of exhaust fumes and set off for the short drive to RAF Coningsby. It was some time before the Sun would appear above the horizon but within the hour the Station would be on a full war footing ready to react to any eventuality.

*

The high pitched alert claxon pierced the night air.

In the small bedrooms attached to the Quick Reaction Alert Facility at RAF Coningsby the crews were instantly awake, aroused from a tenuous slumber by the raucous horn. Bedside lights flicked on as Air Force-issue blankets were dumped unceremoniously onto the floor and partly clad bodies emerged, disentangling themselves from sheets which had wrapped themselves around limbs like an eel. In the aircrew bedrooms, hands groped on the floor next to the bed feeling for immersion suits which had been laid out carefully before going to sleep for exactly this eventuality. Feet slid into the rubberised socks in an unconscious routine, the coarse material of the suit hefted up and over the torso as they struggled into the heavy waterproof survival suits. The rubber of the neck seal felt cold and unforgiving as it tore at sleep-flattened hair before popping tightly around the neck. A quick drag on the heavy zip which cut diagonally across his chest and one rapidly awakening pilot was stepping into his flying boots and stumbling out of the door towards the hardened aircraft shelter, or HAS, which held his dormant Phantom. There was no time for the luxury of tying his laces which dragged in his wake.

DECEPTION

The Quick Reaction Alert sheds at RAF Coningsby lay at the easterly end of the airfield on Echo Dispersal just a short distance from the 8000 foot long runway. For most of the year, the two Phantom air defence fighters sat on readiness twenty four hours a day, seven days a week. The only respite was when the duty passed over to the other southern base at RAF Wattisham in Suffolk. Two adjacent HASs housed the alert fighters, the small brick-built annex providing a temporary home for the aircrew and groundcrew who made up the QRA team.

At this early hour, only the harsh yellow of the sodium lights that ringed the facility cut the darkness of the surrounding airfield. The additional barbed wire of the security fence that surrounded the complex was the only sign of the added importance of this unassuming collection of buildings. The complex provided a "home from home" of sorts for crews who were confined to this austere facility during their frequent twenty four hour sentence.

There was no time to question a hooter once it sounded; just the challenge of a rapidly diminishing deadline in which to have the jets in the air. The groundcrew had already spilled from the annex and the doors of the HASs had automatically slid back, noisily, to reveal the squat and functional profile of the Phantom fighter jets. As the heavy doors clanged to a stop, the sodium light normally trained on the entrance reflected menacingly on the stark white Sidewinder infra red missiles mounted on the wing pylons, the seeker heads still shrouded by the yellow "noddy caps" which protected the delicate internal gimbals from damage until the missiles were energised. Apart from the imposing bulk of the fighter it was the presence of these missiles which emphasised the different stakes at play for QRA crews over normal training flying and they were brutally evident as the aircrew rounded the open doors heading for the cockpits. There was a frantic activity around the airframe which to an outsider would appear as little short of panic. To the players it was a well-drilled routine, each one of them having a precise role. "Readiness 10" meant exactly that because, if scrambled, this aircraft had to be airborne within 10 minutes of the message, wheels in the well and ready to intercept any intruder which strayed into UK airspace. There were no excuses for failure. There would be consequences for anyone who frustrated that directive.

Rushing to the base of the ladder, a tense crew member grabbed the bulky green life jacket which had been pre-positioned on the HAS floor and dragged it over his shoulders. A quick click on the breastplate and the jacket was fastened and the straps tightened. This precious, if bulky, garment contained the flotation collar which would save his life if he was forced to eject on this dark and unforgiving night. He sprinted up the ladder and stepped over the edge of the cockpit onto the Martin Baker ejection seat and dropped onto the hard pad which might be his "armchair" for the next seven hours dragging on his bonedome which he had collected from the canopy rail during his rapid passage. Swiftly plugging the equipment connector, which trailed from his lifejacket, into the housing on the ejection seat he connected the intercom lead and hit the floor-mounted transmit switch with his foot.

"01 is at cockpit readiness."

"01, Wing Ops copied."

"01 maintain," came the disembodied voice of the intercept controller sitting in the control room at the Sector Operations Centre many miles distant in rural Norfolk. Normally under these circumstances the controller would be tracking a Soviet bomber rounding the North Cape and would be scrambling his fighters for the long trek north to intercept them as they entered the UK Air Defence Region. Today the airspace to the north of Norway was clear of any traffic.

"01 maintain," the navigator acknowledged.

At least there would be time for his heartbeat to stabilise before they rolled out of the HAS. Although it had been only a short run from the Q Shed, the bulk of the heavy survival suit despite the help from a hefty adrenaline shot had raised it to an unhealthy level. The sweat had already formed around the leather lining of his flying helmet, sticky on his forehead. He sucked gratefully on the cool oxygen flowing through his facemask cracking the edge of the mask allowing a rush of cold air to cool his face. The Phantom's engines were already spooling and the activity beneath the jet had not yet abated as the groundcrew buttoned up panels and prepared the jet for flight.

"02, cockpit readiness."

"02 maintain."

They had beaten Q2 to the check-in which always raised a certain irreverent satisfaction.

"02 maintain," the navigator acknowledged.

"On intercom," he heard from the front cockpit as his pilot finally found time to plug in his own intercom lead.

"We're being held at cockpit readiness, standing by for instructions."

"Bloody hell what's this all about?" came the grumpy, if still breathless, response. "I suppose a five minute warning to let us get into our immersion suits was out of the question."

In the other jet, the Q1 navigator finished strapping into his ejection seat the pressure somewhat diminished. It seemed like an hour since the intrusive hooter had broken his slumber but in reality it had been less than two minutes. As he glanced ahead across the deserted airfield he could see the warmth of the hangar spilling out into the cold morning air shimmering through the glare of the sodium lamps. He glanced down at his navigation system waiting for the brief alignment sequence to finish. Despite the hold the tension was still palpable.

"QRA this is the Master Controller."

"01 Go."

"02 Go"

"Roger, 01 and 02 revert to Readiness 10."

That was it. No scramble, no apology and no explanation. The Q1 pilot pulled back the tight rubber seal which was already chafing his wrist and checked the time. It was 4.05 AM.

As he pulled back the throttles in response to the stand-down the engines slowly wound to a halt. The begrudging whine as the rattling turbines clattered to a stop was replaced by the incessant hum of the avionics still powered up by the onboard battery. He signalled to the confused liney next to the jet to reconnect the external power set and intercom lead. .

"Clear to switch to external power?" he asked his navigator.

"You're clear," came the frustrated response from the back cockpit.

The letdown after the artificially induced high was tangible. They began the slow process to reset the switches and place the jet back on readiness feeling cheated. If they were to be dragged out of bed at 4 AM at least someone could have had the decency to fix up a target and let them go flying. As the adrenaline buzz faded and more reasoned thought kicked in there were a few more things that did not make sense. If this was TACEVAL, where was the evaluation team? The keynote exercise often started with a Station callout and the inevitable first serial was to evaluate the reaction of QRA. To do that, the first evidence of the start of the exercise would be a knot of aircrew evaluators clutching notebooks assembled outside QRA. The team was notable by its absence. If this was a Station exercise the Station Commander would have had no hesitation in launching them even if it meant the Phantom boring holes in the sky for an hour. So what was the reason for the siren? In the background, it moaned out across the airfield its relentless tone competing with the now subdued noises in the HAS. It was all very odd.

*

In the East Wing of the Officers' Mess Mark "Razor" Keene had been sleeping. As the sound of the siren penetrated his slumber he groaned, tempted just to roll over and ignore the incessant wail. It had only been eight days since the last Station exercise. Why, oh why, was that blessed noise ringing in his ears again? He looked over at the alarm clock on the bedside table. The fluorescent hands stared back. It was 04.01 and the distinctive whine of a jet engine sounded out across the adjacent airfield. He allowed himself another groan before he dragged himself out of bed cursing as he stubbed his toe on the bed leg. There would be a scrum for the showers even though he was supposed to go straight to work. To hell with that for a game of soldiers! He grabbed a towel and made his way from his room.

Along the same corridor, doors were opening and bleary faces emerged muttering threats of violence.

The small rooms had been the height of luxury in the late 1930s when the majority of the officers' messes had been built. The imposing buildings with their large entrance foyers, huge public rooms with high ceilings and grand picture windows looked out onto extensive grounds and well kept lawns. Inside, however, time had stood still since in the 1950s. The furniture, approved by a faceless Defence Logistics Board many years before, had been the height of fashion at some time but was showing its age. En-suite facilities, which could be seen as a basic standard in modern society was a term not yet adopted by the military. The "ablutions" were still located a short walk down the corridor and were a communal arrangement. With the increasing numbers of female officers, the arrangements could be quite "progressive" at times, albeit only by accident or arrangement. At least by the 1980s single officers could elect to move out into the local area and rent accommodation or even buy houses and many chose to do so in the more attractive areas. Razor would follow suit soon but, in the meantime, he was biding his time. The small room with its sink tucked in the corner and regulation pattern bed and wardrobe left a lot to be desired but it was home of a sort. Since his move back from Germany, life had been hectic and he had not had much time to settle down given the hectic exercise schedule. The Mess at RAF Wildenrath had been the social hub for families as well as the single officers but this front line base in rural Lincolnshire was crowded during the working week but pedestrian at weekends.

As he emerged from his room into the darkened corridor Razor tripped over "Stripes", the most pampered resident of the Officers' Mess, prompting a yowl as the disgruntled cat made its displeasure evident. He was not the only one unimpressed with the early morning call. Pausing in the batting room, he filled a bowl and relationships were quickly returned to normal as the cat lapped up the milk contentedly. Finding an empty shower he turned on the water full bore before stepping into the enveloping steam.

*

Back on the Married Patch doors were beginning to open and cars fired up taking their reluctant passengers to work. Across the crescent, as the siren moaned its incessant message, Jim "Flash" Gordon reacted like any of the other officers but this time there was no complaint from his new wife who was equally alert by now. Julie Gordon was an air traffic control officer and, like Flash, would be at her place of duty within minutes. They both scrabbled around trying to find the small bags of essentials, pre-packed and ready to go that made life a little more tolerable during a lock-down.

*

On Echo Dispersal, Paul Anderson pulled into the Squadron pleased to see that he was not the first arrival. Already the duty airman had drawn the keys and was working methodically around the concrete hardened buildings unlocking doors and turning on lights. It had probably only been a few hours since it had been secured at the end of the night shift and he would not have been surprised to see the last tired bodies leaving the dispersal on their way home as he pulled in. It could be a struggle keeping his aging Phantoms serviceable and only his dedicated groundcrew kept them in the air.

He made his way in through the main entrance of the annex towards his office. The adjacent hardened bunker, known as "The Hard", was constructed from four feet thick concrete walls which could withstand the blast of a 1000 lb bomb. The brick-built annexes used for routine operations would be less durable under air attack but provided a more comfortable daily existence. He was already gagging for a coffee but, as he slipped into the chair behind his large leather-topped desk, he hit the direct line to Wing Operations eager to find out what was underway.

"Is the Old Man in yet?" he asked listening to the ops clerk at the other end of the phone line. "OK I'll call him on the direct line." He punched another of the square plastic keys on the comms box marked "Force Cdr".

"Sir it's Paul. I hear this one's not a routine Station exercise?"

"Far from it Paul. Let me fill you in on what we have so far," said the surprisingly calm sounding Group Captain, his day already well underway.

With the handset clamped to his ear and his other hand wrestling with his notepad he missed the door being pushed open but nodded gratefully as his PA placed a steaming mug of coffee in front of him. At least she hadn't faced the dilemma of whether to shave before responding to the siren. He made a few scribbled notes as he listened.

"Let the flight commanders and SENGO know that I want them in here in 10 minutes would you, Jill?" he said covering the mouthpiece. She nodded and pulled the door closed as she withdrew to the outer office.

Some minutes later, the Squadron Execs filed in and dropped into the easy chairs arranged around the office ear wigging the latest conversation, eager for any snippets to supplement the meagre diet so far. As the Boss put the handset back in its cradle the engineering officer piped up.

"I asked the Squadron Movements Officer to sit in Boss. He'll have to get the kit ready for the move straight away so it's best if he listens in now. It'll save a re-brief."

"No trouble. Anyone else need any specialists?"

Heads shook.

"OK, it's still sketchy but here's what we've got. I'll go into the intelligence background in a minute but the headlines are that we are on 48 hours notice to move to Cyprus but expect that to come forward. They want us down at Akrotiri ready to respond to a situation in the Middle East. It'll be six jets and eight crews. We'll have two for QRA, two for the mission and two spares. We'll deploy with a full weapon load and armed guns. We'll need at least two missile reloads per jet including the spares and we're operating from Golf Dispersal as usual. The crews need to be combat ready and ACE qualified on the gun. I know it's a while since we did a gunnery qualification so we can schedule a banner down in Cyprus if any crews need a refamiliarisation. That might be a good idea in any event for all of us. Must admit, I feel a bit rusty myself. Let's make sure the emphasis is on op. shoot profiles not academic. SENGO, you might want to ask the Boss of the resident squadron if we can use their Suu-23 guns rather than drag them down with us. It'll save fuel on the deployment if we can load them on arrival and those guns down there will be prepped and ready to load. It might take quite a while to drag ours out from the Armoury here."

He paused collecting his thoughts. The room was absolutely quiet and notes were being taken rapidly.

"OK, the background. I don't know the full story but a hostage has been taken in Beirut and it seems that MOD wants him back. The mission is to spring him from wherever he's being held. From what I can make out they know where that is and it's a case of some precision bombing to breach the compound walls. For that reason a Buccaneer squadron has been put on notice to deploy with eight jets and that'll be their task. They'll be carrying LGBs and Pave Spike pods for targeting."

"That sounds like shades of Operation Jericho during World War 2, Boss. That was the raid to spring prisoners from Amiens Prison."

"It does and there might be lessons for the "mud movers" from that but we'll leave that to them. I suspect the technology they have these days might make it a bit easier than the original effort. Our role is to escort them to and from the target. We'll get detailed intelligence briefings when we get to Akrotiri so I won't get bogged down on that stuff now. The main thing is that we're planning an escort mission similar to Operation *'Pulsator'* which was staged a few years ago. Some of you might have been involved in the original missions."

He looked around but there were no takers.

"Do I need to assume I have to air-freight everything Boss?" said the senior engineer. Have we been allocated air transport yet?"

"The transop is still in preparation. The warning order went out last night so the tanker and transport fleet planners have already started working on it. One of the squadrons has just finished their armament practice camp and was packed up ready to come home. They've been warned off to stay put and provide any support we need so we can set up for the operation. I'm not sure why they weren't tasked to do the operation but they are at the end of a long detachment so they might want fresh minds on the task. They will leave as soon as we're in place. SENGO, get onto them straight away and discuss what we need. Anyone know which squadron is down there?"

"It's 56 Squadron Boss."

"OK that's good as they have FGR2s so the spares will be compatible with our own jets. Having a spares flyaway pack already in place should help but I'll leave the detail to you. Warn them we might need to use one of their jets for a gunnery sortie. SENGO speak to your counterpart on 56 and make sure they leave everything we'll need."

The engineer made eye contact with the Movements Officer who acknowledged the task.

"We'll tank down behind Victors or VC10s. The new Tristar tankers are not cleared yet which is a shame. That would have given quite a bit more flex with their extra fuel capacity. One Group is preparing the air-to-air refuelling order now and we should have it later this morning. If I was a betting man I'd say we'll be launching early tomorrow morning to arrive down in-theatre just after lunchtime inside the Akrotiri flying window. The Buccs will almost certainly be in the same stream to aid the diplomatic planning so expect them to be onboard as we form up over the North Sea and to transit down there together."

"Boss, I'll get a couple of the navs started on the route planning," said the flight commander. "We can't do much until the air-to-air refuelling instruction comes in but we can get hold of maps for the deployment and the operating area and make sure all our documentation is up to date."

"Good stuff; are there any particular techniques we need to practice in the simulator before we leave? We won't have access to the simulator down there."

"The Syrians have Foxbats, Boss. I know we did some work against Concorde in the late 70s to be able to attack a high flying supersonic target. We developed some intercept profiles at the extremes of the envelope but they were pretty tricky to fly if I remember rightly."

"Get the QWIs digging into those and book a simulator slot for this morning. Have a few crews run through them just in case. There are bound to be a lot more topics come up as you begin to dig into the detail so you can update me when we get together in a few hours. Is there anything we're missing? Are there any problems with the jets that will prevent us selecting six plus two ground spares? Are there any people or particular expertise that we haven't got on the Squadron? If so I need to tap the Operational Conversion Unit or one of the other squadrons."

"We don't have an electronic warfare officer Boss. We have a navigator on the next course but he's not qualified yet. Also we could do with an extra pilot weapons instructor. Our QWI is a back seater so a pilot QWI would be a big help."

"OK, I'll get onto the Boss of the OCU and ask for an extra crew to deploy with us. They have plenty of qualified guys with those specialities. I'll warn them that it's an open ended commitment so they should plan on at least a month away. SENGO, any ground trades that need strengthening?"

"I could do with a few extra radar tradesmen Boss. Plus a big spares pack to go with them."

"I'll ask for that."

"We'll need to brief our crews Boss," said the flight commander. "I can give them a quick walkthrough until the details become clear but speculation will be rife otherwise. I take it this is close hold?"

"Yes go ahead. Just give the brief outline at this stage. Let's look at which crews will deploy so that they can get home and pack their bags. SENGO, get a quick brief together for the troops. Again just make it broad brush at this stage but start to look at trade coverage for the deployment. I don't have any numbers from Group Headquarters yet but assume we can take as many people as we need. It goes without saying that everything about this Op is "strictly need to know" at present. No talk off station. We don't want the press getting hold of it and plastering it across the front pages. It'll be a big enough challenge as it is. If this is what I think it is, we'll need all the help we can get to beat the opposition. We don't want the "Daily Blurb" mapping out our tactics in advance."

"Understood Boss. I'll get them together in the Main Briefing Room right away and prime them for the tasks to come."

"I'll get someone drafting an Op. Order Boss," said the other flight commander. "We'll need a lot of Station support so we need to prime the system. I'll start to make some phone calls."

"Good idea. Make sure the paperwork doesn't slow us down but we all know that we'll need it in place before we can move. Get the Adjutant on that one and tell me if you hit any "Jobsworths". OK that's about it for now. Any questions? No? OK let's get back together at 10.00 for a progress update."

As the executives left the office the hotlock containers from the kitchens on the other side of the airfield arrived and were carried down to the crewroom. Breakfast was served; undoubtedly the high point of the proceedings so far and a fillip to morale. A whoop from the end of the corridor announced the arrival to the captive audience. Appetites would quell inquisitiveness for a few minutes at least.

Across the airfield on the training squadron one crew was just finding out that the carefully scripted schedule for the next three months had just changed out of all recognition. Rather than pushing students through basic radar sortie number one they would be returning to operational flying. One member of the crew was Jim "Flash" Gordon only recently returned from Germany via the academic schoolhouse at RAF Cranwell. His newly endorsed qualification as an electronic warfare officer was about to be put to the test. His Boss had just given him the news that he would be temporarily seconded to the sister squadron and he was already climbing into his car to make his way across the airfield for an eagerly anticipated briefing. He was about to deploy on operations for the second time

Despite the urgency around RAF Coningsby it was not the only place where normal life had been interrupted.

CHAPTER 2

The Ministry of Defence, London.

Deep beneath Whitehall in London, under the Ministry of Defence, is a secretive military citadel known as Pindar. The building programme began in the early 1980s but it would take 10 years to complete at a cost of over £100 million. Equipped with a complex computer system and secure communications it would eventually link the MOD Headquarters with a new centre for military operations, the Permanent Joint Headquarters in Northwood to the north of the city. Despite the ambitious plans a basic crisis management and communications centre had been up and running from the outset and, for the latest operation already dubbed *"Pulsator 2"*, the MOD operations staff would work in close cooperation with the air staff in the operations bunker at Headquarters Strike Command, RAF High Wycombe in Buckinghamshire. For the initial planning meeting, staffs had been drawn from the key subordinate headquarters around the country and had assembled in the underground conference room deep in the basement of MOD Main Building.

The muted conversation around the planning table died, as the Assistant Chief of the Air Staff, a Two Star officer from the Air Force Department in the Ministry of Defence, called for attention. His loud tap against a water carafe brought the meeting to order. As he introduced each of the representatives in turn, the diversity of the operation slowly became clear. As was the norm in central London, a business suit was the dress of the day making it difficult to differentiate between civilian and military representatives The planners from the Air Force Department and the subordinate headquarters were obvious but others less so. Two men remained detached from the main group occupying the seats at the back of the room, avoiding conversation with the others. Unacknowledged, there could be little doubt that they represented the, still secretive departments, MI5 and MI6 and no amount of euphemisms bandied around during the introductions could cover that fact. Yet another small group looking decidedly unmilitary sat alongside. The two groups had worked together on many occasions before but the other attendees would be hard pressed to know. Special forces operatives would blend well amongst a crowd of football fans in the East End but, surrounded by well-pressed suits in an MOD conference room, they looked distinctly out of place.

"Gentlemen," the slightly greying yet distinguished officer began. "You will be aware that we have a situation developing and we need to begin some contingency planning."

The Assistant Chief of the Air Staff was one of the senior RAF officers on the Air Staff in the Ministry and he had been busy for some hours already that day.

"We should be under no illusions that this operation will, almost certainly, be executed so warn your staff accordingly. RAF Coningsby, RAF Lossiemouth and RAF Odiham were placed on alert at 4AM this morning and detailed planning is already underway. I know that many of you were warned-off late last night and have already been planning for some hours. For that I'm grateful. I wanted to get you all together at the outset to ensure that we move forward in a coherent way. Some of the background to this mission will have to remain close hold but much of the detail will be essential if the crews are to be successful in their task. It is not over estimating the challenge to say that this is, potentially, one of the most complex operations we have attempted since the Falklands War and will require precision of the highest order. Let me hand over to DCDI who will give you the background as to why we find ourselves in this situation."

The Deputy Chief of Defence Intelligence cut an imposing figure. A serving military officer, his bearing spelled purpose. As his deep baritone voice filled the small enclosed space he held the attention of every single attendee.

"Thank you, Peter. You will know that we have had a military presence in Beirut for many years. The Multinational Force was dissolved in March 1984 soon after the October 1983 Beirut barracks bombing. Throughout that year tensions were high between Syria and the United States and Syrian anti-aircraft batteries fired on US aircraft as they patrolled Lebanese airspace. Little was reported in the press but two US aircraft were shot down during those months and there were regular exchanges of fire. The US extracted an element of revenge when a Syrian Command Post was shelled by the USS New Jersey killing the Commanding General of the Syrian forces in Lebanon. Late last year a coalition formed known as the "National Democratic Front" bringing together many of the political organisations but allowing the Lebanese Army to take control of Beirut. Sadly, it fell short of establishing full control in the Country and, rather than help, this seemed to provoke the Syrians. Fierce fighting occurred between the two armies in Souk El Garb, and Dahar El Wahech. It came as a surprise when, upset by world opinion, Israel recently pulled its forces from southern Lebanon and set up an occupation zone on the border to try to prevent attacks from its neighbour."

"Are the Israelis involved in this operation?"

"I'll come to that in a moment if I may," he replied.

"Faced with the loss of intelligence after the withdrawal of Commander British Forces Lebanon, SIS agents were inserted into Beirut under the guise of diplomatic activity. This is where our friends from the agencies come into the picture," he said acknowledging the two men at the end of the table for the first time.

"One of those agents formed some very useful links with a contact in Damascus. Now this is the part which is extremely sensitive and should not be repeated outside these walls. He acquired some operational plans which appear to show a rather worrying plot being hatched in Damascus. Allegedly, the plans involve a rapid manoeuvre to retake the Golan Heights and to position Scud missiles on the high ground. With the recent Israeli withdrawal the Syrians obviously feel that they are sufficiently distracted to take their eyes off the strategic prize. Our agent has assessed the plans in broad terms but his initial impression is that they are viable. We desperately need to get hold of those documents so that we can study the detail and form an opinion as to why this latest initiative might work. Unfortunately, three days ago he was taken hostage as he was trying to arrange to deliver the plans to the Embassy and extract them via the Diplomatic Bag. We don't know at this time whether his captors were just lucky or whether they knew that he had acquired the plans and their actions were deliberate in order to avoid them being compromised. What we do know is that he has been taken out of the city and is now being held captive in a compound inside Lebanon somewhere along the Syrian border. We know he is safe for the time being and we are trying to arrange consular access to speak to him. Only then will we know whether he has been compromised."

"Isn't this a task for the special forces?" asked the Director of Air Defence.

"Director Special Forces will be joining us in just a moment Alexander and he'll explain what they have been doing over the last hours. John here is our military representative on the Cabinet Crisis Action Team and he will make the arrangements to ensure that the Israeli Ambassador is briefed on our efforts. That will ensure that they don't disrupt our plans. While we wait for DSF, DCOS Ops will update you on the air effort."

The Deputy Chief of Staff for Operations at Strike Command took to his feet.

"Gentlemen, we have already begun planning in anticipation of a tasking order and I have formed a mission planning group. All the key elements have been identified and air-to-air tankers, fighters, bombers, helicopters and transport aircraft and their crews are on notice to deploy. The Cyprus-based units will be reinforced with additional personnel to support the influx adding fighter controllers and air traffic controllers to their normal complement. We will publish an Op Order later today to formalise the arrangements. You don't need the detail just yet but I will make sure you have access to my staff to get whatever you need for your own planning efforts. A liaison officer has been nominated to work with each of you."

As he sat down the door opened and a burly man entered the room.

"Phillip, perfect timing. Gentlemen, Director Special Forces."

"Thank you, Sir. Apologies gentlemen but I've just finished briefing the Prime Minister and he's just given his go ahead. The operation is on. We deploy at the earliest opportunity so time is short. I assume the question was why have we not already got to the hostage and pulled him out? Believe me we've tried. When he failed to make contact after the rendezvous with the contact from the Embassy, a team of SBS troopers were infiltrated into Beirut. Incidentally, the Embassy man has disappeared. The team had been on readiness in Cyprus for another task and were diverted immediately, going in by sea under cover of darkness. They checked out the planned rendezvous and another safe house which had been nominated should there be a problem at the RV but there was no sign of our man. They stayed at the Embassy while efforts were made to locate him but the opposition beat us to it. The British Ambassador was informed that he had been taken within hours of his disappearance. It has the hallmark of a carefully orchestrated effort but even by Beirut standards it's all a little unusual. Chaos seems to be the normal order of things over there. We heard late last night that he is in a secure compound on the Lebanese border surrounded by half the Lebanese Army on one side and the Syrian Army on the other but neither seem complicit. He seems to be particularly well guarded inside the building but we have no idea how determined that guard force is. They could be the usual rowdies but maybe there's more going on here than we know as yet. One thing is clear. Without air support we have no chance of getting anywhere near the compound to secure his escape. The place is locked down and control of access is tight. That's where you all come in. This is what I think we need . . . . ."

He outlined an embryonic plan. Once complete he made eye contact with a number of men in the room who silently acknowledged the signal.

"I have put a troop of 22 SAS on readiness to fly out with the deployment. The liaison men are here today so use the opportunity to ask questions if you need to. They will have helicopter support from two Chinooks which will be airlifted into theatre aboard a Belfast freighter which has been chartered for the operation. The flight is planned for later today. It will land at Akrotiri to drop the team and its kit."

"Well gentlemen," said ACAS. It looks as if we have some serious planning ahead. Let's get moving and I'll see you back here at 1800 for an update."

At the far end of the table the two SIS operatives were more hesitant than their special forces colleagues and rose to leave as soon as the meeting was closed. Their business would be conducted in slightly less public surroundings and their master would be briefed carefully on the military plans within the hour.

CHAPTER 3

North of Beirut, The Lebanon, the previous day.

Adam Reeves had no idea of his whereabouts. The vehicle taking him out of the city had taken a circuitous route and he was thoroughly disorientated. Sneaking small glances under his blindfold he had, finally, been able to see shadows cast inside the vehicle. Knowing roughly the time he had been taken and by estimating the position of the Sun he had worked out that they must have taken the northerly road out of Beirut. His hands had been bound tightly and there was no way of easing the blindfold to get a better view. His hands were numb and the bindings chafed painfully and, by now, the circulation had almost been cut off. He was conscious of the minder in the seat next to him who had made it very clear that any attempts to escape would be extremely terminal and he had no wish to decide whether that was bluff or not. The fact he was still alive meant they wanted him to stay that way; at least for a short while.

As the journey had begun, the truck had rattled along poor roads for some time. He could, occasionally hear the sea and, by angling his head carefully, he could sense it on his left so he reasoned that they were taking the coast road out of Beirut towards Tripoli. Sure enough, after what he thought was about an hour, he began to hear the sounds of a city around him again and the traffic became heavier. Rattling along rutted roads they left the city behind and he could still hear the noise of the waves surging gently in the background. Soon the truck veered right and the familiar noises faded replaced by the odd rush of a vehicle travelling in the opposite direction. He decided they must be heading inland. By his reckoning they must have just taken the fork near Mqaitaa towards the Syrian border but it was at that point that he became disorientated. Please God don't let them be taking me to Syria he pleaded silently.

The truck drove on for another 30 minutes the drone of the tyres unchanging. If he was right, he had driven this road many times before as he made his way to Damascus for meetings with his contacts. There was little other than small villages along this stretch until the border post just south of Addabousiyah. Usually supremely confident he began to worry.

*

The fortified compound on the Syrian Border was a Hezbollah stronghold. Used for many things including hosting a training camp for "freedom fighters", it doubled as a regional headquarters for the embryonic organisation. It was well defended with large walls and guard towers set at each corner. Outside the walls a deep ditch deterred all but the most dedicated visitor from approaching from anywhere but along the single approach track and in through the main entrance. The huge wooden gate was always closed and a pair of guards on each side of the doorway controlled access. Cameras stared silently at the access point checking and recording anyone who approached and only those with bona fide credentials, or perhaps an RPG, would go in through the gates. The physical barriers were not the only defences. A troop of gunners controlled the arsenal of SA-7 Strela MANPADS which protected the immediate area from air attack. Usually deployed in teams out into the surrounding area, these were by no means the most potent weapons available to the terrorists. A radar-laid ZSU 23-4 Shilka mobile anti-aircraft artillery system spent some of its life in the large compound. At other times it roamed the local area looking for trouble. On this desolate stretch of border it had been used regularly to warn off inquisitive pilots, mostly Israeli but not exclusively. With its quadruple barrels firing thousands of rounds of 23mm shells per minute, directed by the Gundish fire control radar it was feared by most pilots who encountered it.

The truck carrying Reeves rattled to a halt outside with little fanfare. After a relaxed exchange the gates were drawn apart and it moved inside making its way across the wide compound where it drew up in front of the building at

the far end and came to a stop. Today life in the compound moved along at
pretty much the usual pace. It was obvious that his arrival had been
expected. Reeves tensed at the shouted commands as doors slammed and
the rear doors of the truck were dragged open noisily. With his sight
inhibited for the last hours his senses of hearing and smell had been
heightened, compensating for the loss. He was dragged, roughly, from the
back seat and frogmarched inside the building. Still blindfolded he had little
awareness of direction and complied meekly. After a long walk down a
never-ending corridor he heard the sound of a door being unbolted and he
was propelled inside an echoing room. The bindings on his wrists were
removed before he was pushed, forcibly onto a chair. He waited.

There was a sound off to his right and he strained to identify the noise. The
scurrying was more animal than human and he relaxed again. A loud click in
his other ear brought back the familiar tension but it was only the sound of
wood flexing in the oppressive heat. His bladder ached and he realised how
long he had been cooped up in the vehicle bringing him to wherever the
hell he was. His senses were on edge, attuned to the intimate space around
him, working overtime to locate signs of a fellow occupant. Deprived of
sensory input anyone else in the room with him, even one of his captors,
might be welcome. The door clanged closed and he waited for a while
tensing and anticipating the blows he expected to follow. There was
nothing but silence and, beneath the blindfold, the blackness was
overwhelming and disorientating. He had suffered similar treatment during
his resistance to interrogation training but there was a limit to what the
instructors and interrogators at the Survival School at Mountbatten could
do to him. Despite the realism of that training there were limits and
physical violence was beyond the brief and would not have been tolerated.
Here, there were no such rules and he was, suddenly, afraid. The sensation
was new to him. He was used to controlling his own destiny.

Some time passed before his customary bravery returned yet he gave it just
a few more minutes before moving, still anticipating the blow. Nothing.
Easing the blindfold away from his eyes he tensed, the inevitable blow just
one movement away but it never came. Looking around he took in his
surroundings. The small room was sparsely furnished with a bench seat
along one side and a rudimentary cot in the corner. There were no blankets
or pillows nor were there any other concessions to civilisation. The small

bowl under the bed appeared to be his toilet and he gratefully relived himself, glad that he had avoided the degrading consequences. Such a seemingly insignificant victory might be important over the coming hours. Outside the small window that was positioned high on the cell wall he could see daylight. A powerful engine fired up outside reaching a crescendo before it slowly subsided. The noise was replaced by chattering voices, the tones harsh and guttural.

Outside in the compound a convoy of trucks had pulled to a stop and a new contingent of guards bearing AK47 assault rifles climbed from the flatbeds. A few words of Arabic seemed to stimulate the group and they dispersed to points around the walls relieving the bored-looking incumbents from their posts. The now empty vehicles pulled across the dusty yard and came to a halt outside the MT yard. With his cargo delivered the driver lolled against the bonnet of the first truck and began to converse with his compatriot, a cigarette lodged firmly in the corner of his mouth.

Back inside his cell Reeves slumped down onto the bench seat and pondered his fate. The relatively gentle treatment so far was unnerving. There seemed little to do for the time being but sit down and wait.

CHAPTER 4

Echo Dispersal, RAF Coningsby, Lincolnshire.

RAF Coningsby with its east/west runway stood out from the flat Lincolnshire countryside with its sprawling technical site dominated by the 2nd Word War hangars and support buildings adjacent to the main aircraft parking areas. The air traffic control tower sat alongside the 8000 foot runway on the northern side opposite two dispersals on the southern side built at the height of the Cold War. The ugly toned-down concrete structures had grown as the airfield had been equipped to survive a nuclear or chemical attack from the Soviet Union. Self-contained with their own power, water and decontamination facilities, it was hoped that the squadrons could continue to operate despite the cataclysm of a nuclear strike.

At the eastern end of the airfield, Echo Dispersal housed No 29 (Fighter) Squadron operating from a large concrete blockhouse known, not surprisingly but to the chagrin of the navigators, as the Pilot's Briefing Facility or PBF. A taxiway threaded its way through ranks of immature pine trees from the threshold of Runway 26 at the eastern end of the airfield and through Echo Dispersal. It passed onwards through Foxtrot Dispersal close to the opposite end of the airfield close to the threshold of Runway 08. Within each dispersal, groups of NATO-standard hardened aircraft shelters, or HASs, had been clustered around short connecting strips of taxiway. Each HAS could house a pair of Phantoms at a pinch and there were just enough shelters to house each of the 29 Squadron Phantoms individually.

The harsh white of the concrete had been sluiced with dingy brown slurry to make detection from the air just a little harder. It was impossible to hide the bulk of the massive structures entirely but the tone-down and the trees helped, if only marginally. Huge metal doors at the front of each HAS, supported by enormous girder frameworks, slid across the yawning entrance to each shelter allowing aircraft to be manoeuvred in and out of the HAS at will, albeit under tractor power rather than the power of the Rolls Royce Spey engines. Small concrete annexes housed essential services such as the external power sets, vital to operate the complex fighters.

Within the PBF was located the operational accommodation. A huge chemical decontamination area just inside the metal blast doors held racks of flying clothing and aircrew survival equipment. The flying helmets and flying suits positioned on the metal stands looked eerily like figures in repose in the harsh fluorescent light. Once through the decontamination zone, visitors entered the operational and engineering complex. A large operations desk fronted the daily flying programme board where details of who would fly and when were posted. An aircrew officer orchestrated the complex flying programme and ensured it moved along as planned. Today the board was remarkably blank and the desk was noticeably free from the usual throng of aircrew who frequently lurked, hopeful of picking up a stray sortie which might be added to the programme.

The original plan for the day had been discarded as soon as the hooter had sounded. Magnetic tags nominating crews to accept aircraft as they were declared serviceable were lined up in order on the ops board but, as yet, not matched to airframes. Around the dispersal, aircraft were being serviced and armed and were appearing on the engineering totes next door ready for crews to accept. So far, in the absence of any guidance from the Boss, the normal, practised chain of events during a generation exercise had been disrupted. The well-oiled machine was, temporarily, idling.

The cavernous vault opposite the ops desk housed the sensitive intelligence material held on every squadron yet today the door was wide open as it acted as a planning room. This was another indication that events were bucking the trend. The smaller briefing rooms ranged along the internal corridor were quiet. The larger main briefing room alongside would be the venue for the initial briefing which would finally let the crews know why they had been dragged in at "O Dark Early" this morning. In the meantime, they had been dispatched to the crewroom in the adjacent administrative complex to quell the inevitable speculation and to allow things to settle down. Something was amiss and the deception tactic was spectacularly ineffective. For a normal exercise once aircraft were generated and armed, crews were dispatched to the HAS to complete an acceptance and to declare the aircraft "on state" with Wing Operations. It was obvious to everyone that this was not a normal generation exercise and they were curious to know why.

The administrative offices were located in a small brick-built annex alongside the huge concrete structure and in one of those offices the flight commanders had been adding flesh to the bones of the initial plan they had received from the Squadron Boss just minutes before. Secretly they knew that he would lead the detachment and that only one of them would be lucky enough to deploy to Cyprus. For the unlucky candidate remaining behind, he would have the dubious privilege of running whatever was left of the Squadron once the jets flew out. To the rest of the squadron, the closed office doors told a story and, down in the crewroom, speculation was rife. The Duty Authoriser had already warned the crews that telephone calls from the base were strictly forbidden and a lock-down was in force. With the dearth of information it would be impossible to transgress as no one could even speculate over events in the Mediterranean.

"We need to decide on the crews and quickly," said the flight commander. "The Boss of the OCU has allocated the extra bodies we wanted so we have an EWO and a QWI on their way over here. The Boss needs to come clean on whether he's leading. No prize for guessing that answer."

He hit the squawk box and the Boss's terse reply suggested he was still embroiled in negotiations. He sounded strained already.

"Boss are you leading the detachment?"

"Dumb question John."

"Who do you want to stay behind?"

"You're the Deputy Squadron Commander John; that'll be you."

The light on the squawk box snapped off.

"I guess we'll take that as a yes then! Bloody hell, why did I know that I would be Cinderella?"

"That makes it easy then," replied the other flight commander. It'll be the Boss and his nav, me and my pilot and four other crews. We'll need to split the OCU crew up because we'll need a QWI on each shift. Razor used to fly with Flash Gordon in Germany so we can crew them together. The OCU QWI pilot can fly with Razor's usual navigator. I've already got the Boss's nav working on the route planning for the deployment so that works. Our own QWI nav takes his pilot along so that just leaves one crew to choose. Any preferences?"

"You might want to take a QFI along in case you have any check rides fall due while you're down there."

"Good thinking. That's it then. His nav goes with him. We'll schedule some simulator rides today so everyone is current before they deploy. I'll check for any essential check rides that are needed."

The phone rang as he hit the squawk box to the Duty Authoriser on the Ops desk. He gestured urgently to his colleague to pick up the call.

"Duty Auth," came the harried response from the Ops Room.

"Phil, call a briefing in the Main Briefing Room in 10 minutes. I'll update everyone on what we have so far. Can you get Paddy to put together an ops pack-up for the deployment? Get him to put in the usual stuff plus a spare set of order books. I think we might need them for this one!"

He switched his attention back to the phone call.

"That was the operations staff officer at HQ 11 Group. They've arranged for some of the deploying crews to get a session in the Air Combat Simulator at Warton to fly against some of the threats we might face. Defence Intelligence is sending a desk officer up to Warton to run some background briefings for the crews. There's a Devon on its way here right now to fly them up there. It'll be on the ground in 45 minutes. We must be on a short fuse for them to allocate air transport for the task."

He raised his eyebrows not for the first time that morning. Unusual stuff! Best get this briefing done quickly before the crews spread to the wind.

*

It had been barely three hours since the hooter had sounded when the twin propeller driven Devon from the Communications Flight at RAF Northolt taxied onto the squadron dispersal and nodded to a halt outside the PBF. Normally a four hour drive, the small aircraft would whisk the crews to the commercial facility in the northwest of the country in less than an hour. Six aircrew dressed in green flying suits made their way across the taxiway from the PBF towards the stationary Devon. The nearest engine had been closed down and the oval door pushed back against the fuselage allowing easy access to the cabin. The co-pilot beckoned from the doorway and they climbed aboard up the shaky folding steps taking their seats inside the small cabin and strapping in. Without fanfare the door was pulled closed and, as the co pilot slipped back into his seat and strapped in, the propeller began to turn as the engines wound up and the small commuter plane made its way onwards through the dispersal towards the duty runway. Inside the cabin the crews watched as the crew ran through the check list prior to departure. The pilots felt the usual anticipation as the small plane gathered speed down the runway not used to being ferried around. The navigators, thoroughly used to the experience and familiar with the surrounding Lincolnshire countryside paid less attention. A document which had been hastily thrust into their hands before setting off was being circulated around the cabin. The pink cover, stamped "Secret" on the top and bottom gave a clue to the sensitivity of the content. If things had been normal the document would have been signed out through the squadron registry and packaged carefully in double wrappers not to be opened until they arrived at their destination. Today was not a normal day as they avidly devoured the content, whetting appetites for what was unfolding. The small commuter plane settled down at its cruising altitude of 10,000 feet and threaded its way carefully through the airways which split the backbone of the Country, under the control of a military air traffic agency. The pilot chatted amiably to the controller negotiating a direct route to their destination which lay to the northwest.

As the Devon settled onto the runway and taxied across to the small operations complex a bus was waiting to move them immediately to the plush briefing room within the Air Combat Simulator complex. The small coach dropped them at the front doors of the nondescript building and they filed inside.

Squadron Leader John Silversmith rose from his seat and greeted them as they entered the room. Razor and Flash were the first to recognise him having worked with him during their time in West Germany and knowing him well. As they shook hands, a broad smile creased his face and he beckoned them over to the front of the room.

"I have someone with me that I think you'll remember."

Before he had finished his sentence the other officer in the room also dressed in a green, albeit, American flying suit, rose and turned around. To say they were taken aback would be an understatement. Yuri Andrenev, the Soviet test pilot who had defected to the West bringing his Su-27 Flanker to Wildenrath just a few years before, greeted them warmly. The last time they had seen him was as they had closed alongside an RAF HS-125 communications aircraft as it made its way westwards en route for London. Razor and Flash had escorted him out of West German airspace in their Phantom after the momentous events at Düsseldorf airport. It had filtered back during the days that followed that he had been injured in a struggle at the airport but at that point the trail had gone cold. There was no evidence now of any lasting injury. John Silversmith had been the intelligence officer at the Joint Headquarters at Rheindahlen who had taken care of him during those early days of freedom and, clearly, he had not lost contact in the intervening years. In a rapid-fire exchange they greeted him like an old friend eager to fill in the blanks.

"Sorry chaps, I'm going to have to rush you," said Silversmith. I know you have a lot of catching up to do but I know you'll get chance to do that very soon."

His knowing smile suggested he knew more than he had so far revealed.

"We have a lot to squeeze in and you have to be back on the Devon in three hours. The Squadron has already been on the phone asking when they can expect you back. It looks like things are hotting-up back there."

He moved over to the podium and began to speak.

"I'm going to hand over straight away to Colonel Andrenev - Yuri. Some of you know his background but he has some experience which is particularly pertinent to the situation which is developing. Yuri, over to you."

The Russian accent was still pronounced as he began to speak.

"Gentlemen, I don't yet know how much of the detail that you have been given but I've been asked to support you in an upcoming mission. I've only just been briefed-in myself this morning but luckily I was here at Warton helping to configure the Air Combat Simulator so I'm happy to assist and I'm looking forward to working with you again. You might not know but I did much of the testing of the Mig-23M, known to you as the Flogger Bravo, including quite a lot of the development testing on the export variant, the Mig-23MF, the Flogger Golf. I understand that the Flogger is your principal threat for this upcoming mission so, today, we are going to fight against it in the Air Combat Simulator and I am going to tell you exactly how to exploit its weaknesses."

The blank looks on some of the faces around the room told a story and it was clear that even Yuri was better briefed than the crews at this point. John Silversmith interrupted.

"Don't worry too much if this seems out of context. Just treat this as an isolated briefing to get you up to speed on this particular threat. Some of you won't know Yuri's background but I'm sure Razor and Flash will fill you in on some, if not all, of the detail on the way home. It's quite a story but "need to know". Yuri has well over 1000 hours on the Mig-23 so you can assume that he's an expert tutor in every aspect of its capability. After today you can assume that you will have a better knowledge of that aircraft than most other pilots or navigators in NATO."

"Thanks John," said Andrenev continuing the double act. "You will have had many briefings about its capabilities over the years but I want you to ignore much of it for the next 2 hours. If you have questions after the session we'll answer them for you but I intend to give you a focussed analysis to allow you to beat it. Stow what you think you know up to now and we'll put it in context in the simulator. There's a lot of disinformation out there but my knowledge is first hand."

Silversmith interrupted.

"What we have for you is this, gents. Yuri will start with a briefing on the Flogger Golf, its capabilities and equipment. Then we'll split up and fly the combat sim. sessions as crews. Razor and Flash you'll be first. When each crew is in the sim. the others will receive more orientation briefings from one of my intelligence analysts to bring you up to speed on the avionics. Flash, I know you've been nominated as the electronic warfare officer so we have already prepared an assessment of the electronic warfare suite for you which you can take away. You can use that to brief the crews back at base as you see fit. I can't tell you where the information came from but, trust me, it's of the highest fidelity and you can be sure that if you use it in conjunction with today's information it's as good as it gets. We'll fly the first session against the Mig as a split crew against the simulator computer. After a quick debrief, the second sortie will be against Yuri who will be in the second dome flying the Mig. By then you should be able to exploit your superior Phantom tactics to achieve consistent kills. Trust me, this jet has some serious weaknesses."

Already intrigued by the secretive aura the crews were transfixed as Yuri began to delve deeper into the capabilities of the Soviet fighter. From bland descriptions in technical intelligence manuals and grainy photographs garnered from expeditions by BRIXMIS in East Germany, they had suddenly moved into the realms of reality. Compared to previous briefings they felt as if they were being offered access to the Crown Jewels.

"Let's start with a quick description of the Mig-23. As you know it's operated in the Soviet Union but an export version was widely sold both to Warsaw Pact countries and to other nations outside the Pact. Like the West, the Soviet Union pays for its military machine through hard currency earned overseas; but there's a catch and it's relevant to your mission. The ones sold to Syria lacked the Soviet communications and identification equipment, they had no datalink and the radar was downgraded to remove the electronic counter-countermeasures. Some of those systems are crucial to its effectiveness and without them it struggles. You can exploit that deficiency and I'll show you how."

He paused to assess his audience.

"Stepping back a stage, you know it's a single engine fighter powered by a Tumansky R29A turbojet. The engine develops 12,500 Kg thrust that will take the aircraft supersonic. That's its first big positive. It goes very fast in a straight line so if you try to outrun it make sure you set up well in advance for the disengagement or it'll be in your shorts before you can blink. It'll do Mach 2.5 at height and well over 900 knots at low level. You know too well that the best you'll achieve in a Phantom, even if you jettison the external fuel tanks, is 850 knots. Don't try to outrun it unless you have a head start."

He clicked on a new slide on the overhead projector and a picture of a fully armed Flogger filled the screen.

"It's armed with the Vympel R-23, AA-7 Apex missile and the Vympel R-60, AA-8 Aphid," he said pointing out the missiles on the pylons.

"The Syrians normally carry two Apex under the wings and two Aphids under the fuselage, although they have been seen carrying four Aphids on specially adapted launcher rails. The Apex is a medium-range radar-guided missile which relies on a continuous wave signal from the illuminator to track the target and is very similar in overall capability to the Skyflash. You now have the Skyflash which out-ranges the Apex but only just. The Skyflash is also much better in electronic jamming conditions but don't underestimate their electronic warfare capability. Like your own weapon it's semi-active so the Mig pilot needs to stay locked on until impact but if you jam it, the missile can home-on-jam so beware. If it reaches you it has a large high explosive warhead with a variety of fuses and the test firings have shown it to be very reliable with a high probability of kill."

He looked around anticipating questions but so far the room was quiet. He had a captive audience.

"The Aphid is an infra-red guided short range missile. The early versions were uncooled which meant they were quite short range and worked only in the stern hemisphere. The seeker heads on the later versions are cooled and much more capable but the Syrians don't have them. In the B version the Aphid has an all-aspect capability but we only gave the Syrians the A version so they are limited to stern hemisphere shots only. Store that one away because it's another huge advantage. The missile has a range out to 5 miles but realistically if you defend against it by turning, that range collapses to probably two miles at best. It has an expanding rod warhead and it's just as lethal as a blast fragmentation warhead, perhaps even more so. When that warhead detonates it sends thousands of supersonic shrapnel pellets at you. Just a few would destroy an average fighter."

He flicked on another graphic which showed a series of tactical engagement profiles.

"So what does that mean about the tactics you'll face? It means they'll have to get into your 6 o'clock to fire an Aphid. The only head-on threat you face is from the Apex and the pilots are heavily reliant on their ground controllers to set up those shots. If you can disrupt their profiles you'll defeat the shots. If they should get in close, the Aphid can be fired at very close range and the minimum range is quite short. They have a very clever safe and arm circuit which means they can close almost to guns range and still be in the missiles envelope. Sucking him in that close on the off chance that he misses is not a tactic I'd recommend! Keep him at arm's length."

There were knowing smiles around the room and Razor chuckled quietly at the English sayings and mannerisms that Yuri had picked up since he arrived in the West.

"The gun is a GSh-23L 23 mm cannon with 200 rounds. It's accurate, reliable and carries high explosive rounds. We never trained much in air-to-air gunnery so it's not a tactic I'd expect the Syrians to employ. They will be more likely to use missiles so the most important equipment for them is the radar; oh and the ability to be able to speak to their controller. Jam the comms channel and they'll struggle. The Sapfir-23D, or High Lark 4 to you, is quite a clever system and is integrated with the TP-23 infra-red search and track sensor and the ASP-23D gunsight. It has a detection range of about 30 miles against a Phantom, although it's not a true pulse Doppler system because it uses moving target indicator technology, or MTI, to give it a limited look-down capability. The radar scope sits immediately in front of the pilot below the gunsight allowing the pilot to keep his head out of the cockpit and he operates his radar using controls on the stick and throttle. The lesson there is don't think that by flying just below him you will give him a hard time. The radar will cope just fine with a small look down at medium level. If you want to take advantage of that aspect of the radar design you'll need a big height split and you'll need to come in from way below."

There were nods as if he had just reinforced some prior knowledge.

"The infra-red system sits in a fairing under the nose and has a detection range of around 20 miles at best but less against fighter-sized targets. It goes without saying that if you use reheat it will love it and track you all day. The sensor is, effectively, an enhanced missile seeker head so treat it as you would a threat missile and you won't go far wrong. If you show the pilot a hot spot on his display and you will if you use too much reheat – he will see you passively and you'll have no idea he has your location. Most importantly, it's integrated into the weapon system. If the radar is tracking you so is the IRSTS and so are the missiles. We were very good at that aspect my friends and it took you quite a while to catch up over here I can tell you. Are you all still following me?"

In a few cases, the warmth of the briefing room coupled with the 4 AM siren was beginning to take its toll. Yuri raised his voice and at least one head nodded back upright once again alert.

"The navigation system is rudimentary and relies on the RSBN Soviet-built radio navigation beacons. Once over the sea and out of range of the beacons they have nothing. Navigation is a challenge in the Mig other than by using a map and stopwatch, especially if they are not talking to their controllers. Even the export versions are fitted with the Sirena 3 radar warning receiver so assume they will see you coming. The RWR is quite coarse, directionally, but quite sensitive as a receiver. Think of it as a less accurate version of your own radar warner. Whereas you have fine angle indications accurate to a few degrees, the Flogger pilot has only a quadrant warning like your own warning function for continuous wave radars. He knows the general area you're approaching from but not the precise bearing. When you attack he will know you're coming if you lock on, so try to save that for as late in the intercept as possible. The Mig-23 is also fitted with an active jammer, the Gardeniya, which is one of the main jammers deployed on Soviet fighters. The Syrians were sold quite a few of these to combat the Israeli F-15 radars. It's quite old technology but still works well. You should think of it as a brute force solution; not very bright but very

41

strong. It will give your AWG12 radar quite a hard time too so brush up on your electronic warfare drills. Flash is your electronic warfare officer and with the information he just received I'm sure he'll be giving you the low down on its capabilities and the tactics you should use. Any questions so far?"

"Is that assessment of the jammer based on testing?"

"A bit of both. Most of my experience was against our own radar systems in the Soviet Union. We used our own SAMs such as the SA-6 to test against rather than western types but I know it well and I've had a lot of input to the briefing material. It's a very capable jammer and you have done some bench testing of a captured Gardeniya that you picked up in Mogadishu market place and that information has found its way into the report. I think the analysts used an AWG12 for that testing but we'll check. OK let's move back to the tactics."

Even the narcoleptic in row three perked up at this point.

"The Syrian pilots were all trained either in Moscow or by Soviet advisers in Damascus. They adopted Soviet style tactics, although after the Yom Kippur War they adapted them after they learned a few tricks which you'll need to take into account. Soviet tactics are quite simplistic and rely on the ground control. Pilots expect help with the air picture from the man on the ground using the data link system for control. If they go low level they are out of their element and their weapon system is not optimised for that regime. In a one-on-one engagement there's little finesse. He'll point at you and keep the nose on. That makes him hard to see but it also makes him predictable. He'll rely on information from the ground and only lock up when he needs to in order to launch a radar guided missile. That means you'll get a late warning on your RWR so never underestimate a lock as it probably means a missile will be on its way very soon afterwards. They are probably unlikely to take big tactical height splits. If they know your height they'll come to you. You can use that to your advantage because if you change your height in the end game, the ground controller will never keep up. The height finding radars on the ground are inaccurate but that can also mean they are vectored towards you at the wrong height. Multiple aircraft tactics are a whole different ball game and we can brief you on those separately. There are a few set-piece manoeuvres which may be used so you'll be briefed specifically. You have a question?"

He pointed at one of the pilots in the front row.

"How much do they rely on the RWR?"

"Good question. I know many of my peers didn't even look at it unless it showed a solid lock-on indication. They figured that with GCI control, the controller would tell them if there was a threat around them. They barely even snagged the equipment on the squadrons when it failed. I often wondered if it would ever work on the day. However, don't assume that and the Syrians may be different. They have been at war for quite some years now. It would be a brave man who ignored the capability. It's fitted in the jets and we should assume it works, although we have no feel for how well the Syrians look after their sensors."

The briefing continued dissecting each and every facet of the Mig-23 weapons system in exceptional detail which could only have come from someone with an intimate knowledge of what made the jet tick.

"I'm going to finish by giving you the greatest weakness of all. The Mig-23 is a pig to fly! We knew the Americans had been given examples of the Mig-23 by some of their allies in the Middle East. In fact I was lucky enough to fly a Northrop F5 Freedom Fighter at Ramenskoye which fell into our hands after Saigon fell to the North Vietnamese so the practice was not unique to America. This type of evaluation goes on all the time and you may have programmes of your own. The test pilots on the 4477th "Red Eagles" Squadron at Tonopah, Nevada flew a squadron of captured Migs for training purposes and formed their own opinions but I'm about to tell you exactly how it flies. This jet will go fast. The canopy is likely to implode before the airframe breaks up. It will go well beyond the engine placard limits which are carried in the cockpit. The wings sweep between 16 degrees when fully forward to 72 degrees fully back but they're operated entirely manually and there is no auto wing sweep mode. That means if you see the position of the wings at the merge it gives you an instant assessment of the energy levels. If the wings are forward he's slow. If external tanks are fitted the wings are going nowhere. The pylons are fixed so he would have to jettison the tanks to move the wings. The lesson here is look at the wings at the merge and you'll know how to react. The turning performance is about the same as your "hard wing" Phantom so if you exploit your better weapons system you will win. The engine is smoky so you'll see them coming but don't forget that it has a very small head-on profile so, nose on, it's hard to see. The handling is poor and we fought hard to get improvements as it went through testing but with no success. The forces on the controls are high so it never feels comfortable manoeuvring hard. Even though it's a stable aircraft it doesn't tell you when it's unhappy. If you push it to the limits and beyond it will bite. You get little notice of departure from controlled flight and, when it goes, it's vicious and hard to recover. Lookout from the cockpit is poor. The view forward is similar to your own Phantom. The HUD is relatively clear of heavy ironwork but the windscreen is quite thick which obscures the view. The windscreen supports, the canopy arches and canopy rails are all heavy metal and restrict what the pilot can see around him. I've sat in the back of a Phantom and I'd say the Flogger pilot has about the same view as you back-seaters. He doesn't have the advantage of being able to turn around quite so easily because he has to keep hold of the stick. The view down and back is almost non-existent so if you can get into that sector you'll be unseen despite the stupid telescope you can see that was fitted on the canopy. There are limitations of when missiles can be fired under G and that assumes that the pilot is still trying to employ weapons if he has been forced to turn that hard. If he's in a merge he may already have given up the fight as his training is limited."

"That's the first time I've ever been briefed to stay and turn at the merge," said one of the pilots ruefully.

"Trust me, you're no worse off than he is. If you fight the Phantom well you'll beat him. If you push a Flogger pilot hard he'll be working way harder than you are. The most important thing to remember is they don't train in air combat skills as much as you do, if at all. Finally, this aircraft has tried to kill me more than once! Push your opponent hard and you may force him to make a mistake that you can exploit. Right, if everyone is happy let's split up and get into the simulator and fly against this thing."

There was an enthusiastic buzz of anticipation as the briefing broke up. Razor walked into the huge combat dome his footsteps echoing as he climbed the short steps into the cockpit of the air combat simulator.

Around him the dome onto which the world would be projected amplified every little noise and he resisted a childish temptation to yodel. In the adjacent dome his navigator was already in the second cockpit and had plugged into the intercom system. He chatted with the simulator instructor as he waited for his pilot to check in.

"I'm on," said Razor from the primary dome.

"Loud and clear Razor," came the disembodied voice of his nav from the adjacent dome.

"OK guys you're both loud and clear to me," said the instructor. "Right, the domes are in tied mode so you're both seeing the same picture. We'll run the first one against the computer. Yuri's just plugging in now and will talk you through from here."

"How do you hear me?" came the familiar tones of the Russian pilot. "OK, for the first run I want you to point straight at the bogey. At the merge go into a flat turn and try to match his turn rate. He will enter at fighting speed but then slow down and bring his wings forward to 16 degrees and enter a flat turn. Remember, he has no tanks but you are carrying empty wing tanks which will limit your speed and G. If you can match his G you should stay neutral or certainly not lose out too much. With only Aphids he shouldn't be able to threaten you. Ready? OK the fight's on."

The horizon oscillated briefly as the simulation began to run and Razor grasped the stick and began to fly the simulator. He could see the dot on the horizon which represented the Mig-23 and pulled his gunsight onto the target. As the dot began to grow and become discernible as an aircraft he jinked slightly away putting it into the front windscreen away from the ironwork of the gunsight.

"Tally" he heard from the other cockpit as Flash locked his eyes onto the bogey ready to take over if Razor lost sight.

"It'll be a right-to-right pass at the merge," he intoned preparing his nav for the entry to the fight. As the two combatants passed, the bogey would either turn towards or turn away and, depending on which plan his opponent selected, would determine Razor's reaction. He ideally wanted to set up a single circle fight, in other words, both aircraft flying around the circumference of the same circle but in opposite directions. That way he could compare the respective turn rates. His own jet was simulating empty wing tanks so he would be limited to 6.5G and the Flogger would have some extra G available plus the advantage of not carrying external tanks. It was not a fair match and for real if it came to it he would have no hesitation in punching off his own tanks to improve performance. Mind you, this was a simulator so maybe he would. Well, maybe best stick to the brief for now. The Flogger's profile grew rapidly in size and he experienced a strange feeling of unreality as the familiar planform flashed past, close aboard, its top surfaces visible as it banked towards him. It was in a right hand turn and if it kept that going he would reverse his own turn to enter the single circle fight. The next call from his navigator was crucial as the Flogger disappeared into the 6 o'clock. He knew that Flash in the other dome would be reefing around in his seat looking over his shoulder to make the call.

"He kept the turn going, come back left."

A single circle fight it was then. He immediately responded and racked the Phantom into a max rate flat turn which went totally against everything he had ever been taught. Rule number 1 was never to enter a flat fight and always take it into the vertical, preferably upwards. Height was energy. As he hauled the stick to the left leading with his left hand and pushing the engines into full reheat, he switched his attention to the area behind his cockpit as the horizon gyrated crazily around the nose. He checked the turn and pulled to the maximum angle of attack receiving a solid chevron on his angle of attack gauge showing he was at the optimum turn rate. He was listening intently to the patter from the back cockpit calling the progress of the bogey's turn when it popped back into view over his shoulder. Keen not to wash off his energy he held his maximum rate turn keeping the opposing fighter on the horizon and checked his speed again. Perfect at 420 knots and right where he wanted it to be. If they were matching turn rates he would meet the bogey head-on after 180 degrees of turn. Sooner or later that would give him an idea of who had the advantage. The slender wings of his opponent stayed forward meaning that the bogey was following the brief and staying at slower speed. Any hint of those wings being swept might mean it was getting ready to disengage at high speed. It was an instant indicator of intent. As they passed head-on the compass was almost exactly 180 degrees out.

"OK, knock it off," called Yuri from the console. "That was good. You held the turn perfectly and matched his rate of turn almost identically. If that had been for real you could have easily disengaged from the head-on pass and been outside missile range before he could threaten you. How did it look?"

"Fine," replied Razor. "I didn't expect to hold him off in this configuration with him clean wing."

"See I told you so. Right, this time we'll try to exploit the weapons system. The computer will fly the same profile but rather than turn flat, this time I want you to use every ounce of performance and try for a head-on shot. I'm afraid the radar simulation is poor in the sim so it won't be of much value to you Flash but bear with us. After the merge take it up into the vertical but stay with a single circle fight if you can. Pull him back along the canopy centreline and try to get a radar lock. Take the earliest missile shot available to you. OK, fight's on."

The horizon lurched again as the simulator came live and the small dot began to grow yet again. They repeated the scenario but after the merge instead of holding the flat turn Razor pulled hard back, zooming for height and dropping the left wing to keep sight of the bogey over his shoulder. Expecting to see the bogey turning round to point at him he was surprised to see that it had kept the predictable flat turn going. If he didn't know better he would have thought the opposing pilot had lost sight of him. He rolled off the top of a huge oblique loop and kept the roll going and suddenly, the Mig was dropping into his gunsight still holding its "circle of joy". Not even needing the radar he dropped the gunsight onto the target, the Sidewinder acquiring immediately giving its familiar chirp and he pulled the trigger.

"Fox 2, knock it off." He called with a certain amount of surprise and satisfaction.

"Perfect. OK, for the final run Flash you're evicted and you can join Razor in the primary dome. I'm going to fly the Mig manually from the secondary dome and try a few things. Let's see how you both cope."

Why did Razor suddenly feel that he'd not been given everything he needed to know just yet? With the simulator lurching into action for the third time Razor stared at the small dot and carried out the same action he had done for the last two merges. This time all bets were off and it was free play. The dot grew but seemingly not as rapidly as before. As he moved it into the windscreen he struggled to keep sight and it was a few seconds more before it grew appreciably. As the Flogger flashed past on the right once again showing its upper surfaces it looked entirely different. The wings were fully swept and it flashed past in an instant at high speed. As he pulled up into the vertical he heard urgent roll commands from Flash who even from his perch at the edge of the cockpit was struggling to keep sight of the receding Flogger deep in the 6 o'clock.

"More help," he called to the simulated GCI controller on the console.

In your 6 o'clock range 4 miles going away," came the immediate response. The crew instantly knew their error. Despite a turn at the merge they had bled off speed and their opponent had merely extended through and run away at high speed. Even if they dragged the nose around, by the time they could threaten him their opponent would be in the next hemisphere.

As they were about to call a "knock it off" they suddenly heard a call from the console.

"Bogey 240 range 6 miles turning back, continue."

Razor steadied up on the bearing and as Flash was entirely devoid of radar kit perched on the canopy sill, Razor hit the pilot lock mode button to be rewarded with an instant lock and the Skyflash missile indications on the display in the cockpit. The dot was centred, the steering circle had expanded and the missile was in the heart of the envelope. He squeezed the trigger.

"Fox 1." The crew silently counted out the seconds needed for the missile to track the rapidly reducing range to the target.

"Fox 1, kill, on the bogey bearing 240. Knock it off."

"OK guys good work, I'll see you outside."

*

With the final session complete the crews reassembled in the briefing room for the wrap up. A relaxed Andrenev sat at the front of the room with the intelligence officer who had watched each crew as they progressed through the session.

"So let's review the lessons. If you find yourself in that situation you can stay and turn with the Mig-23 but Soviet trained pilots won't stay and fight. If they get to that point without having taken missile shots they will think they have failed. They will try to disengage at high speed. If you don't spot the move he'll be five miles down the road and you'll never see him again. Remember, even sniper pilots on Soviet squadrons are at the same level in air combat skills as the new students on your conversion units. Those skills are never passed on to the export customers. Next; exploit your superior weapons. Soviet air-to-air missiles are robust and reliable but they are intended to be used straight and level. That will change with the Mig-29 and Su-27 but for now you have the advantage. Remember to watch his wings. He has to be straight and level to sweep them. If you keep him turning he'll struggle but in any event it will give you an idea of his energy state and his intentions. That's my best advice at this stage."

"Well that's all we have for you," said John Silversmith as he scanned the contemplative faces in the briefing room. You have one final chance for questions."

"Are you deploying with us Yuri," asked one of the pilots. "I'm going to have a million questions when I digest this stuff and we haven't even had time to talk about the Mig-21 which the Syrians also fly."

"I think you can count on all the support you need. I can't say too much right now but there's a plan in the offing which, if it works out, will give you quite an advantage if it comes to a fist fight with the Syrians. Your Boss will brief you when you get into theatre and I'll probably see you down there."

With that the chairs scraped back, there were brief handshakes and the aircrew filed out ready for the quick trip back to Coningsby. They were now equipped to fight against a Flogger in the Mediterranean. It was time to find

out why the pilots who operated those Floggers were suddenly the bad
guys.

*

As the Devon taxied back onto Echo Dispersal preparation around the site
was hectic. Razor watched the frenetic activity, surprised yet impressed at
the progress in a short few hours. The semi-circular HAS doors had been
opened, the massive structures with their steel supporting gantries
stationary alongside the yawning entrances. Inside each shelter, Phantoms
shaded from the Sun by the concrete shelter roofs were bathed in harsh
fluorescent light. Preparations were already well underway and weapons had
been loaded underneath the jets ready to deploy. Armament trolleys littered
every HAS neck some still loaded with Skyflash and Sidewinder missiles
stacked on top of each other ready to be lifted into place. Armourers slowly
worked around each shelter finishing the loading. Across the dispersal
toned-down shipping boxes were appearing from storage bunkers and
being stacked ready to be filled with spares and servicing kit. A "Queen
Mary" flatbed trailer was pulling into the dispersal ready to accept power
sets and test equipment which would make the journey to RAF Brize
Norton for onward flights to the Mediterranean base ready for the
operation.

As the Devon pulled to a halt the starboard engine died and the fighter
aircrew tumbled out of the open door deplaning after a quick word of
thanks to the crew. The pitch of the engines rose again as the Devon taxied
away making its way to the departure runway and home to RAF Northolt.
With the impeccable door-to-door service they had only a few short yards
to walk before entering the main entrance of the pilot's briefing facility.

Inside, more boxes had appeared littering the corridor that was rapidly
filling with the paraphernalia the squadron would need to operate for an
indeterminate period. Despite the controlled chaos there was method in the
madness as equipment was packed in accordance with a carefully rehearsed
checklist worked out months before. Deployments were a constant feature
of the Cold War and 29 Squadron was used to moving at short notice.
Assigned to the Atlantic Command of NATO, otherwise known as
SACLANT, it was the first squadron nominated to deploy in a crisis
situation.

In the planning room, navigators pored over maps interpreting the newly received air-to-air refuelling plan and translating strings of hieroglyphics into lines on the map and boxes on the charts. Another navigator played with a navigation computer. More commonly known as the "whizz wheel", there were no computer chips or memory cards in this device. This was an old fashioned circular slide rule in a very analogue form which had seen service for as long as Pontius had been a pilot. Fuel figures and distances were carefully checked against expected wind velocities to make sure that the anticipated fuel uploads would deliver the six jets safely to their Mediterranean operating location. With a healthy tailwind expected down the Med, tension had already dissipated and the fuel figures seemed generous.

A list of the nominated crews had appeared on the navigation planning room wall and the fortunate navigators were busily helping themselves to maps from a large pile which had appeared in the corner. The clock ticked down to the nominated briefing time just 20 minutes away. Flash walked into the planning room exchanging banter with an old mate from Germany days and joined the melee. He pulled out a bunch of maps and chose a free spot at the planning table.

*

Just a short time later, the Boss walked into the briefing room and, unbidden, the aircrew rose to their feet.

"Sit down Gents," he said as he took his seat in the centre of the front row. The room quietened instantly everyone fascinated to hear finally why they had been called in. It was, by now, an open secret that they would deploy to Cyprus at no notice. Flight Commander Operations stood up and addressed the audience.

"OK guys, the fact it was a Station call out is obvious. Well done for getting in so quickly. We generated 80% of the jets in just 3 hours which is oystanding and the last jet will be up in an hour giving us almost a full house. The jet in aircraft servicing flight is in the middle of deep servicing so we'll get a spare from the OCU if we need it. Nine jets should do us so I don't think we'll need help."

He watched the fidgeting crowd in front of him.

"OK I'll get straight to the point. We've been tasked to deploy forward to Akrotiri to execute Operation *Pulsator 2."*

He paused to let the significance sink in and was rewarded with an enthusiastic murmuring. Even the aircrew who had not been involved in the earlier shows of force over The Lebanon knew exactly what the Operation was for.

"We'll be providing escort for a force of bombers tasked against targets overland in The Lebanon. We launch at 0400 to join with eight Buccaneers from Lossiemouth. We'll tank down behind VC10s with the troops following in the main party on a C130 Hercules from Brize at 0500. The advance party will be on one of the VC10s and arrive just after the Phantoms so 56 Squadron, who are already in Cyprus on gunnery camp, will see us in on arrival. . . . . I thought that might get your attention."

He smiled at the junior pilot at the back of the room who punched the air seeing his name on the list of nominated crews that snapped into view on the screen.

"These are the crews."

A few groans as some of the aircrew realised they were not on the list.

"This is the broad situation. A hostage was snatched from Beirut a few days ago and is missing. The intelligence bods think they've located him in a compound in the north of The Lebanon close to the Syrian border and they want him back. I have no idea what he knows, why he's important or why he was kidnapped. All we need to know is that we'll be escorting a force of bombers and helos which will go in to suppress the target and to pull him out. It's a hotbed down there right now and anyone following the news will have seen that the Israelis have just pulled back to the southern border. If it's too hot for them it won't be a picnic for us either. I need to stress, this is not a routine detachment. There'll be no playtime for the next few weeks. This is serious enough that we might expect to take losses. Some guys might not come home so take this very seriously. Am I clear?"

He looked around the room at the sober faces digesting the harsh reality of his words.

"OK, enough said. Friendly forces are the eight Buccs, two Chinooks from Odiham and six Phantoms from the Squadron. Olympus radar will provide fighter control. With the short ranges involved we don't expect to need tanking support but one of the VC10s will stay in-theatre just in case. He'll be on station during the recovery phase if we need fuel. There's one additional asset and the crews who flew up to Warton this morning have been given specific briefings on the capability of the Flogger in air combat. I can't say any more at this stage but for those flying the escort mission you will be briefed separately. If you see something unusual operating at Akrotiri – and I don't mean the U-2 – keep your mouths closed."

He paused for effect as the significance sank in.

"Hostile forces are Mig-21 Fishbed and Mig-23 Floggers of the Syrian Air Force. We'll get detailed rules of engagement in-theatre but expect these guys to shoot back. They've been taking hits from the Israelis for months and I wouldn't put it past them to take a cheap shot first and ask questions later. Our mission is to escort the Buccaneers in to the target and deflect any interest shown by those hostile forces. We may need to exercise some discretion with friendly forces if they show too much interest. The politicians tell us that the Americans and Israelis have been warned off. We'll see. There's a NATO exercise going on down there involving the US 6th fleet with the carrier USS John F Kennedy plus assorted helos. The Israelis can be expected to take an interest although the Boss has been assured they'll play along with us. What we don't need is a blue-on-blue engagement so rules of engagement will be carefully briefed. We'll get the full scenario and mission briefing in-theatre so at this stage we'll concentrate on getting packed up and getting down to Cyprus. I don't need to say that this operation attracts the most sensitive caveats at this stage. Any details are "Strictly Need to Know" and that includes wives, girlfriends and lovers! Close hold and I mean close hold! Boss anything to add?"

"I'll wrap up later."

"OK Boss, we'll break now. Back in here in 30 minutes for a route briefing."

Seats clattered as the chattering mass headed out towards the crewroom for a coffee and some reflection of the significance of the briefing they had just received. It would take some time for it to sink in. Within hours they would be within 60 miles of the Syrian coast and things would be a tad more hostile than rural Lincolnshire.

CHAPTER 5

The Foreign Office, Whitehall, London.

The Foreign Secretary sat behind his large mahogany desk leafing through a pink file, the word SECRET prominently slashed across the front and back. Normally fascinated by the daily diet of titbits from the embassies abroad, today his attention was lacking and his thoughts had already turned to his upcoming meeting. The door opened and his aide, with a discreet flourish, announced the arrival of the American and Israeli ambassadors. Rising to greet his visitors he ushered them to the comfortable chairs beside the windows which overlooked Whitehall and motioned for them to take a seat. Setting the right tone would be vital if he was to achieve his aim.

"Thank you for coming at such short notice Gentlemen; tea?"

Perhaps the fact that they readily accepted suggested that both men were becoming somewhat more anglicised than they realised. Without further preamble the Foreign Secretary placed a dossier on the desk in front of him.

"We, and by that I mean the members of my Government, seem to have a problem in the Middle East. Let me be frank with you both and, of course, the following information is highly sensitive. Three days ago one of our operatives in Beirut disappeared. Initially, we were unsure of where he had been taken but two days ago we heard from a contact known to have strong ties to Hezbollah that he was being held at a secure compound close to the Syrian border about 20 miles northeast of Tripoli. We're making efforts to see him but so far we have made little progress. Hopefully, we can gain access soon. The reason for asking you here today is that we have reason to believe he acquired some fairly controversial information from an informant in the Syrian Defence Ministry. We think it might have far reaching implications for your National interests Mr Ambassador," he said turning to the Israeli.

"I'm grateful that you felt you could share this with us Foreign Secretary."

He nodded gracefully, silently reassured by the diplomatic gesture.

"Yesterday, I authorised a special forces mission. We approved the infiltration of a small reconnaissance troop from the Special Boat Service which landed on the coast near Tripoli. They reached the location where we suspect our man is being held easily enough. After a reconnaissance of the facility they concluded that it would be impossible to gain access without a head-on assault against the compound which is heavily fortified and protected. That was unexpected as we'd hoped to wrap this up quickly. I've concluded that we need to allocate more military resources to the problem and I plan to authorise a deployment of combat aircraft to our base at RAF Akrotiri in Cyprus. Under the circumstances we feel it vital to secure his release so that we can delve deeper into the information he has uncovered. Without being able to consult him we will struggle to verify the veracity of the information."

"I can ask our Ministry of Defence to send a ground party should you wish," said the Israeli Ambassador. "As you know, we withdrew to the southern border some months ago but we have forces on readiness to penetrate as far as we feel is necessary. We could probably have a unit briefed within days and use as much force as you deem necessary."

"That's kind, but that wasn't the reason for this discussion."

"Do you need assets from us?" asked the US Ambassador. "We have the 6th Fleet on exercise in the Eastern Mediterranean as we speak. I'm sure we can allocate as much effort as you need."

"I'm grateful to you and I might come back to you if we need specialist help if, or when, it becomes appropriate. No, the reason I wanted to chat is that the PM has asked the MOD to begin contingency planning for a recovery operation. We have no way of knowing how much time we have available and the situation could deteriorate. The hostage could be moved at any time and I desperately want to find out what this operative uncovered. We also run the risk that we might lose contact with him. Time seems not to be on our side. The deployment of combat forces was authorised this morning and preparations to send the force of fighters, bombers and helicopters are already well underway. They fly out later tonight."

"I'm still a little unsure of what you need from us, Foreign Secretary," said a perplexed Israeli Ambassador. "If you don't need combat forces maybe we can offer intelligence assets?"

"That would be hugely useful but my main concern is to ensure that we don't fall over each other in our enthusiasm. I would like to have your experts briefed on the details so that they can pass it on to your forces in the region. I know everyone is under intense pressure and for you Mister Ambassador," he said returning the piercing stare, "such tensions are a feature of daily life in Tel Aviv but I would hate to lose one of our aircraft through simple mistakes in coordination of forces."

"Our cooperation is of course is a given, Sir."

"Could I perhaps ask of the broad nature of your plans so that I can exercise the appropriate leverage on your behalf?" returned the American diplomat.

Of course, although the plans are maturing as we speak. We intend to breach the compound to allow a team to extract the hostage. It will need some bombing of the utmost accuracy in order to succeed. The MOD is concerned at the recent elevation of the alert state in Syria so we intend to escort the bombers to the target to ensure that they are not molested en route. You'll forgive me if I don't go into precise details at this stage and, to be frank, I've not yet been fully briefed but the PM is content and has agreed to the operation in principle."

"Is NATO involved in the operation Sir?"

"No, at this stage this is purely National, hence my discrete enquires today. We will brief the North Atlantic Council at the appropriate time but security has to be paramount for this to succeed. I'm so grateful for your understanding and thank you. Perhaps I could ask you to task your Air Attachés to liaise with my planning team in the MOD. That way they can make sure the information reaches those who need it. Clearly the details need to be protected carefully until the operation is executed but it is absolutely vital that the force can prosecute the attack unhindered. If I understand the concept for the attack it will be complex enough as is but if opposed by well intentioned friends it might become impossible. Meanwhile I will instruct my own Attachés in Tel Aviv and Washington to stand-by to provide assistance and information."

"Please be reassured, Foreign Secretary, that if there is anything more we can do to assist you need only ask," said the US Ambassador. He rose to leave offering a firm handshake.

As the ambassadors filed out, another door opened and Sir Richard Courtney, the Head of MI6 entered the room.

"Could you hear the conversation, Sir Richard?"

"Yes Foreign Secretary, I could indeed. They both seemed genuine. I couldn't detect any subterfuge."

"Likewise. Mind you, I'm sure my briefing will have a few aides rushing around quite soon."

"Indeed Sir. I have news from The Lebanon. It appears we might have made progress and it might be possible to gain consular access to our man. I'm surprised because I would have thought they would be most reluctant to give any confirmation of where he is being held. They have almost telegraphed his location so this is all very unusual. The good thing is that if they intended to do away with the poor chap it would probably already be too late. It might also mean that they will treat him well until they see how we respond. It doesn't do to handle the goods negligently if they plan to sell him back to us."

"Any idea of the potential tariff?"

"If I was a betting man I'd say it will be weapons. They have some low tech stuff but after the drubbing they've taken recently they will be looking for more and better."

"You are much better placed to handle this type of thing than me Richard. It goes without saying that we will make provision for anything that is needed to secure his release. The usual line though. Formally, we don't negotiate with terrorists. Any idea yet of what he uncovered?"

"Not really. His contact in Damascus was a staff offer in the Operational Plans Division and was regularly involved in some of the more outlandish proposals. We think it's a plan to recapture the Golan but without the detail we can't assess its probability of success. The Israelis took the wind out of the Syrian's sails by pulling back to the southern border recently so maybe the reason for this surfacing now is to capitalise on a perceived weakness. The Syrians have little in the tactical inventory which can threaten Israel from Syrian territory so they need to re-establish a position of strength in a forward location. Guile and cunning in operational manoeuvre has never been one of their strong points but it's always foolish to under estimate an opponent. I'd be speculating if I go on. We need to get our hands on those documents and only one man has the key at present."

*

The Israeli Ambassador walked back into his office, his diplomatic facade gone. He barked a few very undiplomatic instructions to his aides generating a flurry of activity as they withdrew to make arrangements for a hastily convened conference call. As well as the inner diplomatic circle from the Knesset, the participants would include high-level members of Mossad, the Israeli Secret Service. It would not be an easy discussion but he was not the happiest Ambassador in London at that moment and he would demand answers.

DAVID GLEDHILL

CHAPTER 6

Air-to-Air Refuelling Towline 5 over the North Sea.

With the Sun still some way below the horizon, eight Buccaneers launched from RAF Lossiemouth in northern Scotland and climbed slowly to their cruising altitude, initially heading across Fife coasting-out near the fighter base at RAF Leuchars before turning southerly towards the first refuelling area. The rendezvous with the Victor tankers over the North Sea directed by a fighter controller from RAF Buchan on the eastern coast had been straight forward with the first bracket flown in total darkness. Still tired eyes focussed rapidly as the bucking refuelling basket had offered its usual challenge. Each of the Buccaneers topped off to prove the fuel system ensuring that the fuel tanks were full before leaving UK airspace. With the Buccaneers impressive combat radius it was almost possible to complete the 2300 mile trip unrefueled in a single hop but with tankers on offer it was unwise to generate additional pressure by refusing fuel. Unexpected adverse winds and a desire to guarantee an on-time arrival meant that discretion was preferable to bravado. The Victor tankers would return to Marham after the first refuelling bracket leaving VC10s to accompany the formation down route once the Phantoms had joined.

The Chinooks had already flown to Brize Norton where a team of technicians had removed the rotors and defueled the cabs before loading them onto huge Belfast transport aircraft. Ironically, the Belfasts had retired from RAF service many years earlier but with nothing even close to a similar capacity in service, the private company now operating the lumbering transports was doing lucrative business shipping outsize loads around the world. The MOD was a reluctant benefactor and it would be many years before an expensive lease programme for Boeing C-17s filled the yawning gap. Well before the Victor and VC10 tankers launched from the same base en route for the rendezvous over the North Sea, the Belfasts had lumbered airborne to begin the long, slow journey down route. With the disparity in speed they would arrive at Akrotiri in the Eastern Mediterranean a scant few hours ahead of the fast jets.

At RAF Mildenhall in Suffolk, an American C-5 transport was loading an altogether more unusual cargo under cover of darkness. The tarpaulins draped over the fuselage concealed the identity of the aircraft from prying eyes. It had been flown in from another more secure and secretive location earlier in the week for an entirely different reason. Its task had been changed after a tentative call from the US Air Attaché in London and its original destination became a distant memory. It was now being readied for an onward trip to the Middle East where it had originally been based many years before.

As the trailing pair of Phantoms rolled down the main runway at Coningsby the afterburners briefly lit the night sky. Ahead, the lead pair was easily visible, although as they began the turn back to the east the discs of intense light from the reheats blinked off and the darkness enveloped them once again. The moment the wheels were in the well the navigator snapped on his radar transmitter and rolled the thumbwheel upwards looking for the leading pair as they climbed to height. The familiar blip appeared on the scope and he moved the acquisition markers over the target and squeezed the acquisition trigger. The radar locked on and began to track the pair ahead. There was little said in the cockpit as the pilot pulled the steering dot into the centre of his dimmed gunsight and began to pursue the leading Phantoms. The navigator monitored progress giving the odd word of encouragement but this was low key stuff until the two sections joined up. Ahead the lead pair levelled off at 15,000 feet to thread through the small gap in the main arterial airway which crossed their flight path. Normally, heavy with airline traffic plying to and from the continent, at this early hour the airway was almost deserted. Once through, the navigators focussed their radar scan on the area of the refuelling towline looking for the approaching formation of Victors, VC10s and Buccaneers.

The Buccaneers had already been topped up to full and had slotted back into a loose transit formation as the package headed south. Once formed up with the Phantoms the formation would cross into French airspace at Mike Charlie One, a reporting point on the French Flight Information Region boundary, before heading down over familiar French cities such as Lille and Dijon, across the Alps to coast-out into the Mediterranean at Nice. Passing west of Sardinia and Corsica the formation would turn east for the long leg down the Mediterranean passing Malta, Sicily and Crete before beginning the descent into the base at Akrotiri. Most of the crews had flown the route many times and it held few mysteries. Often the attraction of an unanticipated diversion en route to exotic places such as Nice or less exotic venues such as Gioia Del Colle held an attraction. On this occasion, with an operation in prospect, they were keen to complete the sortie without drama. A mid morning arrival in Cyprus fitted the bill just fine.

In the darkened Phantom cockpits, bathed only in the red glow of the floodlights, the navigators concentrated on the rhythmic scan of the radar waiting for the first elusive sight of the tanker formation. As they headed out from the coast the tankers flight path would cross the nose allowing a gentle turn to roll out just behind. Staying below the main formation the Phantoms would close in joining alongside the leading VC10. Like the Buccaneers before them they would top off to full to prove their fuel systems before crossing the border into France. On the ground, a spare aircraft waited patiently, the crew more than willing to substitute for anyone unable to coax their serviceable jet down route. After an uneventful join up each section tucked in behind its allocated tanker and topped off.

With the initial refuelling complete, for now, the pilots settled into a loose transit formation alongside the tankers, the red navigation lights winking away betraying the wider girth of the formation to passing airline captains who enjoyed the momentary excitement at the sight. Many would have flown fast jets in an earlier life and probably still hankered after the thrills. The torpidity of the transit flight would be interspersed only by the mad adrenalin-filled minutes reserved for the tanking brackets.

Dawn was breaking as the craggy profile of the Alps became visible in the morning light. The last Phantom pulled out from the basket completing the second refuelling bracket successfully and dropped into formation on the wing of the tanker. As the systems were turned back on the RWR began to warble. A strobe showing a solid India band signal appeared on the beam and tracked steadily round into the 6 o'clock position. Craning his neck, peering back over his shoulder, Flash could see the familiar profile of a Mirage F1 as it closed in. The dark shape with its high mounted stubby wings and wing tip pylons was unmistakable. The weapons visible under the wings confirmed that this was a little more than a courtesy visit as they transited French airspace. At this early hour, a pilot had been woken up from his overnight slumber on Quick Reaction Alert to check out the military formation and, as he pulled alongside, the pilot pulled out a camera and snapped away from a number of different vantage points. Whether for intelligence purposes or whether the shots would eventually find their way into his personal album or onto the crewroom wall, no one would know. The Mirage flew in close formation for about 20 miles before waggling its wings and departing in a flourish rolling onto its back and descending rapidly back to lower levels. If the pilot was lucky he might catch a few more hours sleep before handing over his alert duties. If he was even luckier he might be relieved by a replacement pilot on landing.

Although the formation had filed a flight plan and had cleared the movement through diplomatic channels with the French, it was not unknown for the European neighbours to take umbrage if anything was amiss. Unauthorised tanker brackets or failure to follow the flight plan had resulted in diplomatic protests in the past. The breakaway was tacit acknowledgement that all was well. It had passed a few otherwise boring minutes. As the unexpected guest departed, the ground ahead began to rise and the snow covered peaks of the French Alps appeared ahead of the formation.

With little else to occupy their time until the next frantic airborne coupling, attention turned to personal needs. Breakfast aboard the fast jets this morning would not be a traditional English "full fry". The white cardboard "butty boxes" carefully prepared by the catering sections at the operational bases were pulled from small nooks in the cockpit where they had been carefully stowed. Rummaging through the contents killed five more minutes of the long transit without generating too much excitement. The contents were predictable. Butter and the oxygen which spilled from the masks clamped to their faces were not happy bedfellows so the small clinical sandwiches were dry and unappetising. Exotic items such as sticky fruit or sausage rolls made life in the cockpit unpleasant in the aftermath of the meal so the extras were predictable. A nice, safe chocolate bar would suffice. Masks were dropped, sandwiches chewed and juice sipped before masks were quickly returned to the face to stave off the hypoxia, or oxygen starvation, which might otherwise ensue.

Aboard the tankers breakfast was a far more pleasurable experience. Small trays of steaming eggs and bacon were served up to hungry troops. Inevitably, an item of food was waved through the window at the fighter crews alongside, the joker thinking it was the first time anyone had shared the "jolly jape". Despite being the victim many times before the crews strapped to the ejection seats in the Phantoms burdened by the heavy survival equipment and bonedomes could not prevent a slight feeling of frustration. It would not be the last time.

With three refuelling brackets behind them the formation had progressed well down the Mediterranean on the long easterly leg towards Crete. All had gone perfectly so far and the crews were beginning to anticipate that magic feeling of opening the canopies on arrival and feeling the first rush of fresh air. With one last tanker bracket to complete, the sky had turned a deep, dark blue and the hoses had been trailed for the last time. Behind the lead VC10 the Buccaneers closed in, ready for contact. The lead pair was cleared astern and the plug went without a hitch. The second element leader made contact and his wingman began to close on the opposite hose. The pilot sat very low in the waiting position and, as the rate of closure increased, he began to correct from below but always chasing the basket. The navigator tensed as the probe crept upwards towards the bucking receptacle his cadence increasing trying to persuade the reluctant pilot to climb. The corrections in the front were just not enough. As the probe closed the final inches it struck the canvas frame around the basket which bucked slightly pivoting under the pressure. The rate of closure was too high and, as the probe forced its way past the reluctant rim, it thrust hard into the metal spokes which radiated from the central fuel receptacle towards the rim. The over enthusiastic prod forced the probe tip through the spokes wedging it tight into the flexible structure. The basket lurched alarmingly taking on an unnatural angle in the airflow wedged tight on the probe.

"Spokes," called the navigator highlighting their plight instantly to the tanker captain. In the cockpit the tanker navigator had been peering at the small TV display and had already warned of the imminent danger. Expletives flooded the intercom.

In the Buccaneer cockpit the air was equally ripe with expletives as the crew watched small shards of broken spokes disappear down the engine intake. The Spey engine gave a hesitant cough as the RPM wound down triggering a raft of red and amber captions on the telelight panel. With the engine RPM stagnating rapidly there was little the pilot could do

"PAN, PAN, PAN, RAFAIR 9554, starboard engine failure, dropping back."

The Buccaneer, starved of power from one engine, decelerated rapidly placing immense strain on both the probe and the basket given the high speed of withdrawal. The violent manoeuvre placed extra strain on the damaged basket and more debris rained down the intake as the inner structure disintegrated. The Buccaneer instantly dropped lower and fell below the formation struggling to maintain height. Faced with the complex series of warning captions the crew began to run through the complicated "bold face" drills designed to put the failed engine into a safe condition. With potential damage there was no way they would be relighting the engine before it had been inspected for damage. A diversion was the only option.

"RAFAIR 9541 this is PAN 9554 we have potential damage to the starboard engine, requesting immediate hand off and diversion to the nearest airfield."

Roger PAN 9554, come up 129.35," said the Tanker leader bringing the emergency aircraft across to the control frequency.

The crippled Buccaneer descended ever lower struggling to stabilise and, as the crew checked in, the tanker captain had already warned the air traffic control agency of their plight as the emergency squawk flashed up on the radar screens on the ground. The calm tones of the Greek ATC controller confirmed the crew's analysis that the air force base at Souda Bay in Crete was their nearest safe haven.

"PAN 9554 this is Atheni Centre, how do you read?"

"Atheni, PAN9554 loud and clear requesting immediate diversion to Souda Bay. Stand by."

The frequency fell quiet waiting for the crew to complete their emergency drills but ready to provide immediate assistance should they need it. In the cockpit, switches were set and emergency systems configured and activated. With the situation seemingly stable and the jet now level at 10,000 feet and holding its height the pilot drew breath.

"Atheni, PAN 9554 is at level Flight Level 100 and maintaining level. Request a straight in, priority approach to Souda Bay Runway 11, check the surface wind."

The stiff crosswind from the north came as an unwelcome surprise to the crew but with an 11000 foot east/west airstrip they could make a long straight in approach to land.

"Request range to touch down, PAN 9554"

"50 miles to run, alerting Souda Bay of your problem Sir."

"Roger copied, requesting a gentle descent and non-deviating headings where possible."

"Copied Sir, you are Number One to land. The cables and barriers are rigged and available."

With the rest of the formation receding into the distance, the pilot began to lose height gently, the throttle on his remaining good engine set at about 80%. As the altimeter began to unwind slowly and with the TACAN needles showing a steady lock to the Souda Bay beacon the crew pointed towards the distant runway threshold anxious to put the crippled jet on the ground at the earliest opportunity.

"OK lets go for a slow speed handling check," said the pilot as they approached 5000 feet about 20 miles from landing. If they were to experience any unexpected handling problems he wanted to find out while he still had height in which to recover. With one engine still providing the essential services he gingerly lowered the landing gear without drama. The flaps followed and the aircraft behaved impeccably. Just the hook to go and they would be configured for landing. Again, the hook dropped without drama. With the jet now in its approach configuration he exercised the throttle on the good engine and received a comforting increase in thrust. All looked good. Up ahead, with the outstanding visibility over the eastern Mediterranean the long runway invited their presence.

At 10 miles he began to lose the final height and set the throttle to intercept the ideal glidepath to the touchdown point. He had begun to give himself that smug pat on the back that all would be well. As the altimeter wound down through 1500 feet the TACAN range counter wound down through six miles and he felt another surge of confidence. With the flying controls on the right wing affected by the dead engine his confidence was just a little premature. As the strong northerly crosswind began to affect the airframe during the final descent he found himself feeding in more aileron to keep the right wing up. The gusts were becoming more pronounced as he began to be affected by the rolling countryside below and he was suddenly struggling to stay on the centreline. The jet gave an uncomfortable lurch to the right and he could sense the nervousness from the back cockpit even though the comments were still unsaid. He pushed hard against the rolling moment and the wing came back up and he corrected back towards the runway. Despite more few tense moments during which he strained to keep the wings level, he crossed the piano keys, once more on the ideal approach path. Since the emergency had begun only 10 minutes had passed but to the crew faced with a possible ejection, it had seemed like an eternity. The pilot looked ahead and flared the fighter bomber onto the welcoming concrete.

As the Buccaneer slowed to a rapid halt in the arrestor cable the remainder of the formation pressed steadily east. Already messages were winging their way to the recovery party aboard the sweeper C130 Hercules that they would be enjoying an unexpected overnight stop in Souda Bay. Hopefully, the engine was undamaged or the casualty would be lounging on a Greek island rather than taking part in the forthcoming operation.

*

With the unexpected drama behind them the remaining crews began to anticipate the arrival at Akrotiri. With a solid lock on the TACAN radio beacon the range was reducing slowly and now well inside 100 miles to Cyprus. With all the fuel transferred and the refuelling hoses stowed safely in the refuelling pods the VC10s had bumped up the speed to Mach 0.8 reducing the range at a much more acceptable rate. In the fast jets crews had stowed the paraphernalia which had been spread around the cockpits and were ready for the descent. Uneaten sandwiches were back in the cardboard boxes ready to feed the birds and maps were folded neatly and placed back in flying suit pockets. Formation leaders began to champ at the bit willing the tanker leader to release them to fly on ahead. Eventually, the call came.

"Triplex and Jackal come up on Nicosia Centre on 126.3"

"Roger, Triplex, 126.3, 126.3, Go!"

"Jackal, 126.3, 126.3, Go!"

The formations checked in and after receiving their initial descent clearance began the slow drop into the Mediterranean base. Radars scanned to and fro painting the landmass ahead, the green return from the southern coastline of the island showing distinctly on the radar scopes. Markers moved over the tiny peninsular and navigation systems were updated for the final approach. As anticipated, the weather conditions at Akrotiri were wide open "blue" allowing a tactical arrival, hopefully to impress the locals . . . . . or not. Fighter crews felt it their sworn duty to fly low and fast to appear punchy; the locals felt it their sworn duty to feign indifference. With rising tensions to the east, perhaps on this occasion the locals would be pleased to see a fighter presence on the island.

"Akrotiri Tower, Triplex formation at initials."

"Triplex, Akrotiri, loud and clear. Clear to join runway 11, surface wind 100 at 8 knots."

"Roger, clear join, Triplex. Echelon starboard, Go!"

The Phantoms had skirted south of the base staying over the deep blue Mediterranean and began to move into close formation before turning back westerly for their run-in-and-break. Dark visors had been lowered to shield sensitive eyes from the bright tropical sun as the six aircraft dropped into close echelon formation. The speed had pushed up to 400 knots and would only drop off as they turned downwind to land. As the pilots tightened up their formation positions the turbulent low level air began to buffet the jets causing a slight whip along the line. With the leader rock steady, the minor oscillations were magnified and, by the time the whiplash reached number six, the ride had become positively lively. The formation passed over the threshold and, at the runway midpoint, the leader cranked on 90 degrees of bank pulling hard downwind, washing off the speed as the pilot set up for the landing. Behind him, each pilot counted two seconds, silently, before matching the manoeuvre so that by the time they had steadied up at 1000 feet downwind the spacing between jets was identical.

Final checks complete the leader thumped the Phantom onto the concrete popping the drag chute with his left hand. Each aircraft would land on the right hand side of the runway before easing slowly to the left as each jet reached a controllable taxy speed. Landing six aircraft at the same time on the same runway was tense. If the drag chute failed it would be an automatic "bolter" as, without a chute and with poor brakes, the Phantom was reluctant to slow down. A further approach would be necessary and there was a strong risk that the aircraft would end up in the overrun cable. With the tankers approaching from the west and also eager to use the concrete, a brake parachute failure would relegate the unfortunate crew to a holding pattern in the overhead to allow other aircraft to recover first.

In sequence, the Phantoms landed and, one by one, moved to the slow side of the runway. Overhead, the Buccaneers broke into the circuit but, with its clamshell airbrakes at the rear of the fuselage, the bomber was self contained and also designed to land on a carrier. Its rugged undercarriage would take anything thrown at it and, unlike the Phantom, it had brakes that worked. The remaining jets landed in turn, without fanfare, taxing to their parking slots on Golf Dispersal, the temporary home for the foreseeable future.

*

For one crew looking forward to a leg stretch and a toilet break after the long transit, there would be no respite. As they checked in on the squadron operations frequency, cheerily waving to the controllers in the control tower, their day was spoiled.

"RAFAIR 9564 and 9565 this is Wing Ops, check in."

Each pilot responded immediately.

"9565 and 66, we have trade building to the north. Your mission is to identify. Confirm you are serviceable?"

The delay in response was telling as each crew considered whether they could generate a fault in the next 10 seconds. Professionalism quickly took over as they acknowledged the request; albeit reluctantly.

Roger, complete your turnround and come up on readiness 02 in the cockpit. Check in with Olympus on this frequency with turnround complete. Adopt the callsigns Hawk 1 and 2."

"Hawk 1"

"Hawk 2."

In the cockpits groans welcomed the prospect of a further sortie. It would be some hours before they hit the bar for a well deserved brandy sour.

Once on the chocks frantic preparations began to service the Phantom. The crew unstrapped taking a well deserved stretch in the warm sun. Immersion suits were peeled off revealing flying suits underneath; a smart contingency when travelling down route. At least the next sortie over the warm Mediterranean waters would be flown in relative comfort. The pilot watched the flight line mechanics as they checked the oils and fluids. Another "liney" perched on a small stepladder pushing hard on the replacement brake parachute at the rear of the Phantom forcing it into the small chute bay at the rear of the fuselage. With the pack finally in place he forced the chute door closed and latched it shut. The NCO parked against the external power set alongside scribbled notes and signatures into the aircraft's Form 700. This might be an operation but the paperwork would not go away. As the activity slowed with the turnround almost complete the pilot began to complete his walkround rechecking the airframe and missiles after the long transit sortie. In the cockpit the navigator reapplied the power and began to realign the inertial navigation system ready for the sortie.

To the north, a visitor approached.

CHAPTER 7

Over the Aegean Sea.

The Soviet Illyushin IL-38 May maritime patrol aircraft had taken off from the military base at Sevastopol in the Crimea some hours before. As it routed through the Bosporus Straits, radars on mainland Greece monitored its progress and Mirage fighters at the Hellenic Air Force base at Larissa scrambled to intercept. The fighter provided a welcome diversion from the tedium of the long transit but the crew onboard had no interest in Greece or in the hundreds of radar returns from ships which littered the radar display reflected from vessels plying the waters of the Aegean Sea. Their interest lay much further south in the sea off The Lebanon and Israel.

The maritime exercise had been going on for a week and the crews in the Mays had been monitoring the ships for some days now. A massive task force from the US 6th Fleet steamed relentlessly up and down the coastal waters. The carrier battle group was spearheaded by USS John F Kennedy with its squadrons of F-14 Tomcats and A-6 Intruders. The command and control vessel USS Mount Whitney had joined the Carrier Task Force, or CTF, some days earlier and the commanding admiral had transferred his headquarters staff aboard the custom vessel. From there he directed the activities of the other vessels; the Spruance class destroyers the Oliver Hazard Perry class guided missile frigates, the Tarawa amphibious assault vessels and not forgetting the mighty battleship the USS Missouri. The raft of smaller resupply and support ships were almost forgotten as was the Ohio class submarine which tailed the carrier constantly, watching for inquisitive Soviet submarine captains who may decide to take an unhealthy interest in the exercise.

The Greek air defence forces were not the only ones to take an interest in the flight path of the May. Showing as Zombie 11 on the NATO air defence tote the warfare officers aboard each US Navy ship in the CTF were alert to its progress. As it headed south and closed on the task force, F-14s would be launched from deck alert to shepherd and to ensure it did not stray too close unobserved.

Before its arrival over the fleet, the air defence controller in the British facility on Mount Olympus would be next to provide the crew with some company.

"Akrotiri, alert 2 Phantoms."

"Olympus, this is Akrotiri, Hawk 1 and 2 are on this frequency and listening out."

"Hawk 1."

"Hawk 2."

"Hawk 1 and 2, vector 020, climb angels 25, contact Olympus on Fighter Stud 24, stay feet wet, scramble, scramble, scramble, acknowledge."

"Hawk scrambling."

The Rolls Royce Spey engines were already spooling up through 60% before the scramble message had even been completed. As the starter motor cut out and the systems transferred to internal power the umbilical tying the jet to the ground was pulled. Panels beneath were rapidly buttoned up as the second engine spooled up. Groundcrew crawled from beneath the jet ready to watch the wing tips as the jet rolled forward from the protection of the sun shelter, the aircrew still running through checklists readying for the scramble take off. Some were vital but some would be neglected in order to meet the stringent demands of the scramble time. The engines screamed as the jet moved forward from under the canopy. Radio frequencies were changed and the control tower, already alert to the scramble, moved other traffic aside. Nothing would stop the inevitability of the mission once the hooter had sounded. For once ATC had little or no control over its runway until the pair of Phantoms had rolled. Even the daily trooper flight would find itself sent around if its arrival happened to coincide with the launch.

"Hawk taking the active," called the lead Phantom pilot.

"Cleared for takeoff, wind 120 at 5 knots."

"Hawk 1 rolling."

The wheels barely slowed as the crew rattled through the final pre takeoff checks. As the first Phantom made the sharp turn onto the duty runway from the loop taxiway the afterburners bit throwing debris into the air as the hot exhaust plume rasped along the concrete deflecting back upwards from the surface. The shock diamonds glowed bright as the awesome power of the twin engines rattled windows and doors throughout the base. With the first Phantom easing into the air, its gear and flaps travelling, the second fighter rolled just seconds behind. With the burners still lit the first fighter pulled into a hard turn passing just feet above the security post at the main entrance to the base, turning downwind, climbing rapidly. Its functional planform was easily visible to anyone watching from the ground. The wingman followed the manoeuvre arcing inside the turn seemingly drawn along in the wake by an invisible thread. As the jets were lost from sight the only hint of their passage was the lingering noise of the afterburners still powering the jets to their cruising altitude way up in the deep blue sky.

The Phantoms held a steady heading under the direction of the fighter controller from Olympus Radar. Sitting in his control room at the summit of the Troodos mountains that dominated the Cypriot skyline, he watched the contact on his large circular radar scope as it tracked southerly. The radars in the front of each jet scanned the airspace rhythmically searching for the tell tale contact. Up to now the "zombie" had maintained 25,000 feet but, as it approached the waters east of Cyprus, it had begun to descend. Although he had good coverage out to the northeast, if the track continued its descent it would fade from his scope so he was keen to make the intercept before it disappeared. The controller interrogated the response but it remained stubbornly blank meaning either it was not fitted with an

IFF transponder or it was not transmitting a code. This was not unusual for the Soviet crews who doggedly exercised their rights to fly in international airspace unannounced. Unlike other air traffic they also refused to talk to western control agencies exercising their right to fly under visual flight rules in open waters. By the time the navigators in the Phantoms detected the May it had already descended well below their outbound level so they began a gentle descent to follow. The lead navigator set up an intercept to manoeuvre into the stern hemisphere and as they began their final turn in behind, the "Zombie" had already descended through 5000 feet. It was a bright blue day and the pilots made visual contact with the converted airliner during the turn and took over visually. In the back cockpits the navigators removed SLR cameras from hastily installed housings in the rear cockpit and prepared for their task.

The Phantoms pulled alongside the still descending four-engined aircraft its light blue camouflage scheme blending in almost perfectly with the colours of the sea and sky around it. The huge radome housing the Wet Eye radar prominent beneath the fuselage left little doubt as to the intruder's role. As the Phantoms slotted into formation, one on each wingtip, the Soviet radar was searching the waters ahead of the ad hoc formation, the radar operators in the rear cabin mapping the positions of ships within the American task force to the south. The bright red stars of the Soviet Air Force emblazoned on the fin left no doubt as to its identity.

Flash snapped away with the QRA Pentax camera muttering a few commands into his facemask urging his pilot to ease in a little closer. Peering through the wide angle lens he had little perspective on the real world and, as he lowered the camera from his eyes, he was momentarily startled at the close proximity of the light blue maritime patrol aircraft. His urging had been persuasive but they were now well inside the 200 yard minimum separation distance required by the order books. Leaving the camera to do a little more of the work he zoomed tighter on the bulging radome which housed the surveillance radar capturing intimate details that the analysts would spend hours poring over in the intelligence cell at Akrotiri once the film had been processed.

"Got it mate thanks, you can back out now," he confirmed to his pilot. As they withdrew, a face appeared at the cockpit window. After a few frantic gestures a piece of paper appeared with the words "6th Fleet" clearly visible, written in English. Only briefly noticeable it was replaced by the grinning face once again followed by a few frantic gestures and a thumbs up.

"I guess we know where they're heading then!"

"OK ease it below so I can get a shot of the undersides. I want a close up of the radome from below," the navigator replied cutting off the discussion.

The Phantom moved around the huge airframe as it dropped ever lower towards the surface of the sea. They would have just a few more minutes to get these shots before they risked being dumped into the water sandwiched between the May and the waves as it descended ever lower. The navigator snapped away.

"All done, over to you."

"Olympus, Hawk 1 and 2 alongside. Identify one May heading 170 degrees descending to low level. Request further instructions."

"Roger Hawk 1 and 2, shadow."

"Shadow, willco, Hawk 1 and 2."

The Phantoms stepped up, one on each wingtip, picking up a comfortable loose formation position and began the vigil. They would stay here until either they were called off or they ran down to minimum fuel. The May would, undoubtedly, be in the area longer than the Phantoms and would have to return to the Black Sea base via the same route. By then the Phantoms would be back on the ground, refuelled and ready to launch again if needed. Unexpectedly, the May began a gentle turn onto west.

"Odd, I thought the note in the window said 6th Fleet?"

"It did."

"This is a bloody strange heading to close on the Fleet then," said Razor.

"I wonder if they are checking out the Cyprus Buoy?"

"Maybe so but it's empty. The sitrep said that one of the jets on the banner checked it out this morning and the ship had gone. The visiting Krivak has weighed anchor and is shadowing the task force."

"Can't wait to see what this is for then."

The May eased lower, now only 500 feet above the water as the Phantoms moved out into a looser formation. With his intentions unclear the Phantom pilots were leaving plenty of space. QRA crews often witnessed sonobuoy drops at low level and sitting immediately behind a May at this height could be an unhealthy position.

"There's a freighter up ahead. Looks like we're going to pass right over the top."

The May flew across the bows of the freighter on an oblique angle to its course. From their perch on the right wing the lead Phantom flew directly overhead-only a few hundred feet over the superstructure. Almost as soon as they had overflown the ship the May began a gentle turn to the right positioning a few miles behind and ran back towards it. The second pass took them close aboard down the right hand side.

"They're obviously interested in this guy but I can't see why," said Flash. "I can't see anything unusual. It's just a standard freighter. Pretty unremarkable. It looks like it's called the *Curium Star* but I can't see where it's from. Don't recognise the flag it's flying either."

"Let's take another look on the way home mate."

"Roger that. I'll drop a navpoint into the INAS so we can come back to this point. It's heading 090 so we'll need to look a few miles east of here."

In the back of the May the radar operator recorded the scope picture as his mission briefing required annotating a few notes to his log so that he could identify the plot at the debrief. At the porthole an air crewman poked a camera into the bubble angling it downwards to get a decent image of the small freighter as they passed by, the Cyrillic script captured on film. Motor Vessel Curium Star, 67 kilometres east of Larnaca heading 090 degrees, in company with 2 British Phantoms the navigator scribbled on his chart. As the ship flashed past the port wing the Captain eased the maritime patrol aircraft right and picked up his new heading towards the Fleet.

On the right wingtip Flash had been snapping shots as the had passed catching one picture of the May and the ship in the same frame. He had no idea whether the two were connected but it seemed like a good idea. As they came right and steadied up on the new heading Razor hit the transmit switch.

"Olympus Hawk 1 still in company now heading 120."

"Hawk 1 and 2 Olympus copies. You're clear to RTB, contact me with the field in site."

"Roger Hawk 1 and 2 pulling up and on recovery. Hawk 1 is X Ray."

"Hawk 2 is X Ray."

"Olympus copied will relay to your operators."

"Hawk burner, burner, Go!"

After a short pause he pushed the throttles through the gate engaging the afterburners and the Phantoms surged forward in unison. Accelerating rapidly ahead of the lumbering four-engined aircraft they pulled hard and climbed rapidly away from their temporary companion. They set a heading back towards the coastline.

"Olympus Hawk 1 and 2 we'll run back past the previous ship en route. Just checking it out once more."

Within minutes, the Phantoms rolled out, lined up with the runway and accelerated to 500 knots for the break. The distress frequency burst into life.

"Aircraft five zero miles southeast of Larnaca, heading 120 degrees, this is American warship, 3 Tango Papa Zulu on 121.5. Come up this frequency and identify yourself."

"I wonder who that could be" said Flash as he switched to Akrotiri Tower.

The cat and mouse game would continue all day.

CHAPTER 8

RAF Akrotiri, Cyprus, the following day.

RAF Akrotiri is the jewel in the crown and an important base for the Royal Air Force. Set in its strategic location at the eastern end of the Mediterranean Sea it lies less than 100 miles from the Syrian and Lebanese coastlines. With Turkey to the north and Egypt to the south it acts as the referee amongst the warring factions with the biggest protagonist Israel close by. It was not immune to tribulations of its own, however, and since the Turkish invasion of 1974 it had been separated by "The Green Line" which divided the Turkish north from the Greek south along ethnic lines. Like its big brother, the Inner German Border, the line cuts through the former capital Nicosia. Its recent past had more sinister undertones. Home to a squadron of Vulcan nuclear bombers it had offered a route into the less well defended rump of The Soviet Union via its southern flank. The Vulcans had been withdrawn when the Royal Navy had taken over the British nuclear deterrent in the 1970s. With the demise of the V bombers, it remains an important staging post for refuelling shorter range transport aircraft en route to the Far East, although less important since the Far East Air Force was withdrawn and with the introduction of long range transport aircraft.

The sprawling base lies 10 miles from the Greek Cypriot provincial capital Limmasol. Stunningly beautiful and set amid orange groves and alongside a coastal salt lake populated by bright pink flamingos, the base exudes a relaxed atmosphere. Generally immune from the madcap schedule of

NATO evaluations in Europe, station exercises were a much more gentlemanly affair. The 8000 foot main east/west runway cut the peninsular on which the base was located with the easterly threshold almost on the beach. Stunning craggy cliffs on the southern perimeter look out over the deep blue waters of the Mediterranean.

Since the early 1970s a secretive operation had run from a large hangar on the south side of the runway. Known by the obscure title of "Operating Location OH", its operatives were headquartered in the town of Langley, Virginia in the United States of America. The detachment personnel kept well away from the other military users at the base. Every morning a black-painted U-2 spy plane would be towed to the holding point of the duty runway and prepared for flight. Fitted with sensitive optical sensors the jet would fly its pre-planned route to monitor activity in the neighbouring countries. At 0630 local time, on the dot, its space-suited pilot would arrive in a specially adapted crew bus and be transferred from his portable life support system and plugged into the jet. On the stroke of 0700 the engines would accelerate to full power and the glider-like aircraft would quickly accelerate down the runway. The outriggers which prevented the wingtips from scraping along the runway fell away as the long wings took the load and eased the aircraft into the air. A constant crescendo drowned conversation as it become airborne and began its steep ascent to its operating height on the edges of space well, above 70,000 feet, trailing thick black exhaust fumes at it went. Its route varied daily but its primary mission was to monitor the ceasefire agreement between Egypt and Israel following the Yom Kippur War of 1973. The warring factions had separated but it was an uneasy peace in the early years. Even though the detachment was brought out into the open in 1976 when the U-2 operations were turned over to the 9th Strategic Reconnaissance Wing of the US Air Force, Detachment 3 of the 9th SRW still attracted the nickname conferred by its secretive past - *Olive Harvest*. The mysterious air around the detachment would be perfect for the purposes of the unfolding operation.

Today was no different and at 0700 the U-2 powered down Runway 11, initially heading west before beginning a huge arcing turn back overhead the airfield powering its way upwards into the stratosphere.

*

With little fuss an American C-5 Galaxy touched down on the same runway at Akrotiri some hours later and taxied towards Foxtrot Dispersal at the eastern end of the airfield. Its huge bulk limited the places where it could park and it turned off the runway onto one of the huge dispersals last used by the Vulcans in the late 1970s, well away from the main air terminal. Inside the cavernous fuselage was a cargo that would not be unloaded until well after dark after most of the prying eyes had gone for the night. A powerful tug with a towing arm had been positioned alongside and, as the crew began to supervise the servicing, armed US Air Force guards emerged from the cabin doors and positioned themselves discretely around the access doors. No one would enter or leave the transport jet unless cleared.

As the Sun dropped below the horizon another tug powered its way across the dispersal towards the huge transport aircraft and the massive nose of the C-5 began to rise giving a tantalising sight of its load covered in tarpaulin sheets nestling in the cavernous belly. Hooked up to the tug, the cocoon was withdrawn from the freight bay and began to move across the dispersal towards the *Olive Harvest* facility.

CHAPTER 9

The Hezbollah Compound on the Syrian Border.

The locks on the cell door rattled as it was heaved open.

"Step outside Mr Reeves and keep your hands out in front of your body where we can see them."

He did just as he was asked. So far the experience had been pain free and he much preferred to keep it that way if he could. As he stepped into the corridor a restraint was slipped over his wrists and he was guided firmly towards the familiar small room. Forced to sit, the restraint was cut off and his arms were tied with thin straps to the flimsy chair before a blindfold was slipped back over his eyes. So far it had followed the same routine which had become boringly familiar but there was to be a change. He felt a slight jab in his arm and suddenly felt very tired.

When he awoke his mouth was dry, his head ached and his chest felt as if he had been attacked with a cattle prod. He also had a strange pain in his abdomen as if he'd been cut with a knife. He shook his head to try to clear his thoughts, his arms still held to the chair although the blindfold had gone. All part of the disorientation process he assumed. The "good guy" was sitting opposite. So far it was following the pattern; a refined discussion with this cultured character followed by a verbal assault from the "bad guy". He sensed the additional presence but was afraid to look around to confirm his thoughts.

"Welcome back Mr Reeves. You were quite talkative whilst you were asleep. It's surprising what a small shot of drugs will do to assist."

He felt a growing feeling of dread. What had he said? Cocktails of drugs such as morphine, chloroform, and scopolamine could induce uninhibited revelations about things that he would rather not discuss. Even hardened professionals had been known to speak candidly when under the influence of scopolamine and there was little defence that he knew of.

"I was hoping you would explain something to me. You kept repeating a phrase: "The key is the book". Those were your exact words Mr Reeves and I'm wondering what that could mean. Would you care to expand?"

His worst nightmare. He looked down at the floor and remained silent. If he was to avoid a beating how long would they go on like this? Did they assume that the drug would achieve the same end without violence or was this just a slow work up to the inevitable?

"The key is the book! You had neither a key nor a book with you when we collected you in Beirut Mr Reeves. Please expand and I may be able to make life more comfortable for you."

He kept his gaze averted and the phrase "name, rank and serial number" irreverently formed in his mind. It was drummed into service personnel on the resistance to interrogation course which Reeves had attended many years before and, about now, he wished he had a serial number to offer up. His silence irritated the interrogator who stood up and disappeared from view behind him. The feeling of dread returned. He anticipated the blow but still nothing.

"I wish you were not being so uncommunicative Mister Reeves. My friend is desperately trying to persuade me that other methods would work better. So far I've argued my case more eloquently but I don't know how long I can continue."

It was the moment that he had been dreading but the interrogator was not yet done.

"You should also know what else occurred whilst you were asleep my friend. I took the liberty of arranging a small insurance policy. A device was implanted in your gut. It's perfectly safe providing you follow my rules, Mr Reeves."

He paused to allow Reeves to assimilate the new information.

"It's only a small receiver and it picks up a signal from a transmitter here in the building. It has a very short range; let's say maybe 100 metres but, more importantly, it's attached to a small explosive charge. If it doesn't receive its regular update from the transmitter it will explode. In the position it's been implanted it would destroy most of your liver and part of your digestive system. I would strongly recommend you don't consider leaving us Mr Reeves. You wouldn't get very far. Until I decide otherwise, you fate lies within the range of my transmitter."

The man left the room and, as the door clanged shut, the familiar gnawing sensation returned to the pit of Reeve's stomach. The significance of the pain in his abdomen struck home. So much for a break for freedom, he thought.

Behind him a noise caught his attention and he tensed as feet shuffled across the floor.

DAVID GLEDHILL

CHAPTER 10

Akrotiri Village, Cyprus.

Dimitris Papadakis was a willing worker. The son of a Greek Cypriot family from Nicosia he had moved to the small village of Akrotiri many years before. Like his friends in the village he had a number of jobs, some more lucrative than others. The bizarre tax rules on the island meant that he would pay tax on only one of his jobs and he could decide which to declare. The British did not pay well for his humble efforts cleaning the accommodation blocks so that was the wage he nominated to the taxman. The fact that he ran a lucrative taxi firm which made best use of his contacts on the base and in the service messes was something the taxman had no need to know. As a consequence, his family coffers had continued to swell and by local standards he was well off. His neat house was well equipped with gadgets, air conditioned, nicely furnished and his family was well fed. He should have been a contented man.

His father had been active during the troubles of the 1950s. As a strong supporter of EOKA he had borne arms against the colonialists fighting for the right to self-determination. With the establishment of the constitution in 1960 and the setting up of the new Republic of Cyprus, life had settled into an uneasy stalemate. Rather than opposing the British the new "bad guys on the block" were their Turkish Cypriot neighbours. With his strong Marxist beliefs he had schooled the young Dimitris in his left wing ideology and his son had been a willing learner. As politics developed and the British withdrew to the Sovereign Base Areas of Episkopi, Akrotiri and Dhekelia, the new foe was the Turkish Cypriot community. With the British paying his wages they slowly became the benefactors rather than the oppressors and his affection grew. The troubles in 1974 which resulted in the division of the island into the Turkish North and the Greek South threatened to derail things. He had been careful to protect his interests and, if anything, once the immediate threat had passed and the two sides had settled into an uneasy divided truce, he was even better off. His clientele were now restricted to half the island and his services were even more in demand.

He was a businessman at heart and held no malice but business was business and, in his spare time, he had met new friends in the backstreets of Limmasol. Friends who would pay well for the information he was able to glean going about his normal duties at the active airbase. Dimitris was in reality a paid informer for the growing Soviet intelligence effort on the island and he was paid well for his troubles. His information attracted a premium and his taxis which plied the roads between the base and Limmasol were waved through the security post almost on a whim. His taxi drivers reported drunken conversations from the regular taxi trips and he was, perhaps, one of the best informed people on the base. Little happened without Dimitris hearing about it. For his own part, his ears were always open as he made beds and tidied up the areas in front of the blocks. He was also responsible for cleaning the crewroom at the squadron so at every stage of the day he was involved. He made sure he blended into the background, never questioning but always listening. He became part of the furniture. He would still be around as the crews made their way back to the blocks after flying and he would listen in discretely for any hints of how the days flying had gone and for any dramas which had befallen the temporary residents. The level of detail which emerged from the crews who assumed they were in a secure area was truly staggering.

His real activities would have been a revelation to any of the military personnel who were so dismissive of him. Over the recent years he had installed monitoring devices in each of the areas where the British personnel worked and played and the bugs transmitted their information regularly. Quite sophisticated, they emitted burst transmissions at times when it was unlikely that anyone would expect to see such signals which would in any case be lost amongst the general electronic chatter around the facility. These short transmissions were recorded on a master device which was cleverly hidden in one of the accommodation blocks amongst piles of cleaning products which would otherwise attract little or no interest. He had become skilled at predicting when the RAF Police would carry out the counter espionage sweeps and had made sure that his devices were hidden well and transmitted at discrete times. His habit of sitting and sketching scenes around the base which he often showed to the military officers with apparent pride hid his less appealing habit of mapping the facility carefully and recording each and every aircraft movement. This information was regularly taken to his small house in the village and carefully dispatched to his handler downtown.

Recently, however, he had been concerned at the increased pressure from his contact. Oh certainly the cash still flowed and the promise of more was welcome but the difficulty of meeting the new demands was increasing. He had resisted pressure to install a bug in the main briefing room as he knew that it was regularly swept and could compromise his efforts. Yesterday, a demand to take an impression of the keys to the line hut and the hangar on Golf Dispersal had been unwelcome and risky and he had barely escaped discovery when an inquisitive sergeant had quizzed him on why he was in the hut when his duty was in the crewroom. He hoped his bluster had been effective but it had rattled his confidence. He could not afford to jeopardise his position. The small plasticene block in the tin in his pocket held imprints of the keys and he would have copies cut by a friend in Limmasol later. The charge for this service was going to be high.

*

Since the arrival of the Galaxy the previous evening there had been an increase in the comings and goings from the American hangar. Unlike normal US detachments elsewhere in the world, the cars which lined the parking bays were right hand drive compact cars which would fit in perfectly in downtown Limmasol or in any of the other villages which dotted the southern coast of the island. The men and women who worked there wore jeans and T shirts rather than the more common khaki uniforms of the British personnel. Blending in with the local activity was the watch word. The armed guards were discretely dressed, their weapons concealed but certainly ready for use if needed. Large signs announcing the secure area dotted the perimeter and warned of the consequences of inadvertent access. Such signs had not been in evidence since the nuclear weapons had been withdrawn when the Vulcan bombers had left Cyprus back in the late 70s.

The sight inside the hangar would have surprised even the most apathetic onlooker. In addition to one of the normal inhabitants, a U-2 of the *Olive Harvest* detachment, a new arrival had been carefully positioned. The black bulk of the strategic reconnaissance aircraft with its long slender wings filled most of the rear of the hangar. Its counterpart was, even now, flying high over the Sinai Peninsula capturing images to verify the fact that military units were holding in the positions agreed so many years before. The thin fuselage and tall fin looked relatively normal but the enormous drooping wings terminated in a small outrigger at each wingtip which prevented the tip from scraping along the floor and were far from conventional. This wheel was jettisoned on launch and the wingtips would indeed scrape along the runway as the jet settled back to Earth after its flight. The small wheels would be reinserted for the short journey back to the hanger post flight.

Normally the U-2 was the highlight of any visit to the facility but another more unconventional addition threatened to eclipse the star. Under the glare of the arc lights a Mig-23 Flogger Golf sat on jacks. Its external paint scheme had been skilfully reapplied and it wore the splinter camouflage of the Syrian Air Force with the red white and black badges and roundels prominently applied. Around the jet technicians worked inside access panels which had been carefully removed and lay alongside. In the cockpit another avionics technician ran a test sequence on the Sapfir-23D, High Lark 4 radar system. The radome had been pulled back and test umbilicals had been plugged into the electronics boxes to monitor the outputs from the system. The scanner moved rhythmically left and right and, occasionally, nodded manically as it ran through a test sequence. The technician on the ground gestured to his colleague in the cockpit as the test sequence moved into a new phase. The long white AA-7 Apex missiles had already been loaded onto the wing pylons and were silently communicating with the radar system as the test set ran them through their paces checking the functions of the missiles and ensuring they were communicating with the onboard avionics. The last of four AA-8 Aphid missiles was being manhandled onto the twin missile launcher under the forward fuselage. Once the test sequence had been completed more umbilical connections would be made and a final check of the infra red missiles would complete the preparation. The technicians had no clues as to the reason for its presence in the hangar, nor at this time did they want to know.

Yuri Andrenev, who had flown in aboard the huge American transport aircraft was in deep discussion with another technician in a small cabin alongside the Soviet fighter. They were closely inspecting a small electronic device and the technician was pointing out a number of switches. The box was an IFF interrogator adapted from captured Soviet equipment which was designed to interrogate the identification codes transmitted by Soviet fighters. Unlike the original equipment this black box had been designed by clever analysts at a US Air Force facility in the United States. With the press of a button it would communicate silently with the Odd Rods IFF system aboard a Soviet aircraft and receive a reply confirming the code which was being used to identify the fighter. In the air Yuri would be able to check the code of any aircraft within a formation and guarantee its identity. Once Yuri was happy the box would be installed in the cockpit alongside the radar controls ready for use. The capability would be crucial as the plan unfolded.

CHAPTER 11

Limmasol, Cyprus.

The green camouflaged crew coach rattled past the small piquet post on the main road from RAF Akrotiri alongside the salt lake, dotted as ever with flocks of bright pink flamingos. The raucous chatter inside the bus matched the birds in volume and spilled from the open windows as the bus bounced over the occasional pothole on its way to the local town of Limmasol. The 20 minute journey through the orange groves passed quickly before the bus pulled up outside the local kebab house, a favourite with the crews for years. As they trooped in through the main entrance they were greeted like long lost friends by the owner who had worked hard to attract their custom. The tourists who made their way to this restaurant from the new hotels which had sprung up along the coast road spent well but the regular trade from the base was the real money spinner for him. He suffered the occasional high spirits or even the odd drunk which often caused disdainful glances from rather more staid tourists but when he presented the cheque for payment at the end of the evening it always seemed worthwhile. His recently arrived guests provided a lucrative trade.

After a quick head count, the waiters pulled a number of tables together and the noisy crowd flopped down demanding kokkinelli. Despite the disparity of roles between the squadrons involved in the operation it was a small community. Divided by postings in different parts of the country but temporarily reunited, friendships picked up where they had left off years before. On cue, bottles of the rough red wine appeared on the table along with large wine glasses designed to increase the rate of consumption. Small bowls of exotic dips with Mediterranean names such as Tzatziki, taramosalata, tahini and hummus were joined by yoghurt, olives and toasted pitta bread. The level of conversation slowly grew in intensity in direct proportion to the rate of consumption of wine and inevitably focussed on flying. On a more traditional detachment perhaps the conversation would have drifted onto social events or the best venues to check out at the weekend. On this occasion, and this would probably be the only night to hit town before events turned more serious, work was not far from everyone's mind. The detachment commanders for the Phantoms, Buccaneers and Chinooks had closeted themselves on one end of the table and were deep in earnest conversation, their faces serious. The level of responsibility had almost by default arranged itself along the table with the junior aircrew entrenched at the far end of the table engaged in harmless banter, their problems briefly forgotten.

Razor and Flash had joined old mates from training days now flying the Buccaneer. They were enjoying being reunited as a crew since Flash's posting to the OCU had threatened to break up the old team. This was a surprise bonus. The rate at which Flash's kokkinelli was disappearing emphasised his pleasure at being back amongst squadron mates. Life as an instructor was a far more responsible affair and a break from the routine was proving to be just what he needed. A few war stories about times on the squadron in Germany had already been recounted and the atmosphere was light. Smiles down the table meant that similar stories were flowing thick and fast. Waiters arrived continuously and the first courses of the kebab began to appear. Plates of spicy lamb sausages called sheftalia joined grilled halloumi cheese and small skewers of spicy meat. Later a piece of barbecued chicken and a pork chop would tax the best of appetites. As the kokkinelli bottles emptied they were recharged. These bottles were not vintage and had not been uncorked especially for the visitors; in fact corks were not in evidence. They were regularly refilled from a huge vat of rough red Cypriot wine in the back of the restaurant. No one cared.

To an outsider, it was unlikely that this band of revellers could be about to embark on a, potentially, life threatening mission yet, inevitably, real life would impinge on the temporary levity.

"How come Julie isn't on the detachment with us?" Razor asked his navigator. Julie was Flash's new wife and their brief marriage and a co-located tour at Coningsby was to have signalled a more stable few years. With the unexpected turn of events, here he was, once again, on detachment drinking wine with the blokes. The differences this time were not lost on him.

"She volunteered but one of the other "air traffickers" was due a detachment and got priority. Some of the new controllers haven't even been abroad yet. With a tour in Germany under her belt she was well down the list."

"Happy or not?" Razor probed.

"Probably best that we're apart for this one," he reflected. "Who knows how this will go? It should be easy enough if the intelligence reports are anything to go by. I can't see us being opposed can you?"

"Probably not but the fact the bad guys are on a pretty high alert state isn't normal but what is in this neck of the woods? It's been pretty quiet around here for a while since the Israelis pulled back to the border and they haven't carried out any attacks inside Syria for a good while now. I wonder what's with the higher alert state?"

"They didn't give us much of a hard time last time," said Flash's old mate from across the table. "I was on the original Operation *"Pulsator"* mission in '83. In comparison to this one it was a doddle. Both us and the Americans had quite large contingents of troops in the city and we were supposed to demonstrate that air support was on hand if needed. Our Army guys, wait for it, known as BritForLeb, were hemmed in at a block of flats in Hadath in one of the suburbs and the idea was to make at least two passes across the block to show a presence. I think it was on the 11th September two pairs of Buccs took off from Akrotiri and flew out through the airspace controlled by the American Task Force which was sitting off the coast. That bit is similar. It was only 17 minutes flying time to the coastline and as we coasted-in we flew right over Beirut International Airport. After hitting the flats the first time we turned north over the city before looping back around and past the block of flats on the way back out. We whizzed over the top of Beirut at about 50 feet at 600 knots but there was no real intent to drop weapons. My nav said that he was looking up at the driver of a bus as we flew over the airport on the way out."

"It must have been sporty!"

"Good fun but it was all a bit naive. Your guys, and I think it was one of the Leuchars squadrons, were escorting us and they were not even allowed to load weapons. They came along and held at the coast armed with nothing but a load of ball ammunition in the guns. At least we had an AIM-9B each but a fat lot of good that would have done us against a Syrian Mig!"

"At least this time it looks like MOD is taking it a bit more seriously," said Razor. "We'll have a full war load on when this game kicks off."

"Thank goodness for small mercies. I don't think there will be much of a delay from what the Boss has been telling us. I might slow down on the vino just in case."

On an adjacent table, a man with slicked back hair and knock-off Ray Ban sunglasses was paying rather too much interest in the conversation, straining to hear the details as the crews chatted. His male friend showed little interest in the pile of food in front of them and their lack of conversation might have been a warning had the raucous revellers been paying them more attention. Despite the dire warnings during the briefings, alcohol-fuelled tongues wagged a little more loosely than was wise. The men picked up random snippets of operational information exchanged far too loudly. Occasional gruff warnings from one of the more alert aircrew switched the conversation to less controversial subjects. Operational security and kokkinelli were proving to be tense bedfellows.

The erstwhile eavesdroppers, still feigning disinterest, exchanged frustrated looks as the party opposite began to wrap up. With the food gone, the wine slowing and an impatient driver waiting at the front of the restaurant, the well-oiled crews finally got the message that it was time to leave. After the usual example of advanced O Level mental arithmetic over how much each individual owed, the bill was paid and the slightly happier crowd meandered out through the door sharing the bonhomie with the owner who, as effusive as ever, was keen to see them return.

Within minutes of the noisy departure the two men also settled their bill and followed the aircrew from the restaurant.

CHAPTER 12

No. 280 Signals Unit, RAF Troodos, Mount Olympus, Cyprus.

The military site on the summit of Mount Olympus was the oldest military base in Cyprus. The first camp had been set up as early as 1878 as a field hospital for soldiers injured during the Egyptian campaign and there had been a continuous presence since that time. Now home to a Joint Signals Unit, the real reason for its continued occupation was to house a listening post alongside the air defence radar. Visible from anywhere on the Sovereign Base Areas below, the "golf ball" radome on the peak of Mount Olympus was a familiar landmark. Bright white, it stood out prominently in the ever present sunshine. The fabric of the protective shield hid a number of things from prying eyes. With access to the site difficult, visitors and workers alike were only able to get into the small complex via the tiny road which wound its way up to the summit from the small village of Platres just five miles away.

The main radome held the massive air defence surveillance radar which would otherwise have been exposed to the biting winds atop the 6,404 foot peak. The huge scanner rotated slowly only ever stopping during the short periods of maintenance and from its lofty perch high above the Cypriot coastline, it could see for hundreds of miles in all directions. Its height finding radar was tucked away in an adjacent radome. This was the main reason for the continued existence of the base. Its electronic eye stared out as far as Syria in the east, Egypt in the south and Turkey to the north. With no terrain to obstruct the radar beam its coverage was almost uninterrupted and gave a perfect view of every flight which plied the eastern Mediterranean, civilian or military. It was a unique operating location for the British forces and one which was jealously guarded.

Others with a more strategic interest in military goings-on also had reason to covet the location. Alongside the main radome were a cluster of smaller bubbles. Not only were communications relays located on the site giving a huge increase in the effective range of the transmitters but, in a small building alongside, listening devices were trained on Arab neighbours. A secretive signals regiment operated equipment rarely discussed outside the small enclave. Little of significance happened in the warring countries around the eastern coastline without one of the sensitive receivers overhearing the event. Whether it was a radio conversation, a radar transmission or communications traffic, everything was recorded and anything of interest would be carefully analysed. For the last month those receivers had been carefully targeted at Beirut and other locations within Lebanon always alert and ready to capture the smallest, perhaps significant, snippet of information.

In the small operations cabin the sand coloured KD uniforms of the analysts who dotted the room looked strangely out of place in the dim lights and the chilled air. Huge racks of electronic receivers filled all the available wall space and the background electronic whine was occasionally tempered as cooling fans cut in to keep the operating temperature down. Working in silence, the technicians occasionally tweaked a control knob making notes on pads on the console. Some receivers were festooned with green electronic displays which danced in tune to unseen electronic emission from nearby Syria.

The supervisor, an RAF sergeant, made his way towards the communications desk where a corporal was listening intently to a conversation on a radio circuit many miles distant to the east. His expression was quizzical.

"Got anything?"

"I'm not sure about this. It doesn't fit the usual pattern."

"How so?"

"I'm getting a DF in the area of the terrorist training camp at Berbara but the chat is different. The two words that stand out are guest and package. They've been mentioned quite a few times. I'm also hearing some unusual accents that I can't place. Most of the blokes on the radio are regulars and the dialect they use is familiar. It's almost like an Arabic "Brummie" accent. These new voices sound a lot different and I can't work out the accent. It's almost the equivalent of Oxford English and it doesn't fit the pattern."

"Is there a theme to the chat?"

"Not that I can work out. Just this constant reference to "the package" whatever that means. I know it sounds daft but I'm not even sure it's originating from the camp. There's a different sidetone to the transmissions. The signal is a lot clearer too. If I was a betting man I'd say it's coming from another sender nearby."

"Look it doesn't make any sense to me but that's not unusual. Seeing as we've been specially tasked on this one I'll get the transcripts typed up straight away. As well as our normal customer I'll get them sent back to MOD Defence Ops and see if it rings any bells there."

"Sounds good. I'll let you know if I get any key words coming up."

"Anything on any of the Syrian air defence frequencies?"

"No it's been pretty quiet since that last Israeli raid last week. I reckon they're keeping their heads down for a while. They took a bit of a hammering. Lost two aircraft from what I read in the latest intelligence bulletin."

"They did. I was on watch that day and the Israelis went in mob-handed. The Migs at As Suwayda took it on the chin. F-15s against Fishbeds; no contest really. Anything else?"

"Well there is one other thing. The traffic levels have been up on the frequency used by the Russian Consulate in Nicosia. There's been a lot of traffic between Limmasol and Nicosia which is unusual. It might be a response to this latest operation. The messages are encrypted so I can't make any sense of them so all I know is that people are busy talking."

"So no transmissions in the clear"

"No, no mistakes at all. It's all been coded stuff. One odd thing though. I've been getting the odd hit on a signal from Akrotiri. It doesn't come up often and when it does it's just a burst transmission. Short duration and very directional. If we weren't nearly down the line of sight I'd probably not even have picked it up. We might want to get the Signals Regiment at Episkopi to look into it a bit more. Maybe they could do some defensive monitoring just to make sure there's nothing weird going on."

"Good idea. I'll let them know. Have you got a precise location on base?"

"No but it's in the vicinity of the main fighter dispersal."

"Right, I'll flag it up to them and I'll go pull the tapes and get that transcript sent out. Let me know if you hear anything else."

"Will do."

The NCO turned back to his console and adjusted the headphones. His attention switched back to the low crackle as the sensitive receivers trained their electronic ears on the Syrian border just across the short stretch of the Mediterranean.

DAVID GLEDHILL

CHAPTER 13

As Suwayda Airbase, Southern Syria.

The clock hit 0700 and a Mig-25 Foxbat Echo crossed the easterly threshold of the runway at As Suwayda already passing 1,000 feet in a steep 60 degree climb heading east. As it passed through 15,000 feet it popped up on the radar screens in the operations room at Olympus attracting immediate attention. It held its easterly course as its speed increased, rapidly approaching Mach 1 in the climb. As it approached the Iraqi border it began a lazy turn back towards the west staying inside Syrian airspace before it accelerated and set course. Its new heading would set in train the usual helter-skelter of events.

"Akrotiri, alert one Phantom!"

"Hawk 1."

"Hawk 1, vector 090, climb flight level 250, contact Olympus on Fighter Stud 25, scramble, scramble, scramble, acknowledge."

"Hawk 1 scrambling."

In the crewroom chairs slid back, bodies scattered and the crews ran for their jets, a short sprint away under the sun canopies on Golf dispersal. Although only one aircraft had been scrambled the number 2 would cover the launch ready to substitute in the event of a problem during start up.

The vector was ill advised because high above Syria the Foxbat had already reached Mach 2 and was passing 50,000 feet on its way to its cruising altitude of 70,000 feet. As it left Syrian airspace and coasted out over the Mediterranean it headed doggedly westwards. It was more than the usual feint.

As the Phantom left the runway at Akrotiri the Foxbat was only 25 miles to the east and there was no time for a fully armed Phantom to zoom climb to such a height. With four times the range to the target it might have been possible to reach the high 50s but 70,000 feet was a false hope. With the Phantom passing 10,000 feet in the climb the Foxbat flew overhead and began its photographic run over Akrotiri. The infra red linescan equipment in the avionics bay captured the scene below stamping a seamless infra red image onto film. In the forward camera bay, oblique facing optical cameras added visual images to wet film. The whole of the airfield was captured in high detail recording the precise location and numbers of each aircraft on the dispersals. As the Phantom crew checked in on frequency, the images had already been recorded and the Foxbat was already miles past the island.

"Olympus, Hawk 1 on frequency, Charlie 4, 4, Plus 8,Tiger Fast 45."

"Hawk 1, Olympus loud and clear, your target, bears 270, range 10 miles going away, stand by for further instructions."

The frustration in the cockpit could be heard all the way up the hill at Troodos.

"Hawk 1, Olympus, anchor left in your present position, call me level at Flight Level 250."

"Hawk 1."

The tone of the response said a thousand words. The radar controllers in the darkened ops room could do little more than watch the receding Foxbat. They had wasted little time in launching the Phantom but the recriminations would continue long after the jet had landed. He would sit and wait, although it was reasonably obvious that having watched the Foxbat pop up over the base at As Suwayda that it would have to return there in the not too distant future. There was no doubt in the controller's mind of the identity of the target so the only real question was what to do with it. The line between Olympus and the Air Defence Commander at the Joint Headquarters at Episkopi was hot. There had been no increase in their own alert state despite the warlike preparations going on down on the apron at Akrotiri. There could be no reason to engage an aircraft passing through the airspace without a rise in the alert state even though a track emanating from Syria and flying at Mach 2 plus at 70,000 feet was unusual by any standards. Normally the Syrians kept themselves very much to themselves. A Foxbat heading down the Mediterranean at that height could only mean one thing. He watched the track as it approached Crete well to the west, already close to the limits of his radar coverage. At Mach 2 plus it was eating up the miles rapidly. He could not imagine anything of interest so far down the Med. All the activity was at this end. He waited anticipating a turn back..

"Hawk 1continue to hold in your present position. Bogey is well to the west still heading away at high speed. Expect clearance to identify if it returns."

"Hawk 1."

In the cockpit, the crew began to digest the implications. The standard profile to intercept and identify a high flying supersonic target was difficult in a Phantom, particularly one carrying a full war load of eight missiles and a Suu-23 gun pod. Engaging with a missile was easier. After accelerating to supersonic speeds, a snap up at 25 miles would convert the speed to height and as the Phantom topped out at 50,000 feet plus the Skyflash missiles would snap up the extra height and take out the target. To identify a target so high and so fast was more a leap of faith and well beyond the normal operating envelope of the aging fighter. The navigator began to chew over the likely problems.

"OK, we're not going to detect this thing until about 60 miles if we're lucky. We'll need to accelerate as fast as we can go."

"In this fit with external tanks and a gun we're limited to Mach 1.6. Standby transmitting."

He hit the switch on the throttles.

"Olympus Hawk 1 will we be clear to jettison the tanks. We're speed limited in this fit."

"Standby Hawk 1, checking."

"If this is a Foxbat, which is what I think it is, Mach 1.6 won't be nearly enough. He could be closer to Mach 2.5 at the merge so he'll be opening on us. I had a go against Concorde down the North Sea a few years ago and it was doing Mach 2.2. I seem to remember the QWIs worked out that a turn at 28 miles with a 3G to 4G pull would be needed to try to roll out inside weapons parameters. If he is as fast as that we'll need a lead turn and let him come over the top as we roll out on his heading. There's no way we can get anywhere close to his height with tanks and a gun. He may go off the side of the radar scope in the turn so it'll be fun trying to reacquire him once we roll out. We'll have to be ready because he's going to be well above the contrails layer at that height. It'll be hard to get a visual acquisition to get the identification."

"Hawk 1, Olympus I confirm you are clear to jettison tanks if required."

"Hawk 1 copied, clear jettison tanks, thanks!"

"Bloody hell now that's a first! You ready for this?"

"As ready as I'll ever be! You know what the burners are like at those sorts of heights. If we lose a burner we're only going one way and that's down. If we get anywhere close to his height the chances are at least one if not both of them will blow out."

They waited in anticipation nursing the fuel as the pilot held the gentle elongated orbit to the east of the island. The radio was frustratingly quiet.

"Olympus, Hawk 1 sitrep."

Over 100 miles to the west the Foxbat began a lazy turn towards the south. Even at such extreme height the Foxbat handled the turn, easily holding the height even though such a manoeuvre would have seen most high performance jets returning earthwards. On his kneepad the pilot checked the headings for the final run. It took him well south of Cyprus towards the Israeli airspace. It was the ships of the US 6th Fleet that were the primary interest but he intended to give them a wide berth. He had already stirred a hornet's nest and he fully expected a reception committee on the homeward leg. The Brits from Cyprus would probably have a go and he would be surprised if the alert birds from the US carrier hadn't been launched to meet him. A quick check of the speed and he pushed the throttles up to take him back above Mach 2 as he steadied up on heading.

"Hawk 1vector 270, gate, target bears 270 range 100 inbound."

"Hawk 1steady west, looking. Check the target's height?"

"Hawk 1 target shows Flight Level 700 plus."

"Holy shit, that's the first time I ever heard that on the radio. Here we go!"

With the aircraft still subsonic the pilot knew that to make anything like that height the wing tanks were history. Most of the fuel had gone, sacrificed in the rapid climb to height so they had fulfilled their role. They would end their days at the bottom of the Mediterranean. He leant down to the missile control panel and nominated the tanks for jettison before hitting the red selector in the centre of the panel. He warned the navigator and as he punched the button there was a subdued thump. Below the wings the explosive cartridges in the tank pylons activated severing the link with the aircraft. Suddenly free the tanks tumbled in the airflow dropping below and behind on their long drop towards the surface of the sea below. He eased the throttles forward into min burner and the jet responded instantly now much lighter and more responsive. The speed began to creep up immediately and he began a gentle climb. He would hold just subsonic until he reached the tropopause before pushing over to accelerate the Phantom through the Mach. At that stage it should accelerate away and pick up speed despite the gun pod strapped to the centreline. The tanks were one thing, the gun and missiles would be much harder to explain if he returned without them. He watched the spped build anticipating the point at which he would begin the zoom climb to intercept the Foxbat.

In the back the navigator played with the radar controls as the AN/AWG12 in pulse Doppler mode scanned left and right. His attention was focussed on the small area either side of the centreline looking for the first tell tale smudge of a radar contact. In his mind he was running through the mental calculation of where to position the radar scanner to detect the target way above them. He set the elevation strobes at the side of the radar display in the position which should point the radar beam in exactly to right area of sky. In his headset the fighter controller offered the occasional snippet of information to assist in the search. The target was a long way above him.

"Target range 80."

"No joy," he replied frustrated at the wait. With the Phantom almost supersonic, 80 miles would be covered in mere seconds so there was no margin for error. The radar scope stayed frustratingly blank.

"Range 70."

The range was marching towards at a blistering pace. This intercept, if that's what it turned out to be, would be very brief.

"Contact, range 65," called the navigator.

"Target."

"Judy."

Sixty five miles was a healthy pick up and he was secretly pleased. He could see the blip on the tube and he'd made contact in sufficient time to engineer an intercept. He began to call the parameters to his pilot but rarely had he seen a blip so far up the Doppler display. This target was motoring!

"No place for clever stuff here, come starboard to centre the dot. We're just going to point at him and that'll give you the best chance to accelerate."

The pilot pulled the Skyflash aiming dot into the centre of the radar scope setting up a collision heading. The slight crossing angle would be fine for their purposes.

"It'll be a left right crosser and our final turn will be to starboard. I'll need a 3G pull during the turn. Accelerate high speed and give me what you can."

"Accelerating."

The jet bunted over and the needle on the airspeed indicator flickered momentarily as the Phantom flew through the sound barrier Once transonic the speed crept rapidly upwards; Mach 1.2, Mach 1.3 . . . . .

"Target range 35, stand by for the turn."

Everything in his psyche told him to turn later. During a standard intercept that might be as late as 12 miles but with the high speed Foxbat, unless he started the turn early the target would be long gone by the time he rolled out on the same heading. It would look wrong on the scope but he had to trust his instincts and anticipate the turn.

"Range 28 come starboard hard now, roll out 120 degrees."

In the front the pilot rolled on the bank and pulled gently to 3G. The airspeed indicator showed Mach 1.6 and had stubbornly refused to go higher. The drag of the external stores, particularly the gun pod, was preventing anything more. He had managed to get the reluctant jet up to 40,000 feet and he would try for more once he rolled out after the turn. The Phantom could turn or climb but in this fit it would not do both and to try would lose all the carefully nurtured speed which he needed to prosecute the intercept. The target was still 30,000 feet above them. Listening to the commentary from the back seat he focussed his eyes at the point in space where the target should be. Nothing yet but it was still 15 miles away. He held the G steady glancing regularly at the speed. If he allowed it to drop off they could kiss goodbye to any chance of seeing this thing. The locked up display glowed brightly on his radar repeater as the navigator monitored the progress and he could see that they were pulling well ahead of the target in the turn. Even so, the Foxbat was way faster and was closing down the distance between them by the second. He concentrated on the commentary from the back as the range closed inside 10 miles. There was a brief puff of a contrail in his peripheral vision and his eyes locked onto that position in space.

"Target 60 left at 8 miles 25 degrees high, coming heads out," he heard from the back as the navigator's eyes switched from the radar to the world outside the cockpit. The pass would be fleeting and 2 pairs of eyes were better than one.

They both saw it at exactly the same moment. A pin prick in the deep blue sky magnified in intensity in the rarefied upper air. It was still probably five miles away but closing rapidly as he eased off the bank to hold sight. The intercept had been perfect. They were virtually coincident in space as the Foxbat flashed over the top of the Phantom still 20,000 feet above. The slower fighter clawed for the extra height to get closer still but it was a losing battle and the superior speed and performance of the Foxbat at this height meant the pass would be swift. Even so, there could be no mistaking the distinctive profile as it streaked past, the twin fins shielded from view from this aspect. The giveaway was the square engine intakes and squared off wingtips. They were too far below to see if it carried weapons or to recognise any national markings. As they watched it opened in range, rapidly receding from view. The radar stayed doggedly locked to the receding target.

"Olympus, Hawk 1 identifies one Foxbat heading 090 at Flight Level 700. Hauling off."

"Olympus copied."

As it passed south of Cyprus on its second pass, cameras on both sides of the forward fuselage clicked away. The scene on the ground at Akrotiri was captured for a 2nd time but the southerly facing cameras mapped the ocean between Cyrus and the Egyptian coast in detail. Any ships which appeared on the images would be carefully analysed and their positions would be captured for analysts to pore over. In just a few hours time, a precise sea plot would be displayed in the Defence Headquarters in Damascus. Behind the Foxbat, and well below, a frustrated Phantom crew called for recovery to Akrotiri.

"So it was a Foxbat. Big deal, that was bloody obvious before we made the intercept. What else flogs down the Med at those speeds other than an SR71? And to top it off we just dumped a set of tanks into the Med. What did we just prove?"

The frustration was palpable as the pilot flicked the weapons switches off and began his recovery checks.

"Hawk 1 field in sight to Akrotiri Tower for recovery."

He switched frequency without another word pausing momentarily on the squadron operations frequency to warn the Duty Authoriser to prepare a new set of external fuel tanks for loading..

*

Already close to the Syrian coastline well to the east, the Foxbat was subsonic as it coasted-in. As the sleek jet turned onto finals the support team watched from their position alongside the hardened aircraft shelter poised to recover the vital film. The minute the jet closed down the film canisters were pulled from the camera bays in the fuselage and dispatched to the photographic bay for processing. Within a few more hours, the precious negatives would be in the hands of Syrian intelligence who would pore over the detailed images and decide on whether to respond to the unfolding events at Akrotiri. The outcome of that analysis would decide whether the mission which was being planned would progress as smoothly as the British crews hoped. No one at the Syrian base cared about the diplomatic wrangles that had just begun. The fact that the Syrian Ambassador had been called into the Foreign Office in London to receive a formal complaint about the aircraft overflying British airspace was irrelevant to them. Their job was to develop pictures.

CHAPTER 14

Whitehall, London.

Sir Richard Courtney, the Head of MI6 was ushered into the spacious office on the Sixth Floor of the Ministry of Defence Main Building on Whitehall. The Defence Minister rose to greet him surprised at the speed of his response to the invitation. He showed him across to the comfortable sofas near the windows, the dingy bomb blast curtains weighted with lead spoiling what would otherwise have been a stunning view of The Thames.

Thank you for coming Sir Richard, I know just how busy you must be."

"My pleasure Minister, I thought it best to keep in touch given the speed of events at the minute. I sat in the margins at the Foreign Minister's meeting with the Ambassadors yesterday morning. Quite helpful and most illuminating."

"Do tell."

"He played with a straight bat, although, as we have all agreed, he stopped a little short of disclosing the actual operational plan. All the background was laid out including our predicament with our man in Beirut but he suggested our aim was merely to show a presence at this stage. He told them of the fact that we planned to send a force in order to try to recover our man. The actual plan and the force composition is still close hold. Again, he only offered broad details."

"So what were they asked to do?"

"Merely to deconflict their forces from ours. He asked that their headquarters be warned of the movements and guarantee that there would be no intervention."

"Were they supportive?"

"Incredibly. They both offered as much assistance as we might need. In fact, if anything, he had to ask them to be patient. The US Ambassador was almost falling over himself to provide forces. Even so, I'm still nervous. It's tinder dry down there and one little spark." He hesitated. "You'll know better than I that the 6th Fleet can be a little trigger happy and you only have to look at some recent incidents to know how narrow the margin is for error."

"Surely there are robust rules of engagement to prevent mishaps?"

"Quite so but if they thought it was an attack against the task force I'm sure they would shoot first and ask questions later. Pre-emptive self defence I heard it called once. A wonderful euphemism. We've had a lot of intelligence showing that the pressure on the trigger is tightening. They keep their location quite tight but to be frank, they are boxed into quite a tight area of operations. We don't want our aircraft passing through their zone. They got very close to engaging a Russian maritime patrol aircraft earlier in the week but it hasn't put our friends from Moscow off at all. As usual, the Russians will blunder into the middle of a crisis without any notification or flight plan. They really do push their luck and it's only the fact that they were being tracked by NATO that defused the situation."

"Why don't you give me an update on your plans and progress and then I'll tell you where we are with the operational deployment."

"Of course. Obviously, as soon as we heard our man had been snatched I sent another operative down there immediately. He got straight in touch with our network down there and he's made remarkable progress. I'm not sure if I should be worried or not but Hezbollah seem to be almost crowing about this situation. They've pretty much told us where he is being held and that they would be receptive to a diplomatic approach. Director Special Forces has all the details and he has already had a team infiltrate the area. If it is the compound we think, it's secured tighter than a drum and we won't get even a small force in there. Hence our requests to you for an operational contingency plan."

"Yes, Director Special Forces was in earlier and gave me the latest."

"What I hope is that we can set up a visit on the pretext of consular access and make contact with the hostage. That way we can try to work out where this mysterious package is being held and whether any of the information has been compromised during his enforced stay. With appropriate offers of "specialist assistance"; weaponry to you or I, any commodity has a price in The Lebanon at present. I feel sure we could come to a deal if we can get to him."

"Are you working alone?"

"Let's just say that our friends in Mossad have fairly extensive contacts in the city and are onside. If the terrorist group is receptive we'll make contact and quite soon."

"Good, good, that sounds promising. Well as you know I warned-off forces yesterday and they have already deployed to RAF Akrotiri in the Eastern Mediterranean. The main force has arrived including the helicopters which were airlifted down. The briefings and mission preparation are underway as we speak. Barring mishaps I hope to give the execution order soon. The PM has already agreed and delegated the call to me. How long do you think you need to work on this visit? We can't hold off for long now the jets are in place. It's a fairly overt measure and there can't be many reasons to put that size of force down there. Of course were calling it a routine exercise and suggesting it's been planned for months but that won't hold up to much scrutiny."

"I realise that. I'll chase them up when I get back to the office. You'll have an answer by Five PM."

"Perhaps the time for subtlety is over, Richard? Maybe we just need some gung ho for a change?"

"Perhaps so Minister but if we can do this via good old diplomacy even if it is "under the counter diplomacy", it might be less messy."

"Well they're carrying out some essential pre-mission training today and the briefings are planned for this afternoon. If we speak later we can decide how long your new man will have. I'd suggest that if there's no progress we push tomorrow. It's an ambitious military plan but very bold. I have to say I'm impressed at the lateral thinking that's gone into it. I really do think it can work but time is short."

The two men rose.

"Thank you for coming over and we'll chat again later."

*

To say that the Israeli Ambassador was not happy was a huge understatement and he was making it very clear. The secure telephone connection had been established a few minutes earlier and complex cryptographic cipher boxes made sure that the only recipients of his tirade were the unfortunates at the Israeli MOD, Mossad headquarters and the Foreign Office in Tel Aviv. His aide was scribbling furiously trying to capture the main points as the rhetoric flowed. The nervous tic on the Ambassador's temple was not a good sign.

"Why am I the last person to find out that a British agent has been snatched off the streets of Beirut. I'm only the Ambassador in London and we only pride ourselves that we have that city flooded with agents. You told me only last week that if a pin dropped you'd hear it. What went wrong?"

There were reassuring but apologetic noises from the round teleconference speaker set in the centre of the conference table. The tone on the line surged distorting the voices slightly as the cryptographic boxes scrambled and reassembled the electronic signals in milliseconds.

"I spent the morning offering the British Foreign Secretary help with a problem in our own back yard that I knew nothing of. I was ambushed for God's sake!"

He snapped the pencil he had been playing with.

"Tell me now; who is this agent, what was he doing? Who did he meet? What might he have acquired? We should know this stuff without me asking! I should have been briefed. Was it in the daily sitrep?"

The aide scribbled furiously. The Ambassador barely paused for breath as the line to Tel Aviv delivered the monologue.

"What help can we give them? At least we need to make sure we don't get tangled in their operation whatever it's supposed to be for. Am I the only one who thinks we haven't had the full story. Isn't a show of force in that part of the Lebanon just a little naive at present? After all, despite the kicking we gave the Syrians, even we have had to pull back."

As he paused for breath the back-pedalling from the harassed recipients in Israel suggested that he had struck a nerve. Despite his impeccable diplomatic facade the Ambassador was well known in Tel Aviv and known to be a political heavyweight. His former role in the Israeli Defence Force gave him credibility as well as the moral high ground. He could slug it out with the best bare knuckle opponent and he was on a roll.

"OK so get back to me. I want information from the streets about where this agent is being held. I want to know who he's been seeing and what he might have got hold of. Dig deeper and I want information by close of play today. Good God they even have me using cricket terms! If I get called back to Whitehall I want to be properly briefed this time."

He hit the disconnect button before there was even time for an acknowledgement.

CHAPTER 15

The Hezbollah Compound on the Syrian Border.

Many miles away on the Syrian border there was a surge of activity in the compound. A satellite phone had been provided as a means to communicate with an "overseas contact". With landlines in the region unreliable and with telephone exchanges being tapped by the Israelis the new technology, supposedly, offered relative relatively secure communications. The leader had called his handler.

"Our offer seems to have been taken seriously. Our contacts in Beirut have already been approached and a request for the British Embassy to speak with our guest has been made. It would help our cause if we comply you know."

"Of course and we both agree on that but we need plans in place to move our guest as soon as the meeting is over. We can't risk an effort being made to recover him before we have the package in our hands."

"Of course, that was anticipated and plans are already in place. Do you wish us to communicate directly or is there a cut out in place?"

"We will pass the where and when but the timescales will be short so be ready. If we can arrange if for later today we will. I assume he's secure for the time being?"

"Very. Since he arrived he has not been outside the building. Other than routine traffic at the site there is no way he could have been seen. Just make sure the visitor doesn't have time to make elaborate arrangements. The journey from Beirut is short but we need to keep the pressure applied. We should be careful in what we say. I'm sure if word gets out of his location the move will be harder to execute. Well, more than we would wish."

"Of course."

"Why don't you have our people meet the delegate at the crossroads on the coast road? That way we can escort him into the location and make sure he is alone. I don't want surprises at this stage."

"Consider it done. I'll make the call now and come back to you with a time."

Terminating the call, the leader barked a command and, after a hurried exchange, the aide disappeared to plan the rendezvous. A road move onwards to Damascus had been in his mind from the outset but the conversation added urgency.

Little did the leader know but his actions had just sealed his fate. The satellite call had been monitored and, without encryption every word had been captured in the clear. On the summit of Mount Olympus the NCO had pressed the earphone closer to his ear and listened intently. The recorders captured every word on the satellite communications channel. Once the speaker had been voice printed to ensure his identity the details would be sent to those who needed them back in UK. Almost as soon as the call ended, a FLASH signal with a transcript was on its way to London. As soon as the timings fed through to the political hierarchy the operation would be declared time critical. By agreeing to a meeting, a clock had been set ticking. Soon, the operational planning cell at High Wycombe outside London would be drafting the execute message.

*

Reeves looked around the small cell and tried to get things into perspective. The lack of physical violence was almost unnerving. He had expected from the very first moment he had been taken in Beirut to be beaten. This way was even more subtle and the isolation was beginning to tell. The cot was reasonably comfortable and the thin mattress and sheets that had been thrown in through the door shortly after his arrival had made his stay almost comfortable. He was being fed regularly even if the menu might struggle to make the culinary review pages in the London Evening Standard. The problem was the boredom. From living on his nerves in the Beirut suburbs to his current predicament was a huge gulf and he needed a stimulus to stay sharp. The quiet was disconcerting and the only noises he ever heard emanated from the compound outside. Add to that, there was nothing to suggest any variation from the routine. With only the regular comings and goings of the guards, normality such as it was, reigned. The small bowl under the cot which had been his toilet for the last days stank but his mind was even beginning to tune out that rank discomfort.

He reclined on the bed and his mind wandered back to the meeting in Damascus. The wiry Arab whom he had cultivated for months had actually come up with the goods. He had been at the drop as promised dressed in his military uniform and the tell tale had been placed; not that Reeves had left that to chance. He had monitored his progress, if nothing else, to ensure that he was not being tracked by a watcher. The package had seemed to be what he had promised. The thinly bound operation order had all the correct markings and seemed genuine. The Syrian MOD crest was authentic and the signatures seemed to be those of the officials who would approve such plans. So what had gone wrong? The journey back to Beirut had been uneventful. He had checked the package for bugs and tags and it was clean. The rental car he had secured for the journey was clean. The package had fitted neatly in the compartment under the boot floor and, although the charade at the border was as painful as usual, the guards had barely shown any interest other than a cursory check of the boot and the bonnet. He would probably have bet money that they would not have recognised the documents even if he had waved them under their noses. Mind you, the small wad of dollars that had changed hands in the customary fashion had probably helped smooth his passage.

He had known where he was going to hide the document before he had even made the pickup and had gone straight to the location as soon as he returned to Beirut. His careful routing, completely random and circuitous, had guaranteed that he could not be followed. The occasional sniper fire in the seedier parts of town would also have deterred a pursuer. There was nothing he could identify that should have flagged up his activity to the terrorist team. How the hell had they caught on?

It was at this point he cleared his mind. The direction in which it was moving led towards the key piece of information. Knowing the location of the documents was his only salvation and, the less he thought about it, the less likely he was to give it up if the interrogation went further. He was paranoid about the use of drugs and had no idea how long he could resist. Blanking the thought from his mind he switched to other things.

The pain in his abdomen was a constant reminder of his major dilemma. The revelation about the device implanted in his gut was a serious setback and a devious twist. It didn't stop them moving him around. All they had to do was take the damned transmitter along with him. While he was in this cell and without knowing how the device worked, he could go nowhere. He had no idea where the transmitter/receiver was located. For now, thoughts of escape had been consigned to the bin.

Doors slammed and an engine fired up as another truck drove across the yard outside the window. He ran through his strict mental routine, training his mind to adapt, striving for control of his subconscious. His thoughts were of easier times.

DAVID GLEDHILL

CHAPTER 16

RAF Akrotiri, Cyprus.

It was 7 AM and the dining room in the Officers' Mess was slowly filling up. As the diners drifted in, the harsh sound of Phantoms in full reheat split the morning air. The previous squadron was leaving setting course for the UK behind the fleet of tankers which had delivered the combined force to Akrotiri just yesterday. The noise continued for some minutes as the fighter jets streamed off in close succession, the crews eager to head home.

In addition to the usual crowd of locals dressed in their distinctive khaki uniforms a small knot of aircrew in green flying suits had formed around some of the long mahogany tables in the centre of the room. Tribal as always, the Buccaneer crews occupied one table and the Phantom crews had joined forces with the helicopter crews around a second. Breakfast cereal was supplemented with an English "full fry" looking slightly out of place in this outpost of Empire and somewhat different to the Mediterranean fare which would be served in the plush new hotels on the outskirts of Limmasol this morning. Conversation was muted and the morning newspapers littered the tables as the officers tried to catch up. Today's papers would only arrive on the trooper flight later in the morning and the headlines were already familiar to the crews who had seen them in UK before starting the long deployment flight yesterday morning. As yet, the news of the operation had not leaked and the headlines trumpeted the latest indiscretion by a B list celebrity. How long the lull would last was moot. The MOD was notoriously leaky and few around the tables had any doubt that by the time they set heading for Beirut their mission would be splashed across the tabloids. For now, the slightly bored looking stewards dressed in smart white jackets served up plates of bacon and eggs. A strident call from the doorway announced the arrival of the transport. Chairs scraped and bodies moved towards the door en masse leaving the dining room almost deserted.

There was a bustle about Golf Dispersal as the crew coach pulled up to the front of the operations building. The groundcrew had been at work for hours fixing snags from the deployment flight and running through pre-flight servicing and weapons acceptance checks. A couple of aircraft sat in the hangar their problems proving a little more elusive to fix. The majority of the jets had been pulled onto the flight line pointing out across Limmasol Bay. The Buccaneers had deployed with Pave Spike pods but bomb trolleys were arriving constantly from the Station Armoury carrying the laser guided bombs which would be loaded for the mission. The Suu-23 gun pods left behind by the departing Phantom squadron had been positioned alongside each Phantom. They would soon be fitted to the aircraft along with the Skyflash and AIM-9L Sidewinder missiles which had been pulled onto the dispersal on small trolleys behind a bright white Land Rover.

At the far end of the line a pair of 56 Squadron Phantoms resplendent in the light grey air defence camouflage had been held back when the remainder of the Squadron had departed behind the VC10 tankers at first light. These jets still carried the dark green Suu-23 cannons which stood out starkly beneath the fuselages in the absence of the external wing tanks. They would follow the remainder of the squadron later in the day staging back through an Italian airbase but today they would be used to re-qualify some of the 29 Squadron crews in air-to-air gunnery skills.

In the small briefing room the crews were being reminded of procedures for air-to-air gunnery. It was a skill that they may have to employ for real over the coming days. Even though today they would carry "ball" ammunition, an inert round used for training purposes, mistakes could be fatal. The Canberra target towing aircraft had also remained behind, although with its huge fuel tanks, it had no need for air-to-air refuelling and could make the trip back to the UK in a single hop. It would depart later in the day as soon as the gunnery sorties were complete. By late evening its crews would be safely home at RAF Marham in Norfolk. First, however, it would tow one last gunnery banner for the new arrivals.

The banner was a strange contraption and the procedures a total contrast to the high technology of the fighter jets. Towed behind the Canberra on a 100 metre towline, the huge flag with its black aiming marker comprised of a large net attached to a metal cylinder. Heavy metal weights at the end of the "spreader bar" ensured it flew upright. In order to ensure that the net stayed intact the maximum speed the Canberra would reach during a gunnery sortie was 200 knots. Any faster and the netting would be shredded leaving little to shoot at. The Phantom flew its gunnery pattern at 400 knots and simple maths suggested that with 200 knots overtake, Phantom pilots might find challenges tracking the slow moving flag with the gunsight. Shooting at the banner from line astern might leave the Canberra crew feeling slightly nervous as bullets would pass uncomfortably close to the tug and, more importantly, its crew. For that reason complex figure of eight and circular firing patterns had been designed by the weapons instructors. This ensured that once the trigger was pulled the bullets passed well clear of the Canberra tug, harmlessly. With firing ranges of 300 to 500 yards, the escape manoeuvre, up and over the banner, was dramatic. There was some incentive for the Phantom crews to get it right. Low angle gunnery passes would exact retribution from the weapons instructor and guarantee threats of physical violence from the Canberra crew.

With the warm climate and the equally warm water of the Mediterranean there was no need for the bulky immersion suits which the crews had worn for the deployment flight. As they walked to the jets they wore only a light flying suit, a life jacket and carried a bonedome and a kneeboard. In a "clean wing" Phantom and with the high use of afterburner during air-to-air gunnery, their sortie would be short and they would be landing a mere 20 minutes after takeoff. Normally, a gunnery phase would follow a scripted progression working up from academic shooting into limited operational profiles and then into operational patterns. Today there would be no time for niceties. After a quick academic pattern it would be straight into an operational shoot and the guns carried a full load of over 1200 rounds of ammunition. Those bullets would be expended in mere seconds as the Suu-23 wound up to its fearsome 6000 rounds per minute firing rate. The bullets would leave via the front door whilst the spent cartridge cases would be ejected over the side into the Mediterranean Sea below.

With the Phantom crews checking in and running through their pre-flight checks the Canberra tug pulled onto the runway. The support crew swiftly arranged a banner behind the retired bomber laying it out on the runway behind and clipping the shackle into the housing on the rear fuselage. With a quick acknowledgement the pilot spooled up the engines and the tug trundled off down the runway towing the heavy spreader bar on its small metal wheels. The banner flapped along the runway but as the tug lifted off and pulled up and away from the runway the spreader bar snapped upright in its wake the banner flapping lazily behind, the crack of the fabric audible to anyone close by. After a lazy turn the Canberra and its strange companion headed south towards the firing range just off the coast. The pilot would fly around the range checking for small vessels which were not showing up on the air defence radar on Mount Olympus. Small wooden boats had no radar signature but, despite the warnings, fisherman often drifted into the danger area. A rainstorm of spent 20mm cartridge cases would be an unwelcome experience for an interloper. A hail of 20mm ball even less so. A final visual check to ensure the airspace was clear was the only way to combat their apparent indifference to danger. Content that today they were alone in the range the Canberra pilot transmitted his clearance on the Tower frequency eliciting an immediate response as a pair of Phantoms rolled down the runway to join him off the coast.

The first formality was a banner check to ensure that the banner was upright and stable. With the Canberra holding a steady easterly heading at 5000 feet, each Phantom conducted a slow flyby locking up to the spreader bar and eyeballing the long oscillating net. Their next view of the banner would be far less pedestrian. Happy that it was behaving the second Phantom climbed to 10,000 feet well above the tow and throttled back to watch the first crew go through their paces. The first Phantom had thrown a large orbit and positioned two miles behind the tug. In the back seat the navigator locked to the banner making sure, first of all, that he had identified both the banner and the Canberra tug. To lock to the Canberra would be a cardinal sin.

"Commence. In Hot!" he transmitted.

It would be live from the outset. The Canberra began to turn gently as soon as the navigator made the call. It would turn left through 135 degrees before reversing the turn back to the right.

As the tug followed the pattern the Phantom would arc the turn closing in rapidly, taking a short burst at about 400 yards. Only a few rounds would be expended on this sighter pass and the coloured paint on the tips of the bullets would mark the passage of any rounds which pierced the netting. The Suu-23 emitted barely more than a burp.

"Out. Complete."

Rolling out 270."

The Canberra steadied up on its new heading ready for the operational shoot. There would be no fanfare this time. On the call of "commence" the Canberra would enter an orbit. The Phantom pilot had only 2 full orbits in which to empty the remaining rounds from the gun and during that time he could make as many hot passes as the time allowed. The Canberra pilot would call "rolling out" at which stage the shoot was over. This time instead of the slight stutter of an academic pass the Suu-23 would emit its satisfying extended buzz as the remaining 1000 rounds left the six barrels of the Gatling gun at 6000 rounds per minute. In the event the two turns were superfluous. As the Canberra was barely half way through its second orbit the call came.

"Out and RTB. See you on the ground."

The Phantom pulled off and headed north descending rapidly to mere feet above the waves for the recovery. Leaving his playmate to continue he left the frequency.

"Olympus, 21 is RTB, to Tower."

"21, Olympus, to Stud 1, good day."

Overhead the banner the second Phantom had positioned two miles behind and immediately dropped into the line astern position already locked on to the banner.

"Commence."

There was not time to waste.

As the second Phantom broke into the circuit its exercise complete, the Canberra followed just a few miles behind. It would fly low over the runway offset by just a few yards and cut the towline allowing the banner to fall to earth. The support team would collect the discarded flag and take it swiftly to the squadron where the crews eagerly awaited the delivery. Marking the banner was normally a blood sport and highly competitive with debates over which hits would be awarded to which crew. Colours could be confused and the odd hit here and there could be crucial to achieving a qualifying score. Today there would be no fanfare. The holes would be counted but the crews would fly the mission whether their scores had been respectable or not.

The Land Rover pulled in behind the ops building and the banner was carefully lifted from the back and spread out on the floor. Immediately the crews swarmed around looking for the tell tale holes with the coloured edges. Still wearing life jackets and clutching helmets the second crew were even more interested. The QWI clutched his clipboard and began to count holes verifying each one with a piece of chalk. At the end he announced the tally with a simple call of "requalified". Repeating the exercise for the second crew he reached the same conclusion before returning to the operations desk to release the Canberra and Phantoms from their commitment. Before the week was over, the Suu-23 gun pods may be needed in anger but at least the crews were better prepared.

*

As the first U-2 was pushed back into the hangar after its daily mission the fast-jet crews watched in fascination at the procedure. It was hard to imagine a greater contrast between different jet aircraft. The squat ugly functionality of the Phantom had little bearing on the long elegant lines of the reconnaissance aircraft. Designed for the same medium of flight the two aircraft operated in entirely different regimes. The Phantom was happiest down low travelling at high speed. The U-2 trod a very thin line in the upper air. With its slow speed of little over 130 knots it had a thin margin between maximum flying speed and stall speed. Small variations in either direction could prove terminal. Too fast and there was a real risk of airframe damage; too slow and the aircraft would depart from controlled flight and return to Earth in a less than elegant fashion. The long thin glider-like wings seemed barely strong enough to keep it aloft.

The Phantom crews had been joined by the Buccaneer weapons instructors who would be briefed into a sensitive addition to the cast. Their presence had nothing to do with the U-2. They were here to see the newest resident of the hangar. As they waited for an escort the black jet disappeared from view and the hangar doors were drawn closed. Screens inside had ensured that other occupants were protected from inquisitive eyes. The guard with whom they had exchanged brief words on arrival re-emerged from the hangar and beckoned them over. As they approached the door the familiar face of Yuri Andrenev greeted them, a huge smile on his face and genuinely pleased to see them again.

"One of these days we'll meet in a pub," he quipped. "Let's go take a look at this thing. Hopefully getting hands-on will be better than a dozen briefings in the briefing room and the sim."

The Buccaneer crew looked on quizzically still unaware of the surprise to come. They followed him down the corridor towards the hangar door where the whine of maintenance equipment announced the activity within.

The technicians were still busy with preparing the Mig and the final weapons had been uploaded. Test umbilicals snaked from the avionics bays connecting to ruggedized test boxes ranged across the floor. Yuri sidestepped the activity and began a walkround with the enthralled aircrew in tow. Even knowing of its presence, the Phantom crews were awed at such a personal view of the Mig which looked totally out of place in this small corner of the air base. Pointing out the key features as he went along he explained things in a level of detail which would be impossible to replicate in any technical manual. His first hand experience cut through rafts of irrelevant information. He focussed the briefing exactly on the issues which he knew would concern the flyers. He also knew they would need to know about very specific capabilities as the mission unfolded. Pausing alongside each of the air-to-air missiles he explained the intricacies of the tracking process gesturing occasionally at the cockpit to tie in the way he manipulated the controls to prosecute an attack. They worked slowly around the airframe pausing regularly to focus on each system.

*

As the crews were inspecting the Mig in the hangar the pilot of the second U-2 was well into his mission. It was rare for both aircraft to fly on the same day but events were not normal and the tasking rates had been high this week. As usual the run through the Sinai had been stultifyingly boring and he had suffered the normal restricted view from the dark visor of his spacesuit. He had flipped on the autopilot as he reached top of climb and the mission system had routed him around the familiar track. In the camera bays the precision lenses were trained on the areas of interest and the cameras had snapped away automatically as the spy plane had passed overhead.

Today, however, would be an unusual flight because an additional, very specific target had been added and he would have to fly part of the mission manually. The flight profile had been difficult to plot for a number of reasons. On the normal route he headed south to monitor the disputed border in the Sinai and then recovered directly to Akrotiri. With the new target's proximity to the Syrian border, a huge orbit would have to be flown over The Lebanon yet avoiding penetrating Syrian airspace to the north and east. The flight profile was out of the ordinary and would attract attention from both Syria and Israel. The British would, by now, have briefed the Israelis on the operation but the Syrians would be left guessing. As they were almost certainly complicit in capturing the hostage it was likely that they would be suspicious and would be likely to respond. The planners had reassured him that they would have insufficient time to understand the significance of the deviation before the operation was completed. He loved it when the intelligence analysts were so sure about things. Nothing ever went wrong. . . . .

As he finished his primary detail he felt the autopilot bring the jet back onto north. As he coasted out over the Gaza Strip the autopilot brought the aircraft further right and it hugged the coastline just outside the territorial limit off Israel. At just 130 knots it was slow progress but, as he passed abeam Tripoli which he could see on the coastline below, he took control and made the additional turn taking him into The Lebanon. Skirting the eastern border he turned north before making a tight turn at the northern border remaining just inside Lebanese airspace. His altimeter read a reassuring 70,000 feet. There were a few casual bleeps from his radar warning receiver but nothing that gave him any concern. Once on a westerly heading the cameras clicked away mapping the border at high resolution and in precise detail producing a series of pictures that would be of a much higher quality than any satellite could ever produce. As the coastline approached he flew a lazy orbit to the left before repeating the pass. It was this second pass that caused him the anxiety. The ground attackers' mantra was "never reattack" and, that way, defences alerted during the first pass would never get the chance to respond. What he was attempting went against the grain. This time his RWR was much more animated. Throughout both passes the Spoon Rest surveillance radar inside Syria had continued its relentless scanning. Now a Fan Song acquisition radar from an SA-2 battery just inside the Syrian border took much more interest and tracked his progress. The familiar rattle of the track-while-scan system heightened his attention enough that he flicked on the transmitter of his active jamming system. It would cause diplomatic tension later in the day but far better that than another Gary Powers incident. Unseen in the cockpit the electronic signals he was now emitting played havoc on the ground in the control cabin of the SA-2 system. He could imagine engagement controllers frantically seeking permission from a startled air defence commander to engage the belligerent intruder. It was doubtful that they would receive clearance in time but, if they did, his electronic box of tricks had more programs to employ which would ensure the SA-2s Guideline missile never got anywhere near him. The countermeasures had been carefully tested on test ranges back home and he had every confidence they were effective. Even so, he was glad he didn't have to fly a third orbit. There was no point in taunting them too much. He had played with a bees nest as a kid in the wilds of Kentucky and had no desire to relive the consequences. It was with an unintentional sigh of relief that he coasted out overhead Beirut after the second orbit and set course for the runway at Akrotiri.

As he headed home his attention turned to the recovery. Getting his charge back down on the ground was never easy. The huge wings were reluctant to stop flying and killing the lift was an art in itself. The biggest challenge was the last ten feet of the approach. With its massive lift and his appalling peripheral vision he would have to be talked onto the runway by another pilot in a car which would race down the runway alongside him.

The controller at Olympus handed him back to Akrotiri Approach and he continued his descent to initials. With the runway in sight he transferred to Tower and checked in with the controller and his support crew. With the massive spoilers on top of the wings deployed into the airflow he drove for the threshold watching the altimeter slowly unwind. Passing over Limmasol Bay he began to reduce the rate of descent and picked out his touchdown point. Inevitably he would float beyond it but it was a start. With a stiff breeze from the west it would be even more challenging than usual. Sea turned to scrubland and he covered the short distance to the runway rapidly. As he passed over the piano keys the pilot on the ground began the litany, counting down from ten feet as he eased the reluctant glider back to Earth. Barely registering the event, the single main wheel kissed the asphalt and the massive wings began to droop downwards as they lost lift and the speed slowed to walking pace. As soon as the black jet stopped, its wingtips scraping to a stop on the concrete, technicians swarmed around hooking up tow bars to pull it clear. It took just minutes to extract the pilot transferring him to the air conditioned crew bus, his life support system hooked up to a portable device. Within minutes the jet was returned to its hangar to join its stable mate where it would be safe from prying eyes. The moment the hangar doors had closed and the jet was stationary technicians began unbuttoning panels and pulling cameras from the bays to begin processing the vital film. It would be ready for analysis within the hour but unlike the Syrian operation miles to the east those analysts were thousands of miles away on the continental United States. The secure electronic communications systems meant it would reach those who needed it the minute it was processed..

*

Later as Razor and Flash downed the first brandy sour of the night Yuri Andrenev walked into the bar accompanied by John Silversmith the intelligence officer. Pointing at the large drink in his hand Flash saw the nods of agreement and ordered another round of drinks as the newcomers made their way through the double doors to a table outside on the patio. They had some catching up to do and a discrete distance from the other rowdy drinkers seemed like a good idea.

"So Yuri, what's life been serving up since we last met?" asked Razor as the Russian sat down.

"I'm not sure you'd believe me if I told you," he said "but I will anyway."

Flash deposited glasses of an ice cold yellow liquid on the table the ice cubes clinking against the glass and planted a huge jug of brandy sour in the centre. They would be good for some time to come.

"I figured we might be talking for some time so I got a recharge while I was at it."

The glasses clinked together in a toast as the ice cold liquid hit the taste buds.

"After I got to London I was a guest of John's organisation for some time. The injuries took a little time to heal so I was off flying for quite a while. I spent a long time going through the Su-27s capabilities and how the test programme had gone. Quite a few of the avionics systems had been taken out at Wildenrath and they had been kept safe. We were able to mount them on a test rig and get them talking to each other again. Although it's not quite as good as flying them, the analysts were still able to work out how they operated and we were able to use them for a number of tests against your aircraft systems. You might have seen some of the results from the CTTO trails already?"

"I kind of assumed that would be where all that amazing data came from," said Flash.

"It helped that I was able to point them in the right direction. I'm not sure how accurate it would have been if the scientists had been allowed to make their own conclusions about how it worked. Anyway, the test set up at RAE Farnborough is still up and running and you'll continue to get loads of good information for some time to come. My only recommendation would be not to risk going up against a Flanker in a Phantom if you have the choice. I've flown the Phantom now and I've seen how the Gardenia jammer does against the AWG 12 radar and it's not pretty. I have to say that as much as I love your jet it's no match for the Su-27. If you think about the F-15 Eagle in terms of performance and then think Flanker in the same thoughts you won't be far wrong."

"Deep joy! So once that was finished what then?"

"Once the bullet wound healed I was invited over to Boscombe Down and I got to fly with the Empire Test Pilot's School at Boscombe Down. That's a great organisation and, having flown mostly Soviet types it was a treat for me to fly western fast jets. I flew the Phantom, the Buccaneer, the Jaguar as well as the Hunter. That really is a sweet old aircraft and reminded me a lot of some of the early Migs. Come to think of it, it was way better!"

"It's been quite a while since you came over though. Surely you haven't spent all the time in England?"

"No that's true. I'd been visited by quite a few of our friends from Nellis Air Force Base during the testing and they asked if I could go over there and work with their Aggressor Squadron to write a supplement for their tactics manual. Of course the thought of a few months in Las Vegas seemed like a good idea so I agreed."

"Tough duty Yuri!"

Razor and Flash exchanged knowing glances having both attended the legendary "Red Flag" exercises at Nellis.

"So I was sent to work with the 64th Aggressor Squadron and spent about a month doing similar work with them. They had worked up some simulations and I was able to refine the model and give hints at how to make it fly more like a Flanker. I have to say by the time I'd finished I found it hard to tell from the real thing. I have some contacts over there so maybe next time you're on Red Flag you can get a simulator ride."

"So was it just ground work?"

"No I managed to get quite a few trips and not only in US aircraft. You might not know it but let's just say the Americans have a very unusual Squadron flying from a desert base. They call the programme "Constant Peg" and they have a number of Mig-21s and Mig-23s up there. They use them to give the squadrons experience against the Soviet aircraft. They teach the best tactics to use and how best to fight against a Mig. I was taken up there and got to fly both types again. The aircraft came from various places but I was able to point out the differences between the Soviet domestic versions and the export jets. Let's say my country didn't give away the best examples of each type to our allies!"

"Tell me it's not true!"

"As I said when I saw you at Warton, I was invited to give some advice on configuring the air combat simulator to fly like a Mig. It's going to be used as a trainer for the new Eurofighter and they want to do some development work in there during the design phase. I helped with a Flanker simulation too so they should be well ahead of the game when the new jet arrives."

"Lucky for us that you were on site at the time. It couldn't have worked better really. So how do you feel about getting some live flying again?"

"I can't wait. All this test flying is great but you can't beat the shot of adrenaline from a live operation. Any news on a "Go" yet?

"Still waiting said John Silversmith who had been remarkably quiet during the exchange. "I doubt we'll wait long so maybe I'll go easy on the brandy sours tonight."

"How is your wife Yuri?" said Razor remembering the real reason which prompted the Russian to defect to the West. An unfamiliar frown passed briefly across his friend's face.

"She passed away shortly after I came over but that was to be expected. I might never have made the decision but for her condition. It was a blessing that she did. That was my one big concern that she might suffer for my actions. I don't regret it for one day."

"So are you happy with the way the build up is going? Are you ready for your starring role?"

"We have everything we need and the asset will be ready to go. I have no idea where those missiles came from but they are the front line items. I'd say they are in better condition than some of those I flew with on my squadron! Trust me, if I'm needed I have the tools to do it. I also have one little extra box of tricks up my sleeve which will make sure I know who to engage."

With the Sun well below the horizon, glasses topped off and the bar thinning out the group began to discuss some fine details which would only play out some time later high above the Mediterranean.

CHAPTER 17

Ministry of Defence, London.

The Assistant Chief of the Air Staff ushered the US Air Attaché into his office on the Sixth Floor of MOD Main Building. The Lieutenant Colonel was experiencing a slight feeling of celebrity at the close attention.

Take a seat Terry. Can I get you a coffee?"

The use of his first name heightened the euphoria.

"Sir that's kind but I just had one and I'll be on a caffeine high if I take another."

"Thanks for calling in. I want to brief you personally on the operation that's underway in the Eastern Med. I know you have a large task force down that way and I want to make sure we don't trip over each other."

"The Ambassador gave me a heads up Sir and he wants me to do anything we can to help out. You just need to say the word."

"Just what I needed to hear Terry."

"I hear you lost a guy down there Sir?"

"We hope not. We think he was taken by an extremist group and we have reason to believe he's being held in a compound on the border with Syria. How much Syria is involved is not clear but, if I was a betting man, I'd say quite a lot. We have diplomatic efforts underway to try to gain access but there's no suggestion yet of how willing the terrorists are to speak to us. I have to admit they've been remarkably quiet under the circumstances."

"Any idea why he was taken yet Sir?"

"Can we talk frankly?"

"Sure, Sir."

"We think he got access to some information which would interest our mutual friends in Tel Aviv. If so, we need to find it and get him out of there. So far we've only admitted that he is a trade attaché with the Embassy but I suspect you might know his real role."

"The Ambassador gave me a good steer Sir."

"We've already tried to insert a special forces team to recce the site but its locked down. There's no way to get at the hostage without a full scale frontal assault on the compound. We don't have the troops on the ground for that option even if it was the favoured solution; which it isn't. That's of course assuming he's in there in the first place. What we've planned is a show of force to back up the diplomatic efforts. We've sent a force of Buccaneers and Phantoms down there and they'll mount a COMAO. Briefings are going on in-theatre as we speak."

"I assume the Ambassador also mentioned that you have offered another asset to help out with the plan. We think the force may be opposed by Syrian air defence forces and we want an insurance policy. The people at Nellis have been helping us set it up."

"I got that Sir. It came through on special channels. I know the team are working it as we speak. A C-5 has already flown out of Mildenhall, Suffolk. I think the asset has been delivered."

"That's good. The Olive Harvest Detachment at Akrotiri is hosting the visitors. Everything is set up I hear. The briefings will tie everything together and they'll liaise directly with the crews flying the mission. I certainly don't need the details about that aspect and I hear it's quite close-hold. I've had the staff put together a briefing pack for you with all the operational details."

He handed over a weighty pink file stamped SECRET top and bottom.

"It has all the key stuff in there but what I wanted to discuss are the risks. I know the carrier task force has come under pressure from the Soviets probing the defences every day. Your people must be on a high readiness in any event after the recent Israeli pullback. I just don't want them feeling threatened by our force."

"I can see that, Sir."

We don't need to get into details now but when you've had chance to go through the mission plan I'll arrange for you to go into the nitty gritty with our planning staff. They'll answer any questions you have. The team down in Joint Ops have been working closely with Strike Command at High Wycombe. They have the detail you'll need. We're not exactly flush for time though. If we have our way, "Execute" will be 1247 Zulu time tomorrow."

"You mentioned risks Sir."

"Yes. I foresee a few. Just about everyone in the region has fighter jets on alert. We have a pair on readiness 10 at Akrotiri, you have the deck alert on the JFK, the Israelis have F-15s at Tel Aviv and the Syrians have units at Homs. The minute a package heads at the Lebanese coast at high speed all hell will break loose. If everyone gets airborne we'll have chaos. We've warned off the Israelis and we've pre-warned you. If I can ask you to stay on deck just for that short window which means we only have the Syrians to worry about. We have a plan to keep them occupied and if they show too much interest we have options to make them wish they'd stayed on the ground. There's also the ground based air defence threat. I thought about asking for EA-6B Prowler support but with the limited ground threat I think it would be harder to coordinate than it's worth. If the SAM or Triple A was heavier I might rethink. Can you keep that in mind Terry and maybe speak to the Flying Boss on the carrier for me?"

"Consider it done. Those guys are pretty flexible and they don't even need to talk to your guys. Give them a target set and they'll suppress it. Might be worth thinking about Sir. "

"Thank you I appreciate that Terry. Can you think of anything more you need at this stage?"

"No that's all clear Sir. Is it OK if I call in on Joint Ops before I leave?"

"Of course, my PSO will fix it for you. Thanks again for coming."

As the Air Attaché left the office, ACAS had already turned to the next file on his desk.

CHAPTER 18

The Station Briefing Room, RAF Akrotiri.

"Gentlemen, can I have your attention please," shouted the Buccaneer detachment commander above the noisy clamour. Outside the briefing room, the noise of a Phantom taxying back to Golf Dispersal temporarily drowned out his words.

"Let's get this started."

The overhead projector clicked on illuminating the front wall.

"Operation *"Pulsator 2"* is the codename and it's been called by HQ Strike Command to recover a hostage who has been taken by terrorists in Beirut. Let me introduce Squadron Leader John Silversmith who will start by giving a roundup of friendly forces and an intelligence briefing. John, over to you."

"Thanks Sir. Five days ago an agent operating in Beirut warned us that he had acquired some fairly sensitive operational plans from a contact working in Damascus. Let's just say that the content is political dynamite and could change the strategic map of the region if implemented successfully. He made efforts to protect them and was in the process of trying to get them into

149

the hands of our man in the British Embassy when he was taken hostage by an armed group in the city. He disappeared briefly but after a some effort we've tracked him down. He's being held in a compound in the north of the country close to the Syrian border."

The overhead projector snapped on once more and a map of Northern Syria appeared with a small town on the Lebanese border ringed in red. The image was replaced by the outline of a desert compound, obviously taken from satellite imagery.

"The mission is ambitious. We plan to try to breach the walls of this compound, land a special forces team at a tactical landing zone and recover the hostage. We'll have help from our friends from Hereford who are already here with us."

The implications were sinking in amongst the aircrew and, as heads turned, the special forces team at the back of the room experienced an unfamiliar scrutiny.

"Before you ask, efforts have already been made to extract the hostage covertly and have failed. The compound is too well guarded but the reconnaissance has identified a few weaknesses that, with some heavy metal on target, we can exploit."

He looked around expecting an interruption but his audience was quiet.

"The target, as I mentioned, is well north of Beirut near the Syrian border. The makeshift prison is a fortified blockhouse at the rear of the compound which is guarded 24 hours a day. Our initial assessment was that it was set up as a terrorist training camp but some things have suggested that it may be more sinister. We now think the whole operation may be state sponsored. Which state we're not yet certain but I wouldn't take bets on the possible candidates. The walled compound sits on the outskirts of a small town which provides all the local services. It sits on the main road to Damascus. The compound is circled with high, fortified walls with guard towers at regular intervals. Just inside the walls but well away from the blockhouse, are the guards quarters in a separate block. Also in the compound is the MT yard where all the vehicles are kept. The primary DMPIs for the weapons will be the blockhouse wall and the compound wall. It's vital to breach them although the helo pilots could land inside the compound in extremis. The secondary targets are the guard's quarters and the MT yard. There are a number of comms towers and it would be good to take them out if possible but not essential. The longer we can prevent the occupants from speaking to their masters the better. The bad news is that it's defended by anti aircraft artillery, Triple A. We have seen ZSU 23-4 Shilka gun systems operating locally and the Lebanese don't operate that system so we have to assume they are Syrian. Although primarily an anti-air weapon, the system can be used ground-to-ground in a secondary mode and is particularly effective against slow helicopters. You'll all know it's radar-laid by a Gundish fire control radar. Don't under estimate the threat. I should finish by saying that the Syrians have advanced warning that something is afoot although we don't know how they have found out. Their alert state was increased yesterday and their QRA is primed so expect opposition."

At the mention of the Shilka there were audible groans. The ZSU 23-4 was a fearsome opponent and had extracted many simulated kills during exercise Red Flag at Nellis in the States.

"OK guys lets go over the laydown," said the intelligence officer moving across the podium.

"We already know what assets we have deployed from UK. We're all here and accounted for. Our own forces are the eight Buccaneers from Lossiemouth and the six Phantoms from Coningsby plus two Chinooks from Odiham. The fast jets are working from Golf Dispersal and the helos from Echo. We have one more asset working from the Olive Harvest hangar on Delta Dispersal more of that soon."

He flipped on the overhead projector again and the map of the surrounding airspace lit the screen.

"Olympus will control the mission and the Phantom guys are already familiar with their capabilities but for the Buccaneer crews, the radome on the summit that you can see from here contains the air defence radar that can detect targets down to low level right up to the Lebanese coast. You can expect good coverage for most of the mission except for the final leg overland. With overland clutter at that range I'm afraid you'll be on your own for that bit. The radar is fully serviceable and we've delayed scheduled maintenance so it'll be available throughout our mission. We also have a back up radar head down at Cape Gata on the coast which we can fire up instantly if we hit problems with the main radar. I can't go into other details but let me just say that we'll be monitoring all the key frequencies and if anything moves close to your route we'll know about it. We'll launch a Nimrod for extended search and rescue coverage during the mission and it will act as autocat. The Nimrod is inbound from Kinloss as we speak."

There were a few murmured comments amongst the crews as the intelligence officer continued. The need for search and rescue sounded a little sinister.

"Also on our side, the Israelis are key players and hold Quick Reaction Alert from Tel Nof Airbase at Reehovot which is 12 miles south of Tel Aviv. No. 133 Squadron of the Israeli Air Force, also known as the Knights of The Twin Tail, is an F-15 fighter squadron and they have at least two jets on 10 minutes readiness. That may have increased in response to the Syrian escalation. The US 6th Fleet has a Carrier Task Group, CTG 417, deployed in the area with the USS John F Kennedy as the flagship. It has two Spruance class destroyers fitted with AN/SPS-40 air search radars and armed with Sea Sparrow Mark 29 missiles embedded in the task force. They provide the anti-air warfare assets for the group although JFK has its own, not insignificant, capability. Normal rules apply about operating close to the CTG. They get very nervous if formations of fast jets operate at high speed within their vicinity. We'll update you of their location before you walk but make sure you give them a wide berth and don't push it. Olympus will coordinate with them via the comms nets and data link so, hopefully, you won't get any interference."

The full extent of the political wrangling behind the scenes was lost on the aircrew and went unsaid. The sombre mood in the room was unusual.

"Moving onto the Red Forces. The Syrians have Mig-21 Fishbed Deltas and Mig-23 Flogger Golfs as their main air-to-air assets. They recently bought Mig-29 Fulcrums but they are not operational yet and we don't expect them to be players. I suspect you'll be pleased to hear that."

There was an audible sigh of relief from more than one of the audience.

"No. 675 Squadron of the Syrian Air Force operates Flogger Golfs from the base at Shayrat near Homs. The Phantom crews have been briefed on the capability of the Flogger at length. Your role will be to tie up any air defence opposition if it gets anywhere close to the package. Further south are the Mig-25 Foxbats and the Mig-21 Fishbeds at As Suwayda airbase. We might expect recce over flight as we move to the later stages so dust off your high level profiles," he said pointedly to the Phantom crews at the back.

"Finally, up north are the Mig-21s of 825 Squadron at Al Qusayr.

Most of these assets have combat persistence in the area of operations, although the Fishbeds will be fuel limited. Again, more of that in a minute as I have a potential solution. The integrated air defence structure is comprehensive. They have two air defence headquarters, 25 air defence brigades and 130 air defence batteries dotted around the country. You should assume that the coverage over southern Syria is overlapping so you will be seen even at low level. It extends well across the border into The Lebanon and includes a mix of Soviet systems. As well as the Spoon Rest they have Bar Lock long range surveillance systems as well as the Tall King and Square Pair associated with the SA-5 Gammon long range SAM system. There's an air defence radar site close to the southern border which has good coverage out into the eastern Mediterranean, although not all the way down to low level. I'll give each detachment charts showing the coverage at medium and low level. You can expect to operate unseen at low level towards the Lebanese coast but if you have to pull up for any reason expect to attract attention. I'm not going to cover the air defence structure over Syria as no one should be penetrating Syrian airspace. If you do you're on your own. Let's just say it's extremely effective and the coverage is almost total. You can't move without being seen by at least one threat system, however, we've seen SA-6 Gainful systems deployed in Lebanon and we can't discount the risk of encountering these mobile surface-to-air missile systems along the route. They've been known to operate inside Lebanon and if you see anything on the RWR assume that it's real. The Lebanese operate the SA-7A and SA-7B Grail MAPNPADS and we've had reports they might have been given some of the latest SA-14 Grouse missiles. I'm not sure if they would know the difference between a Buccaneer, an F-15 or a Mig so don't assume they'll see you as friendly. Unfortunately we all know that the first you'll see of an SA-7 is the smoke trail."

A hand went up.

"Can you give us an update on the recommended tactics against the SA-7?"

We've just done some trials back in UK and the weapons instructors have refined the tactics. The SA-7A is un-cooled so it has a rear hemisphere capability only. You can still outrun it if you are at 450 knots plus. The SA-7B is another thing altogether. With its cooled head it has a limited front sector capability so you'd need to be smarter. You need to see it coming but we don't think it has counter-countermeasures so, if you can get flares out, you will defeat it. We'll give you the latest updates later."

"Thanks. . . . . I think."

"They also operate the ZSU-23-4 Shilka which, as you all know, is an armoured, self-propelled, radar guided anti-aircraft weapon system. The turreted barrels are mounted on a tracked chassis which gives it good manoeuvrability across rough terrain. The Gundish radar operates in J Band and provides accurate tracking for the guns. The crew of 4 consists of a driver, a gunner, the radar operator and the Commander. The driver's compartment is up front, the fighting compartment in the middle and the engine compartment in the rear of the vehicle. With me so far?"

Sombre faces stared back.

"The final spoiler is the Soviet presence. The Krivak class frigate that was moored on the South Cyprus Buoy left late yesterday afternoon and is heading towards the US task force. It's armed with SAN-4 surface to air missiles so it's a potent weapon system so don't take liberties. There's no reason to suggest that the Sovs would have a go at you but they have not been briefed on the mission so you will look hostile in their eyes. We've flagged our presence as a routine exercise but don't assume they buy that story. Take care and, if you fall across it, I wouldn't recommend any high speed passes. Our activity here is not exactly covert with all the jets lined up on the dispersal so they will get instant notification from their network of agents in Limmasol once we launch. Expect them to be jumpy. They have been putting a pair of IL-38 May maritime patrol aircraft from the Black Sea Fleet at Sevastopol down into the area every day for a week now. They are interested in what the 6th Fleet is doing but you can bet they'll show even more interest when this kicks off. I just mentioned that they have a strong presence in Limmasol so take care tonight if you're out at the Kebab House. Someone might be listening. Bet on the fact that any indiscretions will filter back to the Soviets downtown so OPSEC is paramount. Finally, they have an AGI sitting off the Lebanese coast, again monitoring the Americans, but it will be hoovering up anything from our normal air to air frequencies. I suggest you use min comms procedures. Any questions for me at this stage?"

He scanned the faces.

"The section leaders will now give some background briefings and a brief rundown on weapons fits for the mission before we go into the mission briefing."

The Buccaneer Weapons Leader stood up and made his way to the podium.

"OK I know you Phantom crews wouldn't know the front end of a bomb from the tail fins but if you listen up you might get an education."

There were hoots of derision from the back of the room the tension temporarily broken.

"We'll do our own internal briefings on procedures but I've been asked to give you an overview on the targeting pod and the Paveway. We're carrying the Westinghouse Pave Spike pod for this mission. It'll be carried on the left inboard stores pylon to give us a precision attack capability. Dumb bombs just won't cut it for this one. It's an electro-optical laser designator pod which we'll use to target the Paveway 2 laser guided bombs. It only operates in daylight, visual conditions but that's not a constraint for this scenario. It has a laser tracker boresighted to the TV camera which displays an image on a cockpit screen in the back seat. The navigator uses a joystick controller to direct the sensors. The Paveway 2 is based on the standard 1000 lb bomb but is controlled by a computer. The guidance unit fitted to the nose contains a laser seeker head and steerable fins guide the weapon once released. The fins deploy after launch from the tail unit. Once the bomb is released it flies into the laser "basket" and the fins kick it onto a course towards the target. It's not powered and uses gravity and momentum to follow its trajectory and the bomb steers towards the reflected laser energy. Providing the "spiker" carrying the pod keeps the crosshairs on the target it will hit with precision. We'll have pods on the primary spikers in the lead pair but it's absolutely vital we have the spikers for accuracy so numbers 3 and 4 will also carry pods and act as back up if either of the primary spikers goes U/S. There's one other weapon specific to this mission. Numbers 5 and 6 will be carrying modified BL755s. As you know the standard weapon is a cluster bomb unit and it normally carries 147 bomblets which are designed against armour. They are simple devices. If they hit a tank they go "bang". If they land on the ground and someone rolls over them they go "bang". The sub-munitions in these ones are different. Once the anti-personnel bomblets land they'll lie dormant for 8 hours. That will give our own people in the target area freedom to move around for a few hours. Once the bomblets activate, any movement within a few feet and certainly any efforts to move them, will make them detonate. After the eight hours, random timers will activate and they will keep exploding at regular intervals for days. It will effectively shut down the area around the target for weeks until they can send in the bomb disposal teams. Even then those things are not easy to clean up. We'll also be carrying AIM-9Gs so best not piss us off in the bar! Any questions?"

As he sat down, the Phantom Weapons Leader replaced him at the podium.

"Let me just run through some key aspects of the air-to-air weapons fit so there's no confusion. You should all be aware of the basic capability of the Skyflash, AIM-9L Sidewinder and the Suu-23 gun so I won't waste time there. If you want more, see me separately. We have a limited identification capability. These jets are carrying the TESS; the telescopic sighting system. It's a telescope fitted in the back cockpit and viewed by the nav. If we lock up to a target, by using the Sidewinder aim dot we can point directly at it and get an identification outside normal visual detection ranges. The scope has six times magnification so at low level we can probably see a target out to about ten miles depending on the visibility. What does that mean to you as bomber crews? You might well see missile launches against targets you can't yet see. You'll need to trust us but listen to any radio chat."

He scanned for questions.

"The next point is absolutely vital so listen up. If we get mixed up in a turning fight and you find yourself in amongst it, there's one call that might save your life. If you hear "*Heads Up*" at any time, check your radar warning receivers carefully. If we get a short range lock and don't have the chance to positively identify the bogey, that shot might be our only chance to survive. We'll probably take it. If you hear the call and suddenly your RWR goes nuts I want to hear a "*rackets*" call; and straight away. If I hear that call I'll kill the CW radar and the missile will be trashed. If I don't, the Skyflash is going to hit whatever it's locked onto."

He sat down replaced by the Mission Leader.

"OK, that's the background, let's get into the main briefing. Everyone listen up. "

The overhead projector snapped into life and he dropped the first slide onto the glass.

"We'll run this mass brief together and then we'll split into individual formations for detailed briefings. Callsigns: we'll use *"Pulsator"* as the overall callsign for the mission. Each section will have individual callsigns. Jackal 1 to 6 will be the Buccaneers, Buzzard 1 and 2 for the escort and Springbok 1 and 2 for the Chinooks. If you hear the callsign Hawk, that's allocated to QRA and will be under the control of Olympus. The mission will be broken down into 6 phases. Phase 1 will be departure and form up. Phase 2 is the anti-air element. Phase 3 is the ingress and attack by Jackal. Phase 4 is the special forces insertion in the Chinooks. Phase 5 is the egress and Phase 6 is recovery. Let's have individual radio checks and a main check in, by formations, at 1515 Zulu. Immediately after check in we'll have a time hack. Don't miss it! Start up, taxy and take off is in individual formations but I want a final check from formation leaders that you're ready to go by 5 minutes prior to taxy. At that time I'll decide whether to wait for stragglers and call a rolex or whether to push on time and let the straggler catch up. Expect a rolex."

He paused to allow a ripple of discussion to end.

"I'm expecting Runway 29 so after takeoff I'll bring the formation downwind heading back east. We've set up a timing trombone and we'll go around the pattern once to get everyone joined up. I'm getting Jackal airborne first but I want Buzzard to push from the datum first, ahead of the package. Buzzard will act as sweep for the formation and engage anything that shows an interest. More of the rules of engagement later. Fred, can you cover the route for me."

The lead Buccaneer navigator stood up.

"OK we'll route from the datum just east of the field direct to the coast-in point here."

An image appeared showing a large headland on the Lebanese coast.

"This is Al Aabde just north of Tripoli. I chose the headland because it shows up well on radar. We know you Phantom boys are not used to a stationary target so we chose something that stands out for you."

A snicker from one of the Buccaneer navigators drew a rude comment from the back of the room.

From there it's a direct track to the initial point but we pass just south of the airfield at Rene Mouwad. It used to be a fighter base but there's been no activity for years other than helicopters so we don't expect any opposition. The IP is a fork in the road just east of the village of Massaaoudiye and it's a straight run in on 145 degrees to the target. On the way out it's a reverse track but offset to the south. Right, on to the targets."

Another image of the compound snapped on.

"OK let's look at the main targets. The DMPIs are the compound wall, the watch tower and the main building itself which is where the prisoner is held – we think. Absolute precision is essential. If we don't hit the walls and breach them the helos will have to land in the compound which will make them seriously vulnerable. If we don't hit the main building, the security at the door is probably impenetrable for the insertion team. We can't risk a fire fight. Our insertion team is only lightly armed. The prisoner is held at the back of the building so don't go high or long or we risk hurting him. I can't stress enough that precision is vital and that's where the "spikers" will come in. More of that soon."

The image changed to a close up of the main entrance to the compound.

"I want my bombs to breach this wall destroying this gate and, ideally, taking out this tower which stands immediately next to it. This tower commands the approaches to the compound so if we drop it they have lost the advantage. It also means the helicopters on the LZ will be less vulnerable to snipers."

Another image appeared of the main building at the back of the compound.

"This is the makeshift prison. You can see from this satellite image that there is always a guard on the door with a controlled access point inside. I want my No 2's bombs to land in his lap. Numbers 3 and 4 have the secondary targets but be prepared to be re-tasked. The main thing is to hit the primaries. If the "spikers" think we missed they'll call you back onto the primaries. You won't have much to do as the sighting picture will be the same so run in as planned. The secondary DMPIs are the guard's quarters, the communications towers and the MT yard. The "spikers" will also have a secondary role. Once the Paveways have been dropped they will run back over the target from the east with the modified BL755s. That will suppress movements in the compound after the attack. It should be some time before the bad guys can get a clear picture of what's happened on the ground but if they don't pay attention those bomblets will spoil their day. Fuel shouldn't be an issue. It's 45 minutes duration so that should give us as much holding time as we need and 20 minutes combat fuel in the area if we're tied up by fighters. OK back to the Boss for the other aspects. Any questions at this stage?"

"Thanks Fred. The first and most important aspect is that the rules of engagement are explicit. This is the only authorised target. If you don't drop first time you probably won't get a chance to reattack. I'll decide on that in the air. There are no secondary targets away from the compound and you are not, repeat not, cleared for any opportunity attacks en route. Is that perfectly clear? OC 29 will cover the air-to-air ROE later."

He paused for effect. There was no doubt in the room that screw ups would not be tolerated or covered up.

"We don't need to know in detail how the insertion team will do its business so I'll leave them to run their own internal briefing. Springbok, the Chinooks, will launch ahead of us all because of their slower speed. We'll call them in once we know how the attack has gone. The responsibility for the call will be the leader of the spikers. Once the helos press inland, the Phantoms will hold at a datum just offshore ready to support if needed. Any hint of fighter opposition and they will be called in. The helos will run in to the LZ, drop the insertion team who will extract the prisoner. Once they lift, they'll return to the datum and be collected by the Phantoms who will escort them back to base. What we do need to ensure is that everyone makes the pre-briefed calls at each reference point. We need to know exactly where every one of the players is at each phase. If you are not where you should be at the planned time let me know. My final point before I hand over is about R/T discipline. First the obvious; It'll be busy on the main tactical frequency. I don't want useless chat. If you don't have anything useful to say, don't say it. The fighters will chop to a secondary frequency if they are engaged. Use min comms procedures at all times. This place is a hot bed. Not only will the bad guys be listening but so will Olympus. If I hear at the debrief of any comsec breaches, I'll have you!"

He looked around the room to press his message home.

"OK over to OC 29 Squadron to talk about the air-to-air aspects."

Paul Anderson stood up.

"Thanks. You've already heard that we plan to fly a two minute sweep ahead of the package. That way we can try to pick up anything that sniffs at us and keep it away from the main formation. If Jackal formation hears a "bogeys" call, listen to the bearing and fly a sidestep. Crank off at 45 degrees away from the threat and leave us to tie it up. Go as low as you can and you should avoid trouble. If there are "leakers" that get past our sweep, give us your position and we'll send the cavalry. Don't even think about engaging. Press on track and only use your Sidewinders if a bad guy drops into the middle of your formation."

There were nods of acknowledgement.

"If we end up with a "fur ball" and the Buccaneers are tied up, try to disengage. Our tactics will be to take it wide and try to engage the bogeys head-on with a Skyflash. If we have you in there with us it makes it harder to guarantee we're locked to the correct target. Finally, as you're carrying AIM-9s make sure you positively identify before you shoot. Once a 'winder is off the rails you can't call it back. We are clear to engage anything we think is hostile. If you're targeted, call it. That will stop us going blue-on-blue. We have Jubilee Guardsman on these jets so we can interrogate IFF before shooting but it's immature technology and it's not foolproof. We have one more ace up our sleeve."

He flipped on a slide of a Syrian Mig-23 Flogger Golf and watched the puzzled faces around the room. The Phantom crews who had already been briefed looked smug.

"There are some things you will see as this mission progresses that I want to remain close hold. We are operating in broad daylight so there's a risk of compromise but let's not help the bad guys by talking about any of this at the Kebab House."

He looked directly at a number of hitherto noisy characters, the warning implicit. He waited for what he expected to be the inevitable question but it never came. The reality of the additional asset had already sunk home.

"If I hear of any deliberate compromises I'll make sure we have our Chinook friends drop you back at the compound!"

He had everyone's interest.

"I'm not going to go into much detail but let's say we have an asset available that will help us run a deception plan if the Syrian QRA launches against us. The details are at a much higher classification than the overall level of this briefing so we'll leave those to the section briefings. If they come our way we'll make sure their intercept doesn't run as planned. Enough said on that one but remember the warnings."

He sat down as John Silversmith returned to the podium.

"Sir, I know you're only tasked to provide two escort and two QRA jets but what chance of you manning up the spares? We've come up with another deception plan which might take some pressure off the main force."

"Let me hear it John."

"The Syrian Northern QRA is provided by Mig-21s from Al Qusayr. We don't think they have the range to threaten the main force to the south but it's marginal so we probably need something to keep them busy. If we can run a feint in the northeast once they commit they'll have to land and refuel before they could be used in the south. They don't have AAR assets. The idea would be to launch just ahead of the main force and run at high speed, high level towards Al Qusayr in the north. That should provoke a launch and keep them tied up while the main force ingresses at low level."

"Can you hold the briefing for 2 minutes while I call the squadron? We'll man up as many as we can but we'll need to use the spares for the primary mission first. If we are all serviceable we'll do it. I'll brief the spare crews when we get back. Olympus will have to live with any gaps in QRA readiness but we can turn the Q jets rapidly if they get scrambled. If we can, we'll do it."

As Anderson returned to his seat the buzz of excitement in the room quietened.

"OK that's it for the main briefing," said the mission leader. Our planned launch time is 1247 Zulu. We'll split down into individual formations for internal briefings and then get back together in one hour for the final coordination briefing. Any questions so far?"

The three sections broke down into individual elements and the Buccaneer crews made their way to the navigation planning room. The Phantom section had by far the easiest planning task. The legs were all oversea and a quick check of the latitude and longitude of the holding CAP and a quick line on the map and they were done. It was almost an afterthought to mark the compound as the target on the map. They would guard against the risk of interference by Syrian fighters by holding just off the coast and it was a short run towards the Syrian border if that eventuality should arise. They would not go overland other than for an unexpected event so the short leg inland received only a cursory check. The time would be spent discussing air-to-air tactics and the Syrian threats they would face.

The helicopter navigation plan would be more complex but unaffected by the details of the target and weapons aspects. Their task was to identify a suitable landing zone close to the compound to give the insertion team the best access. There was an obvious candidate.

The navigation planning room was a relic of the Vulcan era.

Large wooden planning tables with sloping tops were arranged in neat rows across the room. In the nuclear bombing days Vulcan crews would have pored over maps of the Soviet Union plotting their way to Doomsday. The tables would once again see operational use as the lead navigator laid the huge low flying chart on the table and began to plan the detail. He would start in reverse. Already weapons planners in UK had pored over the target images and selected appropriate weapons for each of the desired mean points of impact or DMPIs. The weapons which now sat in the armoury at Akrotiri were the result of that planning. Selected and loaded onto C130 transporters, the dangerous air cargo had been pre-positioned ready for the lethal task.

A preliminary review had confirmed the planning assumptions and Paveway 2 laser guided bombs had been allocated to the primary DMPI, the headquarters building. Fuse settings were verified before the same weapons were allocated to the secondary DMPIs. Modifications to the fuse settings would optimise the fragmentation patterns for the lighter structures of the communications towers. His nominated initial point would be the feature from which the individual sections would begin their run in. When attacking an airfield it was often useful to plan split IPs so that sections approached on different headings and with different timings. In this case a single IP would be perfect for his needs. The road junction was a few miles short of the target, would be easily visible as they ran in and a small chimney would be easily visible for miles across the rolling countryside. After a brief discussion with the leader of the element which would act as laser designators the other navigator began planning the ellipse from which they would target their lasers against the compound. Moving back along track he highlighted the prominent point on the coastline from which to start the overland leg. By selecting such a significant point he would be sure that each section would be on track and on time at that crucial point in the attack. The large promontory on the coast north of the town Al Mahmra was ideal and he placed his strike ruler over the turning point and circled it. Next he marked the timing trombone just off the coast of Akrotiri. This holding pattern would allow him to assemble the formation and adjust the critical timings. If he planned a few orbits of the timing pattern he could bring his times forward or slip them back to account for any unforeseen contingencies. With these critical decisions taken he joined the points and began to draw the timing marks on the map. From that would come the critical fuel calculations for the mission. With an exit route decided the plan was done.

With the map prepared he called the other navigators across and they began to copy their own maps from the master. As they did so, the lead crew moved to a separate table and began to pore over the other documents. They would dissect the mission into small elements and consider each phase in minute but crucial detail starting with the target itself. From 100 feet or lower the walls of the main headquarters building and the guard towers would stand out easily. For the weapon delivery they would execute a loft attack where the bombers would pull to an apex and launch the weapons towards the target. At that point they would probably lose contact but the pressure would transfer to the crew "spiking" the target. With accurate tracking the laser guided bombs would fly into a laser "basket" and strike the designated point. He was confident that the "spikers" would be able to break out the tracking points but never assume - check!. The aim was to drop the walls. An airburst where the bomb exploded prematurely would merely pepper the walls with shrapnel. A delayed fuse would allow the bomb to penetrate and probably blow up the whole building. A contact fuse would do just fine. A smaller bomb might have been preferable but the alternative Mk82 bombs were not fitted with laser heads so a larger Paveway it would have to be. Dropping the front wall of the building would allow the hostage the chance to escape yet protect the rear of the building where his cell was thought to be. They hoped that the intelligence was accurate because if the hostage was at the front he would have little chance of survival. The final surprise for the defenders was the anti personnel bomblets. The "spikers" would be armed with BL-755 cluster bombs and once the main attack was through they would return and pepper the site with bomblets. There would be no contribution to the terrorist effort from that site for a while once Jackal had passed through.

He wished he could call on a support jammer but it was a capability the UK had neglected. Although enemy defences were light he would have loved the idea of an EA-6B Prowler jamming the Syrian air defence frequencies and the option to search for and destroy air defence missile batteries before they could engage with SAMs. Although the 6th Fleet was sailing just off the coast the request had gone unanswered so they would penetrate the target area without the critical protection.

With the final review finished the lead crew turned to the "wotifs". What if one spiker was unserviceable? Could a single "spiker" cover all the tasks? What were the priorities if any of the bombers failed to make the target? What if any section was late? Could the other sections delay to make sure the attack was coordinated? Finally, what the hell would the insertion team be doing as all this went on? So far they had been tight lipped.

So many questions, such a short time.

CHAPTER 19

The British Embassy, Beirut.

Lakin sat down in the screened room in the British Embassy and began to leaf through the briefing pack. He was still suffering the effects of the flight after the mad dash to the airport following the call from the duty officer. It had been a good few years since he had worked from this building and looking at the streets outside little had changed. It was still a war zone and he wondered, idly, whether anything could ever change.

His brief had been simple. Make contact with the terrorist gang and using his diplomatic cover decide whether a negotiation was possible. He had been assured that if weapons were the price, a shipment of Blowpipe portable shoulder launched missiles would be shipped in via the diplomatic bag. How they would reach their destination would be his problem. Reading the briefing notes, had moved him a little farther forward but it was still a mystery. Reeves had logged his contacts and there had been a significant increase in the number of meetings just before his disappearance. With the regularity of his trips up the highway to Damascus it had to be the contact in the Syrian capital that was the key to this puzzle. He considered trying to contact the Syrian MOD official whom Reeves had been handling to see if he could cast any light on where he might have been taken. That was until he dug further into the notes. It was obvious as he read on that any direct contact would spook the man and he ran the risk of not being able to contact him again. He could understand that. The Syrians were not well known for treating traitors well. Showing sympathy for the "plant"; he was slipping!

The terrorist cell seemed to be a faction of Hezbollah which had been earmarked for close attention for some time now but something did not run true. Their way of doing business did not follow the norms for this part of the world and he could see the mark of foreign intervention. Some of the contact techniques had a distinct fingerprint and were more relevant to Moscow than Beirut. This was by far their most ambitious move to date. Past efforts had been confined to coercion on the streets of the capital. Taking on the UK was an escalation, particularly if they knew to whom Reeves reported. So why the step change? A leader had popped up recently and seemed to be significant. The listening post in Cyprus had a voice-print and back in London they were slowly homing in on his history. The results were less than conclusive so far but he felt sure that Dzerzhinsky Square would emerge at some stage.

The report from the special forces team leader who had run the recce mission had just hit the file. Looking at the date-time group on the signal it had arrived in the Commcen within the last few hours and it didn't make good reading. The compound in which Reeves was being held was about as secure as it got in this turbulent country. The single track road to the gates was monitored and covert hides had been found at regular intervals along the road which would protect the guards. The walls were high enough to prevent a team scaling them and thick enough to withstand anything but a 1000 pound bomb. The guard towers gave an excellent field of fire around the approaches and the single access gate was heavily reinforced. An RPG might go through it but it would not destroy it. Without heavy weapons the compound was impregnable. He dragged out a satellite image and laid it out picking up a stereoscope to take a closer look. The flat image burst into life as the twin lenses formed a 3D view of the facility. He concentrated on the large building at the back of the compound. It was the only one big enough to house a makeshift prison. The rest of the smaller buildings ranged along the compound wall were clearly support buildings. If he got chance he would take a closer look at that one.

The most worrying factor was the almost taunting tone of the messages to the Embassy. He formed the distinct impression that they almost wanted Reeves to be released at some stage. It was as if there was a greater goal to the plan.

He needed to try to get some type of tracking device to Reeves so that if they moved him he would know his location. The traditional devices had limitations in this austere environment. A radio-based locator beacon was huge and only operated over short range but the new global positioning system that the Americans had just released for public use had promise. After the Korean Airlines Jumbo was shot down by Soviet interceptors when it strayed into prohibited airspace because of navigational errors, the Americans announced that GPS would be made available for civilian use. A couple of years ago the coarse acquisition code was released and the trackers were slowly coming down in size and complexity. They were not exactly pinhole sized yet but if he could feed a GPS tracker into a book, or something similar, he might be able to give it to Reeves. It was the best he could do and he made a note to get something put together. The most important thing was to try to find out where the information was hidden. There was absolutely no mention in the files of what the package contained or why it was so important. Why the hell hadn't he just dropped it back here at the Embassy and none of this would have been necessary. He felt a moment of guilt as he realised that he had just considered abandoning Reeves to his fate. Maybe there was method in his colleagues actions?

As he mulled over the issues the secure phone rang. It was the only phone inside "the cage" and the number was tightly controlled. Only a few people even had access to the number so there could be only a few possibilities as to the origin of the call. Despite the warbling, garbled connection, heightened by distance and the effect of the crypto devices, he recognised the voice at the other end as one of the regulars on the duty desk in the MI6 operations desk in London. The call was brief but set the clock ticking. A rendezvous had been set up at 1530 that day at a crossroads north of Tripoli. The detail would follow up in a signal that was being sent shortly. He checked his watch. Just a few hours away. He packed away the briefing material and notes, returned them to the security container and spun the lock. He had arrangements to make before he hit the road.

CHAPTER 20

Buttons Bay, The Sovereign Base Area, RAF Akrotiri.

Dimitris Papadakis waited patiently. The engine of his rickety old Austin ticked occasionally as it cooled after the short trip from Akrotiri village. Tucked in the corner of the car park he waited alongside the small harbour which served the base. He preferred to hide in open view rather than sit alongside the road and provoke a challenge. The occasional security patrol passed along the beach road at this time of night but they were infrequent and he hoped the risk of discovery was low during the few minutes he would be here. His presence was unusual as his shift had finished many hours earlier but there was still some traffic returning from the Sailing Club which was located a little further down the beach.

"The Mole" as it was known locally was the small man made harbour and home to the RAF air-sea rescue launch, which acted as the range safety boat. It offered an easy route ashore from the support tenders which came alongside from the occasional British warship which anchored in Limmasol Bay on a port visit. With its substantial concrete walls it sheltered boats from a rarely angry Mediterranean Sea but Dimitris had no intention of using that sanctuary for tonight's task. He had already found an ideal spot in the lee of the walls where a dinghy could pull ashore and remain unseen in the darkness. He could see little of the inshore waters from his vantage point but he was sure that his wait would be short.

The small outboard motor had been cut some time earlier and the shadowy figure pulled strongly on the oars as the inflatable dinghy approached the shoreline. Pausing briefly, he looked down at the fluorescent hands of his watch which glowed in the dark feeling slightly smug that he was almost perfectly on time. The last few days had been eclectic since he had been warned of the impending operation on the base and the pace was quickening, relentlessly. He would be living on his nerves for the next 30 minutes as the contact on base was, hitherto, untested. He had provided enough information for sure but this was a whole new chapter. If tonight's little initiative went to plan the temperature of the Cold War would be taken up a notch but he would rather have been the master of his own destiny instead of relying on the knowledge of a local Greek Cypriot. It was impossible to act alone because, without the knowledge the sympathiser offered, it would be unworkable to gain access to the jets in the hangar let alone navigate his way around the sprawling base. He could hear the waves lapping ashore now as he pressed closer to the still indistinct beach, the tide giving a gentle assistance to his rowing. He slowed his stroke looking again at his watch as the minute hand hit the hour. Glancing up at the beach he was rewarded with a brief flash of light, repeated three times. Adjusting his course he aimed towards the point on the craggy shoreline. It was the signal he had expected.

Dimitris watched as the small boat nudged onto the sand and the dark clad figure stepped ashore. He walked towards the new arrival as the figure grappled with the inflatable, pulling it firmly up the shallow incline bedding it into the soft sand. There was no time for trivialities as he beckoned, silently, for the newcomer to follow. Once safely inside the old Austin he relaxed a little. Dimitris could talk his way out of the situation should they be challenged now as he had been assured that the agent sitting alongside him would be carrying a civilian identity card which would pass a casual security check. There was no time for pleasantries as he coaxed the small engine into life. Accented English would the common language, albeit not the natural tongue of either of the conspirators.

"All is fine my friend. I pass dispersal on way here. Groundcrew working hard to prepare aircraft for mission but it seems quiet now," he said in his strong Cypriot accent, waiting for the reply. When it came the inflection confirmed that this man had not been born in the suburbs of Limmasol.

"Do you have the key?" the man asked.

"Of course, I had it cut earlier and tested this afternoon. It will be fine, trust me."

"Have you met anyone while you waited?"

"No it's quiet since last orders in Sailing Club. Even so, I don't use lights for ride up to dispersal. We see traffic on road or security patrol, I put them on. Nowhere to pull off between here and dispersal and nowhere to hide. Not much cover along road so probably best to act normal. You have ID? They may be watching for drunks."

The Cypriot's fractured English was already grating on the newcomer.

"I do. I'll take your lead if we're stopped. Are you ready?"

The engine missed a beat and the passenger groaned quietly but it picked up immediately and the car moved noisily out of the car

park for the short trip up the beach road to Golf Dispersal. As
they turned off the road which linked the beach road to the
operations complex, Dimitris steered the car off onto an unmade
track which skirted the large hangar. Built to service Vulcan
bombers during the time when Britain's nuclear deterrent was
mounted from the Mediterranean base it dominated the skyline.
Standing over five stories high and painted in a light cream
colour to reflect the usually strong sunshine it was massively
oversized to house the fighters which now occupied the floor
space. More importantly, tonight it shielded the small car from a
casual inspection of the surrounding operational area. The scrub
trees which dotted the bundu acted as a further natural screen so
that the car was virtually invisible from the road as it drew to a
halt. The door through which they would gain access was on the
far side of the building but sat in full view of anyone who might
still be around. By skirting alongside the building and hugging
the front doors they would remain out of sight for as long as
possible. The newcomer hoped the dispersal was empty by now
but only time would tell.

Moving silently they reached the front corner of the hangar, the
concrete dispersal stretching out towards the runway ahead of
them. There were still a few jets parked in a line along the ramp
but no movement from any of the small huts alongside the
parking area. Surprisingly the large arc lamps on top of the huge
stanchions were unlit so the area was bathed only in a weak glow
of light from the infrequent sodium lamps along the taxiway.
They exchanged glances, nodded and broke cover, moving
silently towards the small picket door. Dimitris fumbled with the
lock in the weak light but finally inserted the key breathing a sigh
of relief. The door opened easily and they stepped inside drawing
it closed behind them.

The huge hangar was totally silent but any noise would be
amplified and echo around the vast walls. They would need to
work quietly. Dimitris hung back allowing the stranger to take

the lead. As they made their way across the deserted hangar floor towards one of the jets he unhitched the small rucksack from his back and began to rummage inside. Most of the Buccaneers were parked neatly along the far wall with a few more positioned precisely on the yellow centreline marking down the middle of the hangar. The Phantoms were closest and seemed to be buttoned up neatly already prepared for the mission. Against all normal armament rules, missiles hung ominously beneath the fuselages the red safety flags hanging visibly from the rocket bodies. Towards the back of the hangar a single Buccaneer sat on jacks a number of panels hanging loose underneath. It was this jet that attracted the man's attention.

As he eased under the cavernous bomb bay which, thankfully, was empty of weapons he homed in on one of the rear bays. He pulled a small roll of tools from the rucksack and set to work in the guts of the jet. A further small box was pulled from the bag and he eased it into position clamping it alongside a seemingly innocent cylindrical component. He grunted as he twisted his body to get better access, his large screwdriver disappearing into the mass of ducts and wires. Dimitris watched on with little idea of the significance of his actions. If only he had known what the man was doing he might have been less comfortable. Unbeknown to him the man had attached an explosive device controlled by a timer onto the hydraulic pump. Until power was applied and the jet climbed through 500 feet, it would remain dormant. At that moment the timer would initiate and begin to count down from 30 minutes when it would explode. The small charge would wreck the vital pump causing an immediate hydraulic leak. Without hydraulics the aircraft controls would freeze.

The man crouched down and looked at the area where he had been working. Seemingly satisfied he replaced the tools into his rucksack and looked around for another target. The Buccaneer was the only jet which was obviously being worked on so he retraced his steps towards the door where they had entered. Moving under one of the Phantoms he took out a screwdriver and began to unfasten a panel beneath the jet. As he worked they were suddenly aware of the noise of a vehicle outside, the noise of the engine reverberating through the metal walls. They both stopped. The vehicle doors slammed closed, echoing in the still air and they could hear voices. More worryingly they could hear the whining of a dog. The conversation seemed normal but the unexpected visit was anything but welcome. His task abandoned, the pair moved quickly behind an adjacent Houchin power set and crouched down. They would be invisible from anything except a close inspection but the dog was an entirely different problem. If it entered the hangar the game was over.

The noise of a key rattling in the lock raised the tension. They stayed entirely still as the door banged on its stops and the noise of footsteps could be heard above the echoing clang. The conversation had stopped which probably meant that only one of the men had come into the hangar.

"It looks pretty normal in 'ere mate," called the RAF policeman in his broad Geordie accent. "These jets look pretty impressive with all these rockets. Pity the poor sod that collects these things. Wouldn't like it to be me."

Outside the dog was increasingly agitated and whined loudly.

"What's up wi' that dog?"

The response was indistinct but the footsteps paused as the policeman strained to hear. He walked further into the hangar and the echoes grew louder as he passed just a few feet from the crouching pair, fortuitously shielded by the bulk of the power set. The policeman's boots slapped on the shiny surface of the floor but grew softer as he worked his way towards the centre of the hangar. Outside the dog sounded agitated and the handler's voice rose as he tried, unsuccessfully, to quieten it down.

"Bloody hell mate, is there something out there. Why's that dog so antsy?"

The footsteps grew loud again but, as they passed alongside the Houchin, they stopped. Dimitris held his breath fearful that they had been spotted. The pause stretched to eternity.

"It all looks normal in 'ere mate, I'm on my way back out," said the voice from the other side of the yellow appliance. "Gimme a second."

There was an unfathomable noise and a series of grunts from close by. They held their collective breath expecting to be uncovered at any second.

"Bloody stone in me boot," he muttered before he moved back to the door and let himself out. As the door lock rattled once again the conspirators exchanged glances, beads of sweat glistening in the dim light.

It was some minutes after the vehicle had pulled away before the pair breathed, let alone moved. Eventually they emerged from their temporary hiding place and listened carefully. The newcomer spoke first.

"We'll have to give it some more time before we try to get back to the car. Let's hope they haven't seen it from the road. My guess is they'll go down to QRA for a walk around before they leave. That should be the only place where anyone is still on duty. My bet is it's the best place to get a brew at this time of night. We'll be in plain sight as we come out of the door so better to be safe. Let's sit tight for a while."

With just a nod and a grunt from his worried companion they slid back down alongside the Houchin and waited. The Cypriot eventually recovered his composure.

"Sir," pronounced "Seer" he whispered. "I take you back down to beach and we be caught. My friend move boat tomorrow before patrols start in morning. Police more worried about drunks so they not find it. I take you to Limmasol in car. It much safer."

The man considered it but only briefly.

"Tell him he can have the boat. It's untraceable and I was planning to sink it anyway. Just make sure he doesn't draw any attention to himself by suddenly flashing around the bay. We don't need questions."

The cash register was already chiming in his businessman's brain as Dimitris calculated the value of the unexpected windfall.

"OK, Seer, we go back to car and drive through camp and out of main gate. It look normal. Guards lazy by now. They not check people leaving, just coming into Station. We fine and even if stopped you have ID. I say I have late shift in Officers' Mess. It normal."

The man winced at the decimation of the English language but agreed, anxious to be away, his task done.

CHAPTER 21

The Hezbollah Compound on the Syrian Border.

The rendezvous had gone smoothly and the two men who met him at the road junction outside Tripoli had shown no undue interest in either him or his travelling companions. He was obviously expected and they seemed to take his diplomatic passport at face value and had even backed off when he had refused to surrender it. He was relieved that there had been no confrontation because there was no way he was giving up his travel documents in this God-forsaken backwater given Reeves's fate. The Glock concealed under the driver's seat had been a last minute insurance he hoped he didn't need to cash in but, so far, the diplomatic veneer had held up. The drive up the main highway in convoy had passed quickly and, as they turned off onto the minor road, he was almost relaxed. The euphoria was not to last and, as the gates of the compound drew open he experienced a rare moment of indecision although it quickly passed. At this stage taking off back down the road would be tantamount to committing suicide. His diplomatic cover was wafer thin and the fact that he had been dropped into Beirut in the last hours would emerge during even a cursory inspection. He just hoped the leader was not a regular on the diplomatic circuit or he would struggle.

As he waited in the car, the escorts babbling away in rapid fire Arabic, he steeled himself for the meeting. His driver, a local "bodyguard" had been arranged by the Embassy at his request. He suspected that he would be far more able to protect himself than this meathead if it came to it but a consul from the British Embassy would never place himself in this situation without some form of protection. The other "rent a thug" had roused himself and was nursing his weapon in the back seat not even following the first rule of close protection. He was amazed the "bodyguards" had been allowed into the compound at all, never mind carrying weapons. The whole set up was odd.

The compound guard listened to the rapid fire Arabic before walking around to his side of the car gesturing for him to lower the window. The gestures became more urgent and he assumed that it was a demand for another look at his identification. The hastily produced passport in the name of a regular British consular official, John Lakin, was genuine as was his picture so he had no concerns whether it would stand scrutiny. When pressed, the Embassy staff could produce paperwork in hours and it was genuine but his worry was that someone might decide that two British officials was better currency than one. It was too late for such concerns but he had no desire to join Reeves. After a cursory glance, the driver was waved towards the large building at the far end of the compound. With his passport safely stowed away the driver followed the directions he had been given muttering a few words of broken English, presumably for his benefit, which sounded vaguely like "It'll be fine". If it was, it would be no thanks to these two. A man emerged at the doorway and beckoned. He was flanked by more armed guards who held a silent vigil looking more like a set of bizarre bookends than serious terrorists.

As the vehicle drew to a halt the man walked around the vehicle, opened the door and welcomed him in perfect Oxford English, the clarity of his diction at odds with the surroundings. Lakin was ushered into a room just inside the main entrance where the comfortable furnishings and the elegant artwork on the walls contrasted starkly with the austerity of the compound outside. Beginning to feel like a visiting diplomat, which of course he was, he was shown towards a pair of chairs with a small table set in between. The man took his seat and tea was served by a manservant pristinely dressed in the tradition robes of the local Christian community, the Maranites.

"I see you are interested in the local dress Mr Lakin. I'm not sure if you are aware but until recently, maybe the last 10 years, The Lebanon was not an Arab country. These people are descended from the Syrian Christians and are in truth Aramaic. They only started translating the Bible into Arabic and started teaching their children Arabic maybe 100 years ago. There are a few towns that still speak Aramaic on the borders here. They are a different people to many of my colleagues in Beirut but most cultured."

The polite conversation was unnerving given the circumstances of the meeting but, perhaps appropriate given his cover. It was giving Lakin the time to take in his surroundings. Despite the civility, his minders had been excluded and a distinctly seedy-looking guard had patted him down for weapons before he was allowed to sit. The veneer proved superficial.

"Now Mr Lakin, perhaps we could discuss our little issue?"

"Of course Sir, and I'm so pleased that you could see me at such short notice. I know just how volatile things can be at present."

"Perhaps you would permit me to explain how we came to be in this unfortunate situation, and can I assure you that we are most hopeful that we can resolve the problems at the earliest opportunity. One of our groups was expecting a delivery of a certain consignment. Apparently the courier failed to appear but who should have entered the apartment block at the same time but your Mr Reeves. It was extremely unfortunate but when it was discovered he did not have the consignment with him our men simply took him into protective custody. They assumed he had mislaid the goods as is all too common in Beirut as you know. It appears to be all a simple case of mistaken identity which we are keen to rectify."

"I can see that would be a difficult situation, Sir. I am empowered to try to make arrangements to resolve our problems."

"Reassuring Mr Lakin and, of course, we are keen that Mr Reeves should be repatriated as soon as possible but we must ensure he is fit and able to make the journey before we can do so. I'm sure you appreciate our difficulty. It would be most impolite of us not to ensure his good health before we allow him to go on his way."

The sham was transparent but he had little choice but to play along.

"Of course. Equally, you must be pleased to know that His Excellency The Ambassador is only too keen to ensure that you receive appropriate remuneration for your efforts in looking after our representative and ensuring his safe keeping."

"Indeed, now I'm sure you would wish to see Mr Reeves so you can reassure his family that he is safe and well. You will appreciate we cannot let you see him alone but I'm equally sure you will agree that he is in fine health. Trust me, he has been well treated."

At that moment the door to the room opened and Reeves was ushered in. He was unshackled but held firmly between two armed guards who seemed particularly alert. Lakin knew that this was not the time for futile attempts. He would keep to the script.

A third chair was pulled up for the dishevelled agent. Lakin sought to make eye contact but his head was bowed and his eyes were fixed on the floor. Reeves would not join the diplomatic charade.

"How are you Adam?" Lakin asked. "Are you well? Do you need anything?"

There was little response but Reeves seemed lucid and calm and began to talk without emotion about his captivity. His eyes now firmly fixed on Lakin cleared and a spark of recognition passed between them. Lakin briefly thought about passing on the tracking device which had been inserted into a book but thought better of it for now. The chance of Reeves being allowed to keep anything which was offered during the meeting was slim and the risk of compromise too great. He contented himself with the knowledge that his counterpart had not been mistreated as far as he could see. He turned back to the smiling emissary.

"Would it be OK to give him a few items we brought along to make his stay more comfortable?"

"I'm afraid that won't be possible." The response was curt, dismissive and the false sheen of friendship was gone as fast as it had appeared. Ignoring the snub he continued.

"I'm grateful that you are looking after him so well, Sir. Now perhaps we could discuss a way forward. Did you have any particular ideas about a resolution?"

The man dismissed Reeves with a flick of the wrist and he was removed without fanfare. The door closed behind him with an ominous bang. Lakin hoped that his clumsy move would not presage a downturn.

"Well Mr Lakin, you know we are struggling to protect our lands and we do it in conditions which are a daily challenge for our freedom fighters. They are ill-equipped and under constant threat from our southerly neighbours, as you know. We face daily attack from the skies and have little response but some old Soviet era guns. Now if only I could offer them some American Stingers they would feel so much better able to defend themselves."

"I'm sure we could come to some agreement and perhaps we could have Mr Reeves involved in the handover arrangements?"

"Exactly as I was thinking Mr Lakin; exactly so!"

"Maybe we could spend a little time understanding what you need and I will make enquiries. Even if Stingers are not available I am sure we could find a suitable substitute. How many units would you think I would need to acquire?"

Suddenly the smiles returned and the tea was poured for a second time.

CHAPTER 22

Golf Dispersal, RAF Akrotiri.

"Walking for Oscar and Papa with Zulu and X-ray as spares," called the Duty Authoriser over the squawk box.

"Roger Sir, the see-off crews are at the jets," answered the disembodied voice of the Line Controller.

The crews walked towards the line hut, the whine of the Houchin external power sets drowned out momentarily by the clatter of the twin engines of the Chinooks as they lifted from the adjacent dispersal and flew low over the operations building heading southeast. With the disparity in speeds the first elements of the combined force were already airborne and heading for the distant Lebanese coast. The navigators made their way straight to their allocated jets avoiding the tiny line hut which would be swamped with bodies. Avionics diaries had been carefully scrutinised well in advance and each man had studied the foibles of his designated aircraft closely. They had been allocated their jets for the mission at the briefing and had spent hours in the hangar with avionics and radar technicians fine tuning the equipment hoping that on this occasion it would operate perfectly.

The pilots crammed into the small hut seeking out their individual Form 700s amidst the knot of bodies inside the tiny room. The usual light-hearted banter was missing and the faces wore serious expressions as they leafed through the sections checking and rechecking work that had been carried out to prepare the jets. Now was the last time to make sure everything was ready. The Line Chief watched on in anticipation knowing that it would be a personal affront if he had allowed anything to slip through. He demanded perfection.

Out on the flight line events were running to a well drilled routine. Flight line mechanics, pronounced "Flems", made final preparations and plugged headsets into the receptacles in the main wheel well of a Phantom preparing for the start sequence. As Flash climbed the rear steps with his bonedome and kneeboard in hand he could see little of the ordered chaos around him but, as his head popped up over the huge intake he stared down the line of aircraft, briefly taking in the scene. The line of Buccaneers stretched out in front of him and the navigators were already in the cockpits of the first six aircraft in line. With heads down he knew they were well into their pre-flight checks. He leant inside, dropped his kneeboard onto the console and stepped over the rail onto the hard canvas cover of the ejection seat. After a short sequence of checks, he threaded his way along the canopy arch into the front cockpit watching Razor work his way around the outside of the jet completing the external checks. With live weapons he would wait until his pilot was happy before applying external power. In the meantime he ran through his own pre-power checks in the front cockpit so that he would be ready. A glance up and he saw his pilot standing by the power set his thumb raised, the usual grin noticeably absent. It had been a while since he had sat on QRA having been relegated to instructional duties and the nerves suddenly resurfaced. Climbing into an armed aeroplane was so much different to normal training flights and there could be no margin for errors. He responded with the waggling motion, his two fingers signalling that he was about to apply external power. With a tension he had missed, he flicked the two generator switches to "Ext On" and the raft of telelight panel lights sprang alive as the cockpit came to life.

With gyros noisily spinning up he stood and negotiated his way, gingerly, along the cockpit rail back to his own seat. The bulk of his lifejacket brushed along the canopy as he made his way along the rail threatening to dump him unceremoniously onto the concrete 10 feet below. Flicking the AJB7 compass switch he plopped down on the seat and fired up the inertial navigation system. With the present position of "Golf" Dispersal carefully entered he turned the button to "ALN" and the small light began to flash rapidly signifying the instrument was beginning to align itself with Tue North. It would take a full 12 minutes before it was ready but from then on it would provide the vital navigational information on which success would rely. With much of the run-in over the sea he would need its help to ensure they were where they were needed at the right time. With the familiar ritual underway he stood up yet again and began to recheck his ejection seat. For some reason it received much more attention than usual.

Underneath the jet Razor had finished his walkround. He had prodded and poked the usual control surfaces and pressure gauges but, like Flash, he saved his closest attention for each of the weapons and gave them a 2nd inspection. The four Skyflash missiles nestled snugly in the semi-conformal launchers under the fuselage. He would tune them to the CW radar frequency during the start up sequence but for now he wanted to be sure they were properly fitted. He pulled the pylon safety pins from each missile and handed them over to the "flem" before giving each Skyflash his attention. He glanced over the missile body to make sure each was undamaged and that the wings were locked. He checked the small aerials which would relay signals from the AWG12 radar if he pulled the trigger. With a final check that the rocket motor weather seal was intact he was happy. Moving on to the infra-red guided Sidewinders fitted to the LAU-7 missile pylons, he inspected each missile carefully. It was vital that he identified which type had been loaded. There were two types of Sidewinder in the inventory, the "Golf" and the "Lima". The former was a stern hemisphere only weapon which meant that he would need to slot into a targets 6 o'clock before firing. The more modern and more sensitive AIM-9L was an all-aspect weapon meaning it could be fired in the front sector. This was a vital advantage in air combat and it was the "Lima" which had been allocated for the mission. Seeing the double delta canards of the forward fins he relaxed knowing that the correct weapons were in place. Unlike the Skyflash the Sidewinder was manually loaded onto the rail and slid backward into place. It was held there by a simple locking device which prevented it moving forward until the enormous power of the motor broke the detent. With a quick check of the fins he spun the small rollerons which stabilised the missile in flight before moving on to the most important aspect. A bottle in each LAU-7 provided coolant which lowered the temperature of the seeker head allowing it to sense its warm target against the ambient air. Without it the performance of the missile was severely degraded. The tiny gauge showed full. All was well.

The final check was reserved for the gun. The green Suu-23 hung menacingly underneath the jet. The side panel had been removed and lay next to the gun pod revealing the electronics that controlled the feed and breech mechanisms. Underneath the green fairings most of the space was taken up by the long barrels. The six barrelled Gatling gun was fed by a complex series of belts looping from the ammo canister to the breech. As the trigger was pressed in the cockpit, electronic signals passed to the electronics unit sending shells hurtling around the loops to the breech block where each shell detonated in turn before the spent cases were ejected unceremoniously over the side. The whole sequence took just milliseconds. Razor waggled the barrels checking for excessive movement; a little was normal. The rounds counter showed he had a full load of 1200 20mm high explosive incendiary shells and it was not lost on him that he may well need them before the end of today. With a final check on the electronics unit confirming that the rate of fire was set at 6000 rounds per minute and that the electrical connectors were hooked up he signalled the armourer to close up the access panel. He knew that along the flight line the Buccaneer pilots would be making similar checks on their own weapons.

Flash had begun to align the navigation system. As it hummed away he began his ejection seat checks pulling the first two safety pins and stowing them in the small rack on the canopy arch. He had no idea whether he would re-stow those pins in the seat in a few hours time.

Climbing up the front steps Razor glanced at the back cockpit where Flash's head was buried, busying himself with his left-to-right checks. He would be ready in time and he felt a satisfying familiarity knowing his old mate was in his back seat for the operation. He dropped onto his ejection seat and began his own preparations.

*

"Jackal check."

The Buccaneers were checking in exactly on time.

"Jackal 2, 3, 4, 5, 6." Staccato but precise.

"Call me ready."

"2, 3, 4, 5, 6."

Five minutes to taxi time. There was no drama but once airborne they might not have the luxury of being able to use the radio. With listening posts on every street corner they had no desire to give advanced warning of their approach.

"Pulsator, stand by for time check. 1230 Zulu in 5, 4, 3, 2, 1, Hack! 1230 Zulu."

Down the line, stop watches were calibrated to the precise mission time. In his own cockpit Razor had no need to transmit. A series of hand signals from the Boss in the adjacent Phantom had kept him updated on the progress of the start sequence and all seemed normal. They had briefed a check in time and if all remained normal that would be his next radio call.

Even though the Phantom crews had been briefed about the deception plan and had seen the Russian fighter the next few moments were surreal. The noise of its jet engine had been masked by the combined power of 12 Rolls Royce Speys as it had started up on the adjacent tree-ringed dispersal but its appearance was, nonetheless, dramatic. There would be no radio calls on the active frequency for this movement as the pilot's brief was to remain radio silent and taxy and take off on light signals from the control tower. The first glimpse was through the gap between the line hut and the QRA shed as the camouflaged Mig-23 Flogger eased its way along the taxiway, the pilot's white bonedome standing out through the canopy against the dark blue sky. Looking out of place at RAF Akrotiri, heads swivelled as it emerged from the dispersal and made its way around the loop taxiway to the runway holding point. The two-tone brown camouflage and the red, white and black Syrian roundels on the side of the fuselage had been carefully applied over its original markings. The flying control surfaces waggled as the pilot exercised the controls, closely followed by the wings which swept briefly to the mid position before returning to the fully forward setting for takeoff. No one asked or cared where the Mig had been acquired. For some, exactly where this piece fitted into the mission plan would remain a mystery. Within the Phantom formation all they needed to know was that Andrenev would keep his contract.

As the clock wound down to check-in, the camouflaged jet at the end of the runway pushed up its throttle and the noise of the Tumansky turbojet rose to a climax. The Mig had been preceded some time earlier by a pair of Phantoms which had launched ahead of the main force to fly the feint manoeuvre. The Mig-23 followed, disappearing briefly from sight before reappearing from behind the QRA shed already well down the runway. The afterburner had kicked in and it was accelerating rapidly, the shock diamonds in the plume glowing brightly despite the strong sunlight. As it lifted into the air the tricycle undercarriage retracted into the squat fuselage and the fighter climbed away beginning a hard left hand turn back across the airfield. With its belly away from the watchers the white air to air missiles slung beneath the fuselage were shielded from prying eyes as it climbed quickly away. It passed about a mile south of the dispersal having levelled off at about 1000 feet but still within sight of the formation on the ground. The next time they saw Andrenev in the Mig, Razor hoped he would have played his part.

"Pulsator check."

"Jackal 2, 3, 4, 5, 6."

"Buzzard 1, 2."

"Sword 1, 2."

"Jackal Stud 1, Stud 1 Go!"

The planning was done, the briefings were done. It was time to execute.

"Buzzard, Stud 1, Stud 1, Go!"

With the staccato check-in complete the leader of Jackal formation was already pulling off the chocks and turning away towards the holding point. Leaving the neck of Golf Dispersal, he checked his mirrors seeing three of the Buccaneers following him down the taxiway and the last of his element pulling away from the chocks and turning into line. So far, so good.

The first pair of Phantoms set up to the west and ran back towards the island. In the cockpits, as they powered upwards through 40,000 feet, the airspeed indicators clocked the relentless acceleration. Mach 1.5 was their target speed and as the needle hit the mark the pair spread out into a wide battle formation flying line abreast. As they passed just south of the island the sonic boom could be heard all along the holiday beaches causing tourists to glance up into the bright blue sky; glasses filled with the first drink of the day rattled gently as the pair turned north easterly heading directly for the Syrian airspace boundary. It was only 60 miles beyond and, at this speed, they would cover the distance in minutes.

Back on the ground the formation leader lined up well down the runway leaving space for the remainder of the Buccaneer element to pull onto the concrete behind him. The huge gap between pairs was deliberately built in to avoid risk of damage from debris as the Spey jets were brought up to full power for the engine checks. With the second hand ticking down to the launch time each pilot stared intently at the engine gauges checking and rechecking the temperatures and pressures and willing them to show the correct readings. The raised heartbeats in each cockpit were off the scale in anticipation because no one wanted to miss out at this stage. Slowly, starting in the front cockpit of the number six aircraft, raised thumbs appeared in the windscreen showing that each pilot was ready. The unsaid message rippled up the line until the navigator in the lead Buccaneer craning his neck, watching for the confirmation, finally saw the signal from the number 2 pilot. The leader tapped his bonedome and nodded his head deliberately initiating the take off sequence. The first pair rolled, slowly at first but quickly accelerating down the runway. As they lifted off, barely rising above the ground, the undercarriage retracted and they imperceptibly climbed away in close formation hugging the runway. Behind, the same sequence was repeated as each pair of bombers followed the leader. As the first pair passed over the picquet post on the main road into Akrotiri the leader reefed into a left hand turn his number 2 glued to the wingtip. Turning downwind to depart the circuit, the following pairs arced inside the turn dropping into a "card six" formation in two mile trail. As they hit the coast and headed out over Limmasol Bay they descended even lower to 100 feet above the waves and set course for Beirut.

*

Unbeknown to the British crews an EA-6B Prowler lined up on the forward catapult on the John F Kennedy and the shackle was dragged into position on the nose gear. The engines spooled up the pilot's head buried in the cockpit. Once he saluted the crew chief there was no turning back. Committed, he received the traditional flourish from the deck hand as the steam built up to a shattering pressure. With a massive crash the shuttle was driven along the track taking the jet in its wake hurling it down the short catapult track and over the edge of the deck. It disappeared briefly from sight before lifting steadily into the air its gear already travelling.

As it climbed to height the electronic warfare officers in "the boot" fired up the complex electronic equipment and ran through the mission checks. The target list for the day included

Syrian air defence frequencies which would be neutralised by powerful communications jammers onboard the jet. The AN/ALQ 99 radar jammer would scan the spectrum for fighter radars, SAM tracking radars and AAA tracking radars. Anything that transmitted on their frequencies of interest would also be neutralised. The airborne radars from the Brit fast jets, the AN/AWG 12 from the Phantoms and the Blue Parrot bombing radars of the Buccaneers were allocated on the "no hit" list as were the primary and secondary tactical air-to-air frequencies. The EWOs would make sure that those frequencies stayed clear. They were here to help, not hinder. With the massive power of its jamming suite the Prowler could stand off miles from the Lebanese coast and still be effective. It would set up its jamming orbit virtually overhead the carrier and direct its transmitters towards the unseen targets overland. As it reached its cruising altitude, its jammers were already primed with the crew alert and waiting.

*

"Sir, I make phone call?" the Cypriot labourer asked the Line Chief receiving a nod in reply. The harried chief technician barked out instructions to the troops milling around marshalling them for the next tasks. Even though they had some time before the jets returned they would not be idle. He ran a tight ship and there would be no room for mistakes. Everything would be ready when the jets returned, hopefully, to a triumphant celebration. Had he paid more attention, the phone call would have been of particular interest. As it was, his inattention would be costly.

The labourer spoke softly into the phone his body turned towards the wall to avoid being overheard.

"I finish here at base. It very busy now and maybe you not hear me? Many jets just taxy and take off. Yes, maybe 10; and helicopters. Yes, I see you soon."

The man on the other end of the phone was no Cypriot businessman. In his office in the Russian Consulate in Nicosia he had been waiting for the call. As soon as he replaced the handset he placed another call via a cut-out in Moscow which connected with a controller in the Syrian Air Defence Headquarters in Damascus. His information set up a chain of events as messages flashed all the way to fighter bases in the south of the country.

*

The crews in the first pair of Phantoms had the easiest task of the day. They were flying a simple feint designed to pull the defensive force into the air. The northern alert force was equipped with Mig-21 Fishbed fighters which, once lured airborne and without the ability to refuel in the air, would be at a disadvantage. With such limited fuel reserves they would be out of the equation for at least an hour and, by then, the mission would be nearly over.

The pair of Phantoms was easily visible on the screens of the ancient air defence radars on the mainland in Syria. In wide battle formation and flying at supersonic speeds they seemed to be extremely threatening to the surveillance radar operators. With 10 miles to run, the pilots pushed over and began a slow descent towards the sea the navigators directing the power of the AN/AWG 12 radars at a pre briefed point on the Syrian coast. The radar energy would be detected by a listening post and relayed to the central command headquarters further heightening the perceived threat of attack. In reality, the actual target lay well to the south. As the warning from the sleeper at the Cypriot airbase filtered through, and exactly as the planners had anticipated, the feint confirmed heightened fears and provoked an immediate response. In the alert sheds at Al Qusayr airbase, the hooter sounded and Syrian pilots of 825 Squadron scrambled for their Mig-21s.

*

In the darkened monitoring station on Mount Olympus chaos
ensued. The communications monitors which had been tuned
into the Syrian air defence frequencies for days were suddenly
alive as the pilots at As Suwayda checked in and were scrambled.
The pilots at Homs were brought up to cockpit readiness in
close succession.

Tape recorders whirred as the conversations were captured for
analysis. The NCO immediately hit the direct line to the Master
Controller.

"The alert jets have been launched at As Suwayda. Two airborne
and chopped across to air defence tactical. The alert birds at
Homs are at cockpit readiness but not yet airborne. Standby,
they have just received a scramble message. They're launching
now."

The Master Controller checked his tote and the tell tale plots
marking the Syrian jets appeared, an ominous red, climbing out
from the base at Al Qusayr. Tracking relentlessly towards the
point where the Phantom formation had disappeared it was
obvious that the feint had achieved its desired objective. He
discussed tactics with his intercept controller who was already
monitoring the outbound tracks working out how to play the
Migs. Getting tied up in the north was not part of today's plan.

Despite the rapid response and, even before the wheels were in
the well, the Phantoms were turning around to avoid penetrating
Syrian airspace. Tightening the turn back onto west and
decelerating below Mach 1 they remained in International waters
ensuring they would not provoke the same response from the
Turkish Air Force to the north. If the Migs followed they would
drag them further west making sure to leave a good separation

between the two formations. Only if the Migs reacted to the main package to the south would they turn back and engage. The range would not close to less than 30 miles from the Mig-21s; taunting but keeping them predictable. If the plan worked the short range fighter's fuel would soon be exhausted and, hopefully, it would take time to launch more Migs from ground alert as reinforcements. By then the main force would be approaching the Lebanese coastline.

Unseen by the Syrian controllers on the ground, once the Phantoms reached the anonymity of low level they held their westerly track. As far as the controllers knew they had penetrated Syrian airspace and were, even now, approaching the coastline. The communications between the fighters and their controllers became progressively more confused and increasingly fraught. Coasting out over the deep blue waters the Mig pilots received vectors towards the predicted course looking for the inbound aircraft searching fruitlessly for the ghost attackers. It would be some minutes before it would be apparent that the formation had turned away. In tandem, the short range surface to air missile batteries radars located on the coastal plain scanned the empty airspace without success. On Mount Olympus, the Master Controller watched as the Fishbed fighters orbited aimlessly, patrolling the empty skies seeking a Phantom threat; literally. He pushed a pre-briefed codeword out over the tactical control frequency.

*

"Jackal, on time," called the leader as he approached the first timing check point. This would alert the crews in the Phantoms who had launched a few minutes ahead, of their approach. The tell tale wink of an I band air intercept radar on the RWR in the back cockpit of the leading Buccaneer had already made that fact evident. The Phantom crews on their holding CAP ahead of the formation, had been watching the outbound bombers on their radars since the formation had crossed the bay. The Buccaneer crews had been warned to expect a lock up during this phase and, sure enough, the warning receivers rattled urgently as the Phantom navigator set up an intercept. As Jackal approached the waypoint the Phantoms turned in front crossing flight paths in a sharp descending turnabout, dropping down to low level as they did so. From their new position ahead of the force they would act as a screen. Any hostile fighters which threatened the formation from the front sector would be detected by their radars and would be dealt with. In every cockpit within the formation attention turned to maps and stopwatches. The critical progress check would be as they coasted-in over the headland near Tripoli that was already painting at the extremity of the Blue Parrot radar scope.

"Bogeys, 30 left, no range," came the flat call over the radio from the lead Phantom. "Multiple contacts."

In the cockpits the information was digested. The sudden realisation that talk of opposition might not be hollow took on extra significance. Maybe the mission had seemed unreal until now.

"Jackal, sidestep right," called the Phantom navigator. Immediately, the leader jinked away from track in a southerly direction away from the potential threat. As the Buccaneers diverged from track the Phantoms faced up to the intruders.

*

Some miles to the northeast, Yuri Andrenev was holding on a low level orbit well beneath the coverage of the Syrian air defence radars. He had made his way at low level from Akrotiri in radio silence but had tuned in to the Syrian air defence frequency as he approached his holding pattern. He had listened in as the Syrian Mig-23s at Homs had called for takeoff and, as his nose turned back towards the coast the scanner of his Sapfir-

23D radar pointed towards the airbase looking for the first signs of the outbound fighters. The IFF interrogator which had been installed back at Akrotiri was set up with the codes of the day. He had played with it during the quieter moments since takeoff but his radar had remained stubbornly blank. With potential targets airborne he watched with renewed anticipation. The pre-briefed codes were set but there was always the chance that the intelligence was flawed. They were adamant that Syrian QRA always wore the same codes so when he hit the interrogate selector he should be rewarded with electronic confirmation that his targets were Syrian. If they followed standard Soviet doctrine they would set up a decoy attack profile. As they approached the range at which a Skyflash missile would be launched against them they would turn through 90 degrees away from the attackers. Not only would this defeat the tracking of the Skyflash but it would drag the attacking formation into a long tailchase as the British crews tried to run down the lead formation of Mig-23s. The Russian codeword for this tactic was "Obman" or Deception.

Yuri was nervous about his rules of engagement. Putting him out here had been brave and would test his loyalty. Potentially, he would be firing the first shot so his instructions had been appropriately vague. If the Syrian pilots opened fire the decision was easy; it would be self defence. He had pressed for some more likely scenarios but the best he had been able to elicit was that, if at any stage he heard clearance to engage transmitted on frequency, the game was on. Whether that call would come in Russian or Arabic was a lottery.

As he turned inbound on his third orbit a fuzzy blip appeared in his radar display. His years of experience told him that this was a large formation. He could see more than one contact but it was impossible to break out individual players just yet. The blip showed at 30 kilometres just off his nose. Staying low he took a small turn towards and pushed up the throttle. This was it.

*

In the Phantom formation, Paul Anderson, the Phantom detachment commander, heard his navigator directing Razor and Flash in the number 2. They had set up a classic bracket on the radar contacts and had widened to put a Phantom on each side of the inbound formation. The range crept inside 30 miles and, as he stared at his radar repeater in the front cockpit he could see the fuzzy blips in pulse Doppler mode. He had pushed his own formation up to fighting speed and the airspeed indicator showed 400 knots. As he watched, the navigator flicked into pulse mode and the targets appeared at the top of the scope at 24 miles. The call of "trailers" from the other aircraft meant that he must be looking at the lead pair. If the formation continued driving straight at them it might be his worst nightmare. He must tie them up because any "leakers" might penetrate his screen and threaten the Buccaneers. The only way he could do that was to drag them into a turning fight and slow them down for a while. With the Phantoms engaged, the trail pair would be free and might sidestep the melee; unless of course Andrenev could help. The pair of blips approached 15 miles and the second pair appeared at the top of the radar scope. So far there were only four contacts. Where was Andrenev?

*

Andrenev watched through the top of his canopy as the first pair of Migs flashed overhead many thousands of feet above. He had been reluctant to take a lock and potentially announce his presence so he had no idea of the height of the targets. He hoped that the presence of the Phantoms engaging from the south had diverted the attention of both the Mig pilots and the Syrian fighter controllers. As he broke out the second pair on his radar display he refined the scanner position and was rewarded with a solid contact. If they were following doctrine they were about 10 miles behind.

"Obman vypolnit', Deception Execute."

The familiar codeword took him back to his Soviet squadron. He now knew exactly the intentions of the lead pair and his next actions were suddenly predictable.

*

Anderson's back seater locked up the target on their side of the formation and provoked an immediate reaction.

"Bogeys turning south!"

The closing velocity wound off as the targets on the scope began to track to the right rapidly. They had flown a classic defensive counter to defeat the Skyflash missile.

"Go starboard hard," he heard from the back seat. "Go Sidewinder." His navigator would be switching his attention to the telescope sight, or TESS, in the back seat.

"Looking for the ident."

As the pilot pulled the Sidewinder aiming dot into the centre circle on the radar it would place the distant target onto the weapons boresight along which the rifle scope in the back seat was focussed. It was a simple but effective device to magnify the image.

"Dot centred."

The navigator stared through the telescope and was rewarded with the sight of a fighter jet bobbing up and down in the narrow field of view. The target was not quite distinct; just too far to make out the type yet and he, momentarily, switched his attention back to the radar. Staring too long at the bobbing image induced instant nausea. The radar held a solid lock and the range was reducing rapidly now approaching 12 miles. Any time soon. He moved back to the telescope.

*

Andrenev checked his speed; 550 kph, it should be enough. Pulling hard back on the stick, the altimeter began to wind up rapidly as he converted into a vertical climb. He knew that as soon as he popped up into radar coverage the clock was ticking. Hearing the deception execute call had proved critical as he watched the trailing pair of Migs flash through his gunsight well above. As he pulled through the vertical rolling onto his back, the altimeter showed 10,000 metres and he kept the pull on watching the Migs as they tracked down his canopy centreline towards his windscreen. Still inverted he centred the target in his reticule and heard a brief tone from the R-60 infra-red missile. His target had dropped back from the leader and he could only assume that the guttural commands on the radio were a prompt to sort out his formation. Yuri snap rolled upright, centred the pipper and waited patiently.

*

"Bogeys dragging on 120," called Flash to his leader. As soon as the formation had turned, Flash locked to the bogey on his side glued to the radar scope. The leader was responsible for the identification and he would be staring through his TESS trying to determine whether they were on the Migs. Flash's role was to watch how the formation reacted and to report but he wanted a shot in the air. He was nervous because the trailing formation were not far behind yet, without clearance to fire, his hands were tied. He could do no more than follow this pair until the intentions were clear. If the leader identified a Flogger, a Skyflash would follow. If the identification was late the lead Migs might bypass the screen, free to press the bomber package.

"Buzzard identifies one Manta," he heard over the radio. The codeword for Floggers. The next few minutes would decide whether he made the bar tonight for a brandy sour. It seemed suddenly very attractive right now.

*

Yuri's actions were brutally clinical. The tone sounded, he pulled the trigger and the R-60 sped off in a cloud of smoke tracking unerringly towards its target. The flight time was short; a mere six seconds giving the Mig pilot little chance to react even if he had seen Andrenev's approach which was doubtful. The agile missile passed within feet of the Flogger activating the proximity fuse and detonating the warhead. The thousands of tiny pellets freed up as the warhead fragmented struck the fuselage a few feet along the tailpipe cutting into the metal skin and shredding feed pipes and turbine chambers. The effect was catastrophic as the engine failed instantly, winding down from thousands of revolutions per minute to stationary in mere seconds. It disintegrated cutting control lines and flicking the jet onto its back and out of control. The hapless pilot could not have known his fate. From a mile behind Yuri watched with detached fascination as the jet plummeted earthwards still inverted, trailing a plume of smoke. He reached down and flicked the dials on his IFF box selecting the code which the jet which had just crashed had been transmitting just moments before. With the slow update rate of the huge air defence radar on the ground in Syria, unless the controller was really sharp, nothing had changed on his radar scope. Yuri was now embedded in the Syrian formation and had taken the place of the Mig he had just destroyed. He hoped his new leader was not too talkative as his Arabic was marginal at best. In his head up display two new blips appeared but they were now F4 Phantoms. A barked command on the radio and he saw the leader surge forward his afterburner glowing bright. Yuri pushed the throttle through the gate and followed. His new "leader" locked to the left hand Phantom. Until the game played out, friends could become foes.

*

Unseen to the British crews who had been seduced into following the leading pair, just a few miles behind and hidden deep in the 6 o'clock, the trailing pair of Migs were accelerating and closing rapidly.

"Rackets 6 o'clock, defensive counter," screamed Flash sandwiched between the pairs of Migs. The plan must have gone awry. The Phantoms cross turned, Razor resisting the urge to engage afterburner to aid the turn. The speed washed off rapidly and his Phantom expressed its displeasure but it was preferable to heating up the exhaust pipes and offering a target to an infra red missile. As they crossed flight paths mere feet apart and began to separate, each navigator hit the release button in the back cockpit initiating a stream of infra red decoys into the airflow behind the wallowing jets. Four sets of eyes scanned the airspace behind searching for the source of the threat. Four miles to the southeast the lead pair of Floggers turned around and pointed back towards the merge. The tactical picture was becoming murky.

The time for deception was past. Yuri watched as his leader tracked the Phantom just a few miles ahead. Unless he acted now events would take an unexpected and unwelcome turn. He had no desire to end up in a "fur ball" where the potential to be misidentified by the Phantom crews was massive. He cranked on 90 degrees of bank and pulled his sight onto the Mig-23 alongside; too close for a missile! He switched to guns reversing the turn and steadied his tracking watching the pipper settle onto the fuselage of the Mig which was now centred in his gunsight, the lead computer constantly predicting where the bullets would strike. Tracking, tracking, tracking; the Flogger suddenly seemed to react and entered a half-hearted turn towards him merely sweetening the sighting solution. Whether it was a reaction to his attack or a navigation turn he had no idea. The turn helped massively. The familiar planform with its swept variable geometry wings filled the inner reticule. In this configuration the turn rate was pathetic and he had little trouble keeping the sight on the target. One squeeze of the trigger and he was rewarded with a burp as a burst of 23mm high explosive incendiary shells left the Gsh-23 cannon. He vaguely noticed a few puffs of debris spring from the airframe but he tracked in a gentle arc to the right squeezing the trigger again in a longer burst. His tracking was perfect and chunks of the airframe began to detach whipping past, frighteningly close to his canopy. Smoke erupted from the exhaust as the rounds struck home and the hapless fighter juddered before beginning to lose height rapidly. In a scene reminiscent of gunsight films from the Yom Kippur War, the canopy detached and the pilot ejected leaving his jet to its own devices. There had been no resistance and the kill had been quick. Yuri switched across to the pre-briefed tactical frequency and hit the transmit button.

"Buzzard formation, splash two bogeys bugging out on west; you owe me!" He rolled the Mig-23 onto its back and descended rapidly towards the calm blue Mediterranean Sea below dragging the nose around onto west and heading back towards Cyprus.

Registering the information from Andrenev the Phantoms reversed their turns back towards the remaining Migs. In the back cockpits radar controls flashed as the contacts appeared instantly on the radar scopes. With the range closing rapidly there was no time for erroneous talk

The Floggers pilots in the leading pair faced up anticipating the closing moves of what they assumed was a scripted decoy tactic. If all had gone to plan the trailing pair would already have run down the Phantoms and taken R-60 shots. It should have been a case of rejoining in formation and returning to base with the task completed. As expected a pair of targets appeared but the sudden screech of the Sirena 3 RWR was totally unexpected. The leader stared at the display trying to make sense of the indications. The light glowed solidly in the front left quadrant exactly where he had anticipated but the associated threat light showed a Phantom not another Mig-23. It couldn't be! He stared through the thick gunsight at the tell tale smoke trail as the Phantoms bore down. The plan had gone badly wrong but how? His controller had dried up. Unable to compute the implications he pushed up the throttles and drive directly at the smoke. As the formations closed at a combined closing velocity of well over 1000 knots he made the only decision possible; to run.

The two formations passed within feet of each other at the merge and the Phantoms pulled up into the vertical turning hard around to follow the rapidly receding Migs. In complete contrast, the Mig pilots drove hard for the surface of the sea thousands of feet below with no hint of a reaction. Behind them the Phantoms tracked the descent. In the Mig cockpits the temporary lull from the radar warning receivers was replaced with the familiar screech of a lock on and each Mig pilot tensed in anticipation. What they could not anticipate in the absence of the supporting Migs was that they would be spared. With the Floggers disengaging the Phantoms hauled off and headed southeast towards the holding point just off the Lebanese coast. They had other priorities.

CHAPTER 23

Approaching the Lebanese Coast.

It had been noisy on the tactical frequency as the engagement had progressed but in sharp contrast, the Buccaneer crews had stayed quiet as they pressed towards the coast at high speed and at low level. The escort fighters had done their job and from this point onwards they hoped they could discount a fighter threat. What no one knew was that in the hydraulic bay of the number 5 Buccaneer a timer ticked down relentlessly.

The Buccaneers were spread out in a long "card" formation. Up front the lead pair had dropped even lower using the legendary ability to fly almost in ground effect. On a single call from the leader the IFF transponders were switched to standby preventing an inquisitive air traffic controller from checking their identity. From here on they were unidentifiable. The coastline stretched out across the visible horizon with the city of Tripoli just discernible in the distance. To the north lay the Rene Mouowad airbase, home to a squadron of UH1 Hueycobra helicopters. It had briefly operated Mirage fighters but, as the money ran out in the late 70s, they had been grounded. The main road into Syria passed south of the base heading in a straight line for the border crossing. They would give the base a wide berth coasting in north of the town of Al Mahmra. The lead navigator had been painting the town on radar for some time and they would hit their coast-in point precisely. As they flashed past the airfield at high speed they attracted little response. The leader had expected calls on Guard frequency from the Syrian air defence commander given their proximity to the Syrian border. If they pressed on their present track they would penetrate Syrian airspace in just minutes but the radio was deathly quiet. The initial point, a fork in the road just east of the village of Massaaoudiye lay just ahead. Inside each cockpit the feeling of anticipation heightened. This was the culmination of years of training and the next five minutes were critical.

*

Across the border near the village of Addabousiyah the Syrian SA-6 Battery Commander was beginning to think the alert had been a false alarm. They had been conducting an exercise when they had been pushed forward to the border with Lebanon. The briefing had been precise. It was to look for low level targets in the coastal plain near the border and if sighted, to engage. Why the Israelis would be operating here was a mystery. He was a veteran of the 1982 crisis in the Bekaa Valley when the Israelis had attacked their SA-6s. It had been a bloodbath and 17 of the 19 SAM batteries which had been deployed in an offensive screen had been destroyed. It was recent enough to make him nervous and he had considered the risk to his battery carefully as he had deployed his Straight Flush radar and his four transporter/erector launchers. If these fighters were armed with bombs he fully expected retribution at the first hint of a lock on. He would have to get the first shot away. There was little cover in this flat area on the coastal plain and the thin camouflage nets he had rigged over the command vehicle and the target acquisition radar seemed woefully inadequate. He let himself into the control van just as mayhem erupted.

As the lead pair of Buccaneers hit the IP exactly on time they cranked right and diverged from track. In the back cockpits both navigators had been hard at work since coasting-in identifying the precise offset from the radar fix point on the coastline. This would locate the compound. The village of Tall Hmaire stood out clearly as did the long straight road and the border crossing with its cluster of buildings. Somewhere in the confused mass of ground returns was the target. As they finally refined the information the coordinates were programmed into the Pave Spike and attention switched to the large screen by the left knee. A ghostly black and white image in the centre of the screen was the return from the compound, its layout exactly as predicted at the briefing. Cross hairs moved over the target and using the tracking ball on the control unit each navigator began to follow his own target manually on the screen. For the next 40 seconds they would keep the cursors precisely over the target, the small tracking sensor on the nose of each Pave Spike pod would follow its designated target until the bombs struck home.

*

As the vehicle rattled over another pothole the windscreen was filled with the unmistakable profile of a Buccaneer bomber as it flashed directly overhead at what seemed like only feet above the ground. The ear splitting noise was gone almost as soon as it had come prompting a rapid exchange between the driver and the bodyguard. Lakin had only just left the compound and was barely out of visual range. Just minutes later, as the noise of the first bombs hit his ears, Lakin would have cause to believe that his own welfare had not been considered over-carefully in London. He called the driver to pull over, jumped out and made his way up a small rise from where he could see the compound.

*

The rules of engagement had been clear and unambiguous. As he listened to the familiar ritual the surveillance operator in the Straight Flush vehicle of the SA-6 handed off the contacts to the acquisition controller who began to track a fast moving target on the bizarre linear electronic display. The fuzzy blip was unintelligible to the layman but to the trained operator it was a fast jet. The display turned to full track and he heard the request to engage through his headset. Was that him who had just authorised a missile launch?

*

The spikers held their elliptical course illuminating the point where each laser guided bomb would land. Less than a minute behind, the following Buccaneers passed over the IP and, on the call of "Hack", stopwatches began to count down the last minutes to target. From that point the choreography would be precise and holding a steady track would ensure that the bombs would be delivered accurately. In the cockpit of the spikers they were ready. With one minute to go the bombers would initiate a pull up known as a loft manoeuvre and at the apex, the bombs would be released and tossed onto the target a few miles beyond. Timing was all important because if they were not precise the spikers might penetrate Syrian airspace as they held the illuminating ellipse.

In the cockpit of the third Buccaneer the radar warning receiver began to chatter ominously. The slow ping of the surveillance radar, which the navigator had assumed to be the air traffic control radar at the nearby airfield, was suddenly replaced by a harsh rattle. A warning vector flashed up on the display screen and the track-while-scan light illuminated.

"Mud 6, 10 o'clock, tracking!"

The call would normally have been transmitted and accompanied by a call for a defensive reaction to defeat any incoming missile. At this late stage a diversion from track would mean that it would be almost impossible to press home the attack and the bombs would almost certainly miss the target if they could even be launched at all. They had little choice but to press on and trust the AN/ALQ 101-10 electronic countermeasures pod which hung below the right wing. They had every confidence in the countermeasures experts who had programmed the responses into the pod's electronic brain and they had been assured, repeatedly, that the response against the SA-6 was highly effective and would confuse the missile into a near miss. They had little expected in the warm confines of a Scottish briefing room to have to test it out for real.

"Press?"

"Affirmative!"

They were committed.

*

In the field only 12 miles to the north there was a massive crack as the firing pulse reached the Gainful missile initiating its launch sequence. The target tracking radar had already slewed onto a southerly bearing and gyrated gently following its target in anticipation. A huge plume of smoke emerged from the tail of the missile and it streaked upwards in a long arcing trajectory marking its passage with a white exhaust plume. With the missile engagement team already turning their attention to the trailing formation there was no one to watch it fly out.

*

Inside the ECM pod electronic circuits analysed the incoming signals from the surface-to-air missile measuring the precise parameters and categorising the threat. A techniques generator selected a suitable response from its library of countermeasures and began to transmit a deception signal. If all went to plan the missile would see the intricate response and decide it was far too attractive to ignore. What none of the Buccaneer crews could know was that, well to the west, the sensitive receiver in the EA-6B Prowler had detected the Straight Flush radar from the SA-6 the second it had popped up on frequency. Complex analysis had occurred in milliseconds and the emitter had been identified. More complex techniques generators had been tasked by the electronic brain and electronic programs had been allocated to counter the threat. Within moments a carefully designed countermeasure was being transmitted from the antennas on the pod targeted directly at the missile tracking radar on the Syrian border. As the Straight Flush provided its guidance solution for the Gainful missile, electronic deception was already in play to ensure that it would never find its target.

In the spikers, the navigators kept the crosshairs firmly on the briefed tracking points; one on the jail and the other on the compound walls. Their own RWRs were silent as yet unaware of the drama unfolding in the other cockpits. With the Pave Spike pods activated, laser beams from the sensor balls struck each nominated target reflecting back towards the inbound bombers.

"Pulling up!"

The first pair was into the loft manoeuvre. The lead pilot in the designator Buccaneer stared directly at the target when, suddenly, he saw a flash in his peripheral vision and a smoke trail emerged from a field in the distance. It climbed rapidly forming a white arc before descending back to Earth aiming directly at the target area. The tactical frequency was quiet and a quick check with his navigator confirmed that they were "clean" so who was targeted? He experienced a rare moment of indecision as he watched the SAM enter its terminal dive. Should he call and risk distracting the other members of the formation at a key moment in the attack or should he wait it out and risk that they might be unaware of the threat. In any event, so close to the target what would they do? It was likely they would be committed so he waited.

Twenty miles behind, the Chinook helicopters coasted-in and began to track along the road towards the landing zone.

In the number 4 aircraft the attack was on rails. The pilot checked the pull at 60 degrees nose high watching the weapons symbology as it ticked down to the release point. In the back the navigator monitored his radar display keeping the crosshairs on the offset point. As the pilot pickled the weapons, two laser-guided Paveway 2 bombs dropped from the bomb racks and continued the loft trajectory upwards and forward. Thermal batteries fired up powering the laser sensor in the nose of the weapon. The guidance vanes were released ready for the moment when the autopilot detected the signal. Ahead of the Buccaneers the reflected laser energy diverged forming a "basket" as it moved further away from the target. As soon as the bombs entered the cone, guidance signals would flick the control surfaces holding the bombs on course.

In the cockpit of the number 3 things were tense. Neither crew had the spare capacity to watch the incoming missile nor could they improve matters if they did. The RWR still presaged doom as the familiar rattle of the track-while-scan from the tracking radar urged the crew to action. Despite its warning they followed the profile releasing the weapons exactly on cue. With the bombs in the air they initiated the escape manoeuvre rolling the jet onto its back and pulling hard back towards the ground inverted. Rolling upright and pulling around into an oblique turn to the right saw them reversing their track to return to the coast. Part way around the turn the smoking missile passed within a few hundred feet in a vertical terminal dive and smashed into the ground ahead of their track. They assumed that the ECM pod had done its magic or their timely escape manoeuvre had confused the missile. The truth was that a silent benefactor had secured their passage. All they cared was that their jet was still flying. As they steadied up on a reciprocal track the number 4 was positioned perfectly in battle formation on the left and they made their escape. Behind, the trailing pair was initiating the pull up for the follow on attack.

As the first bombs struck the compound mayhem reigned. The accuracy of the laser designation had been perfect. The bombs from the lead aircraft struck the headquarters building precisely on target dropping the walls around the main entrance. The overwhelming weight of the now unsupported upper floor caused the front wall to implode. The guards who had been stationed at the door were lost in the billowing dust and quickly enveloped by the tumbling masonry. A massive breach appeared leaving the central corridor open to the outside air. Seconds after the first explosion, the next Paveway hit the compound wall opening a massive breach and demolishing one of the guard towers.

The navigators in the spikers switched their efforts to the secondary targets just as the trail pair hit their apex and the second wave of weapons was released. The timing was crucial.

In the compound those who could still hear after the cacophony of the initial attack were suddenly aware of an ethereal whistling as the next weapons sought out their targets. The first pair of Paveways hit the transport building destroying the vehicles inside and causing an explosion as the petrol stored in drums around the walls ignited. The second pair programmed for an airburst, shredded the base of the communications tower toppling it and instantly cutting off radio and telephone communications. It would be some time before a clear picture of events would emerge giving the attackers time to complete the mission.

With both attacks successful, the spikers readied to make their own kinetic contribution. Extending eastwards they drove 10 miles beyond the target before rotating inwards crossing flight paths. In tight battle formation they headed back towards the compound this time maintaining 100 feet above the ground. There would be no loft manoeuvre on this pass. With weapon selectors reconfigured, the two pairs of modified BL755s dropped from the wing pylons as they passed over the yard, the tail fins popping out into the airflow slowing the weapons in flight allowing the Buccaneers to forge ahead. At about 30 feet above the ground the side panels popped from the cases and hundreds of small bomblets scattered over the yard embedding themselves into the shallow dirt. A few exploded on contact but the majority lay dormant. The gun cameras in the Buccaneers clicked away during the laydown attack adding evidence for the later analysis. Video recorders in the cockpits had already captured the earlier weapon strikes and they would be pored over and analysed in great detail later in the day. Their final task was to transmit the situation report to the leader of the helicopter flight. The teams in the rear cabins would want to know the magnitude of their task and whether the mission objectives had been achieved so far. Most importantly, the Chinook pilots would want to know whether they had to land in the bear pit of the compound which had just been hit by heavy weapons or whether they would enjoy the relative safety of the pre-planned landing zone. The codeword signifying success went out over the frequency signalling them to continue as planned.

At the holding point off the Lebanese coast the Phantoms of Buzzard formation orbited patiently watching for hostile fighters and waiting to escort the helicopters back to Akrotiri. Suddenly a blip appeared on the scope and the lead navigator locked up. A quick check against his map put the contact 30 miles inside Syria and it was coming towards at 400 knots. The Buccaneers had already hit the target and would be running back down towards the coast. If this was a late response from the Syrian Air Defence Commander he had missed his chance to hit the Buccaneer force but the helicopters might still be vulnerable.

"Bogeys bearing 060, fast," he called prompting a turn towards.

"Investigating."

Olympus had been quiet and either they could not see the threat or were being dull. Razor nudged up the throttles to fighting speed taking the tactical lead and the Boss moved up into battle formation.

"Range 30."

"Looks like a pair," he heard from the other jet as his wingman staying in search mode looked around the formation for other threats. His RWR blinked rhythmically with a J band vector which could easily be the Jaybird radar of a Mig-21 Fishbed fighter.

"Buster," he called, urging the speed up yet further as the airspeed indicator touched 500 knots in response to his command. As he watched, the closing velocity rolled off and the radar picture shuddered briefly before returning to wide scan. The scope was suddenly clear of contacts.

"Bogeys turned away," he called watching the scope for a short time to make sure that it had not merely been an orbit to throw off his lock. It stayed blank.

"Back to CAP."

The feint had been brief and they would watch for further potential intrusions but at the first sign of a lock it had seemed to dissuade the Arab pilots from pressing home an attack. It was a minor victory.

CHAPTER 24

Approaching the Hezbollah Compound on the Syrian Border.

The Chinooks approached the landing zone staying low, hugging the gently undulating terrain. The ground ahead was rising as the pilots looked ahead for their lead-in feature. Little effort was needed because, up ahead, a pall of smoke marked the compound indelibly. In the rear cabin, the insertion team readied themselves for the landing going through their final checks of their equipment, straps cinched tight and weapons loaded as they waited for the tell tale thump as the wheels hit earth. The radio operator spoke quickly into the handset of his secure radio set. The short transmission would be picked up by the sensitive receivers on the summit of Mount Olympus and relayed back to the headquarters at Hereford before they had even touched the ground. To a man their eyes were locked on the loadmaster who would signal when they could move out. That familiar feeling of apprehension affected even the most hardened veteran as they waited those final moments. It would dissipate the second they kicked off the ramp.

The LZ sat in the base of a small gulley giving the team vital cover as they emerged from the rear of the Chinook. At this stage they could have no idea of the state of the guard force after the attack by the Buccaneers. Hopefully the force would be less than organised from the combined effect of the Paveway bombs and the jet noise. As the helicopters transitioned into the hover, sand from the gulley was thrown up by the downdraught of the massive twin rotors obscuring the forward vision temporarily. The pilots were used to it; the term "brown out" described the phenomenon perfectly. Ordinarily, it offered cover during such an operation but, with the gulley already shielding them from view, it was more of a hindrance for this insertion. The moment the wheels touched, the rear ramps dropped and the troopers, wearing light fighting trim, swarmed from the cabin spreading out and moving swiftly up the incline in the direction of the compound. As they reached the crest of the low ridge they went to ground edging forward on their bellies to gain sight of the compound beyond. It would be the first time they would know how good the intelligence preparation had been.

One of the team on the periphery of the fan of bodies held an Accuracy L115 sniper rifle, the sight pressed to his eye. Accurate out to 1000 yards the weapon fired a larger 8.59mm bullet from its detachable box magazine. Resting on the bipod, he scanned the shattered entrance to the compound satisfied at the mayhem visible through the small spotting scope. As promised, the gates had been reduced to matchsticks by the laser-guided bombs and the guard tower adjacent to the entrance had been dropped. Access to the compound lay wide open so he switched his attention to the second guard tower. A reflection from a spotting scope caught his eye announcing the presence of a sniper on the observation deck. It was a fatal mistake by the terrorist, his head visible above the parapet. Taking the first pressure he homed in on the tiny target and breathed out, holding his breath as he took up the second pressure. He squeezed the trigger. The head dropped from view.

On the signal from the sniper the rest of the troop stood up and ran down the shallow incline towards the gate. Back on the ridgeline the sniper scanned for further movement around the compound walls ready to offer covering fire at the first hint of a response. Nothing else moved. He watched as the troop fanned out making them less of a target during this vulnerable approach phase. He would stay here for the duration of the operation covering his team until they returned to the waiting helicopters.

The team leader approached the shattered gates thankful for an unopposed approach. So far his team was intact and the worst part was over. From now on they were in close contact and on equal terms with the defenders. He would have preferred more unequal odds but he was still thankful for the disruption caused by the air attack. Moving carefully through the gates he surveyed the inner courtyard. Small bomblets littered the ground and he hoped to goodness that the RAF weaponeers were correct and that they were inert for the first few hours. If not, one inopportune contact and it was all over. To his right the building that housed the motor pool was destroyed and vehicles in various states of destruction littered the ground. One truck lay on its roof, windowless after the concussion of a 1000 lb bomb landing nearby.

The plans they had pored over at the briefing were remarkably accurate and the layout was identical. The far wall running the length of the compound was dotted with buildings tucked in its lee. The doors were closed and they appeared deserted as he skirted along the wall. He began to feel nervous because there should be more movement from the guards. It was impossible that all of them could have been taken out in the air attack and he tensed in expectation. The remnants of the vehicles provided good cover on this side but the flanking team would be out in the open if they pressed forward to take the guard's quarters. A signal acknowledged silently by the section leader held them back until they could work out why it was so quiet. Followed by two troopers he edged further into the compound staying amongst the shattered hulks for protection. Suddenly a shot rang out from the guard tower at the rear of the courtyard pinging violently off a metal canister. The source of the shot was obvious and more than one of the troopers returned fire leaving the perpetrator slumped over the parapet. The shot was a presage for violence and rapid fire erupted from windows along the length of the compound. He heard a yelp from behind as one of the troopers took a round. Looking back he was relieved to see him clutching his arm but still moving well. The thumbs up was reassuring and he knew that he would fight on. The defenders were not highly skilled. Occasionally the barrel of an AK47 popped out of a window before the firer dropped back out of sight. There was a scream from one building as one shooter was silenced but the bulk of the fire was coming from the main quarters. They had discussed the preferred response to resistance during the main briefing and it came as no surprise as he heard the low whump of a light anti tank weapon from behind him as the round streaked across the yard hitting the guard's quarters, ripping the side of the building apart and destroying the wall. As the dust settled, a few survivors tried to withdraw to the safety of the main building but were quickly cut down in the crossfire. He signalled for his team to cease fire and all went quiet again.

With the resistance quelled for now, they edged closer to the main doors of the two storey building at the end of the compound where they hoped their goal lay. He silently praised the skill of the crews in the Buccaneers who had dropped the weapons precisely on target. The main door was gone and the gaping hole led directly into the main corridor which stretched out of sight inside. He hoped that the intelligence was correct because anyone who had occupied the front rooms would be dead. If the blast had not got them the concussion from the bombs would have been terminal. The partition walls had gone and shattered brickwork marked their former position. A guard appeared around the side of the building and was taken out instantly before even firing a shot. Unfortunately, the resistance was not quite spent and, suddenly, a volley of heavy fire erupted from the guard tower above throwing up mini sandstorms in the dusty compound. Temporarily pinned down the team took cover. The tower was obscured from sight from his present position it was impossible to return fire. There had been nothing in the contingency plan for this situation and he began to think on his feet. His other section was still bogged down at the gate and, so far, had only been able to offer covering fire. They might have sight but the angles were bad. He grabbed the handset offered by the radio man behind him and transmitted briefly to the helicopter pilot explaining their plight. He couldn't accept that the plan might fail because of a single watch tower but he was seriously considering withdrawal as the only realistic option. As he rattled through the potential solutions the unmistakable sound of the massive transport helicopter could be heard in the background and, as it grew louder, the response became obvious. The green fuselage with its large fins and thrashing rotors appeared above the compound wall behind him and turned side on. The minigun mounted in the rear doorway opened up throwing hundreds of rounds into the watch tower and destroying the structure. Debris rained down into the courtyard below as the supports for the roof failed and it collapsed onto the occupants inside. There could be no hiding place from the savage onslaught. The attack was over in seconds and the helicopter withdrew beating its way noisily back to the landing zone.

Finally secure, the troopers moved quickly towards the shattered entrance and stepped inside past the piles of rubble. They worked swiftly down through what was left of the front rooms clearing the ground. There was no resistance. As they worked into the rear of the buildings the rooms became more recognisable and the occasional door remained on its hinges. These were unceremoniously kicked in and the rooms cleared one by one. Finally only one room remained; the one at the end of the corridor. He pushed inside and was confronted by a man wearing the distinctive headdress of Hezbollah. A single tap to the head dropped the hesitant defender. The only other occupant crouched by the back wall but as he levelled his weapon towards the stationary body instinct caused him to hold fire.

"OK, get up slowly and let me see you hands," he said in English rewarded by instant obedience.

Reeves stood up gently his hands in clear view. Having watched the guard drop he was under no illusion about whether the khaki clad trooper would shoot.

"You Reeves?"

He nodded.

"OK come on let's get out of this place. The helo pilot has to be seriously worried by now."

"I can't."

"Stop pissing about. We've come a long way to pick you up and we haven't got time for Comedy Hour. This place is littered with anti personnel bomblets and they'll start to detonate in about eight hours. No one will be moving around here for weeks after that."

"I mean it. They've implanted a device on me. If I go more than 100 yards from here my internal organs will be rearranged. It's all been explained in gory detail. I'm going nowhere unless this thing and I are separated."

"Bloody hell."

"Now listen carefully and forget me. I'm a big boy and I'll take care of myself. You need to pass this on through the intelligence officer. The plans I secured are easily found. I hid them in the Beirut Library in open view. The book where they're hidden hasn't been withdrawn for 30 years. It's a First Edition by an author called William Forsythe. The plans are tucked inside the front cover. Aisle Six on the Upper Level, it's almost at the far end of the row. You might want to get someone there soonest. They used drugs on me but as far as I know I didn't give anything away yet but time isn't on our side."

"Got it," said the trooper. "Look, are you sure you don't want to call their bluff. He could be talking absolute bollocks you know."

"Not sure I want to test that out. My best chance might be if I can persuade them to release me once they know the plans have been collected. On second thoughts we haven't exactly given them an incentive to do that have we?"

"Last chance mate. We can give it a try you know. We have a medic onboard. He could maybe try to get this device out before we lift."

"No it's too risky. Go. Get that information back to London. I'll take my chances here."

They exchanged knowing glances. The trooper silently handed over a Glock pistol before slapping Reeves on the arm. He turned and ran.

Outside the building the thumping of the heavy twin rotors was audible, although they were hidden from sight behind the tall compound walls. The trooper gave a round up call and the other members of his team emerged from doorways around the quadrangle. A single guard popped into view and was quickly felled by a single body shot. He went down hard without firing a shot. The yard was littered with the lethal bomblets and the trooper was reluctant to believe the assurances that they would be inert for another eight hours. As he threaded his way back towards the hole in the shattered compound wall he gave the evil looking munitions a wide berth. After a quick headcount as they fed through the gap he made once last check around for opposition before following the team through.

The helicopters were 100 yards away and now looked vulnerable. The tail ramps had been lowered and a single crewman was visible at each door armed with SA-80 rifles. In the side door of the nearest helicopter a heavy machine gun rotated on its pintle-mount ready to provide covering fire if anyone followed. The small team split with each section running for their own helicopter. As soon as they had stumbled aboard the sound of the engines picked up and the rotors began to beat furiously kicking up dust and debris as the enormous machines lifted inducing a temporary "brown-out".

Unseen by the crews, the ZSU 23-4 had pulled up alongside a small grove of olive trees and rocked to a halt on its tracks. The sleek turret of the gun system rotated and the four barrels depressed towards the horizon, the circular radar dish following the motion. Inside the hull the crew were chattering animatedly.

The pilot in the right hand seat transitioned from the hover and the Chinook began to move forward across the ground its nose still pointing downwards as it picked up speed. The navigator in the left hand seat was looking at his map and passed the initial heading towards the exit gate on the coast. They had been airborne only seconds when the tell tale rattle of the RWR sounded.

"Rackets, J Band, 3 o'clock. Mud Zulu!"

It was unmistakably the high pitched warning of a lock from the lethal Gundish fire control radar. At this stage there were few options.

"Springbok 1 targeted, putting it down."

The transmission was picked up by everyone on the tactical frequency. He dumped the collective, pulled the stick back and the helicopter slowed to a walking pace instantly. No evasive tactics would have been effective against the lethal fire from the AAA system and he had not even considered it. The only hope for survival was to land and hope the system would be unable to engage at such a low level. Fortuitously, the two Chinooks settled quickly into a shallow ravine as the tracer rounds from the 23mm cannon slashed harmlessly above the rotor heads. The tactic had worked; so far. Looking over, he saw his number 2 touchdown, unharmed, just yards away.

"The Buccaneers have egressed but they're out of weapons anyway. This is not looking good."

"I did a tour on Phantoms," replied the helicopter navigator. "They're carrying Suu-23 gun pods and they have a secondary air-to-ground strafe role. We could call the escort in and see if they can lay down some covering fire while we get clear. They're holding just off the coast. It wouldn't take more than a few minutes to get here."

"Bloody hell, a guns pass against a AAA system. Not great odds mate."

"I hear you but unless someone does something to that ZSU we're toast."

"Take your point. Check with the team leader and see if any of his guys is a FAC. The crews will need all the help they can get. If they can brief them on the problem we might just get out of here."

The navigator released his seat harness and stepped back into the rear cabin. He worked across towards the team leader who was strapped into the metal and canvas parachute seats. A hurried conversation followed as he shouted to make himself heard over the clatter of the rotors. The leader beckoned to another trooper who unstrapped and joined them. More words were exchanged and a few nods before the trooper moved urgently back to his seat and began to assemble his kit. The navigator gestured to the loadmaster and the ramp began to lower once more. Fumbling with his weapon and a radio pack the SAS trooper took one final look towards his leader, gave a thumbs up and ran from the cabin. Once clear of the thumping rotors he began to work his way back up the shallow incline towards the crest of the hill.

"I need to get on the secure radio," the leader shouted to the navigator. "I picked up information in there that needs to get back to London. If there's any doubt that we'll get out of here I need to break radio silence."

The navigator began to protest.

"Sorry mate but if you knew what I now know you'd understand why."

He unstrapped and pulled the satellite radio out from under the seat. Removing the canvas flap he flipped open the lid and fired up the small device pulling on a small headset. Lights winked on as he played with a few switches to synchronise the cryptographic key. With the indications showing to his satisfaction he hit the transmit button and made the call.

"Olympus, Olympus this is Trooper, how do you read, over?"

The frequency was quiet and, initially, only background static filled the headset.

"Olympus, Olympus this is Trooper how do you read, over?"

"Trooper this is Olympus, loud and clear, pass your message."

He began to speak relaying the vital message which would initiate a carefully planned series of events.

*

In the operations room at the summit of Troodos the operator monitoring the air defence nets had been relaxing. His own frequencies had been quiet since the earlier flurry of activity. He switched over to the Israeli frequency hoping for something to break the rapid onslaught of tedium. He was rewarded. Although the actual scramble instructions had been passed unheard by landline the tell tale chatter of a scramble was unmistakeable.

He slewed the direction finder around fixing it to the transmission and the bearing confirmed his assessment. The vector pointed directly towards Tel Nof airbase at Rehovot near Tel Aviv where F-15 fighters held alert. He listened intently as the fighters called for takeoff clearance and headed northwest. As they chopped across to the GCI frequency he followed; the silent sentinel. The heading the pilots were given tied in and would position them in the vicinity of the fighter holding orbit off the coast. It was too close for comfort and he hit the mini comms button to the Master Controller in the main operations room yet again. Introductions were superfluous as the tell tale on the console showed exactly where the call was originating.

"Israeli Q airborne heading for the operational area. Airborne at 35 with a pair. Climbing to Flight Level 150."

"Copied, time to run?"

"Hard to say but 15 minutes maximum."

"Roger that, I think we'll give the guys some extra help just in case."

He turned to his telebrief box on the console pleased to interrupt the incessant metronome if only for a few minutes.

"Akrotiri, Olympus alert QRA."

"Hawk 1 and 2."

"Hawk 1 and 2, vector 120, climb Flight Level 150, when airborne contact Olympus on Fighter Stud 024, scramble, scramble, scramble acknowledge."

There was silence and the controller knew that his action would have started the predictable chain of events at the base on the coast below. Already aircrew and groundcrew would be rushing towards the waiting jets. It would be some seconds yet before the check in. The heading would send them directly into the mêlée.

*

"Mud 7, 8 o'clock!"

The call heightened the already intense concentration within the Buccaneer formation and eyes turned in the direction of the threat. They had almost made it back to the coast as the call was made. An ominous puff of smoke rose from amongst the olive trees and a snaking smoke trail was already visible in the sky some miles behind. The action lay with the navigator who had sighted the missile shot and unless his actions were absolutely perfect there could be only one outcome. As he glanced down at the airspeed indicator the words of the intelligence officer delivered in the calm of the briefing room just hours ago were firmly in his mind. The airspeed indicator showed 600 knots and, if the expert was correct, that should be enough to outrun the missile. He looked back reacquiring the smoke trail. Somehow sitting idly by and hoping didn't seem the best plan of action at this precise moment. A call for more speed would only make the engines hotter and more attractive to the missile. For now he could only guess whether it had been fired at his own aircraft or his wingman. It would only be a few seconds later in the endgame when that would become obvious. He made the only choice which was open to him.

"Counter port, counter port, Go!"

A turn towards the incoming rocket would present the flat topsides planform of the Buccaneer towards the threat. Although the engines were mounted along the sides of the fuselage, the exhausts on which the missile would be homing were buried in the ironwork of the airframe. Viewed from behind the round exhaust cans would be an attractive focus for the tiny missile infra-red seeker head. As the Buccaneers reefed into a hard turn the exhausts were momentarily shielded, at least to some extent, making it much harder for the missile to track its prey. He could only hope that the pilots were not holding the high engine settings once the manoeuvre was initiated or the jetpipes would become an even more attractive target.

"Chill. Flares!"

The vital reminder prompted more defensive reactions within the formation. As the navigator watched the corkscrew smoke trail, the few seconds it took to close the distance from its firing point stretched into hours. Or so it seemed. With events in slow motion, he punched the dispense button on the cockpit console releasing a sequence of infra red decoy flares into the airflow behind the jet. Jettisoned from their dispenser the small pyrotechnics bloomed rapidly, the temperature rising to an incandescent crescendo in milliseconds. The rate at which they deployed had been carefully calculated by analysts and was designed to confuse the inbound seeker. By design and with a little luck, the combination of tactics and technology would keep them alive. Decision made, the navigator could only watch as the

missile homed inexorably towards his own jet. If he had made
the wrong call the outcome would be obvious within seconds;
and he would be the victim.

The Hezbollah fighter on the ground had seen the receding
target and, harried by Israeli jets for days, had wanted
retribution. Twisting the thermal battery on the gripstock he had
fired up the missiles electronic circuits. Tracking the jet he had
squeezed the trigger uncaging the seeker head. With a confidence
tone ringing in his ears he had pulled harder and was rewarded
with a bang as the eject motor had fired. The "Grail" missile had
popped out of the four foot long launch tube persuaded by the
shot of propellant to fly. At a range of only six feet from the
gunner the sustain motor had fired speeding it rapidly away. The
two forward steering fins on the missile unfolded closely
followed by the four tail fins giving the missile a semblance of
stability. As it began its short flight to the target the electronic
brain of the missile began sending commands to the autopilot
tracking the hot spot of the target against which it had been
launched. The complex seeker tracked the target and, as it drifted
away from the boresight, tiny corrections were fed to the
missile's guidance vanes bringing it back to the centreline. The
corrections generated the distinctive corkscrew flight path visible
to the Buccaneer crews. To its tiny electronic brain the bright
spot of heat was the only thing in its universe. Suddenly a second
hotspot, far brighter and more attractive than the original
appeared and its sensor had a choice. A third even more
attractive option presented itself and the seeker deviated from its
course towards the new target. Its small 1 Kg warhead was
designed to explode on contact so in reality it was a "hittile". The
self-destruct mechanism had been armed as the rocket had left
its launch tube and would destroy the missile after about 15
seconds to prevent it hitting the ground if it should miss the
target. As its course was seduced by the flares it would never
make that vital contact with the fleeing Buccaneer and it

eventually passed harmlessly by.

In the cockpit the relief was short lived. Life continued a pace at 600 knots and the celebration was brief.

"I guess we can assume that wasn't an SA-14 Gremlin then," said the navigator his pulse returning to a slightly more normal level.

"Thank goodness for small mercies," his pilot replied grimly. He hit the transmit button simultaneously.

"Ninety starboard, Go," he called to his wingman bringing the formation back onto the egress heading. He pushed the stick forward forcing the bomber even closer to the ground.

*

A short distance from the compound, the gunner in the Shilka depressed the barrels to full deflection but it would not go lower than the horizon. When the designers had configured the system no one had thought to include a setting lower than level. It was designed to shoot aircraft and, at worst a ground target at ground level. He slapped the metalwork in frustration. All they could do was wait and hope the helicopter crews were stupid enough to get airborne and try to run.

*

"Buzzard this is Springbok 1."

"Springbok 1, Buzzard go ahead."

Buzzard, Springbok we've got a problem. Just lifted and we've been pinned down by a Mud Zulu. Both cabs are on the ground, due west of the compound by three miles. Requesting a strafe pass on the Mud Zulu; soonest."

"Springbok, Buzzard stand by."

In the Phantom cockpit there was a momentary silence.

"Bloody hell Boss, said his navigator. "The odds are not good against a ZSU 23-4. That's pretty much a suicide mission. We don't have an active jammer just chaff in the ALE40 dispenser."

"I know, old son but what odds do those guys on the ground have at the minute? Stand by, transmitting."

"Springbok, Buzzard, roger, you've got it. Heading in for the IP now and four minutes to target. Give me the details."

"Roger Buzzard thanks, I owe you! Stand by for callsign "Trooper" on this frequency. He'll give you target info."

"Roger Springbok, stand by, going off frequency for one. Buzzard 2, Stud 20, Stud 20, Go!"

The Phantoms chopped across to the tactical chat frequency.

"Buzzard check."

"Two"

"Loud and clear. OK here's the plan."

*

The trooper dragged himself to the top of the low rise and peered back towards the compound. Hitching his pack from his back he pulled out his binoculars and stared down at the scene below. There was little activity around the compound yard but with the bomblets strewn everywhere that was perhaps no surprise. The intact vehicle sitting adjacent to the MT building had not moved and the points where the bombs had fallen were still smoking, although the piles of rubble were a bigger to recent events. There had been little detail in the rushed briefing in the back of the Chinook. All he knew was that something or someone had directed fire at the helicopters as they had started their exfiltration. He had heard the rounds pass close over the top even above the noise of the engines and suspected a heavy calibre weapon. He scanned the surrounding area. There was nothing out in the open. He trained the glasses on a small olive grove and there it was. A ZSU 23-4 Shilka next to the tree line it's green hull camouflaged well against the trees. From the air against the bright sand it would stand out like the proverbial sore thumb. Stationary and with little sign of any activity the barrels had been lowered to the level position as if it was ready to move. It had to be the source of the attack. He pulled out his UHF combat radio.

*

"How long since you did air-to-ground strafe in the Phantom?"

"Never, Boss. Last time was in a Hawk three years ago," Razor replied.

There was a momentary pause as the enormity of the task sank in. An unplanned attack against a highly effective air defence system by a pilot with no experience in the profile. Anderson hit the transmit button.

"OK, it's the same principle, listen in. Set in 36 mils depression and select air-to-ground fixed on the LCOSS. We'll make it a shallow angle pass at 450 knots using a 10 degree dive angle. Open fire at 2500 feet, cease fire at 2000 feet and pull out at 1000 feet at the VERY latest. The bullet time of flight is less than a second. Understood?"

"Got it Boss."

In the back seat Flash groaned.

"When we're back on frequency listen out for the target details," replied the Boss. "It sounds like it's a ZSU so watch that RWR Flash. If you get even a sniff of a lock, counter and pop chaff. We'll run in from the briefed coast-in point but pass straight overhead the airfield at 100 feet. That'll keep any helos on the ground for a few minutes at least. Once we hit the IP, orbit and drop back into one mile trail for your pass. I'll hit it first. Best of luck."

The briefing had been delivered as they flashed towards the target at 600 knots. The groans from the back seat increased in intensity. What could possibly go wrong? They switched back to the operations frequency and checked in.

"Buzzard back on frequency and inbound," he called. "Standing by for control."

"Buzzard this is Trooper, how me?"

"Loud and clear Trooper. Standing by for target details."

As the crews were assimilating the forward air control briefing Rene Mouawad airfield appeared in the front quadrant of the canopy. Tightening the battle formation the leader aimed directly at the air traffic control tower which stood out prominently against the otherwise flat surroundings. Razor's eyes were fixed on his leader remaining just above his height, his radio altimeter bugged at about 90 feet. If the tell-tale warning went off he would ease up. A glance down at the vital instrument showed he was just 100 feet above the ground. As they flashed across the airfield boundary, one helicopter pilot had chosen an inopportune moment to start up, it's rotors turning lazily. He cranked the stick hard over taking his flight path directly overhead giving a clear message to the pilot below. In his peripheral vision he saw the planform of the lead Phantom as it pulled hard towards and passed close to the control tower. He matched the turn keeping his distance in a loose trail formation.

"Try to see what's on the ground Flash. They'll want to know at the debrief!"

"We're clean," was the only response from his back-seater, eyes glued to the RWR. The instrument was thankfully silent. The radio burst into life again, the forward air controller relaying the final details for the attack.

"Buzzard, I have one target. From the compound it bears 270 range two miles. Target in the open and stationary. Road from the compound passes olive grove. Target is south of the grove by 200 yards."

"Buzzard inbound, overhead in two minutes."

"Roger, call me visual on the target, clear hot."

"Clear hot, Buzzard acknowledged."

"Thirty seconds," Razor heard from the lead. The needles on the navigation kit pointed doggedly to the initial point and as they reversed back onto track pointing once again towards the compound. The needles rotated violently as Flash punched in the new target position quickly interpreting the forward air controller's information. The speed touched 600 knots and Razor idly hoped the Boss would pull it back for the guns pass. Tactically, speed was life but for this one-off shot, too much speed might be a bad thing. A little thinking time would be preferable. The IP flashed past on the left and Razor cranked into another gut wrenching turn as the miles tracked down rapidly as they closed on the target. The G came on and he grunted to stave off the dimming of his vision, straining to hold his jet at 100 feet above the ground. The speed washed off as he carried on the turn opening up some separation on his leader. After a full 360 degrees he rolled out, once again directly overhead the IP and followed his leader towards the target. If the Triple A was going to respond now would be the time. He tensed.

"Buzzard Tally Ho!"

If the Boss could see it why couldn't he? Where the hell was it? There; on the edge of the olive grove with its barrels depressed. Thank God for small mercies. It was tiny and hard to see against the scrubland.

Up ahead the lead Phantom popped up from the safety of low level climbing to the apex of the strafe pass and at 2000 feet it pushed over and entered a shallow dive. In the front cockpit Paul Anderson brought the pipper onto the anti-aircraft gun which had appeared exactly where the forward air controller had predicted. His tracking was good and the altimeter began to unwind as he set up the shallow dive walking the pipper onto the tiny artillery piece. It was a while since he'd strafed but it was like riding a bike. The pipper was tracking perfectly when, suddenly, he detected a belch of smoke from rear of the vehicle. The black cloud enveloped the rear of the tank chassis just as he was about to open fire leaving too little time to correct the aim but he squeezed the trigger anyway. The gun pod erupted in a shower of shells and smoke, dumping spent cartridges overboard as the rounds sped earthwards. The Shilka lurched forward and, as it picked up speed, it was just enough to spoil the aim and the rounds struck harmlessly behind the trundling vehicle. As the rounds impacted behind, the driver reefed hard around rotating on one track pulling to an immediate halt.

"Miss. Shot fell in the target's 6 o'clock, close," called the forward air controller his frustration evident even over the static of the radio channel. As the Phantom rotated into its recovery manoeuvre the Boss cursed under his breath. Did he have enough rounds for a second pass?

In the back of the trailing Phantom, Flash continued his methodical commentary talking his pilot into a visual contact on the compound. They had stared at the imagery during the briefing little thinking they would see it in the flesh.

"Contact; it's slightly right about three miles," said his pilot.

OK, come left from that and look for the track out to the olive grove. It should be on the tree line."

"Got it, TALLY," he shouted as the hull of the AAA piece emerged from the background. "It's moved! It's well away from the tree line now but stationary. Pulling up. Camera's going on."

He flicked the gunsight camera switch and the film began to run, recording the pass. The altimeter wound up rapidly hitting the check height at the apex before he pushed the stick forward inducing momentary negative G. Shit and corruption flew up from the cockpit floor as weightlessness persuaded the flotsam and jetsam to congregate in the top of the canopy. Distracted, Razor held the manoeuvre returning to positive G as they settled into the final pass; the debris returning to its former home on the cockpit floor. Flash returned his attention to the RWR. If the ZSU crew was going to fight back now would be the time. The tiny scope was silent. In the front Razor checked his angle and rate of descent before transferring his attention back to the gunsight reticule. Picking up his references, he began to walk the pipper forward moving it onto the still barely visible target.

"Give me heights Flash."

"1800 feet ....1500 feet," his back seater intoned, the readings from the altimeter reducing rapidly. "1000 feet". . . . .

He should be opening fire but he held off for just that bit longer. There is was, the picture he was waiting for; pipper buried on the vehicle. He squeezed the trigger rewarded with a satisfying buzz as the gun pod emptied its rounds towards the stationary target. He rotated snatching 4G at the bottom of the dive and inched clear of the ground kicking up debris as the afterburners scorched the scrubland below. As the high explosive rounds struck the ground causing a massive sandstorm around the vehicle it temporarily disappeared from view. Passing over the target, still concentrating hard on the recovery manoeuvre there was a huge whoop from the back cockpit. The radio altimeter read less than 50 feet and the warning horn, which had been firing out its strident alert for some seconds, finally registered. It had been a very late burst. The results, however, were spectacular.

"Delta Hotel me old mate! It's a smoker!"

On the ground the high explosive rounds ripped through the thin armour plate entering the crew compartment and striking the ammunition trays. The incendiary in the 20mm shells set off a chain reaction and, as a fire began to rage, the high explosive shells which had been intended for the British helicopters began to cook off. The explosions within the confined compartment killed the crew instantly. The Phantom flew a wide arcing wingover pulling hard back towards the ground and reversing its heading back towards the coast. Up ahead the leader had jinked across his flight path putting them back into battle formation for the egress.

*

The trooper watched the smoke rising from the stricken Shilka and smiled. Not bad for an ad hoc effort. Throwing his gear back into the bag he stood up ready to sprint back down the hill to the helicopters. He unmasked for only seconds when the bullet hit. A sniper on the compound wall needed just a few seconds for the shot and took the opportunity. The round struck his left shoulder ripping the muscles and spinning him to the ground. The pain didn't start immediately but he knew it would not be long before the adrenalin wore off and he would be immobilised. Shock was the killer in this situation. It was a long run back to the safety of the helicopter but at least it was all downhill. More adrenalin kicked in as he dragged the pack with the radio and his weapon onto his good shoulder and set off at a trot.

The loadmaster watched the trooper run down the hill, stumbling as he came. He looked rattled and was making slow progress clutching his arm. The Bergen on his back fell from his shoulder as he stumbled yet again. Within 50 yards of the Chinook he finally collapsed and fell face down. Something was amiss and the loadie thumbed his intercom button giving a quick call to the cockpit before unclipping his harness and microphone lead and sprinting from the rear ramp. As he approached the prone figure he could see the exit wound on the back of the battledress tunic and all was obvious. It had been a superhuman effort to make it this far with those injuries.

"Come on mate, let's get you back onboard," he shouted above the beat of the rotors pulling the injured man to his feet and looping his arm over his shoulder. He took up the weight but even though the trooper was as strong as an ox the run down the hill with his life blood rapidly leaking away had taken it out of him. The last few feet to the ramp were a struggle and the loadie was expecting a response from the defenders at any time. He couldn't know that there was no movement in the compound and that the bomblets would guarantee that there would be no activity for weeks. Over the other side of the hill the ZSU 23-4 was a smoking wreck and in no shape to threaten their departure. As he struggled, other members of the team emerged from the shadows of the cabin and helped drag the injured man over the ramp.

In the cockpit, the pilots were tense and itching to lift. The minute the call came from the loadmaster the captain screwed the collective lever and the helicopter rose just clear of the ground. It transitioned to forward flight throwing up clouds of sand and debris which shielded it during the vulnerable moments. Within seconds the pair of Chinooks emerged from the "brown out" moving swiftly down the gulley, the whoomp of the massive pairs of rotors loud in the morning air. Inside, the troopers ranged down the side of the cabin were tense expecting the thump of explosive rounds from the ZSU at any time. As the small force made its escape towards the coast, the Phantoms flew top-cover above flying tight cross turns ahead of the track clearing the way. In each Phantom cockpit four sets of eyes scanned the countryside looking for further trouble but expecting little.

In the rear of the lead Chinook a medic frantically cut off the injured trooper's battledress tunic to treat the bullet wound in his shoulder. Once he peeled back the blood soaked material he realised that it was not a simple flesh wound. The entry wound was small but the bullet had passed very close to his lung causing damage that would only be apparent once a surgeon opened him up. As the blood loss slowed he began to hope that it had missed the vital arteries but it didn't look good. At this point, the medic could not even feel confident that the man would survive the short trip back to the hospital at Akrotiri. He shone a pencil torch into his pupils and there was a reassuring response but the man's skin was deathly pale and he began to hyperventilate. He gave him a shot of morphine and marked his forehead. It would be touch and go but at least the flight would be, mercifully, short.

*

"Hawk 1 and 2."

"Olympus, Hawk 1 and 2 on frequency."

"Hawk 1 and 2 Olympus, loud and clear, vector 140 and maintain current level."

"Hawk, steady 140."

The QRA Phantoms closed rapidly on the returning formation but whether their arrival would be welcome was moot.

"Hawk, request instructions," called a nervous lead navigator, a mass of radar contacts appearing on his scope. He was about to call the contacts when the radio cut in.

"Hawk, anchor port present position."

"Anchor port, Hawk."

Tactically, it was suicide and the frustration in the acknowledgement was tangible despite the distortion of the Phantom radio as the cockpits filled with expletives, the impact of the instructions dawning on the crews. The Phantoms turned their tails on a confused air situation.

*

The pair of Israeli F-15s headed north along the coastline. Unbeknown to the controller on Mount Olympus their sortie was not in response to the attack on the compound and events further north had yet to filter through. They had been vectored towards the southern Lebanese border to conduct a routine presence run. As the ground forces had withdrawn some months earlier there had been concerns in Tel Aviv that Syrian air forces would harry the convoys. The omni-present F-15s would deter any thoughts of retribution. In a routine clearing manoeuvre, the leader dropped a wing and spotted the low level formation in his 2 o'clock crossing from right to left on the deck. The dark grey fighters merged well against the sea background and it had been a chance pick up. With such a high crossing angle it would have been almost impossible to detect them on radar and the visual pickup had been luck rather than judgement.

"Come up tactical," he called to his wingman. Deselecting transmit on the main radio box he selected the standby radio and transmitted on his second radio box. "Tally 2 o'clock low, follow me down."

He reselected the main radio and transmitted again

"Panther visual. One contact bearing 030 investigating. I'll call you back in two minutes."

As the pair rolled over onto their backs and pulled earthwards the radio call caused panic in the Israeli Air Defence Operations Centre. Rapid cross-checking confirmed that the contact correlated with the track which had been declared "protected". There was a block on any intercept.

"Negative Panther, contact is friendly, haul off."

His instruction was met with silence. The F-15s had already dropped below radio coverage so far from the communications transmitter.

"Panther this is Helmsman, check. Panther, check."

The increasingly urgent calls were futile. There was no reply.

"Panther you are not, repeat not, cleared to engage, respond."

Still no reply. The controller swore and hit the minicomms button to the Air Defence Commander.

The pair of Eagles dropped rapidly keeping the low level formation in sight. The leader counted off the pairs flying in a tactical spread about a mile apart. The lead pair was followed by a second pair about three miles behind. He dropped his right wing followed by the left checking beneath the belly of the fighter as they descended spotting yet another pair a further three miles behind, making six. He couldn't recognise the type but they were low and fast. His wingman had dropped into fighting wing in the descent and, loading up, he manoeuvred to drop in astern the rear pair. As he passed 2000 feet in the descent, he realised he had been spotted as the trailing pair reacted. As the low flying bombers pulled hard towards him he recognised the unfamiliar planform of a British Buccaneer.

*

"Hawk 1 and 2, Olympus, vector 140, maintain flight level 150. You have contacts to the south east range 15. Interrogate but do not, repeat not engage, acknowledge."

"Hawk 1 and 2, roger, interrogate."

The pair of Phantoms immediately cross-turned heading back towards the south east. In the cockpits the reasons for the instructions were unfathomable but the controllers tone had made it clear that all was not normal. The timings fitted with the recovery of the operational mission and, if the formation had been tapped on the way in to the target, trigger fingers would be twitching. Not only were Phantoms embedded but each Buccaneer carried a self-defence Sidewinder. For once, staying clear might be the wise option. The wings of each fighter dropped left and right checking the airspace below looking for the first elusive visual contact, hostile or friendly. At this stage either friend or enemy might be unhappy to see them.

*

In the cockpit of Jackal 5 the navigator had almost begun to relax as the slight chop on the wave tops flashed past the cockpit just feet below. As he craned his head around scanning the horizon he caught the familiar aberration in his peripheral vision as the fighter dropped into his 6 o'clock. There was no time for hesitation; the move looked aggressive.

Jackal 5 and 6, counter port, counter port, Go!"

The flash from the jet, which he now recognised as an F-15, could have been anything; a glint from the Sun on the canopy, a wing vortex in the humid air or a puff of afterburner plume but he mistook it for a missile firing.

"Missile launch, missile break, missile break," he screamed. He hit the flare dispense button for a second time in a matter of milliseconds.

The formation responded without hesitation and, in unison, the pair reefed into the hard turn as the defensive chaff and flares dispensed into the airflow behind the jets. As the G forces increased topping 7G his peripheral vision began to fade and he "greyed out", his tense stomach muscles willing his body to cooperate. That was the last thing he needed at this minute and the straining slowly took effect and his vision cleared slightly. As the G forces continued there was a muffled thump from below the jet which sounded as if they had hit the slipstream from the wingman but that was impossible. The other Buccaneer was well through the turn and they had already crossed flight paths. The sudden blaring of the central warning system was an unwelcome addition to the mix. The master caution caption flashed urgently and the front seater muttered. Never a good sign.

"Hyd. failure on the left side easing off," he heard as the G relaxed. "Hydraulic pressure has gone. Steadying up."

The Buccaneer returned to straight and level flight as the pilot wrestled the now sluggish controls checking the Christmas tree of captions which had appeared on the telelight panel.

"The pressure on the right is fluctuating. This looks bad. Tighten your straps."

The navigator needed no further warning. He pulled the lap

straps tight and locked the go forward lever pinning him to the Martin Baker seat. His head returned square on his shoulders and he braced ready for the unthinkable. They had gone from calm to crisis in seconds. Who the hell was in the other jet that had fired on them? In the front the pilot flicked a few switches running through his "bold face" drills to reconfigure the systems. What neither could know was that the small explosive device planted on the hydraulic lines by the agent at Akrotiri a few days ago had detonated wreaking havoc. Although small, it had ripped out hydraulic pipes and damaged a compressor leaking the precious hydraulic fluid overboard. The blades had separated and flown through the compressor case causing further catastrophic damage to the main hydraulic system and a number of ancillary systems alongside. Most importantly, the explosion had damaged the turbine case of the right engine which ruptured with a massive bang. The airframe shook inducing a wallowing roll causing the pilot to fight the controls even more.

"I'm losing it. Eject, eject, eject," called the pilot immediately pulling his seat pan handle initiating the ejection sequence which would fire the rocket cartridges on the seats and throw them, within seconds, from the stricken jet.

As he slotted in behind the trailing pair, the F-15 leader matched the defensive break. They were not Syrian and he had no argument with them. He flicked the radio to Guard and keyed the transmit switch Intending to call a disengagement he watched in fascinated detachment as one of the Buccaneers levelled out and lurched alarmingly. Within seconds the canopy separated followed by an urgent and slightly panicked transmission on the distress frequency.

"Jackal Lead this is Jackal 6 on Guard, Jackal 5 has just ejected!"

"Say again."

"Jackal Lead, Jackal 6, Jackal 5 is down!"

In the leader's cockpit there was a momentary silence as he digested the information. In the Israeli E-2C Hawkeye above, the call on Guard triggered an immediate response.

"All stations, all stations, aircraft down, alert SAROPS! Stand by for position."

The Israeli pilot responded without hesitation.

"All stations, Panther is on station, assuming scene of search commander."

The Israeli F-15 began a gentle orbit around the site where the airframe had plunged into the water, although already the signs of its terminal dive were gone and the ocean swell resumed its gentle pattern. Ejecting so low the Buccaneer aircrew had spent little time in their parachutes; mere seconds. As he watched, the tri-coloured parachutes settled on the surface of the water a stark contrast to the deep blue. Close by, the aircrew were inflating bright dayglo dinghies and climbing aboard. He waggled the wings in an exaggerated manner to make sure they knew he had seen them. He could have no idea of the accusations being levelled at him from the sea below.

Aboard the leading Chinook the calls posed a dilemma. With a cabin packed full of special forces troopers the pilot's gut feeling was to press for home but one situation countermanded any such thoughts and that was a distress call. It was the one call that could never be ignore nor would he expect anyone else to do so if he was the one in distress. He transmitted.

"Olympus this is Springbok 1, diverting Springbok 2 for SAROPS recovery. Request vector from Springbok 2 to the crash site."

In the overhead the pair of Phantoms orbited, watching events, unable to influence the situation.

*

Aboard the USS Mount Whitney the Admiral was concerned. The details of this operation had come in well in advance over SIPRNET, the classified communications network. He wasn't sure of the source nor did he much care but it had been a particularly comprehensive briefing. His overriding concern was for the safety of the vessels under his command and that would drive his actions. With his force approaching the top end of their area of operations and so close to the Lebanese coast he felt most vulnerable. Not only was he now in range of Syrian fast jets but he was also within range of attack helicopters. Recent reports had suggested that they could be fitted with Soviet anti-shipping missiles. The Kh-29 known to NATO as the AS-14 'Kedge' had a range of nearly 20 miles and, with its laser, infrared, active radar or TV guidance sensors, it was difficult to design a guaranteed countermeasure against it. Although it was normally carried by their tactical aircraft and designed for use against battlefield targets it could easily be adapted against ships. He had seen pictures of it loaded onto a Mil 24 Hind gunship. Pictures were never definitive and just hanging a weapon didn't mean it could be fired but he didn't intend to allow an attack helicopter to get close enough to the force to try.

The Carrier Air Wing Boss aboard USS John F Kennedy had been holding his alert F-14 Tomcats on a high readiness state all day. As the British operation had progressed he had brought them up to "Alert 5" status with the crews on deck in the cockpits ready to launch. It would take one simple command to bring the carrier into wind and to get them airborne. Although he could make that call himself his regular discussions with the Admiral suggested that it might be prudent to defer to the senior officer in this instance. As a precaution he brought the A-6 Intruder tanker up to cockpit readiness. If they did launch he wanted to be able to keep them airborne.

The displays around the operations room aboard USS John F Kennedy would not have been out of place aboard the Starship Enterprise. Vast state-of-the-art colour graphic displays offered instant situation awareness to a team of warfare officers huddled over their consoles. Integrated from a variety of sources any ship, tank or plane which moved within a 200 mile radius of the task force could be displayed. Each expert monitored part of the diverse battlespace above and below the water. The anti-air-warfare officer had been watching the progress of the Brit combined air operation with interest. He had watched the force assemble off the Cyprus coast, the IFF codes marking a friendly mission. A number of slower tracks which he assumed were helicopters had headed out first, quickly overhauled by the faster jets. As the force had approached the Syrian coast a flight of Migs had intervened and there had been some type of engagement. That fewer tracks returned to Syria gave him a certain amount of satisfaction and he had begun to feel a little frustrated that they were not involved. Part of the force had held off the coast while the rest pressed inland. Whatever target they had hit must have been close to the shoreline because they had been overland for only a short time. Already the lead elements were "feet wet" and on their way home. For now, they had been warned off but the attack may be just the excuse the Syrians needed to take a tilt at the fleet. If they did he was ready. The warning order had not mentioned helicopters only that a bombing mission was planned against a terrorist compound. He was happy with that idea and providing they followed the pre-briefed track he had no interest in their mission other than to provide air cover if needed. What he did not understand was why the helicopters were involved. There had been no mention of an insertion team so someone, somewhere was not telling the full story. His requests for information had so far gone unanswered and at this stage would probably remain so. He suspected that some quiet diplomatic questioning would be the only way that those answers would ever surface. Having done a tour in London he knew just which buttons to press when this all died down.

He had not been surprised when the Israelis launched their QRA jets but he had been stunned when they vectored towards the returning bombers. As a former fighter pilot he could only imagine what would go on in the cockpits of the bombers as the fighters sniffed around. He had massive respect for the skill of the Israeli pilots who succeeded against often massive odds but this action had been naive. By now the fast jets were returning on a reciprocal track, hopefully mission complete, although the combat air patrol was still anchoring just off the coast. As he stared at the display the slow-movers coasted out and picked up a heading back to Cyprus. He would keep his Alert 5 crews in the cockpits for a while longer.

At that moment the distress frequency came alive.

*

In the lead Chinook the reply was instant and, as the lead pilot looked across at his wingman, the bulky helicopter had already picked up the new heading and begun to diverge from track towards the ships. The Buccaneers had been well ahead and, given that Jackal had made the call, it had to be one of the Buccaneers which had gone down. He had no doubt that a Wessex would be scrambled from Cyprus as soon as the distress call was received but it would take some time for it to arrive. It was slow and they were still at the limits of its range. In this situation, even in the warm waters of the Mediterranean, time was critical and it would be only minutes before cold hands became useless. Unless the Buccaneer crew was able to board the small dinghies and take protection from the elements, their life expectancy might be short.

Unlike the Wessex helicopters based at Akrotiri his Chinook helicopter was not fitted with a winch system. The large

pontoons which stretched the length of the fuselage were
designed to keep the helicopter afloat for just a few minutes in
the event of a ditching but were not intended to give any
amphibious capability. Setting down on the water was out of the
question and some radical thinking would be needed. In the
cockpit of the other Chinook the same thought processes were
being played out.

"Without a winch we're going to have to take it down and try to
get them aboard through the rear ramp. It'll be a tricky
manoeuvre because our downwash will be brutal so close to the
dinghies. The Chinook is not a great platform for over water
SAR. I'll need to approach into wind and try to trap the life raft
in the wash. Once I'm in close I'll swing around and hold
position with the ramp closest to the survivors. If they can
paddle towards us we can try to pull them aboard. It's not ideal
and if it doesn't work they'll have to wait for the Wessex but I
don't have the patent on ideas. Anyone have a better plan?"

The loadie was remarkably enthusiastic given that it would be
him who would end up in the water if it came to it.

"Look if you can hover a few feet above the water I'll go in on
the end of an extended strop if I need to. Let's assume the
aircrew will have got into their dinghies so all we need is a bit of
help to get them onto the ramp. Hell, if they are smart enough
they may even be able to paddle to us and we can all stay dry."

"It's going to be some paddle against the downdraft from two
Lycoming turboshaft engines at max chat. Let's hope they're not
injured. Look, it's all we've got. Can I have everyone at the
windows and let's look for the dayglo rafts in the water. We've
got 10 miles to run."

In the cabin the loadie gestured urgently shouting at each of the
troopers in turn as they were not on intercom. The briefing
might be vital.

"OK I've got the locator beacon on Guard," said the navigator. I'm DF'ing them now............ Come right 10 degrees for the overhead."

The captain picked up the closing heading and the Chinook bore down on the crash site. As a face at every window scanned the vast emptiness of the sea it was the flight crew who made the first pick up. The small dayglo coloured rafts were bobbing on the gentle swell just a few miles ahead and the helicopter took a closing heading. As they neared a small, bright red flare shot upwards from one of the rafts and burst in the air.

The huge helicopter closed gently on the first raft, the sea beneath the fuselage a maelstrom. The downdraft was fiercest immediately beneath the massive fuselage but the airflow surging out from the immediate vicinity whipped up the wave tops into angry peaks. The pilot edged towards the life raft as the survivor pulled the dayglo canopy from his shoulders ready for a pick up. In the countless drills he had completed in training the next thing he expected was a winchman lowering down from the approaching helicopter dangling from the end of a strop. This would be his ticket to safety. This time the script was running differently. There was no winchman and in fact, no winch. The massive beast lumbered closer and the air was whipped into a frenzy. As the rotors of the Chinook thumped overhead it paused before performing a perfect pirouette in front of the startled survivor. It descended even closer to the water and stopped. Taken aback, he watched for a short time before realising that the rear ramp was wide open and camouflaged bodies beckoned to him from inside. Alongside him only hundreds of feet away the other dinghy was being battered by the downdraft the occupant cleverly still protected by the inflatable canopy. The plan became obvious and he began to row towards the Chinook using his gloved hands as paddles.

He pulled hard but seemed to be making little headway. Each

time he made a few yards the rotor wash pushed him away again. He was tiring rapidly. Just as he thought that failure was inevitable the Chinook took a gentle lurch in his direction still tail on to him. It was obvious that the pilot was unsighted as he had no view of the cockpit from this aspect. He could see the man at the edge of the ramp gesturing and he redoubled his efforts. As the Chinook edged ever closer the rotors trapped him in the downdraft and, suddenly, it was like the eye of the storm. The last yards towards the ramp were almost easy and the raft bumped alongside. Hands grabbed his shoulders and he was pulled aboard the helicopter bodily, the life raft following still attached to his lifejacket by a nylon lanyard. It bucked viciously in the airflow and threatened to pull him back into the water before being restrained by a camouflaged body that attacked it with a dinghy knife, deflating it instantly. He flopped exhausted and wet onto the cabin floor and lay still recovering his breath. The sigh of relief could be heard in Limmasol.

The note of the engines picked up as the pilot positioned the helicopter downwind for the approach to the second survivor. One down, one to go. The PLB from the remaining life raft bleeped incessantly on the Guard frequency.

The procedure should have been identical. As the Chinook closed on the second life raft the downdraft from the massive rotors again whipped up a vicious spray. A bow wave developed which eddied towards the bobbing raft but it was finally too much for the flimsy boat and the rubber flotation chamber flipped in the turbulent air dumping the hapless survivor into the water.

Without hesitation, the loadie inflated his life jacket dragged out the long length of strop from the cabin wall and launched himself from the rear ramp into the water. The reaction had been pure instinct. The intake of breath threatened to fill his mouth with salt water as he reminded himself to tell his combat search and rescue officer on the squadron that the Med was still bloody cold at this time of the year. He began to stroke easily towards the floundering body now separated from his dinghy which had drifted away and was pulling him along like a sea-bound kite. Unless he was quick the man would be towed beyond the limit of the strop. He stroked strongly towards the green-suited body whose white flying helmet stood out against the blue sea. Just a few yards short he shouted for the man to calm himself gesturing towards the shackle on the strop. This would be the tricky bit. Under tension the shackle was unyielding and he needed to put some flex into the line. This meant the survivor would need to do some of the work for him. He gestured furiously for the man to swim towards him holding up the shackle. If he could get them both connected, the life jackets should keep them afloat and the men aboard the helicopter should be able to pull them back aboard. The exhausted man seemed to catch on. The loadmaster paused momentarily realising that this guy had just survived a high speed ejection from a doomed fast jet. It hadn't been his day. As he watched the man inched slowly towards him and he redoubled his efforts.

"Unhook your lanyard," he shouted invoking an immediate response. The life raft skittered away across the wave tops released from its human anchor chain. The survivor paddled slowly back towards him and once within the final few feet the loadie was able to clip the two of them onto the shackle with one last superhuman effort. His arm shot up in the air and there was an immediate pull on the strop. The two aircrew began to slide quickly back towards the stationary helicopter and safety. Please God don't climb now he thought quietly. They struck the ramp with a harsh thump which winded both of them. After more rough handling they were, unceremoniously, eased over the deep lip and flopped onto the surface of the ramp like beached fish. The stark cabin of the Chinook had never looked better.

The lead Chinook pilot could not know that his own schedule

was about to be changed significantly. In the back of his cab the medical orderly finally accepted his predicament.

"Call the Captain mate," he said to the loadie. "If this guy doesn't get immediate help he might not make it back to Akrotiri. Where are those American boats?"

"I'll go check, hang tight."

The loadmaster ran the short length of the helicopter cabin and leaned through the gap between the seats.

"The trooper's in a bad way Boss, he's not going to make it back unless we do something. Don't the American carriers have a hospital onboard? Can we get him there quicker?"

"Bloody hell, that's a challenge; an unannounced run towards the task force. They don't take prisoners you know. I'll have to declare an emergency."

He switched to the emergency Guard frequency and hit the transmit switch, the response conditioned by years of training.

"Mayday, Mayday, Mayday, Springbok 1, Chinook helicopter, presently 10 miles off Beirut. I have taken fire and have one casualty onboard. Respond."

He had no idea of the task force commander's callsign and hoped his urgent plea would elicit a response. It was instant.

"Springbok 1, this is Mike, Zulu Three Foxtrot on Guard, you're loud and clear and identified. Squawk 1641 and vector 240. Homeplate bears 240 range 25 miles."

The Captain breathed a sigh of relief. "Homeplate" was the universal codeword for base, in this case the carrier, and he realised that in giving the urgently needed vector, the task force commander had just compromised the task force position. He could only guess at the mayhem onboard as a result. Fighters, missile systems and guns would be brought to maximum readiness and woe betide any intruder who tried to approach for the next short while.

"Jackal Lead copied, Springbok 1 diverting. I'll advise our operators. Best of luck and see you back on the ground."

The Chinook pilot swung the helicopter onto the vector and began to scan the horizon for the tell tale sign of a ship's hull. It might be a smoke trail he saw first but in the vast expanse of water anything man-made would be welcome.

"Mike, Zulu Three Foxtrot, Springbok 1, my casualty has gunshot wounds and needs urgent medical treatment. Request permission to land-on and deplane the casualty. We'd then like to lift and return to base."

"Springbok 1 approved. We'll take good care of him, buddy."

"Who said there was no special relationship with our cousins?" the captain offered to no one in particular.

A stark profile emerged which rapidly broke out as an Oliver Perry Class frigate a gentle plume of smoke drifting from the stack as it steamed northwards. That wasn't the one they wanted and would be one of the vessels in the screen protecting the capital ship. Another vast profile emerged from the haze and the navigator recognised the command and control vessel the USS Mount Whitney. Still not their goal. Within a short distance the massive bulk of the carrier popped up and the Chinook turned towards. As they closed, the vast size of the vessel became apparent. There could be no mistaking that unique profile of the JFK

"Springbok 1 visual."

"Springbok 1 contact Pri Fly on 345.25 for your arrival."

"Springbok 1 to Pri Fly, thanks Sir."

Checking in, the pilot eased up to about 100 feet and positioned slightly astern the huge vessel approaching slowly along the port side. From his position slightly above deck level the effect of the swell even on this gargantuan ship was obvious as the deck rose and fell in unison with the waves. He adjusted the power and passed over the rear fantail feeling an immediate effect on the controls. On deck, faces were upturned, surprised at the unexpected arrival. They would treat it like any routine US movement. If it had got this far the Captain wanted it on deck.

As he eased back on the power the helicopter settled slowly towards the gently rising deck and thumped firmly onto one of the deck positions marked with a huge white "H". The four wheels at each corner of the bulky fuselage compressed under the load swiftly joining the rhythm of the deck as it rose and fell. He had no idea if it was the slot allocated to him by Pri Fly but what the hell. He'd take the flak later. The minute he pulled the engines back to idle US Navy mechanics snapped shackles onto the tie downs securing the helicopter to the deck. The loadie dropped the rear ramp and the injured trooper was taken out on a stretcher.

"Looks like you guys had a tough ride!" the controller said over the radio. "You sure you don't want to shut down and let us do a once over for damage?"

It was so tempting but, with a contingent of SAS troopers in the cabin, discretion overruled airmanship this time.

"Negative Sir but thanks, we need to get home for debrief."

"Understood, clear lift when ready and Homeplate bears 300 range 60, God speed Sir."

Beneath the helicopter the mechanic unhitched the shackles and emerged from beneath offering a supportive thumbs up. Acknowledging, he rotated the collective lever and the helicopter jumped instantly clear as the deck dropped away on yet another downward swell. Clear of the deck they turned onto the heading offered by the controller as the navigator dialled up Akrotiri TACAN. At this range it might be a few more miles before the beacon locked on but it should be plain sailing from here. He was sure that, despite the fact the trooper would receive the best treatment in this part of the world, everyone on the helicopter felt a nervous anxiety at his fate. Hopefully they would see him soon.

As events unfolded, not only were the operators in the listening post on Troodos capturing every move but operators poring over electronic receivers on the Israeli and Syrian coasts had listened equally closely. Scribbled notes were already winging their way to operational headquarters in each country.

DAVID GLEDHILL

CHAPTER 25

Off the Lebanese Coast.

Aboard the converted trawler in the waters off Tripoli the pace had been relentless but had reached a crazy peak within the last hour. Bristling with aerials this boat would be hard pressed to land a decent catch. With its squat and ugly lines, it served the Soviet Navy as an AGI, short for "Auxiliary General Intelligence" and, packed with sensitive listening devices, it was the front line of the intelligence war. Tracking the 6th Fleet for weeks it had been holding a respectful distance. It had no need to approach too closely as its radio receivers, which scanned the whole of the electronic spectrum, could capture every transmission from a safe distance. Occasionally the Captain was allowed a little game of cat and mouse by his masters in The Kremlin. If he manoeuvred into the path of the aircraft carrier, the rules of the sea said that the larger vessel should give way, even if it was engaged in launching or recovering aircraft at the time. It was a good way of relieving boredom but had to be used sparingly. The Americans normally responded with high speed flypasts in the early hours which played havoc with the sensitive receivers onboard the AGI. Emissions security was good among the naval vessels in the area and most communications which radiated from the task force were encrypted. Out here on the high seas they were certainly invulnerable to decoding and, whether the regiments of analysts back in Russia could crack the traffic was another matter. Despite the undoubted prowess there were some things that took the power of a supercomputer to crack and the embryonic 286 computers, whilst innovative, were hardly up to the task. What they hoped for was the odd snippet of hot intelligence transmitted openly on a tactical frequency as the Fleet exercised. It was this type of information which would be of interest to their masters back in Moscow. Just small details pieced together could give a remarkably accurate picture of what was going on in the operations rooms of the ships just a few miles across the water.

In the belly of the AGI ranks of technicians pored over oscilloscopes, fine tuning frequencies waiting for the slightest slip in operational security. Although not blessed with the same situation awareness as the American Admiral, the Captain of the AGI could gain a decent picture of the tactical position around him. Years of practice helped. His operations room kept a simple plan of which aircraft were airborne and plotted their tracks because, sometimes, his survival might depend on it. These were hostile waters for the unwary. The fact that the NATO air defence air picture had been compromised and they were able to display the tactical situation on a brand new computer monitor which had been fitted before they sailed from Sevastopol, helped a lot. There it was in glorious Technicolour and, like his American counterpart, he had watched the combined air operation develop. The IFF transponders which fed the picture had been turned off as the package approached the coastline so as the force edged in overland their activity had become invisible. As they coasted-out abeam Tripoli the IFF signals popped up again and the picture had updated. There had been a lot of cross-chat on the tactical frequency over the target and something had occurred. He had yet to discover what that was. The Phantoms being called in was surprise because there was no sign of any air activity in Syria after the first inelegant lunge at the package by the Migs had been repulsed.

The exchange on Guard had been illuminating and his analysts were trying to piece together the sequence of events as the British force egressed from the target. Israeli F-15s had approached what he assumed were the bombers and within moments of closing, one track had disappeared. This coincided with the rapid exchanges on the distress frequency and Springbok's request to divert. There could be only one conclusion. The Israeli fighters had shot down one of the British bombers. He moved quickly to the communications room to send out a "Flash" signal to Moscow. With the signal winging its way, the operators returned to their other priority task; listening to the frequencies of the, by now, decimated terrorist camp on the Syrian border.

Well to the northeast, the two Phantoms which had run the first deceptive feint had been holding at low level. Their briefing had been to remain undetected and to stay clear of the outbound route. With the increased chatter on Guard all pretence of stealth had passed and the leader began a gentle pull up to medium level. Not wishing to provoke any more reaction from the Syrian air defence system he turned his formation southerly away from the coast. His track would cross at right angles to the returning package and he would look less threatening to the bombers and, more importantly, the Phantom escort.

In the operations room of the John F Kennedy, already buzzing with the arrival of the British helicopters, the surveillance radar operator suddenly detected the pop-up contact off the Cyprus coast and passed it to the anti air warfare officer. He rifled through his mission plan which he thought he had memorised perfectly looking for a mention of any friendly activity in that area. There was nothing. The plan had only the main force and its embedded escort flying a route from Cyprus to The Lebanon and returning via a similar route. He hit the comms button connecting him to the air defence commander. The discussion was brief and the commander hit the scramble button almost instantly. The warning was almost superfluous as the crews had been on deck in the cockpits for some time and little prompting to launch was needed. Curiosity had overtaken discipline. As the scramble instructions were relayed, the sound of jet engines broke the relative calm and the ship's crew felt the huge carrier turn into wind. Within seconds the pair of F-14A Tomcats were lined up on the bow catapult and thrown off the front of the vessel. In the compartments below the sound of the shuttle returning to its starting position reverberated through the spaces.

There was little activity in the Phantom cockpits well to the north. With no further part in the plan they had been monitoring their fuel burn, careful to leave enough reserve to ensure they did not interrupt the recovery plan. As they headed south the RWRs were silent and even the fighter controller at Olympus had been quiet for some time.

Fifty miles to the south edgy F-14 crews had detected contacts on their AN/AWG 9 radars as soon as they had taken up their outbound vector and already were pressing their equally apprehensive fighter controller.

"Bogies heading inbound, strength two, fast, request clearance to engage."

"Negative Player 22, identify and report," came back the reply from the harried controller.

"Do we have a friendly squawk on the bogies?"

"Affirmative Player 22, coordinating with Olympus, standby."

In the cockpit, the radar intercept officer cursed, realising that his failure to interrogate the contacts could have been catastrophic He hit the interrogate button but the track remained stubbornly hostile on the radar display. Switching to his visual acquisition system known as the TCS, the massive optical sensor mounted under the nose of the Tomcat slewed to the radar scan and, as he designated the target locking the beam to one of the inbound Phantoms, a gently gyrating image appeared on the tube.

"I can't make this out but it don't look like a Flogger or a Fishbed to me. Stay weapons tight."

"I hear you but if this guy locks up I don't have too many choices. He's coming pretty fast."

The pilot eased the heading a few degrees towards the threat cutting across the circle to the intercept point, willing the controller to get the message through to the Brits on the island. His wingman followed his manoeuvring. In the back cockpit the radar warning receiver analysed the radar signals which emanated from the distant Phantoms. A small diamond had appeared on the warning display denoting an F4. The fact they suspected who was pointing at them was not helping their dilemma. The RIO locked up to the nearest target.

In the Phantom cockpit the calm was shattered as the RWR burst into life.

"Rackets, 12 o'clock!"

The lock provoked a rapid selection of switches on the control panel as the navigator listened to the rasping audio tone assailing his ears, trying to identify the new signal.

"Relax, it's a friendly. Looks like an F-14, mate."

In the Tomcat cockpits the scenario was less relaxed and the apparent identification had not altered pre-conceived survival instincts.

"Bogeys range 25 miles. Request instructions."

The opportunity for a long range shot with the AIM-54 Phoenix had passed. They were moving into Sparrow territory which made them more nervous. Unlike the active Phoenix the Sparrow was a semi-active air-to-air missile and they would have to track the contacts to the merge drawing them into a fight. The crews, given the option, would rather have followed a smoking missile into the fight but if the controller was right these were friendlies.

"Are we squawking?" asked the navigator in the lead Phantom.

"Shit no," replied the pilot turning the mode selector on his IFF box to Mode 3. The simple electronic identification which would identify them to the control agencies had remained silent since they had launched. Designed to camouflage their identity from the Syrian air defence system, failing to turn it back on now they had pulled up was a critical mistake.

"Parrot on," he called to his wingman prompting him to activate his own IFF box.

The response was instant in the carrier operations room. As the friendly electronic signals suddenly changed the tactical picture the weapons controller relaxed. In the F-14 cockpits, fingers were still poised over the trigger, ready to launch . At the hint of a lock from the inbound fighters master arm circuits would be made live.

"Player 22 flight, weapons tight, repeat weapons tight. Contacts now showing friendly. Intercept and identify acknowledge."

The relief in his voice was palpable.

"Player 22, identify, roger."

As the tension lifted the familiar profile of a British Phantom formed on the TCS display. The pilot switched his radio to the international distress frequency and transmitted.

"Aircraft operating 80 miles south of Cyprus, this is Player 22. Come up GCI Common, 364.2 and identify yourself."

There was a brief delay before the frequency sprang to life.

"Player 22 this is Hawk 3 and 4, how do you read?"

Tensions evaporated at the sound of the British voice on the radio. The discussion coincided with the visual pick-up and the pilot recognised the two Phantoms and pulled hard towards.

Hawk 3 and 4, this is Player 22 Flight, loud and clear and visual. Joining on the right."

The F-14s rolled in behind the Phantoms which began a gentle turn back onto a northerly heading allowing the Tomcats to turn inside and close into loose formation.

"You gave us quite a worry there buddy," the F-14 pilot called over the radio. "We had you down as the bad guys."

"Roger that Player. Glad you worked us out. We'll debrief it on the ground."

The potential adversaries flew along in loose formation for a short while suddenly appreciating technology. It had been a hair trigger moment; literally.

As the pilot touched his bonedome in a final salute the F-14 broke upwards and away from the Phantom to begin his recovery to the carrier. A case of "blue-on-blue" fratricide had only narrowly been averted but outside the maelstrom of the operational area, no one would ever be aware of the dilemma aloft nor would the incident ever reach the headlines.

The Phantoms set up a holding orbit at medium level waiting for their turn in the recovery plan. Below them, the remaining Buccaneers, now one aircraft short, flashed past and checked in on the air traffic frequency, calling initials preparing to break into the circuit. With the helicopter flight split, the escort Phantoms had little further to contribute and were following the Buccaneers just minutes behind. They too would be on the ground in short order. With Olympus radar monitoring the surrounding airspace the pressure was easing.

As he flashed over the flat calm Mediterranean Razor glanced over at the Boss's jet in tight battle formation. During the relative calm of the last few minutes he and Flash had dissected the engagements scribbling hasty notes on kneepads ready for the debrief which would follow as soon as they landed. It was hard to take in the fact that only minutes before they had been tied up with Syrian Migs and yet now they were back over the familiar landmarks on the peninsula. With Limmasol Bay approaching rapidly it was time to think about priorities.

"OK recovery checks coming up. Let's put this thing on the ground."

As the last of the fast jets touched down, relieved crews hit canopy selectors allowing the warm Mediterranean air to wash over them. Oxygen masks dropped from sweaty faces and with after flight checks done they taxied back towards the dispersal. There would be much to discuss and little time to reconstruct what had occurred. Questions were already being posed.

CHAPTER 26

RAF Akrotiri, Cyprus.

With the jets after-flighted and the unused weapons downloaded and returned to the armoury, Golf Dispersal was quiet for the first time in days. Inside the huge hangar the dormant airframes had been hastily arranged in neat rows. Some were serviceable but some carried snags from the mission. Rectification would come later before they lined up behind the tanker for the long trip home. In the meantime exhausted crews had returned to the accommodation blocks eager to celebrate.

There had been a feeding frenzy amongst the media since the events had hit the wires and, already, the first contingent of hastily accredited reporters had made their way from the Larnaca International Airport, along the coastal road, through Limmasol and onto the Sovereign Base Area. Military flights, often open to journalists had, remarkably, been "overbooked" delaying the arrival a little and giving the media spokesman time to prepare. With excuses running out, the first press conference had been hastily convened at the main Headquarters at Episkopi and Commander British Forces Cyprus had revelled in the exposure expounding a carefully prepared line. The questions had been skilfully handled and the basic facts outlined in a way to garner support whilst diverting attention away from some thorny and, as yet, unresolved issues. Some of those facts, hopefully, would never be revealed. The identity of the hostage had been presented thus far as a peace envoy embroiled in the murky politics of Beirut. Time would tell whether the real story would emerge. What was certain was that once the reporters gained access to the aircrews, a party line would be harder to police. In any event, the reason for the mission was almost secondary to the clamour for some Hollywood style headlines. With the marketing for the new movie "Top Gun" hitting the box office banners, real world exploits were just as marketable as the fiction.

While the media circus developed its momentum, one asset which would never be discussed at any of the press conferences was already being loaded onto a giant C-5 Galaxy transport. The Mig-23 airframe neatly covered in tarpaulin was already being loaded into the cavernous cargo bay and secured for another flight. This time it would not fly under its own power but rely on the giant transport to return it to its secretive home. The handling team would rather have completed the loading at night but with the media frenzy building, the decision had been taken to secure the load early. Once aboard there would be no questions and no risk of inopportune pictures leaking to a hungry press. A carefully constructed cage had diffused the distinctive lines if the fighter and, as its bulk was pushed up the massive ramp, it might have been any one of the hundreds of items of cargo which moved in and out of Akrotiri every day. Its destination was unknown to anyone on the RAF base and it would not be revealed through inspection of the flight plan the crew had just filed. Ostensibly bound for the ICAO destination coded KLSV, otherwise known as Nellis Air Force Base, Las Vegas, Nevada, its real destination was in the Nevada Desert some miles distant from the bright lights of Las Vegas. The flight path would be amended once the Galaxy was safely back inside US airspace where fewer questions would be asked.

*

Outside Block 140, one of the accommodation blocks which lined the road to the beach, the post-mission party was underway. Crates of Keo beer and bottles of Keo brandy, lemon squash and lemonade, the ingredients of the perfect Cypriot brandy sour were stacked high. A raucous gathering of aircrew and engineers had cracked the first beers the ring of the fire bell, which was acting as an impromptu bottle opener, marking each celebration.

Although the individual exploits during the mission were being amplified ten-fold, inevitably conversations turned to the casualties. The Buccaneer crew had been airlifted back to Akrotiri by helicopter, met on arrival and transferred immediately to the Princess Mary's Hospital on base. Suffering from compression fractures after the ejection they had been immobilised during the rough flight and were already being assessed. Apart from being an inch shorter, there was unlikely to be any lasting damage. There was no news yet from the American Task Force on the condition of the SAS trooper who was being treated for his wounds in the hospital on the carrier. There was one unspoken player in the scenario and news of his fate had been ominously absent. Although no one knew his name, the hostage had been the whole reason for the operation and, as yet, urgent requests for information had gone unanswered.

As the beers flowed a lone officer dressed in an American flight suit joined the party seeking out Razor and Flash who had found a gap amongst the bodies on the low steps. Yuri Andrenev gratefully accepted the beer which was thrust into his hand and bottles clinked.

"Some sortie Yuri," Flash reflected.

"It brought back memories of the day I came across the Inner German Border. I've never had any real affection for the Syrians but it was still strange to sit in behind a Mig-23 and pull the trigger. Old loyalties still surface you know."

"I can see that but don't be too hard on yourself. Unless someone stands up to these terrorist gangs, the Middle East will be a basket case for decades. The Syrian Government is orchestrating the party you know."

"Did you get a kill?"

"No, after you engaged the first pair we got tied up with the lead element. They flew through and we followed them out but they had no intention of staying to fight. We let them go home. We got a ZSU-23-4 which decided to have a go at the Chinooks. Took him out with a strafing pass. As the helicopters lifted this guy decided to try to take them out and we were called in as cover. How about you, was that your first air-to-air kill Yuri?"

"It was if you don't count the Mig-21 in East Germany but it doesn't feel as good as I thought it would," he replied. There was a momentary pause as each reflected on the sentiment. "So what's next for you Razor?"

"If they clear us to go home it's the endless round of exercises coming up. We have TACEVAL in a few months so the hooter will be going off every week in the build up. Can't say it'll be fun playing with gas masks again and it'll seem a bit of an anti-climax after this."

"Maybe not fun but it's probably safer to be ready for it. With current Soviet doctrine it might get messy quickly if the Red Army rolls through the Fulda Gap."

"Let's hope I never need to find out. How about you?"

"I'm sure John will have plenty of work for me. He's been lining me up for some analysis work of the new Eurofighter against the Su-27. It's one of the design drivers and they want me to advise them on performance to make sure the evaluation models are accurate. Sounds a bit dry if you ask me. The Americans want me to go back to Nellis and help out the Aggressor Squadron prepare for Red Flag. I hear they would like a squadron of Flankers based at Nellis to act as enemy forces. Maybe I could be a squadron commander again? Who knows, if Gorbachev keeps the push for "Glasnost" going he may even sell them a squadron. It's amazing the power of a blank cheque."

"Now that's a job I'd be happy to do. Let me know if you need any pilots."

"I might just do that," the Russian replied. They clinked bottles and drew heavily on the cold beer, the short pause in conversation relaxed and easy. Around them the raucous celebration continued. Suddenly the fire bell rattled quelling the noise and a harried flight commander demanded attention. The volume died slowly.

"Gents, I don't want to spoil the celebration but you need to know a few things. The place is flooded with journalists so watch out what you say if you meet them. The public relations team is trying to keep them in one place but don't put it beyond one of them to go walkabouts. Look; there's no easy way to say this but we just heard that the hostage didn't make it. He wasn't aboard the helicopters when they landed. No details yet as to why but it was nothing we did wrong so no reason to feel bad. The insertion team made contact but they weren't able to pull him out. Keep that close hold for now and certainly not for dissemination to the media until I say so. I'm going back to the press conference now so expect them to want blood once this is public. My recommendation would be to stay clear of the admin areas until this dies down a little. The execs will field the questions today but you might find a microphone in your face tomorrow."

He turned and walked back to the Land Rover which he had left idling at the kerb and took off down the road. The conversation slowly picked up to its former crescendo as the revellers digested the information.

As more cold beer fuelled the celebration, the journalists were gathering in the Station Briefing Room and the detachment commanders were preparing to face the onslaught. The flight commander entered the room and nodded to his Boss receiving a brief acknowledgement that the message had got through to the crews. With details which had only hours before been stamped "SECRET" swilling through their minds they prepared for the grilling.

The public relations expert parachuted in from Episkopi to choreograph the event was marshalling the reporters ineffectually and the low burble heightened the air of anticipation. So far things had been "close hold" but the media sensed, and had been promised, that this was when they would be able to satisfy the itch and, more importantly, their editors' demand for copy.

"Ladies and Gentlemen, can I have your attention. You heard from Commander British Forces Cyprus earlier. Can I please introduce to you the squadron commanders of the Phantom and Buccaneer detachments and the lead helicopter pilot who flew today's mission. They will give you as much detail as they can but you'll be aware that some of it is still highly sensitive. If we stray into areas where we are uncomfortable I'll make it clear at the time. We'll open with a background briefing on the situation in Beirut and why the operation was necessary and then the mission leader will open with a brief description of the operation. There'll be time for questions at the end. Gentlemen over to you."

What the assembled journalists could not know, nor would they ever be told, was that the invaluable "package" that had been the catalyst for the momentous events was safely in the hands of MI6. Although retrieving the package conferred a tenuous victory, the plight of the hostage would take some explaining to an inquisitive press corps if the facts ever leaked out.

The rapid fire questioning began the moment the speakers sat down.

DAVID GLEDHILL

EPILOGUE

ACAS's Office, Ministry of Defence Main Building, Whitehall, London.

"Come in Alexander , take a seat. It's been one of those days."

"Thanks Sir, replied the Director of Air Defence dropping tiredly into the chair. "if I have to give one more senior civil servant an update on the operation, I'll mount a new one with this building as the target."

"I've just got back from Number 10 myself. At least the conversation was brief and stayed on operational matters. I'm afraid you'll need to go over it just once more for my benefit."

"I managed to speak to the Station Commanders at both Coningsby and Lossiemouth so I got the story pretty much direct. The good news is the crew of the Buccaneer which went down are safe and well. They're both suffering from the usual compression injuries after the ejection but I hear it didn't stop them hitting the bar later in the day. They're in good spirits despite their swim."

"Any news on the cause yet?"

"That's the odd thing. The wreckage went down in deep water so unless we spend a big sum on a recovery operation we won't get the main fuselage. In any event, the Bucc doesn't have an accident data recorder so there's only so much we'd add to the story. We did get a lucky break though. A section of the wing was found floating on the surface. . . . . I should step back. The Israelis are convinced the F-15 had something to do with the loss but the hot debrief doesn't support it. Both of the crew thought they saw a missile shot at the time and that's what we told the Israelis immediately following the incident. Unfortunately that's set a false trail going. The Buccaneer navigator was carrying a recorder which caught the cockpit intercom and we've had chance to listen to the transcript. We can hear a distinct noise just before the master caution went off and the hydraulic pressures began to fall. The boffins at RAE Farnborough are suggesting it sounds like a small detonation. Our first assumption when we realised that the F-15 was not involved was that the Bucc had lost its outer wing panel. You know we've had a few failures recently and the fleet was grounded for a while. This time the outer wing section came off clean and there was no evidence of structural failure; or at least not metal fatigue. The jet rolled left before impact and it would have to have been the other wing which came off to cause that. We can discount a wing fold mechanism failure. That means the back end separated because the crew are adamant that there was a major airframe break up."

"So we can discount a structural failure and a missile shot?"

"And I think it safe to assume that the rear fuselage didn't fail. The Bucc is built like the proverbial brick-built shit house."

"So it had to be sabotage?"

"That's what we're working on."

"Any ideas?"

"The Provost Marshal is on it but it doesn't look like an inside job. The morale on Cyprus is good. That said, the local politics are a mess and I certainly wouldn't discount a disaffected local."

"Any evidence for that theory?"

"No. They checked the hangar where the jets were secured before the mission and no sign of a break in. There were no reports of insecurities. It's a mystery. They've increased the alert state and added extra security patrols but the horse has bolted. I'll let you know if anything surfaces."

"What of the Israelis? Are they playing hard ball as usual?"

"Oh yes. They've offered up the HUD film and I've had my guys review it. One of my staff flew the F-15 on exchange and he's given it a clean bill of health. There was no missile launch."

"Why the hell did they get involved?"

"Probably no big surprise. The 6th Fleet is pulling a major exercise in their back yard so they make sure we all know they are on the case."

"Well I'll make sure our aircrew who were involved are taken care of. The crews did well and we should make sure that they get some recognition. The American contribution was quite impressive too. I'm looking forward to seeing the report on the deception tactic. Wish I'd watched that live!"

"Come now, you know the cut and thrust of MOD politics is more fun than flying Boss."

The two men smiled ruefully.

"Well I'm going to break a habit. A wee Malt?"

"I think that might be just the ticket Boss, thanks."

*

MI6 Headquarters, London.

Sir Richard Courtney, the Head of MI6, glanced at the TV tuned into the BBC News in the corner of his office, the "talking head" explaining the air operation in precise detail, despite having absolutely no inside knowledge of what had unfolded. The media had been given the facts about how the combined force had been employed but it would be far too early for them to have digested the full implications. Sir Richard might even have been convinced that "the expert" knew what he was talking about if he did not know to the contrary. At times like this he was thankful for ill-informed speculation. It would give him time to weave the elaborate sub-plots which he had been planning carefully over the last hours. The newspaper headlines made for a useful bargaining chip:

"Israel shoots down British fighter bomber; crew saved from certain death" or some such dramatic by-line.

He had already seen the transcript of the crew debrief and he was well aware that the Israeli fighter jet could not have been involved in the loss of the Buccaneer but he could keep that little fact quiet for the time being. The Israeli Ambassador had already been tap dancing at the Foreign Office explaining that the F-15 had a full complement of weapons aboard when it landed. They had even offered some very impressive gun camera video of the interception as proof of innocence. There was little doubt that the jet had not launched a weapon but the mysterious flash clearly visible on the images from the F-15 head up display showed some type of detonation which had ripped apart the rear fuselage. It was a conundrum that no one had yet resolved satisfactorily. His contacts in the Defence Ministry had told him that the real reason for the Buccaneer's loss would not be obvious unless the wreckage could be raised from the sea bed.

Efforts were underway but the Mediterranean was deep in that area so there could be no certainty that they would ever recover the wreckage to know the truth. The Board of Inquiry had already been convened but it would be far too straight-laced for his purposes. Truth was the mantra for such proceedings and even he could not distort that outcome. He could keep his cohorts guessing for while yet and, in the meantime, he would call in a few favours.

It had been some minutes since he had been called to the Foreign Office to update the Foreign Secretary and he knew he should be on his way. In a vague attempt to crystallise his thoughts he made the odd note in his briefing pack. It was not for him to second-guess the Defence Minister who would give the official line on the incident. The facts were still emerging slowly and his role would be to ensure that he gained the maximum leverage from what could have been, and might yet be, an embarrassment. It was not good to lose an agent, particularly in the Middle East. It was a horrifying development that the terrorist leader had resorted to a surgical procedure to immobilise the agent and this had upped the ante in the war of attrition. If he could prove complicity he would have some real leverage but it was a delicate line to follow. If another intelligence agency was implicated in the kidnap he would need to make sure his displeasure was felt. So far it seemed unlikely.

The way the story had played out had been truly gruesome. After speaking to Reeves at the compound Lakin had gone to ground and had continued to watch the movements in and out through the gate, although the bomblets dropped during the raid had slowed movement significantly. He had relayed information back via the monitoring station on Mount Olympus including battle damage reports on how the air attack had succeeded in decimating the stronghold. The Troodos team had listened as hasty arrangements were made to move Reeves to Syria. With the chaos wrought by the attack the terrorist communications had been disrupted badly and messages had flowed thick and fast in the clear. It had been a simple task for the analysts to piece together a comprehensive picture and the picture was not pretty.

Whatever had really gone wrong at that point might never surface. As the vehicle carrying Reeves had set off through the shattered gates there had been a massive explosion and the vehicle had been left to burn for hours. Lakin had watched for survivors but no one emerged from the shattered hulk. The trooper who had spoken to Lakin in the compound had been quite graphic and, if the story about the explosive device being transplanted into his skin was true, someone had failed to make it safe before trying to move him. How could they have implanted enough material to cause such a catastrophic explosion? Maybe it was Reeves' final act of defiance and he had found some way to take his captors with him. Either way he was dead and, at least he had taken an important decision-maker with him. Being purely selfish, Sir Richard was relieved that he had gone in a blaze of glory; literally. His agents became wary when the system was seen to fail. Every effort had to be made to extract agents from a predicament. The fact that Reeves had died fighting would be good for internal morale. When, of course, he allowed the facts to leak; but leak they must.

The documents had proven easy to find once Reeves had given the information to the SAS trooper. It really had been a masterstroke because they were hidden in open sight. The book was an obscure volume by a little known British author and had not been loaned from the Beirut Library since 1976. It would probably have been a safe depository for years, secure other than by a chance discovery. The contents of the documents had been a revelation. In a carefully crafted plan the Syrians had devised an operational strategy which would have changed the balance of power on the Golan Heights. Employing Soviet style deception techniques, "Maskirovka", they planned to shut down the command and control links, seal off the escape routes from the

Heights and neutralise the Israeli force holding the strategic
ground. His strategists had analysed the detail and they assured
him that, given the right amount of force, the Israelis would have
struggled to hold out for much longer than a few days, if that.
With the high ground back in Syrian hands the northern plains
of Israel were once again under threat of attack. Attacks had
slowed since the Yom Kippur War and the locals had become
accustomed to a more normal existence as much as was possible
in that part of the world. He imagined the Israelis must have
war-gamed the contingency many times but he was still at a loss
as to how the limited forces, and particularly the limited logistics
supplies, could have held out. The plan was fascinating and very
un-Syrian like! He pondered, briefly, whether other forces might
have been at work in the planning.

One aspect would be easy. The Defence Minister would take
little persuading that the crews who had flown the mission
should be warmly applauded. A little media coverage to highlight
the skills they had shown would be kudos for the cash strapped
Ministry and would divert attention away from any risk of his
own potential debacle. There should be little risk of his losing an
agent coming to light. A "D Notice" would ensure that this
particular side of the operation stayed quiet. The public would
enjoy the exploits of the aviators and the special forces and his
own contribution would stay shrouded. When all was
considered, he had, after all, recovered the Syrian plans and
would use the contents wisely to steer the political agenda. The
information operation would have to be steered carefully and the
facts manipulated to his advantage.

Sir Richard gathered up his papers and placed them into a black
official briefcase. He secured the straps and locked the heavy
brass clasp placing the key safely in his pocket. Picking up his
rolled umbrella he made for the door checking his watch. It
wouldn't do to keep the Foreign Secretary waiting.

*

KGB Headquarters Lubyanka Square, Moscow.

The KGB Headquarters on Lubyanka Square in the centre of Moscow glowed bright in the sunlight, the vivid yellow main building a contrast to its drab neighbours. Often seen on television, the landmark had become a vivid symbol of The Cold War set alongside the onion domes of The Kremlin. Taken over by the Bolsheviks in 1918, the seemingly innocent exterior hid a dark past. Since 1984 and with moves to improve the KGB's image, tourists were encouraged to visit the KGB museum in a new annex in an adjacent building. Even though the ground floor was now used for conferences and social events the upper floors still housed the offices of the secretive KGB. One particular office on the Third Floor was close to the seat of power alongside others on the corridor formerly occupied by KGB leaders who had gone on to chair the Politburo; the seat of Soviet power and influence. Grand strategy had been planned in these corridors and those days were not yet over.

The two officials had been closeted away for some hours and the topic of discussion had been wide-ranging. The recent British operation had been dissected in great depth but already they had moved on to more weighty matters. In keeping with other officials in the corridors of power in London, Washington and Paris the topic of the Israeli nuclear deterrent was never far from mind. An official with a florid complexion nursed on a diet of scotch and caviar was holding court. His girth suggested that his diet was untypical of the average Muscovite.

"Of course you know as well as I that Israel is thought to have had a nuclear weapons capability since 1960. It has slowly developed its nuclear arsenal over the intervening years and from a humble start has developed quite a robust capability. Our intelligence analysts in the GRU estimate they have between 200

and 400 nuclear warheads available now. They have ballistic
missiles, aircraft, and submarine-launched missiles to deliver the
weapons and the political will to use them if their National
survival is threatened. Unlike their neighbours in the region, the
test firings that have been conducted have been notably
successful. Their access to American technology has helped that
aspect considerably."

"A worry indeed but their neighbours have not been idle,"
mused the other official, his manner deferential.

"True but we all know that power unchecked becomes
dangerous. Egypt was a good balance for many years but that
fool Sadat changed all that. The threat from the Sinai has been
largely neutralised leaving Syria as the only real opposition.
Jordan has also become rather too compliant. We have for some
time thought that the only way to rebalance would be to
intervene as it would be far too risky to give Syria an equivalent
capability. The regime in Damascus is far too unpredictable;
possibly more so than Tel Aviv. There are too many hotheads in
Damascus."

"Do I sense an undercurrent?"

"Let me try to explain it this way. A cornered lion is dangerous
but predictable but when it breaks out and strikes, it becomes
lethal. With its power and speed it can take even its handler
unawares. But what if you can put a chain on the lion? It might
cause injury but its capacity for carnage is reduced. We needed
some way to hold Israel in check and yet avoid antagonising the
USA. The President would not act against American interests in
the region and the nuclear dimension worries the planners in
The Pentagon."

"True and needing oil from the Arabs is always a good leveller."

"Yes but that in itself is not enough to turn them against their old ally. I needed more. The Golan operation was simple Maskirovka; pure deception. I had to make the West think that Israel was under threat. I also had to make sure Israel was focussed on its northern flank. Meanwhile in the south I had grander designs."

"So the leak from the Syrian MOD was planned all the time?"

"It was. The contact in the Syrian MOD, turned by the British agent, was my man. He had been working for us since he came to Moscow for a technical course a few years ago. Let's say his indiscretions at that time meant that he was more than compliant when we offered him his options. He could either go home in shame after spending most of his time in Moscow bedding a westerner, drinking alcohol and engaging in debauchery, all of which was captured on film of course, or he could provide the occasional service and be well rewarded for his troubles. He was easily convinced. The plans we developed were, obviously, realistic because he, subsequently, became a military planner so he was able to add that aura of credibility. The writing materials were genuine and they were properly logged in the records as genuine contingency plans. The ones which found their way into the hands of the British were, purportedly, copies of the master plan. When I saw them even I was thoroughly convinced."

"Masterful. I'm impressed."

"It still took quite a bit of setting up. I could hardly hand them the documents on a plate. I had to make the agent work for his snippets. A few low grade offerings whet his appetite but we had to sacrifice some real information. I had to establish credibility first but once he was convinced, the deception was more believable."

"How was the Buccaneer bomber brought down? It was certainly the most persuasive element and made wonderful headlines in London."

"I had one of our people in Nicosia infiltrate the British base and plant a device. It was a simple timer mechanism designed to remain dormant until after takeoff. It was easy enough to set the delay to ensure that it would detonate after about 45 minutes. With the short flight times that would be after they had hit their targets. I must admit, I was fortunate there. The timing with the F-15 arriving in the vicinity could not have been more perfect but was total luck. The fact that the Israelis were in close proximity at the time meant there was no need to plant further incriminating evidence. They scored an own goal by being too inquisitive, particularly after the Brits had asked them not to intervene. I did suspect that the request would be ignored."

"So tell me about the rest of the plan. You said there is a strategic motive here but I'm struggling to make the connection. Is that why you were referring to their nuclear arsenal?"

"All the aircraft rushing around was a mere smoke screen and I had loftier ambitions. A tactical nuclear device was taken in via the diplomatic bag right under their noses. A ship, the motor vessel Curium Star flying a flag of convenience, sailed from Limmasol and docked in Haifa on the day of the operation. Such vessels make that journey almost daily. The device was part of a larger shipment and was moved by road to Tel Aviv after its arrival in country. It's now installed in a safe house in Jerusalem. It will stay there, hopefully, never to be needed."

"You never cease to amaze me, Gregor. So the plan worked but I'm still not sure I see why the tactical deception was needed?"

"Quite simple; the whole operation by the British was simply unnecessary. There was never any plan for the Syrians to retake the Golan Heights. I'm not even sure the Syrian Army is capable of such action. I needed attention focussed away from Tel Aviv while the device was being inserted. There would be no way the Israelis would have allowed the British to attack a target on their doorstep without them paying close attention. I knew that by setting up something obviously flamboyant in the north that they would devote much of their intelligence effort to monitoring events. Under those circumstances, my surreptitious move in the south would go unnoticed."

"You took a gamble using the Hezbollah cell. They are new and relatively untested."

"The terrorist leader was easily controlled. We funded the camp in the north and most of the money found its way to the leader via a handler in Beirut. Cash still talks in The Lebanon given the troubles. That said, the whole operation was tightly controlled from here and my team kept a very close watch on his activity. We devoted a lot of effort and the AGI off the coast was not only concentrating on the 6th Fleet you know. We kept a very close eye on his activities as well."

"So it all proved easy?"

"I had one nervous moment. The shipment was detained briefly at Haifa but it proved to be just a paperwork issue. Once I played the diplomatic card it was released almost immediately."

"So you hold the Aces to follow your poker analogy?"

"I do. The thing is, with the Brits convinced of a potential operational plan to disrupt the strategic balance and the Israelis believing they somehow caused the loss of a British aircraft there is now a perfect sub-plot running. Neither trusts each other nor will they for some time. Despite that, each has a reason to negotiate and in the meantime, the device is in place."

"I'll alert the Embassy in London to pay close interest in the discussions. We have some good contacts there who will dig deep."

"So, what I achieved was to run a tactical deception to cover a strategic plan which will guarantee that we hold the bargaining chip should we ever need to intervene in the political mess in the region. How could the Knesset ever exercise their nuclear option now? If the time ever comes, the Israeli Government will find that, if they should ever decide to use their nuclear strike capability, it is not without consequence. That consequence would be the wholesale destruction of the capital, its theological heritage and half of its population. The device is small enough to contain the damage and the fallout but large enough to deliver the threat. All in all, a good few weeks work."

*

Mossad Headquarters, Tel Aviv.

Mossad Headquarters in Tel Aviv is a sprawling yet unremarkable 1970s era office complex. The only real clue to its function is the raft of antennas and satellite dishes which crowd the roof space pointing to all areas of the globe.

The two casually dressed men walked across to the shaded table in the courtyard outside the building. Surrounded on four sides by walls, they could be confident that their conversation was private but, even so, they found a spot away from the main throng of bodies.

"So what alerted you to the shipment?"

"There was something odd about it from the get-go. The Soviets don't bring in big shipments like that through Haifa Port. Everything is normally airlifted in through Ben Gurion Airport in an IL-76 from Moscow. They know about our defensive monitoring at the airport so they must have thought that we would be less prepared elsewhere. I can only assume that they were unaware of the set up at Haifa which is just as efficient as the main operation. It proved to be a critical underestimation.

The shipment arrived from Limmasol which is not completely out of the ordinary but unusual. It was enough to trigger interest in the consignment. As soon as it went through the sensors we spotted it. We have some pretty sensitive screens in the Customs shed and one of them went crazy when the diplomatic bag went through."

"It detected nuclear material?"

"Yes, it was pretty well screened but there were enough residual emissions to set the Geiger counters singing."

"So what happened then?"

"We quarantined another part of the shipment as a cover so we could check it. The consignment, including the diplomatic bag was diverted into a secure facility, and that set off a frantic reaction from the Soviet diplomatic staff here in Tel Aviv. There was no diplomatic courier escorting it which was a little stupid of them and completely out of the ordinary. They must have assumed that a low key entry would divert attention but, as soon as the diplomatic bag was identified, we moved. They squealed of course and started making noises about diplomatic privilege but it was easy enough to insist on them providing some additional documentation before we would release it. We had a team at the port within the hour and it did what needed to be done. Our contingency plans are quite well established for this eventuality, although we'd always assumed it would be a terrorist gang not a Nation State. Of course as soon as the correct paperwork arrived from the Soviet Embassy we had to release the consignment immediately."

"No security tags on the device?"

"No, surprisingly. We expected sealing tags on the case of the device but there was nothing. Maybe they thought that would have attracted too much attention; and it would. We got access to the weapon easily enough and our experts are familiar with that type. Let's just say we've cooperated on similar programmes overseas. We inhibited the trigger mechanism so there's no way that thing will hit critical mass. It might make a small hole in the ground but the core won't explode. It's safe enough even if we might have to clean up after it went off. No, it's been neutralised and marked. We have a special dye that will show up if any one handles it. That may make a future cocktail party at the Knesset interesting. If anyone should show up with that stuff on their hands we would know immediately. It's better than a UV light at a disco. We've also fitted a tracker so we know where it's stored and we can tell if it ever moves. If they follow doctrine, this little present will be secured in a safe house and go untouched for years. They don't attract attention to their leave-behind devices. Our "Cousins" have some experience of these things and have become quite adept at making sure they know how to control them. We learned quickly from them"

"There'll be hell to pay if they know you tampered with the diplomatic bag."

"The seal on the diplomatic bag was a little harder to fix and it took one of our best men to reseal the consignment. He has some pretty effective tools to help that we picked up recently when the Soviet Consul was kidnapped. I think if we ever get to that point they'll know that we're not best pleased about their little ruse. They'll have more to worry about at that stage than a minor diplomatic infraction."

"Indeed; let's hope the situation never arises. I think we can all rest easy in our beds tonight. More Lemonana?"

*

Later that night, The US Embassy, London.

"Good evening Mr President."

"Andrew, thanks for calling, have we had word?"

"We have Sir. Admiral McAuley just called from the JFK."

"Was it as we suspected?"

The speech was difficult to understand distorted by the complex algorithms of the STU-2 secure phone and the Ambassador struggled to interpret his Commander-In-Chief's questions.

"It was, Sir. A Type 3 device. The insertion team landed back just minutes ago with the hardware.

"How did the switch go?"

"No problems at all. The team had copies of each of the typical Russian suitcase bombs and they only had to substitute the correct one. It was fortunate that it was one of the types that they've used in the US so it was a straight swap. We had to transfer a tracking device that the Israelis had fitted but that's now safely attached to the copy device."

"Can they tell it's a copy if they inspect it?"

"No way Sir. It's a perfect match even down to a slight trace of nuclear material which should fool even the most sensitive Geiger counter. I have to say the Israelis were playing with fire. There's enough material in the original to have made a serious mess if it had detonated, even though the trigger mechanism had been disabled. If that had gone off in Tel Aviv it would have closed down a couple of blocks of the city and the fallout downwind would have killed thousands. I can't believe they left it in place. They only had to ask us and we would have helped them dispose of it. I can only think there's another reason that they didn't want the Soviets to know they had tampered with it."

"I worry sometimes you know. For smart people they make some dumb decisions sometimes. Make sure the Admiral knows how pleased I am. It was a text book operation and there was big potential for a screw up. Did the Israelis not detect the helicopters going in?"

"No Sir. We had an EA-6B Prowler on station monitoring all the air defence frequencies and not a blink. They'd be devastated if they knew but the pilots didn't have to go all the way in. Our man in Tel Aviv had positioned the device at a desert strip just outside the city. It's fairly remote and it's unlikely anyone would have thought twice about helicopters flying at night. It's a pretty common occurrence around there. The markings on the helicopters would have confused a casual observer but they went in covertly. We did, after all, sell them AH1s in the first place."

"Good, good. So it looks like the situation's stable?"

"I think we can say that Mr President. Business as normal."

"And what about the Brits?"

"Oh I think we'll need to offer a few crumbs from the table to keep Sir Richard happy. He's still trading in a few favours with the Israelis who are a little vulnerable over the loss of the Buccaneer bomber. I'll speak to our Station Chief and have him discuss a few ideas. We have a few juicy intelligence projects on the go that we can offer up to keep him happy. The MOD is still celebrating the success of the mission but I'll have the Air Attaché drop in later to grease some wheels."

"Well done Andrew. Let me know if there are any more developments. I'll have the British Ambassador over later this morning and we'll talk it all through. I'm sure I can find some good news for him. Maybe I won't tell him that his whole operation was a waste of time. What was it called? *"Pulsator"*? Hell of a name for an operation if you ask me.""

"Indeed, Sir it sounds more like a sex toy. Who dreams them up?

"Maybe we should let them bask in the glory for a while longer. It's a shame their man didn't make it out. He was a good agent."

"Always casualties in this game," the President reflected tiredly. "Anyway I need a few hours shut eye. Goodnight Andrew."

"Goodnight Mr President and sleep well."

GLOSSARY

AAA. Anti-aircraft artillery.

AARI. Air-to-air refuelling instruction.

ACE. Allied Command Europe.

AGI. An intelligence gathering ship normally a trawler or commercial vessel to appear innocent.

Anchor. Establish a combat air patrol in the position given.

APC. Armament Practice Camp where crews learned air-to-air gunnery skills.

ASMA. Air Staff Management Aid. An early computer network and communications system.

Autocat. Airborne radio relay facility to extend the range of airborne communications.

Avtur. Aviation jet fuel.

Barrier. An arrestor net stretched across the end of a runway.

BL755. A cluster munition carry small bomblets inside a bomb carrier.

Blue-on-Blue. An engagement against a friendly target.

Bogey. A codeword for a hostile target.

Bold face. Initial emergency drills in the cockpit.

Bonedome. Slang for flying helmet.

BRIXMIS. The British Liaison Mission to the Group of Soviet Forces Germany.

Bullseye. A reference point nominated by a control agency to give a reporting datum from which all contacts can be called.

Cable. A wire stretched across the runway designed to stop a fast jet in emergency using a hook fitted to the aircraft. Also known as the arrestor cable.

Charlie 4, 4 Plus 8, Tiger Fast 60. A code used to indicate weapon state for a Phantom. Charlie denotes two external wing tanks, four Skyflash missiles, four Sidewinders and a gun. With the advent of AIM-9L an additional number was added to indicate how many missiles were all-aspect capable. In this case, the Phantom would be carrying AIM 9Ls.

Chop or chopped. To switch frequency.

Clean. Not illuminated by a threat aircraft. Sometimes the term "naked" can be used.

Clear Hot. Cleared to make a live weapons pass.

COMAO. Combined Air Operation.

CTG. Carrier Task Group.

CAP. Combat air patrol.

Commcen. Communications Centre.

Comsec. Communications security.

CTTO. Central Tactics and Trails Organisation. The forerunner to the Air Warfare Centre.

DCDI. Deputy Chief of Defence Intelligence.

DF. Direction finding. A means to establish a bearing to a transmission. Many military radios are fitted with a DF function.

DMPI. Desired Mean Point of Impact. The aiming point where a bomb is intended to land.

DZ. Drop Zone.

EA-6B Prowler. An electronic support aircraft fitted with electronic receivers and jammers.

ECM. Electronic Countermeasures.

ELINT. Electronic intelligence.

EWO. Electronic Warfare Officer.

FAC. Forward Air Controller.

Feet wet. Remain over the sea.

Flight Level. A height in thousands of feet. Fight Level 250 is 25,000 feet.

Form 700. The aircraft servicing log book.

Fur ball. A multi aircraft, turning engagement.

GCI. Ground Controlled Interception.

GRU. "Glavnoye Razvedyvatel'noye Upravleniye". The Soviet

Army Intelligence branch.

Guard. The international distress frequency.

"Hard". Concrete buildings built to withstand attack by heavy weapons.

Hard Wing Phantom. The FG1 and FGR2 versions were not fitted with leading edge slats just leading edge flaps that could not be used in air combat manoeuvring. Slats gave extra manoeuvrability at high angle of attack. Slatted versions of the Phantom were called soft wing.

HAS. Hardened aircraft shelter.

Homeplate. Home base also used in the context of an aircraft carrier.

HUD. Head up display.

IFF Identification friend or foe. An electronic identification system.

IFF Interrogator. An electronic system to interrogate an IFF transponder to read the transmitted codes.

INAS. Inertial Navigation and Attack System.

Initials. A visual entry point on the runway extended centreline at 5 miles.

IP. Initial point. The start of an attack run. A reference point some miles from a target from which fine details of track and timing are set.

IRSTS. Infra red search and track system.

Joker. A codeword signifying an aircraft has reached recovery fuel.

Jubilee Guardsman. An IFF interrogator fitted to the British Phantom.

KD. Khaki drill uniform. Normally worn only in warm climates.

Knickers. A codeword for dropping a bomb to catch a pursuing fighter in the blast fragmentation zone.

LZ. Landing Zone.

Leaker. A fighter which has penetrated a defensive screen.

Loadie. Air Loadmaster responsible for the cargo and passengers in the hold of a transport aircraft.

LOCOSS. Lead Computing Optical Sighting System – the gunsight.

MANPADS. Man-portable air defence system. A shoulder launched surface-to-air missile.

Maskirovka. The Soviet Union's military doctrine of surprise through deception.

Max mil. Maximum military power. Full power without selecting reheat.

Merge. The opening position in an air combat engagement when the opponents meet.

Mode Charlie. A function on the IFF system which records the height of the transponding aircraft and displays it on the controller's radar screen.

MT. Motor transport.

MTI. Moving target indicator. Electronic processing which gives a limited look down capability by processing moving targets.

NCO. Non commissioned officer.

OCU. Operational Conversion Unit. The Phantom training squadron.

Opsec. Operational Security.

PAN. An emergency call denoting urgency but short of a Mayday situation.

Parrot. A codeword for an IFF transmitter.

PBF. Pilot's Briefing Facility.

PLB. Personal Locator Beacon fitted in the lifejacket to provide an emergency location signal to search and rescue.

Pickle weapons. To pull the trigger releasing the weapons.

Pipper. The gunsight aiming marker used for weapon aiming.

Port. Left

Pri Fly. Primary Flying Control on a US aircraft carrier.

PSO. Personal staff officer.

QFI. Qualified flying instructor, rated on type.

QRA. Quick Reaction Alert.

QWI Qualified Weapons Instructor.

Rackets. A radar warning receiver alert.

Radalt. Radio Altimeter which uses radio waves to measure height rather than barometric pressure.

RIO. A US Navy term for a fighter back-seater; a radar intercept officer.

ROE. Rules of Engagement.

Rolex. Delay to a planned time. Rolex 30 means slip the event by 30 minutes.

RPG. Rocket propelled grenade launcher.

RSBN. Russian Radio Navigation System.

R/T. Radio transmission.

RTB. Return to base.

RWR. Radar warning receiver.

SAR. Search and rescue.

SAROPS. Search and rescue operations.

SAS. Special Air Service.

SBS. Special Boat Services. The Royal Navy special forces.

SENGO. Senior Engineering Officer.

Sidestep. A tactical manoeuvre to fly an offset course away from track to avoid a hostile fighter.

Sidetone. The background noise during a radio transmission.

SIGINT. Signals Intelligence.

SIPRNET. The Secret Internet Protocol Router Network. An American secure data and communications system.

SIS. Special Intelligence Services.

Sitrep. Situation Report. A summary of the tactical situation.

Soft. Unprotected buildings made of normal construction

materials.

SOF. Special operations forces.

SF. Special forces.

Splash. An air-to-air kill.

Squawk. To transmit a selected code on the Identification Friend or Foe system.

Squawk Ident. To transmit an identification code on the Identification Friend or Foe system.

Starboard. Right.

Stud. A preset frequency on the radio box.

TACAN. Tactical Air Navigation System. A radio receiver in the aircraft which gives a range and bearing to a known radio beacon.

TACEVAL. Tactical Evaluation Exercise. A NATO-sponsored combat readiness evaluation of tactical units normally conducted annually.

"Tally." Short for "Tally Ho" a codeword for visual contact with a hostile target.

Transop. Air transport tasking order.

UHF. Ultra High Frequency.

U/S. Unserviceable.

Visident. A visual identification. Often used as a descriptor for a radar controlled procedure to close in on a target.

Weapons free. Authority to engage delegated to lower levels of command. Hostile targets could be engaged.

Weapons tight. Authority to release weapons not granted.

X Ray. A code to denote the aircraft is serviceable.

Zombie. A potentially hostile track.

DAVID GLEDHILL

AUTHOR'S NOTE

The setting for much of the novel, the RAF base at Akrotiri, sits on the southern tip of the island of Cyprus within one of the Sovereign Base Areas. These overseas British territories were retained by the British Government under the 1960 Treaty of Independence agreed between the United Kingdom, Greece, Turkey and representatives from the Greek and Turkish Cypriot communities. At the same time, the Treaty granted independence to the Republic of Cyprus.

The base is an important strategic site providing not only a staging post for transport aeroplanes but an operating location for military combat aircraft and helicopters. Home to fast jet detachments conducting armament practice camps and a work-up base for the RAF Aerobatic Team, The Red Arrows, it is also a popular destination for crews conducting overseas operational navigation training exercises. The principal reason for its attraction is that the weather factor is outstanding allowing almost unhindered operations. Mount Olympus housed an air defence radar for many years and controllers assisted deployed fighters. The activity of the secretive signals unit in the book is fictional.

The real Operation *"Pulsator"* was conducted in 1983 and was symptomatic of a certain political naivety at the time. Despite the fact it came just after the Falklands conflict, the delicate balance of the Cold War meant that operational crews were placed in a less than comfortable tactical scenario. The crews were asked to fly over potentially hostile and certainly volatile territory in The Lebanon with limited armament. After recent conflicts this would be unthinkable. Although military operations in the Gulf region became commonplace, the operations of the early 1980s were perhaps the first time the UK exercised its expeditionary capabilities despite Cold War tensions, albeit from existing bases.

The scenario for this tale is of a force of Buccaneer bombers escorted by Phantom fighters operating over The Lebanon in 1983 and, although fictional, a similar force flew across the city of Beirut in a show of force to support ground troops and to demonstrate political will to the warring factions. On that occasion, no weapons were dropped. The Phantoms, unbelievably, flew unarmed in perhaps the most hostile airspace in the world at that time. The Buccaneers were armed with older generation AIM-9B Sidewinders even though the more capable AIM-9G and hugely more capable AIM-9L missiles were in the RAF inventory. Happily, all the crews returned safely and the mission, undoubtedly, had the desired impact.

The story also touches on the plight of a hostage snatched by Arab militants similar to real events in the 1980s with the most famous being the religious aide Terry Waite, held captive from January 1987 to November 1991. Although an intelligence agent is the hostage in the story, life on the streets of Beirut at that time was dangerous and a hotbed of political intrigue.

Many aircraft types make an appearance in the novel but one, in particular, has a strong link with the island. The US U-2 spy planes operated from Akrotiri for many years under the Olive Harvest programme. Once extremely secretive, they first came to the public eye when, on 7 December 1977, a U-2 veered off the runway and demolished the air traffic control tower making national headlines. As well as the pilot, the Senior Meteorological Officer and four locally employed civilian assistants were killed and a number of RAF and civilian personnel suffered terrible injuries. The detachment was officially recognised when a statement was made in Parliament in June 1990 by Archie Hamilton, at that time a junior Defence Minister. More recently, during the 2010 "Wikileaks" revelations, the details of operations Highland Warrior and Cedar Sweep in which the U-2s of the 9th Reconnaissance Wing flew surveillance missions over The Lebanon, relaying information about Hezbollah militants to Lebanese authorities was disclosed. The revelations brought to the fore British ministerial concerns over use of the UK sovereign base areas without proper ministerial approvals.

Deception is the theme of the novel but many might be surprised to know that it is a fundamental tenet of modern warfare. The stories of Operation Overlord during World War 2 when masters of deception persuaded German military planners that the allies were about to attack over the Pas de Calais are legendary. Modern reality, with perhaps the exception of the Second Gulf War, is less ambitious. Military deception at the tactical level can be a simple as a decoy airframe, maybe a decommissioned fighter, parked on a dispersal to attract a less than wary bomber pilot. At the operational level who can forget the grand plans which made Saddam Hussein think that Norman Schwarzkopf would attack using Marine expeditionary forces landing in Kuwait rather than the full frontal armoured assault through the desert. Governments engage in strategic deception and not only during wartime. Maybe the USA was intent on fielding the Strategic Defence Initiative, otherwise known as "Star Wars", in order to defeat the Soviet nuclear threat. It certainly hastened the end of the Cold War but was it a grand deception plan? Was the money and the technology really available? The Soviet Union decided it could not afford the risk but was it the grandest bluff of recent history? As an operational planner I would analyse a campaign in minute detail and decide on a number of potential courses of action to defeat the enemy. As a deception planner, I would offer up a rejected course of action as the most effective deception plan. If a military force might execute the strategy it should be easy to persuade an opponent that it could happen. When you read the novel and, particularly the climax, you can decide whether the protagonists were right or wrong and whether their deceptions at all levels worked. True to the title it is a recurrent theme.

I hope you enjoyed the tale but, equally, I hope you ask the question: could these events have occurred?

ABOUT THE AUTHOR

Dave Gledhill trained as a navigator and flew the Phantom and Tornado F3 on squadrons and as an instructor. Eventually becoming the Executive Officer on the Tornado Operational Conversion Unit he also commanded No. 1435 Flight in the Falkland Islands. As a staff officer he was responsible for operational requirements, fleet management and operational testing of many of the aircraft operated by all three Services, both in the MOD and at The Air Warfare Centre. He served overseas with Royal Air Force Germany and as an exchange officer at The Joint Command and Control Center in San Antonio, Texas and The USAF Warfare Center at Nellis Air Force Base, Las Vegas, Nevada. He was also the Senior Operations Officer at The Balkans Combined Air Operations Centre at Vicenza in Italy.

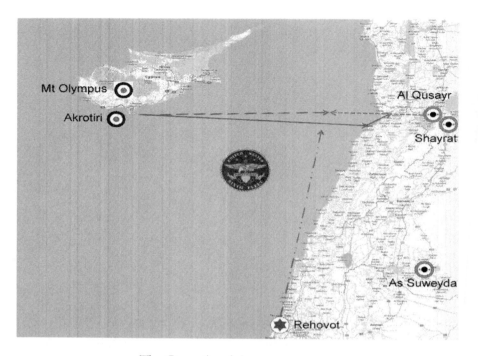

The Operational Area

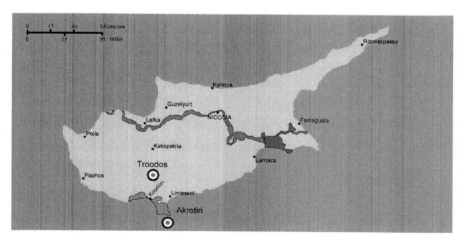

Map of Cyprus.

Golf Dispersal (copyright Google Maps)

OTHER BOOKS BY THIS AUTHOR

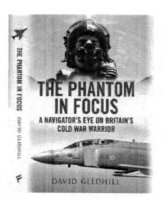

Have you ever wondered what it was like to fly the Phantom? This is not a potted history of an aeroplane, nor is it Hollywood glamour as captured in *Top Gun*. This is the story of life on the frontline during the Cold War told in the words of a navigator who flew the iconic jet. Unique pictures, many captured from the cockpit, show the Phantom in its true environment and show why for many years the Phantom was the envy of NATO. It also tells the inside story of some of the problems which plagued the Phantom in its early days, how the aircraft developed, or was neglected, and reveals events which shaped the aircraft's history and contributed to its demise. Anecdotes capture the deep affection felt by the crews who were fortunate enough to cross paths with the Phantom during their flying careers. The nicknames the aircraft earned were not complimentary and included the 'Rhino', 'The Spook', 'Double Ugly', the 'Flying Brick' and the 'Lead Sled'. Whichever way you looked at it, you could love or hate the Phantom, but you could never ignore it.

"The Phantom in Focus: A Navigator's Eye on Britain's Cold War Warrior" - *ISBN 978-178155-048-9 (print) and ASIN B00GUNIM0Q (e-book) published by Fonthill Media.*

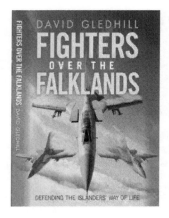

Fighters Over The Falklands: Defending the Islanders' Way of Life captures daily life using pictures taken during the author's tours of duty in the Falkland Islands. From the first detachments of Phantoms and Rapiers operating from a rapidly upgraded RAF Stanley airfield to life at RAF Mount Pleasant, see life from the author's perspective as the Commander of the Tornado F3 Flight defending the islands' airspace. Frontline fighter crews provided Quick Reaction Alert (QRA) during day to day flying operations working with the Royal Navy, Army and other air force units to defend a remote and sometimes forgotten theatre of operations. The book also examines how the islanders interacted with the forces based at Mount Pleasant and contrast high technology military operations with the lives of the original inhabitants, namely the wildlife.

"Fighters Over The Falklands – Defending the islanders Way of Life" - ISBN 978-17155-222-3 (print) and ASIN: B00H87Q7MS (e book) published by Fonthill Media.

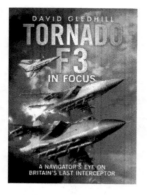

The Tornado F2 had a troubled introduction to service. Unwanted by its crews and procured as a political imperative, it was blighted by failures in the acquisition system. Adapted from a multi-national design and planned by committee, it was developed to counter a threat which disappeared. Modified rapidly before it could be sent to war, the Tornado F3 eventually matured into a capable weapons system but despite datalinks and new air to air weapons, its poor reputation sealed its fate. The author, a former Tornado F3 navigator, tells the story from an insider's perspective from the early days as one of the first instructors on the Operational Conversion Unit, through its development and operational testing, to its demise. He reflects on its capabilities and deficiencies and analyses why the aircraft was mostly under-estimated by opponents. Although many books have already described the Tornado F3, the author's involvement in its development will provide a unique insight into this complex and misunderstood aircraft programme and dispel some of the myths. This is the author's 3rd book and, like the others, captures the story in pictures taken in the cockpit and around the squadron.

"Tornado F3 In Focus – A Navigator's Eye on Britain's Last Interceptor" - ISBN 978-178155-307-7 (print) and ASIN B00TM7480E (e book) published by Fonthill Media.

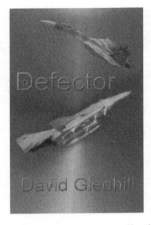

Colonel Yuri Andrenev, a respected test pilot is trusted to evaluate the latest Soviet fighter, the Sukhoi Su27 "Flanker", from a secret test facility near Moscow. Surely he is above suspicion? With thoughts of defection in his mind, and flying close to the Inner German Border, could he be tempted to make a daring escape across the most heavily defended airspace in the world? A flight test against a Mig fighter begins a sequence of events that forces his hand and after an unexpected air-to-air encounter he crosses the border with the help of British Phantom crews. How will Western Intelligence use this unexpected windfall? Are Soviet efforts to recover the advanced fighter as devious as they seem or could more sinister motives be in play? Defector is a pacy thriller which reflects the intrigue of The Cold War. It takes you into the cockpit of the Phantom fighter jet with the realism that can only come from an author who has flown operationally in the NATO Central Region.

"Defector" - ISBN 978-1-49356-759-1 (print) and ASIN B00EUYEUDK (e book) published by DeeGee Media.

Combat veteran Major Pablo Carmendez holds a grudge against his former adversaries. Diverting his armed Skyhawk fighter-bomber from a firepower demonstration he flies eastwards towards the Falkland Islands intent on revenge. What is his target and will he survive the defences alerted of his intentions? Crucially, will his plan wreck delicate negotiations between Britain and Argentina designed to mend strained relations? Are Government officials charged with protecting the islanders' interests worthy of that trust or are more sinister motives in play? Maverick is an aviation thriller set in the remote outpost in the South Atlantic Ocean that takes you into the cockpits of the Phantom fighters based on the Islands where you will experience the thrills of air combat as the conspiracy unfolds.

"Maverick" - ISBN 978-1507801895 (print) and ASIN B00S9ULA30 (e book) published by DeeGee Media.

The Panavia Tornado was designed as a multi-role combat aircraft to meet the needs of Germany Italy and the United Kingdom. Since the prototype flew in 1974, nearly 1000 Tornados have been produced in a number of variants serving as a fighter-bomber, a fighter and in the reconnaissance and electronic suppression roles. Deployed operationally in numerous theatres throughout the world, the Tornado has proved to be exceptionally capable and flexible. From its early Cold War roles it adapted to the rigours of expeditionary warfare from The Gulf to Kosovo to Afghanistan. The early "dumb" bombs were replaced by laser-guided weapons and cruise missiles and in the air-to-air arena fitted with the AMRAAM and ASRAAM missiles. In this book David Gledhill explores the range of capabilities and, having flown the Tornado F2 and F3 Air Defence Variant, offers an insight into life in the cockpit of the Tornado. Lavishly illustrated, Darren Willmin's superb photographs capture the essence of the machine both from the ground and in the air. This unique collection including some of David Gledhill's own air-to-air pictures of the Tornado F2 and F3 will appeal to everyone with an interest in this iconic aircraft.

"Tornado in Pictures - The Multi-Role Legend" ISBN: 9781781554630 (print) published by Fonthill Media.

Made in the USA
Charleston, SC
16 December 2015